The woman leered at Marty perversely. She began to change. Her legs melded together growing thick and black; scales formed and glittered in the dim light making her lower body thick and coarse, like that of a snake. Her legs, bound into one, began to lengthen and taper before his eyes. When Marty blinked, her legs were now one long solid tail. The tail began to coil around Gillian's body. Slowly, patiently, the serpent's tail wrapped around her. There was no hurry; Gillian was oblivious to it all. When the tip of the tail reached Gillian's neck, it stopped.

The creature studied Marty before she spoke. Her voice shocked him more than her body. Her voice was deep and full, that of a woman who was used to being in charge. "Martin, if you come to me, I will spare her."

His eyes grew. He could not hide his astonishment. It was not the tone or the temperament of her voice. It was not the pitch or the accent. It was, in fact, Rachael's voice. He could not respond. His mouth was dry but his skin was clammy.

Without warning, Gillian's eyes cleared. Marty could see the confusion as she struggled futilely against the coils surrounding her.

The creature looked at Gillian. "There is no need to struggle, my dear. I will make this quick."

Marty could see the coils begin to tighten. He could see Gillian's eyes change from fierce to fearful. It was a look he had never seen in her eyes. Gillian opened her mouth to speak but she could not, she could only mouth the words to Marty as she was crushed to death by the coils, *I love you.*

Praise for Darren Swart

"This book captures your attention from the very beginning and will NOT let you put it down. I felt I would miss something if I did. *In The Shadow of a Dark Planet* is so well written, is such a captivating and thrilling book that I read it in one night! You will truly miss a great book if you do not read it. And anything else written by Darren Swart."

~Opie Moore

"A coming of age tale hidden in the pages of a wonderfully written adventure. The next page will suck you in as easily as the last."

~Clint White

"This novel is so exciting! You feel like you're right in the middle of the action. By the end, you're left panting and ready for more."

~Cindy Swart

In the Shadow of the Dark Planet

by

Darren Swart

In the Shadow of Destiny, Book 2

This is a work of fiction. Names, characters, places, and incidents are either the product of the author's imagination or are used fictitiously, and any resemblance to actual persons living or dead, business establishments, events, or locales, is entirely coincidental.

In the Shadow of the Dark Planet

COPYRIGHT © 2021 by Darren Swart

All rights reserved. No part of this book may be used or reproduced in any manner whatsoever without written permission of the author or The Wild Rose Press, Inc. except in the case of brief quotations embodied in critical articles or reviews.
Contact Information: info@thewildrosepress.com

Cover Art by *Debbie Taylor.*

The Wild Rose Press, Inc.
PO Box 708
Adams Basin, NY 14410-0708
Visit us at www.thewildrosepress.com

Publishing History
First Fantasy Rose Edition, 2021
Trade Paperback ISBN 978-1-5092-3439-4
Digital ISBN 978-1-5092-3440-0

In the Shadow of Destiny, Book 2
Published in the United States of America

Dedication

Dedicated to my sister, Ann.

Faced with a lifetime of adversity,
she has maintained her faith and love of family.
Throughout my life she has been a fount
of quiet fortitude.
She is today and continues to be
an inspiration to me and so many others.
I am awed by her courage and proud to be her brother.

Prologue

Upstate New York
Thirty Years Earlier

Fred cursed under his breath. It was going to be a bad year. The soil was too wet. Half the blueberries were so large they split their skins; the remaining half were whole, but tasteless because of all the water. The sun darted behind a cloud and threatened yet another unwanted shower.

The migrants had asked for another dollar per acre to pick. Half of them were as old as he was. They worked slowly and painfully, taking twice as long as the younger workers who remained in the South where there was more money in tobacco. He would do well to break even this year. He just hoped demand for blueberries would hold when the crop came in. It was a bad year indeed.

Fred ignored the noise as the jets flew overhead most days. After they built the new runway, the air traffic increased steadily over the years, as the airport grew more popular as an east coast hub. The low airplanes were so common that he took little notice of them these days. But today, there was something different about the noise.

Absently, he looked up from the berries in his hand for the source of a decidedly different sound. His gaze slowly scanned the orchard. His eyes widened, and a chill ran down his spine at the surreal scene that manifested before him. The shock of the rapidly growing DC-10 nosecone paralyzed him. His only thought was the nose of the plane looked different from this angle. Blueberries tumbled unnoticed from his fingertips.

The old man couldn't remember when he started to run. All he could see was the round cone coming toward him from the distance. It grew larger with each passing moment. His lungs heaved at each step, screaming in protest. A cold, clammy sweat washed over him like a river. He could feel his heart hammering in his ears. His legs burned as he strained to run for the first time in decades. *This is insane.* And yet, his feet continued to pound through the mud. He could hear the screaming of the engines behind him now. He didn't want to look again, but he couldn't resist. He glanced over his shoulder to see the DC-10 was nearly on top of him now.

His feet slapped the sodden ground in cadence. He cleared the row of blueberry bushes to an open field. From the corner of his eye he saw the migrants scattering like so many cockroaches in the night. There was no organization, just people scurrying for cover as the silver behemoth bore down on them. It was so close now he felt the pressure from the heated breath of the turbines which tried to suck him in. Debris began to rain down on him in sodden chunks, kicked up by the wake of the approaching jet.

The plane plowed a slow angry furrow through his neatly trimmed hedges of blueberries as it careened wildly back and forth in a muddy path behind him.

Fred kept running.

The two forward engines exploded like sticks of dynamite as mud and debris snuffed them out like birthday candles. The plane began to arc in a long uncontrolled course away from the old man. Like a dancer, it turned in a long slow pirouette gliding into the waiting granite face of the mountain behind the farm. Moments later, the crescendo of groaning metal and debris smashing into the evergreens and the rock face of the mountain just beyond replaced the sounds of the plane roaring past him.

As quickly as it started, it was over. An eerie silence settled into the valley. The usual twitter of cardinals or robins or the deep punctuation of dogs barking in the afternoon calm were gone. Crickets lay still in their thickets leaving only the sound of the wind across the plain. The old man fell to the muddy ground panting. On all fours, he heaved air into his burning lungs.

He stared at the mud, watching the droplets of sweat fall from his head and disappear into the sodden ground beneath him. Over the ringing in his ears, he could just make out the sobbing of migrants in the distance. He would join them in a while, but for now he had to rest. Far away, he heard the wail of an ancient siren beckoning volunteers to the fire station. He sat back in the mud, wiping his brow with his sleeve. Help would be here soon.

****

Carl stood over Fred, imploring him with an oxygen mask. "Fred, are you sure you don't need some oxygen?"

"Get away from me with that damn thing." He

growled. "Go help some of them people on the plane why don't ya'?"

"Uhhh…"

Fred glared up at him from a sitting position on the ground. Sharply he asked, "Well?"

"There ain't no one to help, Fred."

"What do you mean? Plane had people on it, didn't it?"

"Well, yeah. But there ain't nobody left alive."

The old man stared at him for a moment while the statement sank in. His head slowly lowered to his waiting hands. All those people, all those lives… His body shook as the tears started involuntarily. Fred had seen his share of carnage from grisly farm accidents to men lying dead on the battlefield; none of those scenes held a candle to this.

Carl asked gently, "Fred, are you all right?"

Fred lifted his head and wiped his eyes with a sleeve. "Yes, dammit, I'm fine. I was thinkin' of all those poor bastards on the plane over there." He jabbed his thumb in the direction of the wreckage.

Carl nodded. "Yeah, I know what you mean."

Fred's temper got the better of him. He clenched his jaw so tight he thought his molars would shatter. He sucked in a deep breath through his nostrils that made a whistling noise. He fought to hold back the tears as he looked back up at Carl. He narrowed his eyes to slits. "Do you, boy? I don't think you do. Until a jet nearly stripes your back in your own backyard, I don't think you ever will!"

Fred regretted it as soon as he said it. Carl had spoken thoughtlessly, but he meant no harm by it. Neither man spoke for a while. Fred could make out shouting in the distance. He saw Carl look in the direction of the smoking wreckage. “What is it, Carl?” The old man strained to see from his sitting position.

“Well, I’ll be. It looks like someone did make it off alive.”

The old man was off the ground and moving before Carl could assist him. Fred’s legs throbbed with pain, but he ignored it and kept running. He could smell the burning fuel before he rounded the bushes. The sky was black with smoke. For the first time this year, the blackness wasn’t caused by storm clouds on the horizon. For the first time this year, Fred wished the clouds were rain instead of smoke. He tried to process the panorama before him as he cleared the end of the row. Silos of smoke ebbed into the sky from small fires all over the open field. Hose trucks struggled through the mire of the muddy ground as they moved from one fire to the next. It was an exercise in futility. The smell of burning jet fuel and scorched flesh would be something that would stick to the old man for months, maybe forever. Bits of fuselage draped with clothing and mud littered the field. Bodies and body parts were scattered as far as he could see. The sheer mountain face, unchanged in over a millennium, was now charred and blackened from the impact.

He turned his attention to a small contingent of paramedics as they struggled to cross the rough terrain with a gurney. He could hear a child crying. That didn’t make sense. *How could a child survive this madness?*

As tired as he felt, he sped up. Fred could hear Carl wheezing behind him, struggling to keep pace. Despite himself, he couldn’t help wondering if Carl might not be better suited to another line of work. Perhaps he would be better as a dispatcher? In Carl's defense, he was lugging the heavy jump bag.

As he moved closer, Fred could hear the unmistakable sound of a child's voice now. He was not crying, but Fred could hear the rising panic in his small voice. "Where's my mommy?"

The paramedic facing the boy clenched his teeth and struggled with the gurney. The small caravan stopped when they saw Fred moving toward them. The little boy had strawberry blond curls that framed a cherub face. He looked up questioningly at the paramedic, still waiting for a response. Fred reached them a moment later. The paramedic looked at Fred no less imploringly, than the boy. He was at a loss for what to say to the child.

Fred managed a grin for the little boy. He motioned for them to unstrap the child from the gurney. He eased up to him. Smudges and flecks of dirt could do little to hide the angelic quality of the child's face. His small, rosy, round cheeks melted Fred's heart. The only thought Fred could muster was that this was a miracle child.

The little boy looked up at Fred and asked solemnly, "Do you know where my mommy and daddy are?"

Carefully, he placed a callused hand tenderly on the side of the little face. Using his thumb, he flicked away a speck of mud from the little face. The small face smiled. With eight grandchildren, he knew what the boy needed. An oxygen mask and blood pressure cuff were not it. He stepped away from the gurney and crouched down. Opening his arms to the little boy he said, "Come to Uncle Fred for a minute."

The little body climbed off the gurney and scooted across to the old man. The small form clung tightly to Fred's neck. He could feel the shudder from the tiny form in his arms. The little boy buried his face in Fred's neck, sobbed silently for a moment, and was still. The old man could feel his own tears streaming down the crags of his weathered cheek. He didn't try to hide them from the others. He pulled him back slightly, so the boy could see his face. He tried to smile through the tears. "Everything's going to be just fine, little fella."

The child repeated his question. "Where are Mommy and Daddy?"

"Your mommy and daddy can't be with us right now. They've gone to be with Jesus. But we're going to take good care of you while they're gone, okay?" Fred could see the child studying him. He rewarded the child with the special lopsided grin reserved for his grandchildren.

The little boy nodded. "Okay."

Fred asked, "So, little fella, what's your name?"

The boy looked at him with deeply serious eyes. "Mar-tee."

Fred nodded. "That's a fine name. How old are you, Mar-tee?"

Marty held up five chubby little fingers. "This many."

Fred grinned at him. "Well Marty, in the whole wide world who do you love to visit the most?"

With virtually no thought he responded "My Grandma Barb. Is she okay, or is she with Jesus too?"

Fred swallowed hard; he prayed silently she wasn't on the plane.

With a leap of faith, he replied, "I'm sure she's just

fine. We're going to take you to her, is that okay?"

The tiny head bobbed up and down. "Okie Dokie!"

He hugged the old man around the neck again.

"In the meantime, let's go up to the house and see if we can find a nice piece of blueberry pie. What would you say to that?"

Without looking up, he heard the tiny voice say, "Okay."

He scooped the child up and threw a blanket from the gurney across his shoulders. He carried him carefully across the rough terrain toward the house. The boy seemed as light as a feather. The paramedics walked with them for a distance. Fred looked at one of them and asked quietly, "Is he okay?"

The paramedic responded equally as quiet. "Yes, sir. No outward signs of trauma. Not even a bruise."

Carl eased up beside Fred. "We'll let the government men know where to find him. Is that okay, Fred?"

"That's fine, Carl. We'll get him cleaned up and make plans to get him home. I'm sure Irma's got some extra clothes from one of the grandkids we can round up."

Fred walked slowly back to the house with the small figure clinging tightly to him. Fred watched the tiny face; the boy's eyes took everything in. Fred could sense it; this was a miracle child.

Chapter 1

Present Day

Sharp edges of manacles bit into his flesh as Marty Wood strained against the shackles that chained him to the floor. The shackles were unusual, carved from obsidian; they were shiny and glittered in the dim light of the cave. Each time he strained against them, they cut a little deeper into his flesh. The blood from his wrists dripped onto his legs. Marty didn't care.

Gillian stood out of Marty's reach. Her naked skin was in stark contrast to the dark walls behind her. Her eyes drove Marty insane. They glowed bright purple in the feeble torchlight. She stood still, locked in a trance. She was oblivious to him as he shouted to her to run. Marty sensed another presence in the room. He felt the goosebumps rise on his arms and legs.

A form emerged from the darkness behind Gillian; it was a woman of startling beauty. At least, that was until he saw the blackness in the woman's eyes. The woman circled Gillian, her long fingers explored the curves of Gillian's naked flesh. She stopped when both Marty and Gillian were in full view. Ever so gently she placed a hand around Gillian's neck. A forked tongue slid from the woman's mouth and tasted the flesh of Gillian's cheek. Goose bumps rose on his skin, the sensation was electric. The woman leered at Marty perversely. She began to change. Her legs melded together growing thick and black; scales formed and glittered in the dim light making her lower body thick and coarse, like that of a snake. Her legs, bound into one, began to lengthen and taper before his eyes. When Marty blinked, her legs were now one long solid tail. The tail began to coil around Gillian's body. Slowly, patiently, the serpent's tail wrapped around her. There was no hurry; Gillian was oblivious to it all. When the tip of the tail reached Gillian's neck, it stopped.

The creature studied Marty before she spoke. Her voice shocked him more than her body. Her voice was deep and full, that of a woman who was used to being in charge. "Martin, if you come to me, I will spare her."

His eyes grew. He could not hide his astonishment. It was not the tone or the temperament of her voice. It was not the pitch or the accent. It was, in fact, Rachael's voice. He could not respond. His mouth was dry but his skin was clammy.

Without warning, Gillian's eyes cleared. Marty could see the confusion as she struggled futilely against the coils surrounding her.

The creature looked at Gillian. "There is no need to struggle, my dear. I will make this quick."

Marty could see the coils begin to tighten. He could see Gillian's eyes change from fierce to fearful. It was a look he had never seen in her eyes. Gillian opened her mouth to speak but she could not, she could only mouth the words to Marty as she was crushed to death by the coils, *I love you.*

Marty screamed through tears of rage and grief as Gillian's eyes rolled back. Her head held aloft by the tip of the creature's tail so that Marty could see the faint blue color creep up Gillian's neck and into her lips.

Suddenly, Marty's hands were free. He blinked. He was sitting up, confused and in the dark. He turned his head back and forth as he tried to orient himself. He felt the cold sweat on his body, which made him shiver. The steady clink of the ceiling fan overhead registered in his brain. He was in his room. His left hand immediately shot out to the opposite side of the bed. It landed on a familiar fanny. A drowsy voice sounded from his side. "Do you mind?" Her voice made him breathe again.

"Sorry. Just had a moment."

"Um-hum. Maybe later." Gillian snorted once and resumed her soft snore.

Marty swung his feet over the side of the bed. The hardwood felt cool on the bottoms of his feet. He walked quietly to the bathroom and flicked on the lights. Dark circles under his eyes stared back at him in the mirror. He twisted the antique knob on the cold water and cupped his hands. The cool liquid felt refreshing on his face. He glanced down at the sink at the red stains gathering in the bowl below him. For a moment he stared at the red splotches in the basin. Slowly he raised his hands to see a multitude of cuts on his wrists. The slow, but steady drops of blood turned the water pink in the basin. He stared in disbelief. A single chilling thought struck him: *Only part of it was a dream.*

****

Marty, Gillian, and Jacob sat at the table eating breakfast. Jacob stared at his father wearing a long sleeve shirt at the table in the middle of July. "Dad, what's up with the shirt?"

Marty took a bite of eggs. "Darn Mabel decided to escape from the barn this morning after milking. By the time I got to her, she was caught in the barbed wire below the barn. I got scratched up getting her out of that mess."

It sounded convincing, but Jacob knew better.

Marty changed the subject. "So, buddy, what do you want for your eleventh birthday? No sports cars please, we've still got a mortgage to pay."

Jacob picked at his hash browns with his fork. He knew his father was lying. It was not the kind of lie you tell when you're cheating an elderly couple out of their life savings—it was the kind of lie you tell when you're trying to keep someone you love from being hurt. Jacob had his own lies. He knew his father's tell sign—change the subject.

Jacob stabbed the hash browns and eggs and pondered his father's question as he chewed. "Can we take a trip?"

Marty looked at Gillian. She gave him a non-committal shrug. He looked back at Jacob. "What kind of trip?"

Jacob replied, "Someplace really cool."

Marty thought for a moment. "Can it be someplace cool that we can make the trip in one day? We still have the farm to consider."

Jacob took a sip of milk and paused. "If we get Harry to watch the farm, we could take a couple of days, right?"

Marty blew on his coffee. "We could certainly ask. It would all depend on Harry's schedule." This would be the first time Marty and Gillian had left the farm for any time since they were married. Maybe it was time.

He smiled at Jacob. “So what did you have in mind?”

Jacob’s blue eyes were serious. “Petra, in Jordan.”

Marty sat back. Gillian stopped in mid-bite and set her fork back onto the plate. Their surprise was evident to Jacob. Gillian squinted at Jacob. “Where did you hear of Petra?”

Now it was Jacob’s turn to lie. “The internet. I was browsing and ran across it. It looked completely awesome.” He wasn’t about to tell his parents he had a dream about a girl he met in the desert. They would think he was nuts.

Marty and Gillian exchanged looks. It was Marty that broke the awkward pause. “That is a pretty tall order. Are you sure there is nowhere closer you would like to go?”

He nodded. “I’m sure.”

Marty took a sip of coffee. “So you do realize that Petra is in the Middle East. We have to have passports, travel arrangements, and the cost is going to be phenomenal.”

Jacob nodded. “Uh huh.”

Marty grinned. “Can I recant my first statement? A car is looking attractive right now. In all seriousness, son, that is a very long and private conversation between your mother and me. I can’t say *yes*, but then I’m not saying *no*. Can I get back to you on this?”

Jacob smirked. “Of course.” He took a big bite of buttered toast with marmalade.

Gillian did not smile.

****

From the kitchen window, Gillian watched Jacob mow the lower field on the old Ford tractor, leaving a row of hay in his wake. Marty picked up the dishes from the sink and dried them as Gillian rinsed. She stopped rinsing a saucer and looked him in the eye. “Have you told him?”

Marty shook his head. “We agreed that when the time was right, we would tell him. We also agreed to do it together. But there’s something we didn’t plan for. I had a dream last night. It was like the dreams I used to have when I received prophecies.”

Gillian set the saucer in the sink. “What kind of dream?”

Marty removed the bandages from his wrists and held them up for her to see. “The kind of dream where part of it follows you home.”

She turned off the water and took his hands in hers. “How did you do this?”

He looked outside to make sure Jacob was still mowing. “I was shackled to the ground. A monster held you in its grip crushing you to death. Every time I pulled against the manacles, they cut me. I didn’t really care; I was trying to get to you.”

She looked into his eyes. “Sweet. But totally disturbing. Is that why you patted me on the butt last night?”

Marty nodded. Gillian turned back to the dishes. “That’s disappointing. I was flattered last night.” She gave him a sideways look. “Annoyed, but flattered after I thought about it. How is this possible?”

Marty put away a plate in the cabinet. “I don’t know. But I’ll bet you I know someone who does. I think I’ll pay Rachael a visit.”

Gillian looked at him. “I think you should.”

****

Marty hiked up the small mountain behind the farm

on a narrow trail etched through ground cedar. He continued until he reached a ledge that overlooked the town of Green Lake. It was his thinking spot as a boy. Today, it was a place of meditation. The breeze was cool in the mid-morning sun. Wrens rustled in the undergrowth searching for beetles and grasshoppers. The occasional gust whistled through the craggy scrub cedars.

He found a thick patch of lichen on the rock ledge and sat down with legs crossed. He closed his eyes and opened his mind. He pictured an ancient wooden door. The timbers were held together by black iron strips and rivets. In the center of the door was a flat iron image of the Ark of the Covenant. It took some effort to pull the door open, but as he did, light streamed out from the other side. He walked through. A couple stood waiting for him. Through the powerful light behind them he could only make out their shapes until his eyes adjusted. As he drew near, Rachael and Digger looked the same as they had ten years ago. Today, Rachael chose the image of a twenty-five-year-old woman. Long straight blonde hair streamed over her shoulders. Her eyes shimmered in sapphire blue. They both came forward and greeted him with smiles and hugs. Their touch was warm and comforting.

Marty wasted no time with pleasantries. “I’m sure you know why I’m here.” Rachael looked down and shuffled her feet. It was the first time she had ever looked away from him. Marty reached out and lifted her chin. “I need to know. What is this thing that is invading my dreams?”

Behind them, soft overstuffed seats materialized out of thin air. Digger sat on a purple loveseat and

Rachael curled up next to him. They made a nice couple. Her voice was soft, yet clear. "I suppose it is time for you to know." She raised her hand and made a circle in the air. As her hand swirled, the center filled with blackness. From the blackness, an image of a dark-skinned woman with long dark hair appeared. "For every light, there is a darkness. I was sent here to protect this world. My sister, Jeez, was sent to bring misery. We were never meant to interact directly with humans, at least never like this. She crossed the boundary first. Her first contact was an earth woman known as Eve. She touched Eve in such a way that it changed mankind forever. For that, Jeez was banished to the Dark Planet. She waits there, seething in hatred for all that is human. Her only desire is to destroy all that is good in this world. But she is trapped there. Her only doorway to this world is through the shadow world of dreams. There she has power to influence. That is where she seduced the Duke. She convinced him that she could grant him unlimited power. All he had to do was open the portal. What she did not know was when we opened the portal from Earth, it went only one way. The Duke could travel to her; she could not leave the dark world of Oronas. She failed with the Duke, so she is moving to the next most powerful human she knows of. You."

Marty scowled. "Me? Hardly. Why would she want me? I'm a farmer?"

Rachael brushed the dark circle away with a flick of her wrist. She reached across from where she was sitting and placed her hand on his. It felt tingly. "Marty, you have always denied who you really are. Why do you do that? Do you think your power is limited to channeling with omnipotent supernatural beings? She seeks you because you are the instrument of her escape."

Marty was silent for a moment. "But I have no power to help her escape."

Rachael sighed and settled back beside Digger. "You are so much greater than what you believe you are. You fail to see."

Marty looked into her eyes. They swirled like vast blue oceans, deep and welcoming. Being in her presence made him believe. She looked demure, almost fragile, yet he knew she was anything but that. Her eyes now crackled with energy. She reached out and touched his forehead with her forefinger. He felt the jolt go through him. Rachael removed her finger. She traced her hand along his arm. "You will need this for the future. Jeez is a seething creature made of pure evil, but she is not unstoppable. Her weakness is in self-centeredness—she uses others but trusts in no one. It will be her downfall."

Marty thought for a moment. "Can you defeat her?"

Rachael considered the question. "Defeat is a human concept. It implies win or lose scenarios. We are equals. When equals collide, for one to overcome the other, something must tip the scale. My tipping point is faith. As trite as that sounds, it is a concept that is alien to her. She will use your own fear against you as a weapon. If you can defeat your fear, you can break her hold on you. Because faith is as powerful as fear within the spectrum, it undermines her power. She does not understand faith, nor can she use it to her advantage. That is her weakness—she cannot conceive that I would have faith in humans. That is my secret weapon. As I protect you, you will in turn believe in me, it unleashes a hidden reserve of generational compounded energy. You could tell her this, but she would reject it, she has never accepted the concept of trust or faith. She has forsaken her Master; it will be her undoing."

Marty nodded. "So what do I need to do?"

Rachael's expression changed; normally she had the impish look of a child, but her expression was solemn. "You must go to her. She will bring you misery until you do. By then, you may be too weak to challenge her. Your spirit is strong, you will lead her to her demise—but you must believe. You cannot lose your faith."

Marty took a deep breath and tried to look brave, though he didn't feel it. "I died once for mankind. The second time should be easier, right?"

Rachael's expression never changed. "This will not be like that. She will make you doubt your existence. She will make you doubt every good thing you have ever known. It is all an illusion though. She cannot change who you are, she can only make you believe that she can." Marty looked at his wrists. In this place, they bore no scars. In this place, there was no pain. Where he would go, there would be nothing but pain. He chose not to think about it.

He felt a tremor within. "I must go."

Digger had remained silent the whole time. He reached over and gave Marty a hug. "I am there with you in spirit. You are my brother. I will always be there for you."

Marty hugged Digger back. "We are kindred spirits, you and I."

Marty blinked. As he looked out over the ledge, a hawk soared, circling in a pocket of air. Marty squinted against the bright sunlight. Something did not feel right. He rose and hurried down the trail. As he approached the farmhouse, the tractor was stopped in the field. Jacob was nowhere to be seen. He picked up his pace to a run. As he cleared the back door into the kitchen, the scene froze him. Gillian lay on the kitchen floor. Her body convulsed and twitched. Jacob held her head in his lap. He looked up to Marty. There was a look of helplessness in his eyes.

It had begun.

Chapter 2

The doctor entered the room. Marty looked at the top of his bald head as the doctor stared at the chart in front of him. Finally, he looked up at Marty over the rim of his glasses. "Are you related to the patient?"

Marty's look was steady. "She's my wife.

He looked back at the chart. "Is she taking any prescribed medicines?"

Marty's eyebrow furrowed. "No, she isn't taking any medicine."

The doctor continued, "Do you know if she has taken any illegal drugs?"

Marty felt Jacob's hand slip into his. "No, she is not taking any illegal drugs."

The doctor asked, "Did she experience any violence in the home?"

Marty took a deep breath. "No. To my knowledge she was not subjected to any violence."

The doctor looked up over his glasses. "What do you mean, 'to my knowledge'?"

Marty looked him directly in the eye. "I was on a walk, when I arrived at home, I found my wife on the floor experiencing a seizure." He looked down at Jacob. "Son, can you help with any information?"

For the first time, Jacob spoke. He wiped the tears from his eyes. "No, Dad, I just found Mom on the floor. I didn't know what to do, I'm sorry…"

He hugged Jacob. "It's okay, son. None of this is your fault. The doctor is going to tell us what is wrong with Mommy, okay?"

Jacob nodded.

The doctor stared back at his clipboard and resumed his questions. "Does the patient have a history with seizures?"

Marty replied calmly, "No, no previous history."

The doctor looked up. "Our protocol is to do a CT scan with contrast. I can order it if you will consent."

Marty held his temper in check. "Yes. How long will it take?"

The doctor scribbled on the chart. "I'll write the order. We'll have to prep her with dye. It will take a few hours."

Marty looked at Gillian. She was resting comfortably. "Will you move her to a room?"

The doctor looked up. "We'll keep her overnight for observation. I'll find her a room."

Without looking at the doctor, Marty said, "I need to talk to my son. I'll be in the cafeteria."

Without waiting for the doctor to respond, Marty led Jacob from the room. "Jacob, your mother and I have been waiting until you were old enough to tell you this. It appears that this can't wait any longer. I'm sorry but it may be difficult for you to understand."

Jacob's expression was strange. His face was neither confused nor frightened. He almost looked relieved. "Honestly, Dad, I need to tell you some things too."

Marty cocked his head in surprise. "Well, son, this should be an interesting conversation."

They sat with soft drinks and popcorn in the

cafeteria. Marty began, "It happened before you were born. I inherited a jewel that is connected to the Ark of the Covenant."

Jacob interrupted, "You mean, like the Ark from the Bible?"

Marty replied, "Precisely. When your mother and I recovered this sapphire, we discovered that it unlocked dormant supernatural powers in both of us. We stopped a man who wanted to use the power of the Ark to become powerful, like a god. He wanted it for himself. We still have those powers today, even though we returned the jewel to the Ark."

Jacob's eyebrows furrowed. "And the man, what happened to him?"

Marty shrugged. "He was sucked into a portal that transported him to another place…beyond Earth. We have not seen or heard from him since."

Jacob pressed Marty for more. "Could he come back?"

Marty sipped his cream soda. "I suppose. We don't really know where he ended up. There is an entity that lives in the Ark. Her name is Rachael. She opened the portal and sent the Duke, that was what we called the man, to another place. It would seem someone, or something, would have to send him back. Why?"

Jacob sat without touching his snack. "I need to tell you something, Dad."

Marty placed his hand on Jacob's shoulder. "You can tell me anything, son."

Jacob took a swig of his soda. "Will you promise you won't get mad?"

Marty was intrigued. "I promise that if I do get mad, I'll control it."

Jacob nodded. "Fair enough. Dad, I have powers. And I've been having dreams."

Marty sat back; his fingers stroked his chin for a moment. "Okay, son, let's start with the 'Dad, I have powers.' And we'll work our way forward from there."

Jacob looked around. There were only a few people in the room besides them. When no one was looking, he imagined an energy ball in his mind the size of a golf ball. He focused on the chair beside Marty and mentally threw the ball. The chair fell back onto the floor with a loud clatter. People looked over at them. Marty reached over and picked up the chair. "That's pretty impressive."

Jacob nodded. "I can also understand foreign languages."

Marty replied, "Really? How many?"

Jacob didn't smile. "All of them. I've never heard a language I didn't understand. For years, I didn't realize that there were other languages. When I started taking social studies in school, I realized that other people couldn't understand foreign languages."

Marty arched his eyebrow. "That's impressive."

Jacob looked at him. "That's not all. I can sense when other people have powers like ours."

Marty regarded him for a moment before responding. "Do you mean you have met other people like us?"

Jacob nodded. "You know Pastor Fred?"

Marty responded, "Yes. What about him?"

Jacob replied, "He's like us. He can read people's pain. He knows how to read weakness. And you, Dad. You have a new power that you didn't have this morning."

Marty's eyebrow furrowed. "How could you possibly know that? I don't even know."

Jacob shrugged. "I don't know how. I just know when you left this morning, you had two powers—channeling and connecting to animals. Now you have another one. It is a strange power, involving energy—something like a lightning bolt."

Marty nodded. "I reached out to Rachael this morning because of a dream I had last night."

Jacob pointed to his wrists. "The one where you hurt your wrists?"

Marty nodded. "You know about that, huh?"

Jacob's expression was dubious. "Yeah. The story about Mabel running away from you was farfetched. She's like a pet around you. You couldn't get her to leave your side if you tried."

Marty laughed. "You're probably right. When I reached out to Rachael this morning, she touched me. When she did, I felt a shock go through my body. I'm not sure what she did, I just know I felt it."

Jacob stared at him. "I can see it in you. It's like you have tiny lightning storms inside you now. It's kind of neat and scary at the same time."

Marty responded. "All things being equal, I don't feel any different. All that aside, we need to go check on your mom."

They made the long walk back to the room. When they walked in, Gillian was sitting up. She smiled when she saw them.

Marty kissed her on the lips. "How are you feeling?"

She gave him an encouraging smile. "Not too bad. What happened?"

Marty shook his head. "They're not really sure. Jacob found you having a seizure on the floor. I called emergency services and the doctors are running tests to isolate the cause of the problem."

Gillian looked tired. "How long do I have to stay?"

Jacob sat on the bed beside his mother while Marty replied. "They're not really sure. I'll round up the doctor. He said something about a CT scan."

A large nurse tapped on the door and entered the room. "Hey, guys. My name is Alice, I need to draw blood."

Gillian gave her a droll look. "Of course, you do."

The nurse ignored the comment and began to prep her arm.

A slender redheaded nurse arrived in the doorway. "Mrs. Wood?"

Gillian never flinched as the nurse stuck her with a needle. "Yes?"

The second nurse responded, "My name is Rhonda, I'm from Radiology. I need to prep you for the contrast dye for your CT scan. I need to ask you some questions. Is this a good time?"

Jacob stared at the two nurses. "Hmm. One taking out, one putting in."

Gillian reached over and squeezed his hand gently. "Yes. Go ahead, Rhonda."

Rhonda read her questionnaire for the dye. She finished and left the room with Alice close behind.

For the first time since she had been in the hospital, the three were together. Marty looked at Gillian. "I talked to Jacob. I'm sorry, but we were unsure about what was going to happen. I thought he needed to know."

Gillian nodded. “I understand.” She looked at Jacob. “How do you feel about all this, honey?”

Jacob’s gaze was steady. “I’m a little scared about you, Mom.” He looked down. “I told Dad the truth and now I guess I need to tell you.”

Gillian looked surprised. “Truth about what, son?”

Jacob looked up. “When Dad was telling me about the both of you having powers, I told him about my powers.”

Gillian looked intrigued. “*You* have powers?”

He nodded. “I can send an energy ball at things with my mind. Do you want to see?”

Gillian shook her head. “No, honey. Not in the hospital. When we get back home, okay?”

He nodded. “I can do other things. But they aren’t as cool.”

Gillian studied Jacob’s face. “I’ll be the judge of that. What else?”

He replied, “I can understand foreign languages—all foreign languages.”

Gillian nodded in approval. “Can you speak them?”

Jacob shrugged. “I don’t know. I’ve never tried.”

Gillian continued to probe. “What else?”

Jacob responded, “I can read what powers people have, like you and Dad.”

Gillian stopped smiling. “Who else do you know has powers?”

His eyes took on a more serious look. “Pastor Fred.”

Gillian raised an eyebrow at Jacob. She looked at Marty. “Is this true?”

Marty nodded. “I connected with Rachael this

morning. She unlocked another power in me. I didn't even know I had it until Jacob explained to me what it was."

She took Jacob by the hand. "Son, you can never tell anyone about this, do you understand?"

Jacob cocked his head at his mother. "Mom. I didn't tell you and Dad until he said something first. I've known this since I was five."

She nodded. "I know, but there are people who will try to exploit you. You must protect your powers at all costs. This is our secret, do you promise?"

Jacob nodded. "I promise."

There was a tap at the door. Rhonda came in with an IV stand. "Hello, Mrs. Wood. We're going to start the IV drip to boost your fluids since we were unable to prep you on fluids by mouth earlier. Once I've started the drip, I'll be back in an hour to take you down for the CT scan. Your family can wait here in the room if they like."

Marty nodded. "I've got to call Harry to take care of the girls."

****

Gillian shifted uncomfortably in the bed. "I sure wish they would hurry up. I need to get out of here."

Marty patted her on the arm. "The doctor promised he would be here as soon as he had the results."

There was a tap on the door. Dr. Rosenthal from the radiology department entered the room. He held a manila folder in his hand. "Mrs. Wood?"

Gillian held out her hand. "Yes, doctor. What information do you have for me?"

Dr. Rosenthal took her hand. His grip was firm. "I'm afraid that I'm quite perplexed at your CT scan."

Gillian's eyes narrowed. "How so?"

The doctor placed the file on the bedside table. He looked at Marty and Jacob. "Are you family?"

Marty nodded. "I'm her husband." He motioned toward Jacob. "This is Jacob, our son."

The doctor nodded. "In twenty-five years of radiology, I've never seen anything like this. I ran the results twice and did a test sequence to see if there was a system issue."

Gillian looked him in the eye. "Well, what is it?"

He opened the file. "Our machine only sees images in black and white. When we ran your CT, this is what we saw." He pointed to the silhouette of a black cobra profile with two red glowing eyes between the two hemispheres of the brain. "It appears you have a growth between your hemispheres that is causing interference, much like what we see in patients with epilepsy. However, our imager does not allow for color. How we got two red dots on the scan is beyond me. You wouldn't happen to have an implant of some type, would you?"

Gillian shook her head. "No. No implants."

Marty looked at the image on the scan. He was quiet for a moment. "Doctor what is the course of treatment?"

Dr. Rosenthal looked at Marty. "We could try radiation. Where it is located, it would be impossible to remove surgically."

Marty nodded. He knew there was only one answer. He had to stop Jeez. It was Gillian's only chance.

He shook the doctor's hand. "Thank you, Dr. Rosenthal. I think we need some time to discuss this."

The doctor nodded. "I understand. I'll be available when you need me."

The doctor pulled the door closed as he left. Marty looked at Gillian. "I know what this thing is."

Gillian furrowed her brows. "What?"

Marty's lips were tight. "I spoke to Rachael this morning. She told me something I didn't know. There is another entity named Jeez. She is Rachael's sister. Her heart is black. Jeez is who I experienced in my dream last night. She is trying to draw me in."

Gillian frowned. "Draw you into what? What is the objective?"

Marty looked up, deep in thought. "She wants to destroy Earth. She was banished to a place called Oronas. Rachael can send me there. It's the only way to stop Jeez."

Gillian held out her hands toward Marty. "Sweetheart, I love you. I cannot send you off to a foreign world to fight a demon. I'm not worth that."

Marty met her gaze; he held her hands tightly. "You are to me."

Marty and Gillian talked, argued, laughed, and cried into the night. Jacob sat quietly listening to his parents' debate. When they finally stopped bantering, in a quiet voice, he broke the silence. "I have an idea."

They both stopped and turned to look at him. His legs were crossed in the hospital chair. His hands rested in his lap. He looked like a Buddhist monk. "What if I go to this place? Then Dad could take care of you, and I could fight this demon for Mom."

Gillian held out her hand to him. "Oh honey, no. We couldn't send you to do something like that. We'll figure something out. I promise. Don't you worry.

Everything will work out."

Jacob frowned. "No, Mom. It's not. This is different than anything you've ever faced. If it is a different problem, we must have a different solution. This demon would never expect me. I would have an advantage."

Gillian studied his face. She thought back to when she was his age. She had sat in a hospital room, much like this, having the same conversation with her own mother. She would have done anything to save her mother. Her mother had responded, "Let the doctors handle this. They'll figure this out and it will be okay." She covered her mouth as the impact of the thought resonated within her. After a moment, she said, "We'll talk about it."

****

Gillian swung her feet off the bed and walked to the bathroom. She had been home from the hospital for two days. The doctors had proposed several tests. All of which she rejected. She and Marty recognized something the doctors had no ability to detect—she was being attacked by a malady that had no origin on this Earth. She brushed her teeth and leaned over to spit. When she stood back up, she saw Marty's face in the mirror behind her. She could feel the warmth of his hands on her shoulders.

He asked, "How are you feeling?"

She turned toward him and put her arms around him. She could feel his strong arms pull her close. "What are we going to do?"

He responded, "You're going to call in some favors and I'm going to the root of the problem."

She held him tight. "We can't fight this thing

alone."

He replied, "I agree."

Chapter 3

Fredrick Lindenspear sat on the Throne of Shame which overlooked a festival of debauchery. His seduction had been subtle, almost imperceptible until it was too late. Jeez had seduced him. She made him believe he would ascend from his mortal form into that of a god. He would leave behind all the pettiness of earthly trappings and evolve to what he should be, a deity worthy of worship. It was all a lie. She was sultry, with a curvaceous figure, deep violet eyes, and long black hair that glistened. When she discovered he had been infected by the parasite known as the serqet, she laughed at him. The larva had wormed its way into his body. It had probably saved his life, such as it was. His men had been hunted down and killed one by one by the rippers that inhabited the grasslands. He could only assume all were dead.

It was weeks after he had passed the threshold of the Nexus that he had appreciated the shift. Forced to accept that he had gone from being puppet master on Earth to a puppet on Oronas, he realized that Jeez was the antithetical Geppetto here.

For years, Fredrick had witnessed the Festival of the Chosen. The faces had changed but the outcome remained the same. Older hosts ascended the Altar of Enlightenment and the host and serqet were liberated from each other. The indigenous people had been programmed to believe that serqets, once liberated, carried the soul of the human host in harmony and the two were merged as one. The reality was that the human host was slaughtered to free the serqet which then was sent underground to the crystal mines.

The creatures were masters of milking the human's endocrine system. They fed off the hormones of pleasure. Now, when the host should be most fearful, they were programmed to believe just the opposite. The human host died without so much as a flinch. The room reeked with the stench of death. Dried blood was spattered on the walls and floors. None of this seemed to matter, the hosts remained blind to their fate.

Fredrick was the exception to this carnage. His parasite was stunted, struggling to grow within him. Fredrick controlled his emotions rigorously. He was not to be the typical serqet incubator in this world. Rumors about him drifted among the locals; they shunned him as an outcast. He was the only one here who did not willingly succumb to the serqet's manipulation. The people who were the most emotionally charged were the chosen, not the pragmatists. Pragmatists were subjugated to the mines, where they worked as slaves until they died.

The more disciplined Fredrick kept his mind, the more stunted the serqet within him remained. The creature within him rarely rested, and it constantly tried to push him to produce dopamine and oxytocin. Fredrick had learned to tune into the creature's habits and wait until it was asleep to plot his return to Earth. If he could learn where the alien crafts were held, he could fly away from this place, assuming he could obtain a bearing for Earth. It was a remote plan, but he held to it to keep his sanity in this insane world.

Fredrick had learned much about Oronas in his ten years here. Their language, customs, habits were the same as humans ten thousand years ago. He was the oldest among them by far, which is why he held the throne. The throne he sat upon was one of shame, not honor. No one spoke to him. He watched as a blonde Oronian girl danced before him. Her blue eyes sparkled in merriment as she undulated seductively before him. Fredrick sat stoically, forcing back his primal urge for her to prevent the serqet from stirring within him. After a while, she moved on to the next man who might please her.

While the rituals of the indigenous people perplexed him at first, the greatest adjustment was the polarity of the planet as compared to Earth, where the axis seemed inverted. The sun never truly set here or rose. It was like living in a perpetual North Pole in the summer. He had studied the horizon for countless hours. There were no mountains along the skyline, and the range of colors here paled in comparison to Earth's. He tried to account for the different colors but could only deduce there was another spectrum at play, almost as if for every color in Earth's spectrum, there was an opposing color here. The headaches during the first month were blinding as his ocular nerves adjusted to the new light and color patterns. Eventually, it led to incredible visual events like a perpetual Aurora Borealis.

He had never seen it rain, but there was plentiful undergrowth. Vast subterranean oceans of fresh water vented with enough regularity to create periodic dense fog which supported the grasslands and the few scrub trees. Short trees dotted the plains around the city blackened by a form of alien lichen.

Herds of large bovine beasts, the orn, wandered the landscape unmolested. They resembled a purple hairy crossbreed of bison and moose and provided a sustainable source of meat. Predatory animals were unknown to the people in the metropolitan area, so the orn grazed peacefully on the plains unafraid. As the beasts slept standing, the aerial robots would swoop in and pluck them like grapes from the vine. The beasts were whisked away to an unseen processing center where they were converted into a protein paste that everyone seemed to eat. The creatures never realized they were being harvested. The rippers would not come within the boundaries of the city.

Fredrick was able to stitch together enough information to estimate the population to be only in the hundreds of thousands in a few cities like the one he was in, versus the billions inhabiting Earth. Fredrick speculated this must be what it was like at the dawn of the Iron Age on Earth.

In his former life as the Duke, he had never taken the time to enjoy the pleasure of art or music. In this place, there was little more than marketing for the serqet incubators. Jeez had masterfully deceived countless breeds of aliens to enter this world in order to create the perfect army; the aliens, on the other hand, had their own reasons for coming here. Like Fredrick, the seduction of evolving beyond the confines of their own mortality outweighed their ability to see the whole picture. Some fled, some died, while many were subjugated to the mines. In hindsight, Fredrick had to face the inconvenient truth that he was nothing more than one of many pawns. Now, as he faced an almost certain death from the spawning demon seed within him, he had no choice but to resolve that he was an arrogant fool on Earth. The thought lay bitterly on his mind. Now, the only thing he could think about was dying on Earth among his people. Even the realization that people hated him on Earth outweighed the anguish of living another day in this place.

He learned that the serqets shared a hive mentality and remained steadfastly loyal to Jeez. She provided them with an endless supply of hosts, and the serqets led Jeez's robot overlords through the dark, dank subterranean caverns where the red crystals were harvested by the Oronian slaves. With time and the limitless resources in this world, Jeez had built an impressive army of human-like robots. The mechanical precision of their design was self-evolved. The robots now built robots.

At first, it had fascinated Fredrick that there were no prisons here. After several years, he realized there was no need. All dissidents were either executed or sent to the mines. Children were screened at puberty. Emotives, children with measurable emotional swings, were reserved as serqet hosts while non-emotives were subjugated to the mines. There were few people above the surface who lived past the age of thirty. It was a simple life: eat, sleep, party, and mate. There were no jobs here, no debt, no work, no education. Humans were relegated to having babies or hosting serqets. The robots worked tirelessly to carry out all the work on the planet freeing the hosts for an idyllic life.

Deep beneath the surface, a harsh subterranean world was ruled by centurion robots unlike the robots on the surface. These were large ungainly automatons with onyx faces and ruby eyes. Few humans lived past the age of fifteen in the mines; sometimes they died of natural causes, many by accident, but most by suicide. The Red Crystal mines lay deep beneath the vast underground freshwater oceans of Oronas. The air in the mines was reputed to be thick and polluted. The food was little more than a nutrient paste rationed daily. The shafts and crystal chambers remained cold. As miners died, their bodies were stripped of clothing almost immediately, so the others could wear additional layers for protection from the frigid temperatures. Occasional tremors would rock the mines. As a tremor struck, a sudden stillness would fall over the chamber. Dark eyes would meet, as each miner wondered if this would be the shock that would cause the roof to fail and bury them all. Sometimes it did.

On Oronas, you lived in heaven or hell; there was no middle ground.

Fredrick had witnessed the only dissident to survive, the Woodcarver. When he first arrived, Fredrick witnessed a brutal robot named Nuuse chain the man to the arena wall and force him to watch, as her strong mechanical fingers strangled the life from his wife and two small children. She was an artificial being with defined emotions. Her dazzling pearly smile stood in stark contrast to her deep red hair. Sadistically, the last thing the Woodcarver saw was her dazzling white smile as she blinded him with the ruby lasers embedded in her eyes. The Woodcarver was released and staggered off across the prairie. All presumed he would die, and yet, Fredrick still heard rumors about the old blind Woodcarver had survived in the wasteland. It was a place where nothing lived, an arid plain with no oasis. It had little more than a few clumps of straw grass and rocky ground. Even the orn would not graze there. Somehow, alone and blind he survived. To what end, no one knew.

Fredrick heard the music amp up a bit as the two hosts of the week danced toward the Altar of Enlightenment. A cheer rose from the crowd as the couple, Pau and Rau, excitedly ran up the steps toward the stage high above; they waved to all the Oronians below them as a cheer went up. There, robots waited patiently for them to arrive. The hosts disrobed and stood naked before the waiting crowd whose cheers reached a deafening roar. One man, one woman. Each with a distended belly of the perverse pregnancy. From his vantage on the throne, Fredrick watched the altars where the hosts lay back head to head on dual rose marble Altars of Ascension. Below, the audience could not take in the entire scene as Fredrick could. With mechanical efficiency, the robots injected each host with a spinal block, immobilizing them on the stone tables. A woman's voice sounded above the din of music and frivolity in the arena:

"In the tradition of the elders, all those who ascend this mortal plain, shall have everlasting life! Join me in welcoming the ascension of our brother and sister to the plain of immortality! Like the butterfly freeing itself from the cocoon, watch as we release the host to the next level of being!"

In one synchronized motion, both robots slit through the skin of the hosts and removed the grown serqet from the hosts. The translucent soft outer shell showed the three beating hearts within the creature as it shivered in the open air. The crowd cheered, as the voice spoke again:

"Welcome the new body of Pau and Rau! Welcome them to the eternal life!"

The blood discreetly drained down the small channels built into the altar from Pau and Rau unnoticed by the crowd below. Fredrick could see Pau's eyes cloud and grow dim. The serqets were handed off to another pair of robots garbed in ceremonial attire who then wrapped the fledgling serqets in silk blankets. The identical blond robots then descended the stage allowing the crowd to gently touch the serqets, whispering blessings to them as they passed to the sacred chamber. Fredrick did not watch the procession of the serqets. He watched as the robots covered the lifeless bodies of Pau and Rau with black sheets. He tried not to ponder the bitter reality that one day, he would be the one under the black sheet, and no one would know or care.

People began to filter out of the temple to attend the orgies which inevitably ensued after an ascension. In the thinning crowd, the blonde Oronian girl with blue eyes resumed her dance before him. She grazed his lower leg with her fingers. Fredrick felt a surge of passion course through him as he shifted on his throne, uncomfortable at the sudden lack of control. He watched for a while before asking, "What is your name?"

She flashed a dazzling smile showing her pearl white teeth. "Luna. And I know you, Fredrick of Earth. Everyone knows of you. You are the oldest serqet host alive."

Fredrick studied her. "And what are your feelings

about that? Do you not hate me, as the others do?"

Her eyes never left him as she twirled around his feet. "I do not hate you, Fredrick. I do not hate anyone. Do you wish to come with me to my bed?"

Fredrick caught himself as his breath drew in rapidly. He watched her supple body move past him. "I suppose I may, if you will not kill me in my sleep."

She stopped and raised an eyebrow as if puzzled. "Why would I kill you, Fredrick? I have no quarrel with you."

Fredrick could see her shapely body beneath the gown now as she stood in front of him. "I mean you no disrespect. Most people shun me."

She placed her hand on his. It was soft and warm. He felt another surge go through him. She responded, "I am not most people."

Fredrick nodded. "Indeed, Luna."

****

Luna's sexual appetite was voracious. Exhausted, Fredrick rolled off her. She immediately straddled him. Both Fredrick's and Luna's serqet bumps glowed amber through the skin in the dim light of her cube. The serqets suckled the dopamine from their hosts, squirming comfortably under their skin. Luna was a vision to behold on top of him. Her blue eyes glowed in the soft light. Her blonde hair framed her high cheekbones and olive skin. She was beautiful in any light. He heard her respiration become shallow and rapid pausing for a moment in a sudden shudder across her body. She placed her hands on his chest and gently kissed him on the lips. He felt a minute charge of energy as she kissed him. A wave of calm passed over him, unlike any he had ever experienced.

She lay beside him, spent from lovemaking. The experience was unique, even for an Oronian. Fredrick propped up on one elbow beside her as he studied her face for a moment before asking, "Are you an empath?"

Her eyes grew large, her lips thinned. The glow from their lovemaking left as quickly as it came. She turned away from him. Fredrick placed his hand gently on her shoulder and tried to soothe her. "I'm not judging, nor will I tell the centurions. I'm just curious."

Luna turned to face him. Tears wet her face. He reached over and wiped them away. She took a deep breath. "I am different. The centurions don't know, no one knows except for you. I read thoughts. I can…change thoughts in others. If they learn this, I will be taken away. I don't know what would become of me or my baby." She rubbed her stomach.

Fredrick narrowed his eyes. "The thing in you is not a child. It is an abomination. If I ever escape from this place, I will have it ripped from my body and burned alive."

Luna's eyes widened in fear. Fredrick lowered his tone. "I am not of this world, but you know that. These creatures inside of us are parasites, nothing more than oversized leeches. Jeez keeps them because they are useful to her. When her need of them wanes, she will abandon them like everything else she touches." He tried to keep the bitterness from his voice.

Luna's soft hand touched his face. "She hurt you deeply. She hurt you to your soul."

He studied her face. She was beautiful and right. He replied, "Yes. All I want to do is leave this place and get this thing out of me."

Soothingly she said, "Or, you can accept your fate

and deliver your child."

Fredrick could feel her invading his mind. He forced her back out. She pulled her hand back. He grabbed it. "Let me save you, Luna. Help me to save us both."

She looked puzzled. "How did you resist me?"

He replied, "I am not without my own abilities." A small shell lay on her bed stand. He focused on the shell until it rose from the stand and floated toward them. He directed her hand up as the shell dropped into it. "As I said, you are not the only one."

She stared at the shell, and then her eyes met his. "How is this possible?"

Fredrick concentrated on the shell once more. He lifted it from Luna's hand and moved it back to the bed stand. He gazed into Luna's blue eyes. "Help me escape from this place. We can live together. I don't know how or where or even how long, but I've never felt this way about another person."

She gave him a sly look. "It's just the pheromones talking."

Fredrick shook his head. "No. I've never felt like this. I'm not some star-crossed sentimentalist. I don't have those kinds of feelings."

They locked gazes for a moment. He leaned over and kissed her gently on the lips. In return she grabbed the back of his head and pulled him toward her hard. There was fire in her kiss. He could feel the tingle of electricity as it passed between them. When she pulled back, she placed her hand on his cheek. "I believe you, Fredrick of Earth."

Chapter 4

Fritz the Estate Manager handed Gretchen a handful of mail. On the top was an official looking document marked: *Deutsche Post Einschreiben Rückschein.* This was significant in two ways: One, Fritz never delivered the mail, and two, registered mail was never a good sign.

She looked at Fritz over her glasses. "Is there anything else, Fritz?"

Fritz responded, "No, ma'am. I just wanted to make sure you received the registered letter in a timely manner."

Gretchen nodded. "Thank you, Fritz. I can handle it from here."

He turned and walked out. Gretchen inspected the envelope carefully before opening. She didn't particularly trust Fritz. The young man always seemed to insert himself into conversations that were not his responsibility. He had worked his way through the ranks from being a scullery butler to becoming Estate Manager. He was tall and thin with a handsome face, but a man with a weak handshake, which concerned Gretchen. He still complained that he was under appreciated, even though he had rocketed through the ranks. She suspected he was doing something underhanded, but she couldn't prove it, nor did she have time to pursue it. She turned her attention to the envelope in her hand. She slit open the top and revealed the court-sealed page. A motion had been filed against the Duke's estate succession, moving that the assets should be transferred to Baron Dagobert Von Meier.

She placed the document on the polished Baroque walnut desk in front of her and sat back. The Duke's wife, the Duchess, had died mysteriously one month earlier. Her lifestyle in the south of France could be described as nothing less than debauchery; however, Gretchen did not believe that her behaviors had led to her demise. This was the third attack by the Baron on the estate. Nothing short of the return of the Duke would ward off the legal attack. She had faithfully protected Wilhelm, the Duke's son, after helping him vanish before the Duke's disappearance. After ten years in hiding, it was time to bring him in from the cold.

She balanced the problem in her mind. She was, by all rights, the head of the most powerful network of private spies in the world. Her identity remained hidden even from the agents in the field. If Wilhelm were to suddenly appear during the legal battle ahead, it would put the spotlight on her and her spies. The Baron was not stupid; he would figure it out. Gretchen suspected him of killing the Duchess.

A soft noise from the hall broke her from her reverie. She pulled up the hall camera on her computer. Fritz stood around the corner just out of sight. At least she knew who the mole in her organization was. The thought occurred to her; he might prove to be useful. Her private phone rang on the desk. She picked up the receiver. "Hello?"

The Baron responded, "Hello, Gretchen. I trust you have received the morning mail?"

There was no value in playing games with him. She responded, "Yes, Baron. I received the court notice."

He replied, "I trust you will help us make the proceedings go smoothly?"

She fought against cringing at his nasal response. "I will comply with what the court requires."

She could hear him smack his lips before he spoke. "If you treat me well, I will consider keeping you on to help manage my new empire. Do you like the sound of that?"

She could not keep the sensation of her skin crawling at the thought of it. She replied, "You are most kind, Baron. I will certainly consider your offer."

He replied, "Hmm, please me, and I will take care of you, *personally*."

It was the vilest thought imaginable. "Baron, as you can imagine, we have much to do, so I will not keep you. Have a good day." Without waiting she hung up the phone.

Fritz was still standing in the hallway. She could see him smiling. Gretchen could not decide if she wanted to have him killed or tortured until he begged to die. She would have to decide.

****

Gretchen cruised north on the Tauern Autobahn. She spoke carefully on the secured line to Dominic. "We have a time critical operation. A legal motion has been filed to turn Duke Fredrick Lindenspear's estate over to Baron Dagobert Von Meier. We suspect the Baron is responsible for the murder of Duchess Abigail Lindenspear, the late wife of the Duke. The Duke is still missing, presumed dead. We need to determine if there is evidence to link the Baron to the Duchess's murder."

Dominic responded, "Has the Suerte been engaged?"

Gretchen replied, "No. The local authorities have been paid off and the official statement is it was a drug overdose. It has been ruled accidental and closed."

Dominic replied, "Is there any evidence left on the scene?"

Gretchen responded, "The scene has been sealed since the event. A full set of forensic samples have been preserved for analysis. The information has been uploaded to a secure cloud server."

Dominic worded his next question carefully. "What is the desired outcome of the operation?"

Gretchen didn't mince words. "We need enough plausible evidence to implicate the Baron. We are not interested in prosecuting him, just the correct amount to cast a reasonable doubt over him."

Dominic asked, "What is our timing to completion?"

Gretchen did the math quickly. The first hearing was in two weeks to hear motions, her team would ask for an extension. The delay would buy them a month. "You have five days."

Dominic didn't flinch. "Is there any buffer built into that number?"

Gretchen replied, "No. Turn over the forensics to the legal team, they will build the case."

Dominic paused for a moment; Gretchen could hear him scribbling notes. "I will speak to you again in five days when we have the data."

The call disconnected. Gretchen dialed a number in America.

A female voice answered, "This is Gillian."

Gretchen was to the point. "Hello, Gillian. This is the Director. I have an important mission for you. You will not have a liaison on this case. I will be giving you instructions directly."

Gillian responded, "Hello, Director. Marty and I were just talking about you. Proceed with the instructions."

Gretchen paused for a moment. The statement threw her off. She responded carefully, "What do you mean?"

Gillian replied, "Marty would like to visit the Relic. I am free to complete the mission."

Gretchen considered the request. It added a layer of complexity, but she could leverage using Marty as a distraction to the Baron's team, possibly throwing them off the trail. She responded, "Very well, we will proceed with the plan for you to fly to Lisbon, Portugal, and take custody of the man you will escort. You will connect at the Coconut Groove Bar on da Rosa. Take him by train to Vienna. A team will take over at the Museum Judenplatz and you will transfer custody of the subject."

Gillian asked, "How will I know the subject? How will I know the team?"

Gretchen replied, "I will text you a picture of the subject. I will provide him with a picture of you. He will respond to 'Bill.' The team leader in Vienna, Hans, will provide you with a business card. On the back it will read: *Rose Thorn*."

Gillian responded, "And Marty?"

Gretchen replied, "He will have a plane waiting at the Lisbon airport. They will fly him to Jordan. A jeep will be waiting for him there. I can't promise much more."

Gillian replied, "Fair enough. He may have an extra person with him, is that a problem?"

Gretchen responded, "No. I don't care. Just don't let anything happen to the subject. Am I clear?"

Gillian replied, "Crystal. When do I leave?"

Gretchen responded, "You will need to be in Lisbon in three days."

****

Gretchen called Wilhelm. She regretted calling him so soon after his mother's death, but the situation was desperate. There was music and the din of conversation in the background when he answered. "Hello, Frau Stahl."

Gretchen replied, "Where are you now?"

Wilhelm coughed. "Huelva, Spain."

Finally, a stroke of luck. "I need to bring you back in, there's a situation."

Wilhelm sighed. "What?"

Gretchen replied, "Your cousin, the Baron, is trying to lay claim to the estate."

Wilhelm cursed softly. "I suppose it's because Mother is dead, correct?"

Gretchen replied, "Precisely. Without you, there is not a clear heir to the empire. Dagobert is filing a motion as the only living heir to the estate."

Wilhelm was quiet for a moment before he asked, "Do you think he killed my mother?"

Gretchen replied carefully. "I am investigating the matter privately. I cannot say for sure, but it seems suspicious."

Wilhelm responded, "Bert always was a wanker.

All right, who do I need to meet, where do I need to go?"

Wilhelm returned to the bar where Chris was nursing a beer and Cutty was trying unsuccessfully to pick up a Spanish bar maid with an angelic face and a low-cut blouse. Wilhelm turned his beer up and emptied it. He looked at Chris and said, "We need to talk outside."

Chris nodded. He tapped Cutty on the shoulder and dropped a twenty Euro bill on the neon and chrome bar. "Let's go, Cutty."

Cutty whined, "But I was just about to hook up with this girl." He jabbed his thumb at the barmaid.

Chris raised an eyebrow, and in a soft Jamaican accent he replied, "The only thing you're going to hook is your mouth when she reels you in for all your cash, you bum."

Cutty snorted. "Whatever!"

On the cobblestone street outside, the three walked and talked. Wilhelm looked at Chris. "I have to go back."

Chris shook his head. "You know you're always welcome to stay with Mama on the island. She loves you like a son."

Wilhelm nodded. "I know, but this is different. If I don't go, there will be people after me, and there is nowhere they can't find me. I can't put your family in danger."

The tall Jamaican put his hand on Wilhelm's shoulder. "It's your family too; we adopted you, brother."

Wilhelm's eyes were unwavering, like steel. "All the more reason."

Chris laughed. “We can always give them Cutty.”

Cutty glared. “Hey! I’m standing right here, ya big goon.”

Chris continued, “So what do we need to do?”

Wilhelm thought for a moment. “We’re meeting in Lisbon, let’s sail up the coast.”

Cutty piped up, “Yea! Portuguese women are the best.”

Wilhelm looked at Cutty. “Man, do you ever think of anything else?”

Cutty rubbed his chin. “Not since the Corps, man. When your life is on the line, you jam in as much livin’ as you can. There might not be another chance. Did I tell you about the girl in Barcelona name Lucinda? Now, if I were ever going to settle down with one woman, she would be the one.”

Both Chris and Wilhelm looked at each other and laughed at the same time.

Cutty looked confused. “What?”

Chris looked up at the night sky. “It’s getting late, let’s hit the racks, get up early in the morning and buy supplies. We can be on open water just after sunrise.”

Cutty furrowed his brow. “But the night’s young.”

Chris put his arm around Cutty’s shoulder. “We’re on a mission now. Remember MOM from the old days? Mind on mission, all right?”

Cutty took a deep breath. “Right. Mind on mission.”

The three wandered toward the port. Wilhelm thought to himself, *these are the best friends I’ve ever had*. He looked at his friends and said, “How about one more for the road, aye boys?”

Cutty broke into a big grin. “Now you’re talking

like a Marine!"

Chris shook his head. "I'm probably going to regret this."

Chapter 5

The Baron carved out a large bite of beef dumpling, swirled it with sauerkraut, and stuffed it in his mouth. His double chin wobbled as he chewed. He savored the tartness of the kraut for a moment before taking a large drink of a lovely New Zealand sauvignon blanc. As he raised his fork for another attack on the dumpling, a young woman approached his table. He carefully placed the fork down and motioned to her to sit beside him, so she wouldn't obstruct his view of the Danube.

The young woman bore a striking resemblance to Gillian Wood in both her body and face; in fact, the two could be twins. She greeted the Baron. "*Guten Tag*."

To which he raised his hand. He responded, "In English please, Ella."

The timbre of her voice and pronunciation was identical to Gillian's. "Good afternoon, Baron."

She was perfect. "So it appears our operation is about to begin. Do you have all the necessary arrangements in order?"

With cool precision she recited the details. "Meet the subject in Lisbon and eliminate. Cremate the remains at Figueira. Ensure there is no traceability from the cremation with our asset in Figueira."

The Baron smiled and took another sip of wine. "Excellent. And what of Frau Stahl?"

Ella replied, “I have a pair of assets, they call themselves M and M, short for Mark and Mike. One has been assigned to Gillian Wood, the other to Gretchen Stahl. Wood will be eliminated in the most expedient method possible; Stahl will appear to be an accident.”

The Baron wiped his mouth with a linen table napkin. A young server appeared with a bottle of wine, filling his glass and gracefully gliding back into the shadows. The Baron sipped the wine. He replied, “When I have confirmation of the success of the operation, deposits will be made in the Swiss accounts within eight hours. Is that acceptable?”

Ella’s face never changed expression. “Those are our usual terms.”

The Baron again picked at his dumpling with his fork. “Who is assigned to neutralize Wood?”

Ella’s eyebrow raised slightly. “Does it matter?”

The Baron set his fork down gently. “Yes, it does. Wood is quite cunning and a formidable adversary. We need to ensure we have assigned the best asset to deal with her. There can be no mistakes.”

Her expression was neutral. “These men are professionals. They have one hundred kills between them. I trust them both equally. If it would make you feel better, you can pick the one you like.”

The Baron shook his head. “No, that won’t be necessary. So long as we are clear on the importance of a flawless operation.”

The young woman nodded. “We’re clear.”

The Baron nodded. “Excellent. Would you care for some lunch?”

She shook her head. “I have details to finish up. I’ll

contact you when it's finished."

The young woman stood. The Baron stabbed at his dumpling and swirled it in kraut. He watched her as she walked away without a word.

****

Marty sat on an ugly gray faux leather seat willing himself to be calm. Jacob wandered around the terminal looking in the various shops and at the variety of items offered. He patted Gillian on the arm. "Mom, what is the C-shaped thing?"

Gillian replied, "It's a neck pillow. They're pretty handy for long trips when you lean back in the seat; it gives your neck support."

He thought for a moment. "Do you think it would help Dad?"

She kissed him on the head. "I think he will appreciate you're thinking about him. He hates to fly. He had a horrible experience as a child."

Jacob nodded. "Let's get three."

She agreed. "Good idea."

Marty looked up as Jacob approached with the pillow. "What's this?"

Jacob held out the pillow. "I thought it might help you feel better."

Marty reached out and took the pillow from his hand. He placed it on the top of his head like a hat. "Humm. Now that you mention it, I do feel better."

Jacob laughed. The gate attendant called for the first boarding. Marty stood, grabbing his black backpack. "Okay, gang, this looks like our ride."

Jacob tugged his sleeve. "Dad, your, uh, hat."

Marty grabbed the tartan neck pillow from his head. "Thanks, son."

The three sat together in the middle aisle. The flight would take them to Heathrow and then to Lisbon. It would be a very long day. The people filed in around them while Marty opened the tiny port to allow airflow over him. The hiss of air felt good against the cold sweat dotting his forehead. He closed his eyes and tried to visualize another place. The vision took him by surprise. He could see the plate of food before him. He observed as the view changed to a riverfront scene. The view changed again as a woman approached. It was Gillian. But she spoke in German. He realized it was not his wife, but a double. He listened carefully as she described the plan. The vision ended. Marty opened his eyes. He looked at Gillian and said, “We have a problem.”

****

Ella sat in a straight-back chair at the table, in an apartment with only a kitchen table, a chair, and a bed. There was no food in the refrigerator, no other furniture in the living areas. The table behind the laptop was littered with papers and maps. She dialed a number on a disposable phone. The voice on the other end answered, “This is Mark.”

Ella responded, “We have a time and a place. We need to meet face to face to go over the details.”

Mark responded, “When and where?”

Ella replied, “The old cannery on the abandoned wharf in Lisbon. Bring your partner. Eleven a.m. tomorrow.”

Mark replied, “We’ll be there.”

The line went dead.

Ella sat back and considered the options. She would be responsible for Wilhelm. Mike and Mark would handle Gillian Wood and Gretchen Stahl. Wood was a deadly adversary. Of the two, Mark should handle the contract. She would put Mike on Gretchen Stahl; it would be less complex, and Mike's assignments were artfully done, they always appeared to be accidental. He was an artist in the world of homicide.

Ella stood from the chair and walked to the bathroom. She stared at her reflection in the mirror. A stranger's reflection stared back at her. She had been paid a lot of money to transform her looks so she doubled for the American woman Gillian Wood. Ella wondered if it was worth it or if she would change back once the American was dead. Her old face was on several watch lists, but then the face she had now was not unknown. Gillian Wood had terminated several of her colleagues. Her problem now was she didn't know who her enemies were. It seemed more problematic for the future. Perhaps she would change to yet another face when it was over, a new face altogether. There would be time for that later.

****

The room smelled of cigarettes and cheap perfume. Mike leaned on the belly of a naked busty bleached blonde prostitute next to him, to grab the phone from the nightstand. The hooker grunted and pushed him down, so he lay on her pelvis. Mike answered the phone. "Yeah?"

Mark responded, "Hey, we've got a job. How soon can you make it to the abandoned wharf in Lisbon?"

Mike replied, "I'm in Monaco. I can be there tomorrow."

Mark instructed, "The old cannery at eleven."

Mike grabbed a pack of cigarettes from the nightstand and lit two. He handed one to the hooker. She took it from him and took a long drag. He replied, "Got it. Eleven, at the old cannery." The line went dead. He looked at the prostitute. "Got time for another round?"

With the cigarette clinched between perfect teeth, she grinned and opened her arms. "You like it if I blow smoke on you?"

"Oh yeah, baby."

****

Mark's wife, Grace, eased the door open and entered the room. He closed the laptop as she walked up behind him. She hugged his neck. "Supper's almost ready."

He swiveled the chair to face her and kissed her on the lips. "When is Tommy's soccer match?"

Grace looked thoughtful for a moment. "It's Saturday, a week."

Mark nodded. "Good. I got the call; I must leave for an important sales trip. I will be back here in time to watch his debut as goalie. Are they playing at Lake Taylor?"

Grace stood up straight. "I think they are."

Mark stood. "We'll go get ice cream afterward."

Grace touched his cheek. "He'll like that. Where are you off to now?"

Mark looked down. "Lisbon. It's a major contract, very high profile. The CEO asked for me directly."

Grace looked impressed. "Maybe you'll get a big bonus."

Mark looked thoughtful. "I'm pretty sure of it. So what's for dinner?"

Grace replied, "Lasagna."

Mark nodded. "Mm. My favorite."

She turned, and he patted her on the bottom. "Maybe Tommy will have an early night tonight."

She turned and gave him a sly look. "Maybe."

****

The old cannery had been abandoned for years. The gray timbers creaked under foot as Ella moved carefully up the stairs. Somewhere behind her, pigeons took flight, startled by her on the stairs. Even after ten years of standing empty, the building still smelled of rotting fish. Rats scurried along the wall, leaving her on edge from all the small sounds. Mike sat on an old kitchen chair in the middle of the expansive room. The chair's chrome legs now ensconced by rust; the flowered vinyl was peeling along the edges. His feet were propped up on a rusting conveyor as he smoked a cigarette.

Ella looked around before asking, "Where's your partner?"

Mike studied her but said nothing. A voice sounded in her ear as Mark said, "Behind you."

She whirled around to see him leaning against the rail.

Her brow furrowed. "Man, you're quiet!"

Mike replied, "You hired us to be discreet."

Ella nodded. "Point taken. Now, let's get to it."

She moved to an old wooden worktable and pushed the old cans and papers covered in dust onto the floor. She laid out three dossiers. "I don't suppose I need to tell you this will be the highest paid contract we've seen yet."

Mark asked, "How much?"

Ella placed a dossier in front of each of them. “One million US, each.”

Mike let out a low whistle. “Sounds like a retirement gig to me.”

Ella narrowed her eyes. “Only if we succeed on all three targets. If we don’t, we will be the targets.”

Mark opened his packet. The photo looked like Ella staring back at him. His brow furrowed. “Is this some kind of joke?”

Ella replied, “I was reconstructed to look like the subject. It is the only way I can get close enough to my target.”

Mark began to understand the complexity of the operation. “So how do I make sure I have acquired the correct target?”

Ella reached into a tapestry shoulder bag and pulled out a black leather vest sporting a large golden dragon with a rainbow-colored wings emblem on the back. “I will be wearing this. It’s the only one like it. I had it custom made. It’s a ballistic vest underneath.”

Mark nodded.

Mike opened his Dossier. Gretchen stared back at him. “Dame’s pretty hot. Seems a shame to off her.”

Ella held her temper in check. “Stay focused. If you have an issue with this being too direct, do it remotely.”

Mike shook his head. “No issue with it, it just seems like a shame.” Mike flipped through the dossier to the plans to her apartment. He studied the utilities. It seemed straight forward enough, work on the gas line into the apartment, rig a remote detonator, wait until she entered, hit the button; done and done.

Ella handed M and M a pair of disposable phones.

"We will not meet again after this. There are account numbers in both dossiers for numbered Swiss accounts. When you have confirmation of the kill, text a verification picture to the contact in the phone. When the client has received all three verifications, the money will be wired directly into the accounts. Any questions?"

Mark shook his head. "Seems pretty straight forward."

Mike rose from the chair. "I'll send out confirmation in three days."

Ella nodded. "Good hunting, men."

Mark walked away without a sound.

Chapter 6

Marty, Gillian, and Jacob disembarked the seven-forty-seven in Lisbon stiff from the long flight. Gillian rented a car while Marty retrieved the bags. The open ceilings and vast, white-tiled floors made the terminal look immense on the inside. Jacob held Marty's hand tightly as they moved toward the baggage claim area. "Dad, this place feels weird."

Marty pulled him closer. "It's okay. Foreign countries are just different. The same is true for people coming to America for the first time. We'll be fine."

Jacob looked up with deeply serious eyes. "Are you sure?"

Marty looked reassuringly. "I'm positive."

Gillian met them halfway to the exit with car keys dangling from her hand and they walked side by side out the terminal. Jacob was jammed in the back seat with the bags in a tiny red Fiat. Gillian maneuvered out of the terminal like she had driven it one hundred times. Marty watched her drive. It was remarkable to him how comfortable she was driving in foreign traffic, as she careened from side to side to the Tings Hotel. The hotel was a beautifully comfortable old place with arched balconies overlooking the city to the ocean. The smell of the ocean breeze seemed to clear away the fatigue.

As they settled into the room, Jacob slung open the doors and flopped on a comfortable settee in the corner.

He called out, “Mom, Dad, can we move here?”

Marty chuckled. “We’ll talk about it.” He looked Gillian in the eyes. “We need to call Gretchen. We’re all walking into a trap.”

Gillian nodded. “I’ve got a scrambler. I’ll make a secure call.”

****

Mike looked furtively right and left as he picked the lock on Gretchen’s apartment. He eased the door closed behind him as he walked to the kitchen and found the gas valve to the stove. He closed the valve and unscrewed the connection; a puff of gas smelled briefly and dissipated. Deftly, he attached a three-dimensioned printed solenoid-controlled valve on the pipe and reconnected it. He removed a small remote-controlled detonator and glued it to the wall. The parts would all melt in the fire that ensued, leaving no trace other than the ruptured line. He left the apartment swiftly down the fire escape. The aged rental van was positioned just in view of the apartment entrance. Mike settled into the seat and waited for Gretchen to return home.

After two hours, he shifted uncomfortably as he struggled to stay awake. The monotony of it was maddening. He rubbed his eyes to wipe away the drowsiness. A large BMW sedan eased into a parking space in front of the apartment and Gretchen stepped out. Her skirt slid up almost to mid-thigh causing Mike to sit bolt upright in the seat. His eyes were riveted on Gretchen. He watched her every move, trying not to envision her dying in a hellish inferno. An elderly woman walked toward Gretchen as she waited on the steps to the Brownstone. As the woman approached, they spoke. Gretchen helped the woman carry her grocery cart up the small stair to the apartment and held the door while the elderly woman entered. Mike found himself smiling as he considered that the old woman would die as well; he was sadistic, which is what made him such a refined assassin. This continued to get better. He looked at his watch; he would wait five minutes for her to enter the apartment before he initiated the explosive.

****

Gretchen kicked off her Italian heels as she entered the apartment and dead bolted the door behind her. Removing the band around the tight bun on her hair, it cascaded over her shoulders. The apartment smelled like lemon oil where her housekeeper, Greta, had cleaned earlier in the day. She thumbed through the mail as she walked down the hall. Most of it was sales correspondence, none of which she had any interest in. One from her Alma Mater asking for donations, which made her smile at the memory of college. She dropped the pile of mail on a small credenza in the hall and moved to the bedroom. She needed a hot bath to take the edge off. She walked into the spacious master bathroom from her bedroom and turned on the water as hot as she could possibly stand it.

She exited the bathroom and stopped dead in her tracks. A man sat comfortably in the corner of the bedroom in a leather wingback chair. His face was concealed by a hooded black cloak which framed a red and black kabuki mask. She scanned the room for something to defend herself. The closest object was a leaded glass lamp at the bed stand.

Before she could move, the man said, “You are in

great danger; you have two minutes to leave the apartment or you will die. Change your clothes to something you don't normally wear out in public and grab your wallet. Don't bother with your car keys."

She challenged him. "So I suppose you're going to watch me change?"

The man stood. "One minute fifty seconds. You must move faster, we don't have time to discuss this."

She stood still, edging toward the lamp. "And what are you going to do, if I don't follow your instructions?"

The man opened his hands to her. "Nothing. I am not the one you are in danger from. One minute forty seconds. If it will ease your mind, I will step out of the room. But please hurry." The man stood effortlessly and seemed to glide from the room. His feet didn't seem to touch the floor.

Gretchen considered the situation quickly. There was something familiar about the man. She had no reason to trust him, but her instincts told her she must. She ripped the tan business suit off, rushed to the closet, and grabbed a navy-blue sweat suit and sneakers. She pulled on the sweat suit. She pulled the shoes on without socks. The voice from the hall called out. "One minute."

She ran to the hall and grabbed her wallet and keys. The voice sounded like it was everywhere now. "Leave the keys. Just take the wallet and your planner."

She ran to the front door which was still bolted shut. The voice was in front of her. "Use the back door. Forty-five seconds."

She bolted through the apartment and into the kitchen. The smell of gas was almost overpowering.

She jerked the back door open and began to sprint down the fire escape into the alley below. She neared the street below when she heard the man's voice behind her. "Time's up." The violence of the explosion threatened to cause the fire escape to collapse. It trembled all around her. Flaming debris fell around her. Her heart was pounding in her chest.

When her feet touched the ground, impossibly, the cloaked figure stood on the street waiting for her. He said, "Hide in Old Town, use only cash."

This time she didn't question. She ran past the man and didn't stop until she was in Old Town. She didn't see the cloaked figure evaporate behind her.

In Old Town she slowed to a walk, periodically doubling back to see if anyone was following her. Tourists milled about which made everything seem ordinary. She stopped at a coffee vendor on the street and looked toward her apartment. The black plume of smoke was visible even from where she stood. She headed away from the smoke. She ducked into a small hotel wedged between a lady's boutique and a schnitzel restaurant.

Inside, a plump woman greeted her warmly. "Welcome to the Hotel Bredleberg, my name is Ada. How may I help you?"

Gretchen scanned the lobby, which was small, but tidy. "I need a room for a few nights while my apartment is fumigated."

Ada nodded in understanding. "Of course. Forty euros a night."

Gretchen pulled out two-one hundred Euro notes. "I'll check back in a few days and let you know if I'm staying longer." She looked Ada in the eye and asked,

"Is that all right?"

Ada took the bills and handed her a key. "Whatever you need, please let me know."

The hotel was quaint but well kept. She opened the window to the fire escape and tested how much time it would take to exit. She closed the window and drew the drapes. As she walked past the small desk, she grabbed the wooden desk chair and dragged it to the door, then she dead bolted the door and wedged a desk chair underneath the knob. She took inventory of what she had as she spread the contents of her wallet across the bed. She had three thousand Euros in cash. It would last her for several days. If she surfaced using a credit card, whomever was trying to kill her would know she was alive. There was not a television in the room. She would have to catch the news elsewhere. In the meantime, she needed to contact the team.

She sat back against the headboard for a moment. She tried to slow down the blur of the last hour in her mind. The thought struck her quite suddenly, Frau Schmidt, her neighbor, lived right beside her. She had probably not survived the explosion. A flood of emotion flowed over her; she couldn't hold back the tears. She grabbed a pillow to muffle the sobbing. She had not cried since the Duke had killed her sister over ten years ago. She didn't know what to think. The mysterious stranger in her apartment, the attempt on her life, being cut off from her network. The realization she was no longer in control of the empire created a knot in her stomach. She took a deep breath. She had survived the constant pressure of running the Duke's empire for the last ten years. She was accustomed to stress, but not the kind of stress where people were trying to kill you.

Now the pressure was personal, it felt different.

She wiped away the tears. She needed a phone. It was time to regain some control over the situation. She sat on the bed thinking. There were so many things to do, and yet she could not rise off the bed.

****

Mike took a photo of the inferno that was Gretchen's apartment and texted it to the number. He cranked the van and eased away from the curb and past the screaming fire trucks. He drove slowly down the street trying to remember where the red-light district was in Innsbruck.

****

Light streamed through the window at daybreak. Gretchen went to the bathroom and washed her face with cold water. She hardly recognized the reflection staring back at her in the mirror. She scrounged through the pockets of her sweat suit and found a hair band. She smoothed back her hair and tied it into a ponytail.

Downstairs Ada greeted her warmly. "Here, my dear." She handed Gretchen a voucher for breakfast at the *Haus Schnitzel* next door. Gretchen forced a smile. "Thank you."

The street was quiet in the cool of early morning, but the Schnitzel restaurant was a beehive of activity. She found a quiet corner table and sat with her back against the wall. A young woman with long black hair and an embroidered top offered her coffee. Without looking at the menu she ordered muesli with fresh fruit. Gretchen sipped the steaming coffee and considered her next move, contacting Gillian was imperative. It was obvious the Baron had laid traps for all of them. How he knew about Wilhelm, she didn't know. Within a few minutes, the dark haired server returned with the muesli. She asked the girl, "Is there a store close by where I can buy a phone? I dropped mine in the tub last night."

The young woman nodded. "It happens to me all the time. There's a variety store one block down. They sell no contract phones. I've bought three from them."

Gretchen mumbled "*Danka*" while she ate the muesli. She didn't realize how hungry she was.

Outside, more tourists seemed to be on the streets. Inside the variety store, she picked up a phone and headed back to the room. Safely inside, she keyed in Gillian's number. The response calmed her a bit. "This is Gillian."

Gretchen replied, "We've had an incident. They tried to kill me last night."

Gillian responded, "Are you injured?"

Gretchen replied, "No. I made it out. I don't know if they think I am dead. I'm cut off. I can't resurface without letting them know."

Gillian responded, "Stay low. I will pick you up after I have Wilhelm."

Gretchen was quiet for a moment. "What if they kill Wilhelm?"

Gillian's voice was tight. "We'll have to make sure they don't. I am going to assume that I am the next target. I plan to meet Wilhelm tonight. I'm in Lisbon now. I will call you back at this number when I have him."

Gretchen replied, "Good luck."

Gillian responded, "You too." The line went dead. Now it was a waiting game.

****

The ocean was deep blue with a hint of chop. At fifteen knots the south wind kept a full sail and pushed them steadily up the coastline. It was Wilhelm's turn to make lunch. He baked Jerk Chicken while pea soup simmered on the stovetop, it was Chris's favorite. With any luck they would be in Lisbon at three p.m. Cutty was below deck tuning the engine. Chris steered the boat and enjoyed the wind and sun. Wilhelm looked out the port window and watched as dark clouds drifted past on the windward side of the boat. He guessed the storm would pass south of them leaving them with smooth sailing all the way to Lisbon. It would be their last day on the boat together for a while. It would be a memorable one.

Wilhelm yelled for Cutty to come up for lunch, while he carried a tray of food above deck along with Portuguese beers from their stop in Sines. On deck, no one spoke as they tore through the chicken and beers, a testament to Wilhelm's cooking. They sat back on the deck and basked in the sun. Wilhelm enjoyed his last hours of anonymity. After today, it would all change. He looked at Cutty for a moment and asked, "Cutty, where did you get a name like Cutty?"

Cutty grinned. "My Dad was a scotch drinker, his favorite was Cutty Sark. My mom had a hard labor, so she was still under anesthesia when the doctors asked my dad for a name. He said 'Cutty'."

Chris laughed. "What did your mother think of that?"

Cutty chuckled. "According to my dad, she wanted to kill him. If she could have gotten out of the hospital bed, she probably would have. It worked out for me though. I was a military brat and joined as soon as I turned eighteen." He picked at his back tooth with a toothpick. "Did I ever tell you guys about the time I took out a baby killer?"

Chris and Wilhelm exchanged looks. Cutty didn't talk about his time as a sniper in the Marines. Wilhelm and Chris shook their heads. Cutty continued. "He was a known explosives expert in a terror cell in Afghanistan. He didn't care about who he hurt—women, children, old people. They were all the same to him, a number. I watched him for fifteen minutes waiting for the shot. He was to the north, so I adjusted for the Coriolis by three clicks to the right. He just stood there running his mouth when I took the shot. No more running his mouth, no more baby killer."

A chill went up Wilhelm's spine.

Chris asked, "Why did you think of that today?"

Cutty broke from his reverie. "It was like this. Clear, blue, a perfect day. We didn't get many of those in Afghan. Sand got into everything there."

Wilhelm changed the subject. "Where will you guys go after today?"

Chris was thoughtful for a moment. "It's a good time to sail to Kingston. I haven't seen Momma in a while."

Wilhelm smiled at the thought of Chris's mom. She was a large loving woman with a fondness for color. Their home looked like a rainbow inside. Every room was a different vibrant color. She spent her time sewing and cooking for whoever stopped in. Wilhelm was wearing a shirt she had made for him. It was soft and tropical; he wore it often. He missed her Jamaican Bun. When it was warm from the oven with cream cheese all melted, it was an explosion of wonderfulness. It was a good memory. "Give her my best."

Chris formed his large Jamaican grin. "Indeed. She will miss you."

An hour later, tall white structures with red terracotta roofs appeared on the shoreline as the outskirts of Lisbon came into view. It was beautiful and terrifying at the same time. A tightening in Wilhelm's stomach made him pause. It was the first time he had gone back to Germany in ten years. He would miss the sea.

****

Gillian kissed Marty long and deep. It was a luxurious kiss neither wanted to end. Gillian cradled Marty's face in her hands. "I need you to leave now."

Marty looked surprised. "Why?"

Her gaze narrowed. "Because Mama's got to go to work."

****

Gillian stood in the side alley at the Coconut Groove Bar. The smell of garbage and urine permeated the air. But it allowed her to observe the street leading to the entrance to the bar. She could keep track of the players from this vantage point. She sensed the presence in the alley with her. The voice inside her head warned her: *He's behind you. He has a garrote.*

She could sense it was Marty, warning her.

Strangling a professional is very tricky business. Especially when the victim is aware. She could only assume Marty was channeling. She took a deep breath and willed herself to relax. *He's closing in. His arms are raised. He's over your head...*

The timing would have to be perfect. The assailant's knee would come up as the garrote dropped.

The way he would center his knee in her back would make it difficult to defend against it. Most victims would try to put the hand in the way of the garrote. She would not. At the last moment, she could feel the energy of the wire and the knee coming toward her. She dropped straight down, riding his thigh to the ground. She landed on her shoulders with her arms outstretched to absorb the fall. In a lightning fast move her legs shot back, striking the assailant in the solar plexus, punching him backward into the large dumpster behind them. She pushed her legs upward, righting herself and spinning backward in a vicious kick, striking him a second time.

The assassin dropped the garrote and reached in his blazer for a knife. Almost instantly, he clicked the switchblade open and moved to attack. Gillian was not prepared for what happened next. She became a spectator to her body's actions. The assassin lunged with the knife. She watched as the blade moved toward her in slow motion. She observed her hand grab the assassin's wrist and hold it with ease. The assassin's fist came toward her. Her own parry was so powerful it snapped his arm like a dry twig. There was a sickening crack as the arm broke. She grabbed the assassin by the throat and lifted him off the ground as if he were a rag doll. She held him off the ground watching him twist in the air like a bizarre puppet. She tightened her grip on his knife hand and felt the bones in his hand break like twigs. She turned his own blade back toward his chest. He had no will to stop her as the knife slowly pierced his clothes, sliding though his skin like tissue paper and ever so slowly into his pericardial sac where his heart beat frantically within his chest. The knife pierced his heart and caused it to explode in his chest. He went limp in her hand. Holding him aloft in one hand like a sack of garbage, she threw back the lid to the large waste container with her free hand and tossed him in effortlessly.

A new voice sounded in her head: *You are mine. No one may take you but me.*

Gillian slumped to the ground unconscious.

****

Mark was surrounded by white light. Faces came into focus. The light began to change to amber and then to red. The faces surrounding him were those of his victims. Their laughter thundered in his ears. The face of his last victim, Garrick Kemp, faced him with black angry eyes. Kemp's voice thundered in his ears. "Welcome to Hell, Mark! Everyone here is waiting to feast on your flesh and dance on your bones. Ha! Ha! Ha!"

****

Gillian regained consciousness in the alley. Her head pounded. She looked at her hand in the dim light; she could see the blood on her left hand. She scanned the rest of her body. She could feel no pain, and she did not have blood anywhere else on her. She would have to enter the club. She grabbed an old newspaper off the ground, wiped the blood off her hand, and threw it backward into the trash container. She looked at picture of "Bill" on her phone. The picture was old, his dark piercing eyes glared at the camera. His black hair was in disarray, and his face was thin. Aside from looking seedy, he was really handsome. She stuck the phone in her pocket and picked the lock on the side door slipping unnoticed into the Coconut Groove.

The Blue Haired Leach band was on break, so the

tunes of smoky jazz played over the house speakers. Aqua up-lighting cast bizarre shadows on the limestone block walls, contrasted by a surreal gloss on the parquet floors. People languished about with drinks, occasionally breaking through the music with raucous laughter. The bar lights rotated with bright LED lights to the left of the bandstand. Three men sat at the bar facing outward. The one in the middle was the subject. Gillian almost didn't recognize him. He had filled out and sported a tan. He was tall and muscular. His body had been shaped by work and not in a gym. Gillian watched from the shadows, surveying the room. A tall man with slicked back black hair flashed a pearly white smile and walked toward her. She regarded him coldly as he began to speak in Portuguese. She shook her head and raised her hands. In broken English, he asked, "I am Andre, do you like our beautiful bar?"

Gillian nodded. "It's nice." She focused on the three men at the bar behind him. The local eased over in her line of sight. She placed a firm grip on his arm and moved him to the side.

Andre's jaw dropped as she applied pressure to his arm. To her surprise, he didn't walk away. Instead, he asked, "Are you a tourist here in our beautiful city?"

Gillian never broke her gaze on the bar. "I'm here looking for the right man."

Andre grinned broadly. "Then you have found him! It's me!"

She broke her gaze for only a moment and gave him a thin smile. Andre was going to prove useful.

Andre continued, "And I am so lucky to find such a *bonito amante.*"

When Gillian saw the woman approach from the

right side of the bar, she drew in her breath. Andre misinterpreted the gasp and drew closer. Gillian was looking at a mirror image of herself. Marty had warned her about her double, but she was surprised at the resemblance. The woman walked straight to the subject and struck up a conversation with him. Gillian could sense she would lose them very quickly in the confusion.

Gillian turned her focus to Andre. "Do you dance?"

He grinned broadly. "Like you have never seen?"

She led him out, carefully positioning herself so the subject could not see her. She swayed to the jazz, undulating her hips suggestively. Andre followed her every move. He really was a great dancer. She looked up at the mirrored ceiling. They danced even closer to the bar. Gillian blinked slowly and said quietly, "Spin me, lover." She held out her hand. He took her hand and spun her deftly around him. As she came around in a circle toward the bar, she lifted herself into a spinning back kick centering her doppelganger in the chest.

Ella fell back dazed. Gillian was in Wilhelm's face. "Gretchen sent me, that woman is an imposter. We need to leave; your position has been compromised."

Cutty was on his feet. "Everybody down!"

Gillian looked back to see Ella holding an automatic pistol. Before she could react, Ella pulled the trigger. Cutty dove in front of Gillian and fell to the floor, blood oozed from his forehead. Ella aimed at Gillian. This time Gillian was ready. She concentrated on the gun, as Ella pulled the trigger Gillian concentrated on the round in the chamber. It spun in the barrel but did not come out, fusing it in the tip of the barrel. Ella did not wait she pulled the trigger again.

The slide exploded in her hand sending fragments into her skull. She fell backward crashing into the floor. There was a momentary stunned silence in the bar, before a tall dark-haired girl screamed. Pandemonium ensued. People ran screaming, patrons dove into the floor. Gillian turned back to Wilhelm. "We've got to get you out of here."

Wilhelm looked at her for a moment. "How do I know you're not the imposter?"

He felt Chris standup behind him. He imagined his friend at his back, a head taller, and one hundred pounds heavier.

Gillian's expression did not change. "In your father's castle there is a guest room with gold relief Fleur de Lis wallpaper. If I could have killed him, I would have."

Wilhelm raised an eyebrow. "Yep. I think that sums it up."

He looked at Chris. "Are you coming?"

Chris placed his hand on Wilhelm's shoulder. "No, I need to look after Cutty."

Their attention turned to their friend on the floor. A growing pool of blood surrounded his head. Chris dropped to his knees and cradled Cutty's head in his lap as he held pressure on the wound. He looked up at Wilhelm. "Go now, brother. Take care and know the family loves you."

Wilhelm placed his hand on Chris's shoulder and followed Gillian out of the back as the police stormed into the front. In the street behind the bar, they could see the glare of police lights.

Gillian looked at him and said, "Walk, hold my hand, and don't look back." Wilhelm did as he was told.

Two blocks away, the noise of the crime scene died in the background. She turned to look at Wilhelm as they walked. “I was sent by Gretchen. They tried to kill her as well. I was assigned to take you to Vienna by train. I think traveling by train would put you in greater danger. I suggest we drive. What are your thoughts?”

Wilhelm considered the question for a moment. “I agree. But how do we get a car?”

Gillian gave him a knowing look. “Leave that to me.”

Chapter 7

He watched the screen in front of him. The match was at half time and his team had not scored a point. He had bet heavily on the German team and goal shots were weak; the goalie appeared to be asleep.

The Baron threw the phone against the wall, breaking it into pieces, barely missing a commissioned portrait of himself. All the careful preparation flushed down the toilet in a botched operation. He had two dead assassins and was no closer to completing the objective. He sat back in his leather chair heavily and weighed his options. He had tried to be discreet. It didn't seem to be working. His other option was brute force. He picked up his desk phone and dialed his secretary, Hilda. Her voice was low and weary. "Yes, Baron."

He tried to keep from shouting. "Get me Bruno. I want to see him as soon as he can get here."

Hilda replied, "Yes, Baron."

He slammed the phone down. His face was red. He opened his right desk drawer and pulled out a box of Belgian chocolates. He flipped the box lid off, pulled out a wrapped chocolate truffle, and popped it in his mouth. While he chewed, he unwrapped another chocolate. Halfway through the box, his face was less red; it was more of a deep pink. The phone on his desk rang. He snatched the handset up. "Yes?"

Hilda's tired voice replied, "Bruno will be here in

two hours. He's driving here from Munich."

The Baron replied, "Let me know the minute he gets here!" He hung the phone up. It was six p.m. He unwrapped another candy and stuffed it in his mouth. He turned off the soccer match in disgust.

****

Bruno was a large raw-boned man, with a square jaw, a long scar from his cheek to his jaw, and a twisted nose deformed by numerous fights. He had risen out of the container slums of Frankfurt by his wits and his fearlessness. His network of pickpockets and drug dealers stretched from Frankfurt to Hamburg. He was without a doubt the most enterprising criminal in Germany.

The Baron offered him a Cuban cigar from a gold box on his desk. Bruno sniffed the cigar for a moment before biting the end off and spitting it on the floor. The Baron raised an eyebrow but said nothing. Bruno lit the cigar and blew a plume of smoke in the air. His voice was like a cheese grater dredging through gravel. "So what is so urgent, Bert?"

The Baron helped himself to one of the cigars, clipped the end into the trash container, and lit it. "I have a people problem. I tried the quiet approach. Now I need someone who can deliver results."

Bruno was not an egotistical man, but he recognized an opportunity when he saw it. His gypsy roots had taught him that. "So what do you want from me?"

The Baron replied, "I have two people I need you to make sure they vanish without a trace. They are leaving Lisbon and will arrive in Vienna in six days. I don't want them to make it to Vienna. The contract is worth five hundred thousand, US."

The tip of the cigar glowed red and Bruno inhaled. "I don't like killing people. It brings too much attention. It is bad for business. No less than one and a half million."

The Baron scratched his chin. "I'll entertain one and a quarter million."

Bruno stood, preparing to leave. The Baron motioned him to sit. "All right, one and a half million. There can be no trace of them left. I don't care if you use fire, acid, or shoot them into outer space, there cannot be any evidence."

Bruno nodded. "How do you intend to confirm the kill?"

The Baron considered this for a moment. "I will witness the killing, then you can do whatever you need to for disposal of the bodies."

Bruno replied, "Very well. We will take payment at the time of death. Cash only."

The Baron stood and extended his hand. Bruno ignored the Baron's hand and stood. "I will call you when we have them. Not before. Do not call me."

The Baron drew back his hand. "Very well. My secretary will provide you with dossiers on the way out."

Bruno left the office without looking back. He hated the Baron, but taking his money was as sweet as honey.

****

Gillian negotiated with Klaus, an independent driver for hire, who was pleasantly surprised when they gave him twice what the car was worth new. Klaus stared at the cash as he handed over the keys. It was more money than he had made all year. The blue compact was in decent shape with good tires and brakes.

Gillian navigated her way through Lisbon, avoiding places where the local police might be stationed and into rural Portugal on the way to Madrid. The long expanses of pasture gave way to the sun illuminating golden wheat fields punctuated by vineyards. They chose small sleepy towns which dotted the roadside and allowed for fuel and an overnight stay in a hacienda before they reached Madrid. The course would take them to Barcelona, and then they would hug the coast into France. The days were warm and sunny followed by nights thick with the floral fragrance of countryside. The landscape was far from the excitement waiting for them. On the third day of travel in the South of France, Gillian's phone rang. Gretchen's voice sounded tense. "Have you encountered any problems?"

Gillian replied, "None. Why?"

Gretchen was silent for a moment. "The Baron has placed a bounty on your heads. If they bring you in alive, there's a one-million-dollar reward. Every corrupt cop, street hood, and drug dealer in Germany is looking for you. As soon as you cross the Austrian line, there will be people swarming around you like hornets trying to get their cut."

Gillian thought for a moment before responding. "Then we need to give them what they're looking for."

Gretchen's voice rose an octave. "Say what?"

Gillian replied calmly, "We'll let them capture us."

Gretchen replied, "Why on earth would you do that?"

Gillian's response was both reasonable and

ludicrous. "We would be taken to the person who is initiating this. It is far easier to deal with one person versus one hundred, is it not?"

Gretchen's tone was desperate. "And if you're wrong, the odds of you making it out alive are one million to one."

Gillian calmly replied, "I'll take those odds compared to five million to one in the open with everyone looking for us."

Gretchen's voice was tense. "I think we need to find another way."

Gillian's tone was resolved. "If you figure out another way, you call me. Otherwise, we'll be ready once we reach the border."

Wilhelm looked over at her from the steering wheel. "So I take it we have a warm welcome waiting for us?"

Gillian's voice was distant. "It appears the party is waiting for us."

Wilhelm nodded. "Then I have a suggestion of a nice place in Milan to stop."

Gillian replied, "Sounds good."

The car was quiet except for the hum of the tires on the road. Gillian asked Wilhelm, "Do you have any contacts left in Austria?"

He nodded. "Yes, but not the kind I could trust." He glanced at Gillian; she had a wicked look in her eye. She replied, "Good. That's precisely what we need."

Wilhelm's voice was uneasy when he replied. "You do have a plan, right?"

Gillian responded, "I'm working on it."

The following day they entered the outskirts of Milan. Traffic was controlled chaos. Horns blared all around them as cars weaved in and out of the city traffic. Gillian navigated deftly around cars like she was raised in Italy. Wilhelm directed her to the Mascato House near Piola Station. It was a comfortable older hotel with stained glass and parquet floors. Their suite was immaculate with fresh flowers in each room. Wilhelm opened the windows and allowed the long white sheers to billow as the late afternoon breeze carried the fragrance of a large rose garden below their balcony. It was a perfect Italian afternoon.

Wilhelm's demeanor changed as he entered the room from the balcony. He seemed lost in a memory "Mother and I used to come here in the spring. We would stay for weeks. It was our time."

Gillian asked, "Did your father ever come with you?"

Wilhelm shook his head. "Father was too busy running the world to appreciate it. There was always something pressing. He was either meddling in the politics of a small country or he was trying to find some relic that was going to turn him into a superman or something. We never knew. When it was just Mother and me, we had good times. When I grew up, he wanted to prep me to be his successor. The thought of living in his shadow made me ill. So I moved away. I found my shelter in drugs and women. Mom, she went a little crazier every day. When I disappeared, and then Father, she lost herself."

Gillian nodded. "I can relate. My mom died of cancer when I was eleven. My dad was in the Special Forces. After she died, he signed up for every suicide mission available. When he didn't die, he decided he needed to make me self-reliant, so he started training me like a Navy Seal. I spent a week going through Hell-week with the BUD/S. I spent the night of my sixteenth birthday up to my neck in freezing mud. I wasn't even supposed to be there. On my eighteenth birthday, he finally succeeded in getting himself killed on a mission. By then, it was too late for me to back out, I was in too deep covering covert operations all over the world. I came back and went to college, thinking I would leave it all behind, but I was too good at it. Different agencies kept pulling me back in as freelance help."

Wilhelm replied, "Sounds like we both need a break. I know a place down by Piola called *La Tavolo Divino*. Let's go have a decent meal and commiserate."

Gillian smiled for the first time since she'd met him. "Sounds like a plan."

****

Wilhelm's Italian was smooth and practiced. He knew the cuisine and the customs. He ordered for both. Their server, Giovanni, kept the wine flowing, fascinated by Gillian. He placed a gentle hand on her back as he poured the Moscato. Hot plates of *ossobuco* with steaming *risotto alla Milanese* was a welcome change from the gas station food they had been surviving on for the last several days. The meal seemed to last forever. Wilhelm was charming and cultivated. Gillian felt like a barbarian across from him. But then, she was not assigned to protect him because of her table manners. They walked back to the room in the cool of the evening, trellises of blood red roses mingled with the flavors of the different restaurants, making a delectable combination of aromas.

It had been an incredible evening; the only thing missing for Gillian was Marty. Wilhelm walked and talked about Jamaica and Mama Robinson, Chris's mother. The way he spoke of her, it was as if he were describing his own mother. She lived in a quaint middle-class home in Kingston, where there was always a pot of something on the stove, whether it was turtle soup or brown fish stew, there was always a welcome atmosphere. Mama sat in her favorite chair by the window always sewing for someone. There were potted African violets on tatted table doilies throughout the house. She never missed Mass and when Wilhelm was there, neither did he. Mama, Chris, and the five siblings had been his family for the last ten years. And, in retrospect, they had been more of a family than his own.

The twin beds had been turned down. Gillian could see the look in Wilhelm's eye as they turned in. She raised an eyebrow. "I sleep with a gun, ya know."

Wilhelm swallowed hard. "Good to know." As he rolled over.

Gillian lay staring at the ceiling. Tomorrow would be a difficult day. She closed her eyes and sent a mental message to Marty. *I love you.* She drifted into the blackness.

****

Gillian stood in the center of a large cavern; the black sand felt cool beneath her feet. A bright light from above shown down bathing her in light. She stood face to face with a beautiful dark-haired woman with violet eyes. Both she and the woman held crafted Katanas. The woman readied her sword. She pointed straight at Gillian. Gillian stood with her sword at her side. The woman lunged forward awkwardly. Gillian sidestepped her. They faced each other again. This time, Gillian positioned her sword forward, matching her opponent. The woman lunged and struck. Gillian parried and watched as sparks rippled across the blades of the crossed swords. The blades locked at the hilt as the women circled each other almost nose to nose. Gillian could smell the woman's fear. The woman sprang backward and unlocked their swords. Without warning, Gillian lunged forward striking with blistering speed. The woman parried to the best of her ability, but she was too slow to defend herself against the lightning volley of strikes Gillian delivered. With one well-placed blow, Gillian knocked the katana from the woman's hand. It fell uselessly into the sand. Gillian did not hesitate. She chopped quickly at the woman's neck. The cut severed her jugular vein. The woman's eyes rolled back into her head as she crumpled to the ground mortally wounded. Gillian removed a silk handkerchief from her back pocket, wiped the blood from the blade, and tossed the red stained handkerchief across the woman's neck. The handkerchief quickly turned red from the ebbing flow of blood from the woman's wound. The blood disappeared into the black sand beneath her. Gillian walked away, she felt nothing: no fear, no remorse, no regret. She walked toward the light of an opening which seemed far away. As she approached the wall of the cavern, a gilded gold-framed mirror hung from a rusty spike. Gillian stopped and looked at herself in the mirror. The reflection caused a pit of panic to grow deep within her gut. Her reflection was the face of the woman she had just killed. The same violet eyes glowed eerily back at her.

****

Gillian sat straight up in the bed screaming.

Wilhelm leapt from his bed and sat beside her. He touched her face tenderly. “Gillian, it was dream. You’re okay.”

She turned toward him. Through the veiled light streaming through the sheers, she looked past him in the mirror. Her eyes glowing violet in the dimness. He drew back, surprised.

In a flat tone she said, “Take me.” Her arms wrapped around his neck and pulled him close. The passion from her lips was electric. Wilhelm was on fire from it.

With all his will, he pushed her arms down. “You have a family, are you sure?”

Gillian arched an eyebrow. Her voice was deeper, throatier. “Don’t be stupid. I am here. I am willing; I must be satisfied.”

With ease, she flipped him over onto the bed and straddled him. Her hips ground against him. She lowered her lips to his; her kiss consumed him; his skin flushed like he was on fire. Wilhelm could not resist her. Gillian ground on him with abandon, her body responded to him with passion, born of desperation. Wilhelm was lost in the moment, he could not think, he simply responded in kind. Of all the women he had made love to, none compared with such vehemence.

She pinned his arms down with the strength of an Amazon. He watched with fascination as her eyes changed from violet to blue to ruby red. He felt her tighten and quiver on him in a moment of release. And as suddenly as it began, her body went limp and collapsed on top of him, burying her face in his neck.

She lay for a moment panting, until her breathing slowed, and she relaxed. While gratifying, the dead weight was becoming oppressive. He touched her shoulder gently. "Gillian?"

She was silent. Her breathing was steady and rhythmic. She was asleep. Wilhelm eased himself out from under her and let her rest. He was sure there would be a price to pay for this.

****

Light from the morning sun streamed through the sheers casting beams of white light across the bed. Gillian awoke with a start, sitting up in bed, she scanned the room from one corner to another. The small hairs on her arms stood out as if charged with static as she heard whispers all around her in the room. After a moment, the buzz of weird voices dissipated, and the energy seemed to subside. She swung her legs from under the sheet and was startled to find she was naked. She pulled the sheet around her bosom and sat up. Wilhelm slept in the bed next to hers with his back toward her. She looked down to find her nightshirt lying on the floor at her feet. She snatched it from the floor and slipped it on and padded quietly to the bathroom. She felt sticky all over. She closed her eyes and shook her head. *What have I done?* She tried to remember what had happened. All she could remember were glowing violet eyes reflected back at her. She stared at her own reflection in the mirror for a moment before the overwhelming need to retch propelled her toward to the toilet. Her body trembled on the cold tile floor. She took a deep breath and stood. The water from the sink was cold and welcome on her face. She took a deep breath and climbed into the shower.

The steam rolled from the shower as she washed away the thoughts of what *may* have happened the night before. She dried herself absently until she reached her shoulder, a sudden nagging pain at her clavicle made her pause. She looked at the reflection along shoulder in the mirror and was surprised to find a red mark where her clavicle felt tender. She touched it gingerly and winced in pain as she touched the pink flesh. As she walked out of the bathroom drying her hair, Wilhelm sat on the side of the bed. He patted a spot beside him. "Let's talk."

Hesitantly, she sat beside him. She looked him in the eye. "What happened?"

He held out his hand for hers. She looked at it for a moment before resting her hand in his. "What I can say, is we made love. What I cannot say, is why. You awoke from what appeared to be a nightmare. I went to your bedside and you…well…took control. It's the only way I can describe it."

Gillian looked down. She tried desperately to remember. "Did I say anything?"

He nodded. "It was as if you were a different person. You didn't sound like yourself. The weirdest thing was your eyes changed color."

Gillian's eyes narrowed. "How so?"

Wilhelm took a deep breath. "They were glowing violet."

Gillian jerked her hand back as if she had been stung and stood. She walked over to the window and stared at the courtyard below. "That's all I can remember from the dream, violet eyes."

Wilhelm responded, "You were incredibly strong. I realize you're physically fit, but this was different. It was like you had the strength of ten people."

Gillian turned to face Wilhelm. Her face was

expressionless as she said, “We’ve got a long trip ahead of us. Let’s get some breakfast and hit the road.”

Gillian poked at her focaccia halfheartedly. The espresso was strong and cleared her head. She tried to put the events of the previous night out of her mind and focused on the mission. Wilhelm took a large bite of a small croissant with marmalade almost halving the small bread. Her voice was flat as she went through the details. “As we enter Austria, there will be network of criminals looking for us. There is a bounty on your head. To collect it, they must bring you in alive. We’ll make it a little difficult for them to take us, but not too hard. When we’re facing our captors, I will deal with them.”

Wilhelm raised an eyebrow. “I take it my role is to stay alive.”

Gillian looked him in the eye. She didn’t smile as she said, “Stay low and you won’t get hurt. No matter what happens, don’t try to help me.”

Wilhelm dropped his croissant on the plate. His hand shook as he took a sip of espresso. He sat back and pushed his plate away from him.

It was early afternoon when they entered the outskirts of Innsbruck. Gillian watched the surrounding traffic and waited. She knew it would only be a matter of time before they were spotted. She watched a half-white, half-rust Mini fall in behind them. A large black Beemer fell in behind the Mini. She changed lanes. The Beemer matched her move; the Mini did not. It wasn’t long before a gray Mercedes was traveling beside the Beemer. The older man in the Mini was arguing with a large woman in the seat beside him. The old man’s mouth opened wide, and suddenly, the large woman backhanded him. The car swerved slightly but stayed in control. As they entered the Bergisel tunnel, the Mercedes accelerated and swerved in front of the Mini. The old man reacted by slamming on the brakes, swerving into the Beemer behind Gillian. Two other cars slammed into the back of the Beemer, causing it to turn sideways, jammed against the other cars in the pile up. The Mercedes moved forward toward the small Ford. Gillian sped up. She knew it was only a matter of time before the Mercedes would catch them.

Without taking her eyes from the road, she said, "Move your shoulder harness under your arm, and lean toward me when I tell you to."

She felt Wilhelm's shoulder move closer. The end of the tunnel was ahead. The Mercedes was coming up fast in the opposite lane. Gillian swerved, straddling the lane, keeping the Mercedes from passing. The big car moved to the right; she countered deftly. They cleared the tunnel, and the Mercedes jerked back to the left swiftly. This time she didn't counter, allowing the Mercedes to position itself beside them. Gillian's voice was calm, like she was ordering a meal. "Get ready for it."

Wilhelm felt the heavy impact of the other car and the Ford began to lose control. Gillian's voice was eerily calm. "Now."

Wilhelm lay over the center console. Gillian lay in front of him. Wilhelm felt the violent shudder as the Ford flipped over and over down the highway. He covered his head with his hands. A crescendo of breaking glass and exploding airbags filled his ears, and then all was quiet. He could see and hear the melee of the violent crash around them, and yet, they remained virtually untouched. It was as if they were inside of a bubble. The car came to rest on its side. Wilhelm was hanging by his seatbelt, he groaned under the pressure. Gillian's voice was flat, toneless as she said. "Hang tight, they'll have us out in a minute."

Three beefy men exited the Mercedes and walked over to the steaming Ford. They heard a guttural tone. "*Eins, zwei, drei!*"

The car rocked slightly, and then fell, jolting them into an upright position again. Gillian whispered, "Play dead."

Wilhelm closed his eyes and tried to stay calm. He could feel the air blast in as the door was wrenched open. A click from a switchblade sounded before the seatbelt was blissfully free from his waist. A large meaty hand grabbed his arm and pulled him up. The hand grabbed his belt and arm and lifted him up carrying him into the air before being carried on the man's shoulders. There was a sudden jar as he landed in the trunk of the Mercedes, it was more painful than the car crash itself. Suddenly, Gillian was crashed on top of him. He grunted as the trunk lid slammed shut.

The pair rolled around in the trunk as the Mercedes accelerated rapidly from the scene of the wreck. Wilhelm realized all his belongings were still in the trunk of the Ford. Including almost three hundred thousand in cash. The thought struck him, for the first time in his life, he had only a handful of cash to his name. It was stranger than the thought of being an orphan.

Chapter 8

Marty sat on the bed with his back against the headboard. He stared at a mural on the wall across from him depicting a surrealistic planet where people stood on three sides in completely different environments. One side depicted sea bass walking on land. The next scene showed astronauts standing in a desert. The third was a living hell of drug abuse and torture, in a colony of red macaque monkeys in loincloths. The painting matched his mood. Jacob sat on the balcony watching the late afternoon bustle on the winding streets of Amman. The late afternoon sun cast an orange glow over the city, making it as surreal as the painting. The air from the balcony was as stifling as an oven. Marty barely noticed.

Jacob returned to the room and closed the door quietly. "Dad?"

Marty broke from his reverie as he looked at Jacob. "Yes, son?"

Jacob's young eyebrows were furrowed. "What's wrong?"

Marty motioned for Jacob to come to him. "I'm just thinking through all the logistics of the trip tomorrow." It was a lie, the best one he could come up with on short notice.

"Dad, if we're going to make it through this, you have to be honest with me. You know as well as I do that you're not worried about the drive tomorrow."

Marty patted a spot on the bed beside him. "You're right. Come and sit beside me."

Jacob moved to the bed and sat cross-legged facing Marty. Marty sat up straight. "You're right." He sighed. "I haven't been able to contact your mother for two days now. It's like I'm being blocked somehow."

"Is it Mom blocking you?"

Marty shook his head. "No. It's something else. I'm worried. I want to go to her."

"Is it the thing from the other world?"

"I think it might be. I don't know how to stop it."

"I think we do know. It's just scary to think about it."

Marty leaned over and grabbed his son in a bear hug. "You are wise beyond your years, boy. I'm a lucky dad."

Jacob hugged him back. "So we leave in the morning, right?"

Marty realized he was hesitating. "Yes. We leave in the morning."

It was early when they rose, just after the speakers sounded the prayer call. They packed all their gear and got ready to leave. Marty took a last look around the room. He studied the drugged out red monkeys on the painting before he pulled the door to. It was a bizarre scene, but one that he suspected would pale in comparison to what he and Jacob would encounter. The morning air was cool and filled with the smells of falafel and manakish. Street vendors were busy serving the morning rush. On the street, they grabbed Kaek Bread Sandwiches and hot tea before meeting Omar for the drive to Petra.

Omar was a stout middle-aged man, with a knitted *kufi* covering his bald head. He always wore a white, long-sleeve shirt, black vest, and brown trousers. He looked no different from the last time Marty had seen him ten years ago. As Marty approached, he pushed his round, black-rimmed glasses back up on his nose with his index finger and grinned broadly.

"Hello, my friend, where do we go today? Perhaps the beach at the Dead Sea?" He winked. "Many women there, maybe a new wife for you and the boy."

Marty shook his head. "No, friend, today we travel to Petra."

Omar spat in the street. "Ugh. Nothing there except deathstalkers and sand. You're sure you do not want to go to the beach?"

Marty nodded. "Quite."

The aged Range Rover bounced along the winding road to Petra while Omar lamented about the increasing number of refugees and the struggling economy of the country. "The king is a good man, but he fights to keep us whole in the face of protests and refugees. We all struggle in the end. But that is life, no?"

Marty replied, "I think every leader who has ever lived has struggled against the same issues in one form or another."

Omar laughed loudly and used his free hand to backhand Marty on the arm. "You are right, my friend. We never change, do we?"

Omar turned off the main road to a dirt path on the way to Petra. They bounced along until they arrived at the entrance to the Siq. Omar pulled out a newspaper. "I will wait for you over there, Martin."

Marty looked at him somberly. "Not this time,

friend. I have another ride coming to pick me up on this trip."

Omar looked surprised. "Is it something I said?"

Marty shook his head. "No, my friend. I have arranged to meet friends here. They will bring me back." He handed Omar two-hundred dollars. "I will catch you on the next trip, all right?"

Omar nodded. He reached forward and shook Marty's hand. Marty said, "My best to Fatima and the kids."

Omar replied, "You must let me know when you come back, we will drink wine, feast, and tell stories like the old days."

Marty smiled. "Indeed. Until then."

Omar replied, "Until then."

Marty and Jacob started the long walk to Jebel Madhbah. Omar watched them as they entered the opening to the Siq and were swallowed by the chasm. He reached for his phone and dialed Fritz's number.

A German accent greeted him. "Da?"

Omar responded, "This is Omar. I have news."

Fritz replied, "What is it?"

Omar took a deep breath. Marty had been his friend once, long ago. Before his heroin addiction; before Fatima left him and took their son; before he had been pulled into a web of lies by the Baron's organization. "Wood has just entered the Siq."

Fritz replied, "I will wire you the money this afternoon. No further contact unless I call you first. Understood?"

Omar replied, "Yes. I understand."

The line went dead.

****

"Enoch."

The old man kept his eyes closed. "Yes? Lord?"

"Enoch, open your eyes."

The old man opened one eye and squinted at the cloaked figure in the corner. "Lord?"

The cloaked man replied, "No, Enoch. I am only a messenger. It is time."

The old man opened his other eye. "Time for what?"

The cloaked man responded, "Time for you to protect the treasure. They are coming—like before."

The old man's eyes opened wide. He sprang from the one thousand-year old tapestry beneath him. "Is it the shadow man, again?"

The cloaked figure shook his head. "No. These are different people. They do not know how powerful you are. You must stop them before they reach the summit."

The old man stared intensely at the cloaked man. "How will I know them?"

The cloaked man replied, "They follow Wood. He comes to meet with you. He must commune with the treasure. It is important for you to help him; he seeks to protect us all."

The old man's eyes narrowed. He had been deceived before. "How do I know you tell the truth?"

The cloaked man responded, "Wood returned the Sappir to you. He has protected your secret for many years. I am warning you to help you prepare. I know many things about you. The most important aspect I know is you almost lost your faith when Franz betrayed you to the shadow man. Benjamin will walk through your door in twenty seconds. Protect Wood on the north trail to the Altar of High Sacrifice."

The cloaked man faded from sight leaving Enoch alone in the room. A knock on the door sounded. Enoch asked, “Who is it?”

The voice on the other side of the door replied, “Benjamin.”

Enoch’s gaze never left the corner as he responded, “Enter.”

****

Marty handed Jacob a canteen and urged him to drink. Jacob looked bravely at his father. “I’m okay.”

Marty didn’t waste time trying to argue. “Drink. It’s one-hundred-ten degrees out here. If you wait until you’re thirsty, it will be too late. It will get more difficult as we start to climb.”

Jacob looked at Marty. “Climb?”

Marty nodded. “Yes. We will need to climb a mountain to reach the hidden location.”

Jacob drank the water. “How far is it?”

Marty placed his hand on Jacob’s shoulder. “A few miles. We’ll take it easy. It shouldn’t be a problem. There will be people there to help us.”

A drone flew over their head. It was one of several they had seen. Jacob eyed the drone suspiciously. “What’s up with those things?”

Marty shrugged. “It could be anything. They might be mapping the ruins; it might be a tourist advertisement or anything in between. Don’t worry about it. Let’s keep moving.”

They passed gaping maws in the sandstone which once served as a gateway to a thriving city. The opening hid a narrow trail which snaked upward just past the structure. It looked unchanged from the last time Marty had been here: a blanched landscape of rocks and scorpions set against an unforgiving slope. Another drone buzzed past them in the heat like an angry hornet. They began the ascent. Cross trails and blind corners were confusing. Marty could feel Jacob remaining close to him. The terrain was unforgiving with loose rocks and washouts in spots. They carefully traversed the mountainside, pacing themselves to avoid overheating in the blistering sun. Marty found a sheer wall which offered partial shade and stopped.

He looked at Jacob. "This is as good a place as we'll find for lunch, son."

He removed his backpack and removed bundles of paper tied with string. In one there were dried dates and camel jerky. They tore at the jerky and washed it down with water, still warm from the hike, and rested in the narrow shade.

After what seemed like only moments, Marty stood, and Jacob followed; they began the climb again. They had not passed anyone all morning; the trail appeared to be abandoned. The ground leveled out and passed into a narrow canyon, the walls sloped toward them. Even though they could see the end of the gorge, it felt claustrophobic because of the slope and the dim light.

A figure appeared in front of them and moved toward them from the end of the canyon. In the narrow ravine, it would be difficult for them to pass. Marty felt a twinge on the back of his neck, there was something wrong about this. He stopped; Jacob almost ran into him. He looked behind them at the opening of the ravine; there was now someone behind them. They were trapped. There was nothing to do but move forward, the walls were too steep to climb.

He muttered in a low voice to Jacob. “Stay close, this may get rough.”

Jacob nodded and looked up above them. There was nothing but loose rocks and dirt on the walls.

As they got closer to the figure in front of them, they could see it was a man, dark skinned, with a black beard. He wore a black *kufi* stained with the dirt. The man wore a long knife at his side. He didn’t look like a tourist; he did look like a bandit. The man behind them was closing fast. He looked like the brother of the man in front of them. The bandit drew his long knife.

Marty stopped. He looked behind him as the man to their rear did the same.

Jacob focused on the rocks above them. A rock the size of a loaf of bread above began to tremble and shake, the dirt around it began to shower down. Suddenly, the rock rolled down and toward the bandit. The bandit looked up at the shower of dirt and debris moving toward him and dove forward barely missing the stone as it smashed into the trail behind him. He regained his grip on the knife and stood, heading toward them once again.

Marty removed his backpack and held it before him, it was his only defense. The bandit in front of them was now twenty feet away; his leer showed bad teeth and cracked lips. His eyes were bloodshot. The knife was pointed straight at Marty. Marty placed one foot forward and prepared to attack. At ten feet, the bandit stopped. His knife arm dropped to his side, he fell to his knees and then face forward. It was then that Marty and Jacob saw the arrow precisely located in his back where his heart would be. There was a dim figure ahead in the canyon. He was dressed in black, his face covered. He removed another arrow from the quiver but did not draw the bow, the bandit behind them was lying face down in the dirt as well, another archer was moving toward them.

The archer in front motioned them forward. Marty picked up the knife and stepped on the back of the bandit causing a groan from the stricken man. He reached back for Jacob's hand. The boy shuddered and jumped over the growing bloodstain on the man's back and followed his father. Marty held the long knife as they approached the archer, who had re-quivered the arrow and slung the bow across his back. When they were close, the archer said, "I am Jaro. Enoch sends us."

As Marty and Jacob approached, Marty stretched out his hand. "Thank you, Jaro. Things were looking a little dangerous for a moment."

Jaro dropped his veil so Marty could see his face and nodded. "There are many bandits on the trails. They seek to rob unwary tourists. This man is not someone I have seen before."

They waited outside the canyon for the other archer behind to catch up. Marty recognized him. "Hello, Benjamin."

Benjamin shook Marty's hand. "It has been many years, Martin Wood. You look well."

He patted Jacob on the back and asked, "Is this your son?"

Marty nodded. "Yes, this is Jacob."

Benjamin nodded. "Jacob is a strong name. Welcome to the Edomite tribe, friend."

Jacob stared at both men and then at his father. A mixture of awe and pride for his father filled him.

"Thanks."

They moved out. Jaro led them, and Benjamin followed. It was late afternoon when they reached the grotto.

Enoch met them at the mouth of the cave. He and Marty embraced warmly. "Hello, Martin. You look well."

Marty replied. "As do you, Enoch."

The old man led them inside the cave. "It has been a long journey for you, would you care for tea?"

Marty replied, "Yes. We can talk over tea, if that's okay?"

Enoch placed his hand on Marty's arm. "Of course. I'm sure you're here for a reason." He linked arms with Marty and Jacob. "But first, you must tell me about this young man here." He nodded in Jacob's direction.

Marty responded, "Indeed we shall. It appears my son has a few tricks up his sleeve which I didn't even know about."

The women served tea in a chamber where tapestries covered the walls and electric lamps created an amber glow. Their *tznius* clothing was subtle in the dim light. A dark-haired woman with deep brown eyes gently caressed Jacob's curly hair as she poured his tea. "You are far from home, what is your name, little one?"

Jacob studied the woman for a moment before responding. "Jacob, ma'am."

She ran her fingers through his hair. "Enjoy your tea, Jacob Ma'am."

He blinked but did not try to correct her.

Marty sat cross-legged on a carpet and sipped his tea. Enoch offered him a plate of dried figs, honey, and *saluf* bread. Marty wasted no time in eating two helpings of the warm *saluf* and figs, washing it down with the strong tea. It had been many years since he had shared tea with Enoch. There was a comfortable familiarity about being here.

The old man looked at him and asked, "And what of Gillian? How is the girl?"

Marty took a deep breath. "Well, we married not long after we left here. Jacob is our son. And she's the main reason why I'm here."

Enoch cocked his head. "How so?"

There was no easy way to say it, so Marty blurted it out, "She is sick. The kind of sick where doctors cannot help her. I know this will sound crazy, but I had a vision of her being attacked by a demon. The demon was from another world. It made her sick here. If the Ark can send me to where this demon is located, then I must go there and stop it from hurting her more."

Enoch nodded. "You have been given a vision. And now you must follow your calling. I respect that. Most men never recognize or never even have a calling. You are a blessed man. A prophet."

Marty shrugged his shoulders. "I don't feel like a prophet. I don't even know if I'm doing the right thing. It goes against everything I've known. I just know I can't fight this thing here; I've got to go to it. Gillian's life depends on it."

Enoch removed a talisman from his neck. "Prophecies are always frightening at first. You are on a sacred mission." He leaned forward and placed the talisman around Marty's neck. "Take this. It was handed down to me from my father and his father before him. It is a sacred object and will protect you from evil."

Marty shook his head. “I can’t accept this from you, it’s too important.”

Enoch pressed. “You must. As my father handed it to me, he said I would know what to do when the time came. I have never known until this moment. You must take it for your journey.”

Marty bowed his head to Enoch. “I don’t know what to say.”

Enoch lifted Marty’s chin so he could look him in the eye. “You are going on a dangerous journey. My heart tells me what you face is greater than all of us. You will face many perils; it is only your faith that will save you. You were able to restore my faith, by returning the treasure. Now, you must listen to me. This demon you face can break your body, but not your heart. Remain strong and it will wither at your feet. If you allow it to make you afraid, you will be defeated. Remain strong and return to me.”

Marty was silent for a moment. “I will remain strong.”

The old man stood. “Then there is no time to waste. Let us go.”

Marty and Jacob followed Enoch through the labyrinth to the chamber; he carried a single oil lantern which danced against the walls making strange shapes in the striations of sandstone. They reached a point where the tunnel seemed to end. Enoch turned, and the opening seemed to appear from thin air. They stood in the chamber lit by luminescence from an unseen source. The light reflected off the Ark of the Covenant like moonlight on the surface of the ocean. A thousand beads of light winked off the beaten gold casing of the Ark causing it to shimmer in the dim light of the grotto.

Marty heard Jacob gasp behind him. It was the first time he had ever seen anything like the Ark. It reminded Marty of the first time he had seen the reliquary in the Duke's castle. It was still amazing and nothing like anyone had ever depicted in pictures.

Marty could feel the hum of the Ark resonate within him. He wondered if Jacob could feel it as well. He looked at his son and asked, "What do you think?"

Jacob never took his eyes from the Ark as he responded, "It's the most incredible thing I've ever seen."

Marty turned Jacob toward him. "Son?"

Jacob broke his gaze with the Ark and looked at his dad. "Yes?"

Marty looked Jacob in the eyes. "I have no way of knowing what will happen next. It seems a bit reckless, but I'm being drawn to do this. You can stay with Enoch. The Edomites will take good care of you. Are you sure you want to go through with this?"

There was a look of resolve in Jacob's eyes. "Dad, Mom's life is worth the risk. She would do the same if it were you or me. I can't explain why, but I feel like there is another world and it needs me for something. I'm with you to the end."

Marty hugged his son and kissed him on the forehead. "I love you, son."

Jacob hugged his father back. "I love you too, Dad."

Enoch removed a small wooden box from his robe and placed it in Marty's hand. Enoch placed his other hand under Marty's and held it there. He looked Marty in the eye. "This is the Sappir, the mother to all the other keystones. You are connected to it, as no other human. When you insert it, it will ignite the power within the Ark. I cannot be here with you. This is your journey. I will leave you with my blessing."

Enoch began to chant: "*v'yishm'recha*"

When Enoch had finished the blessing, Marty asked, "What did your blessing mean?"

Enoch replied, "It is the Keep Blessing. It means, *By His own work, He binds and overpowers the destroyer using His authority in His hand.*"

Marty nodded. "Thank you." The box in his hands felt light as he watched Enoch walk toward the end of the chamber; Enoch seemingly melted into the wall vanishing from their sight. He wondered if he would ever see his old friend again. He looked at Jacob. "Before we open the portal, I need to acquaint you with the Sappir."

Jacob raised an eyebrow. "Acquaint?"

There was a glint in Marty's eyes. "Yes. Acquaint. I realize you have natural abilities, but this will take you to another level. I have never tried what we're about to do. Your mother and I both experienced the Sappir separately, I am going to touch it with you. Trust me, the experience will be strange, but it will help you see clearly."

Jacob shrugged. "Okay. If you say so."

Marty kept telling himself his son was only eleven. He sat in the sand of the cave next to the Ark. Jacob sat across from him cross-legged. Marty opened the box, inside the Sappir nested in yellow satin. He placed the box between them. He looked Jacob in the eye and said, "We're going to count to three and touch the stone at the same time, okay?"

Jacob nodded. Marty began to count. "One, two,

three…"

They touched the stone. Nothing appeared to happen. The room remained unchanged. Jacob raised an eyebrow at his father. Marty looked at him calmly. "Stay on it."

The room dissolved around them. They were no longer sitting in a cave. The floor beneath them was smooth, polished marble. They stood and faced a modern overlook of a vast runway surrounded by a causeway of running water at the edge of a deep forest of evergreens. The air was thick with the smell of spruce. Rachael and Digger walked up behind them. Marty hugged Rachael and then Digger. Jacob stared, unsure of what he was experiencing. Rachael lowered herself to Jacob and pulled him close. Her hug was comforting like his mother's; she smelled like honeysuckle in the spring.

She stood up straight and kissed him on the forehead. "Welcome, child."

Children ran up to them laughing. "Come play with us, Jacob!"

Jacob looked up at Marty. Marty nodded. "Go have fun." Jacob and the children ran away giggling.

Marty turned to Rachael and Digger. "I know this is going to be more difficult than anything I've ever done, but I must stop Jeez from attacking Gillian."

Rachael reached for the talisman he wore from Enoch. "I see the Holy Man has given you his charm."

Marty looked down in time to see a small electric charge pass from her hand to the charm.

Rachael continued, "I can help you travel to the dark realm, but I cannot help you return. There is a way to return, but it will be perilous."

Marty replied, "I understand the danger. I've discussed this with Jacob and Gillian. As a family we have decided this is what we must do."

Rachael's smile was soft, her eyes empathetic. "I know this is difficult for all of you. None of this is your fault. Nothing you've done has caused this. I will help you any way I can, but once you are in her realm, I will have no power there."

Marty replied, "I realize that. I was against bringing Jacob, but he seems to have powers beyond anything I have. He convinced me we should travel together. I need your guidance."

Rachael took Marty by the arm and they walked along the overlook to a stair to the lower level. Her voice was soft. "Jacob is an extraordinary child. He has abilities beyond any human I've ever seen. All my children are gifted; they will help him understand his abilities as they play. Let's take a little trip."

Rachael turned and said, "Come children, we're going to the desert."

As if by magic they appeared. Jacob seemed different. Marty looked at his son. "Are you okay, sport?"

Jacob grinned; his eyes glowed blue. "Heck yeah! This place is great!"

Jacob rarely played with other children. Somehow this was a welcome release from all the pressure they had been under. They descended stairs to the platform below. Digger climbed into the open hovercraft and walked to the controls. Marty stood beside him. "So how are you, my friend?"

Digger depressed buttons on the craft making it rise silently on the pad. "Amazing. I built this machine.

It operates on an antigravity propulsion system. It's quick, and it's clean. The kids and I take it out on trips."

Marty looked back at the children. "Are they always this happy?"

Digger gave him a sideways grin. "For the most part."

The craft began to move. It jetted forward at an unbelievable speed, and yet there was no wind or gravitational forces throwing them back. It was like a virtual reality chamber. Rachael sat with the children in a U-shaped red-and-white diamond tuck seat. It looked like something from a sixty's era theme restaurant. Marty pointed his thumb at the seat. "What's up with the upholstery, dude?"

Digger laughed. "Everything doesn't have to be about physics, *dude*." They both chuckled.

They talked as they traveled beyond the evergreen forest, deep into the dunes of the desert. They began to slow as they approached an enormous circus tent at the top of a dune. A three-pole white canvas tent rose high above. The end pole left to erect. Digger slowed the craft and nudged Marty. "Watch this."

A group of men in loincloths stood at the base of the tent holding a rope tethered to the top of what appeared to Marty as a telephone pole laid over for the last section of tent. The men ran, taking the slack out of the rope. As they ran together the pole began to rise. Another group of men stood waiting in the distance. As the runners reached the waiting group, the second team grabbed the rope as if in a relay race and pulled it tight around a large stake in the ground. It was so fluid; it looked like a performance. The children behind them laughed and cheered as the tent stood complete before them.

Digger closed the gap to the tent and slowed to a stop and lowered to the ground. The children raced off the hovercraft and into the waiting tent.

Marty, Digger, and Rachael followed. Inside, it appeared everything was in place, even though they had just witnessed the tent being erected. The rules of logic did not apply in this realm.

The interior of the tent was spacious and filled with treasures. Artwork and sculptures surrounded them. The floor of the tent was a solid base of polished marble. Dark, intricately carved wooden cases with glass shelves glowed with amber light and illuminated items on the shelves: gem encrusted vases, Greek busts, and crystal dioramas of alien worlds. To the side stood a lone display—a studded vest encrusted with rubies, diamonds, and emeralds. Beside it, there was a weathered rectangular block of wood. It stood out as being the plainest piece on display; was it left over from setting up the tent?

Rachael placed her hand on Jacob's shoulder. "You may have any one object you desire."

Jacob looked at her curiously. "Anything?"

She ran her fingers through his hair. "Anything."

He moved from each priceless item to the next, each more valuable than the next. The children followed him; each child pointed to a piece and said, "Pick that one!"

Jacob stopped at the plain block of wood. Marty watched him from a distance, curious at what his son would choose. Jacob picked up the block and examined it. He looked up at Rachael. "Can I have this?"

She eyed him keenly. “Why that one, Jacob?”

He rolled it over in his hands and then looked up at her. “I don’t know. There is something about it calls to me. I can’t really explain it.”

Rachael touched Jacob gently on his forehead. “It is because it calls to you in the song of the ancients.”

Marty watched with fascination as the item that looked like a drab table leg transformed to a crystal rod which glowed with a pure white light. Jacob’s eyes grew large. He stared at the rod and then up at Rachael. “What is this?”

Rachael replied, “This is the Ki. It is one of the most powerful artifacts in the world.”

Jacob asked, “Why?”

“The power of the Ki is beyond my knowledge. It chooses its own form. It is neutral in the balance of power between good and evil, meaning whoever holds the Ki, tips the scale in the direction whosoever holds it.”

Jacob looked at Rachael with deeply serious eyes. “Can you save this for me?”

Rachael replied, “Of course. It will be here when you return for it.”

The other children gathered round. Each wanted to touch it. Marty watched in amusement as the children mobbed his son and he orchestrated giving turns.

Marty turned to Rachael. “So you will open a portal for us?”

She replied, “Yes. All you must do is place the Sappir in the keyhole. It will begin to glow. Close your eyes and think of the Dark Planet. You will be transported there.”

Marty asked, “Do I need to say anything?”

Rachael shook her head. “Jacob knows the ancient words. Let him recite the words.”

Marty looked surprised. He looked at Jacob. “Son, do you know the words?”

Jacob nodded. “Oddly, I do.”

Marty replied, “Then, it is time.”

Marty hugged Digger and then Rachael. “Goodbye, my friends.”

Rachael replied, “Our blessings go with you.”

Marty closed his eyes. When he reopened them, they were in the cave with the Ark. Jacob blinked at him. “Dad, was that real?”

Marty looked at him. “Touch yourself where Rachael touched you.”

Jacob touched his forehead. “It feels tingly.”

Marty nodded. “Then it was real. Are you ready?”

Jacob nodded. Marty removed the Sappir from the box. There was one empty setting left on the Ark. Before Marty placed the Sappir in the opening on the Ark, he looked at Jacob. “You will need to close your eyes for this. Begin repeating the words Rachael taught you when I tell you, okay?”

Jacob replied, “Okay.”

Marty positioned the Sappir over the slot. He instructed Jacob. “Close your eyes now.” Jacob did as his father said, after which Marty did the same. He pushed the Sappir into the slot and withdrew his hand as a small charge of energy coursed through his hand. A loud hum filled the room. Marty instructed Jacob, “Repeat the liturgy.”

Jacob replied, “The what?”

Marty spoke louder over the hum, “Say the words!”

Jacob recited the ancient words in perfect intonation. "*Etok, jux retol ekt nonin hu miteral som.*" The hum subsided but was replaced with a charged atmosphere. Marty felt his body pulled suddenly and tossed like a doll in the wind. He lost his grip on Jacob's hand as he tumbled and tossed for what seemed like an eternity before landing on the ground with a jarring thud. The turbulence around him subsided. All was calm. He opened one eye, squinting at the light that assaulted his eye. He lay for a moment in what felt like dry grass. Again, he eased his eyes open. A pink glow covered the landscape like dusk. As he blinked, he looked for Jacob. The boy was nowhere to be seen. He called out, "*Jacob!*"

He was met with only silence. A sinking feeling settled over him; his son was alone on an alien planet.

Chapter 9

Gretchen sat in the dark room in silence, her knees pulled tight against her chest. The door was barricaded with a chair from the dinette table. *This is stupid.* She could not live out her life in a hotel room in old town. She would have to reach out to her team, or at least to those she thought she could trust. The one person that came to mind was Rutger. He had been shelved as a special operations team leader to head of Security. Since the departure of the Duke, it had become a boring, meaningless job. She called his number. It rang three times before he answered. "Da?"

Gretchen greeted him carefully. "Is it safe to speak?"

Rutger's response was practiced. "No, we cannot accept your delivery at the castle. You are not an authorized provider. We will need to prepare the proper authorization codes for you. I will call you back when I have the correct authorization code for you."

The line went dead.

Gretchen relaxed a little. Rutger had followed proper protocol on an open line. It was five minutes before her phone rang. She answered, "Da?"

Rutger asked, "Where are you? Are you safe? We thought you were dead."

Gretchen responded, "I'm fine. Is this line secure?"

Rutger snorted. "Of course. Now, what is going

on?"

Gretchen took a long breath. "We have been infiltrated. Fritz has a direct line to Baron von Meier. I was preparing to bring in Wilhelm to prove he is the heir to the estate. That's when they made the attempt on me. I have an operative bringing Wilhelm to the court proceeding in Vienna. I am concerned about the operative's state of mind. I may need you to intervene."

Rutger replied, "It's about time. May I deal with Fritz? It would be a personal pleasure to take care of that situation."

Gretchen responded, "No. Not yet. We still need him. I believe the operative's plan was to be captured in order to get closer to the person orchestrating this. I hadn't intended for the operative to neutralize the Baron, just bring Wilhelm in. This has gone a little too far. We need to take control."

Rutger replied, "No problem. I'll find the location and take a team there. We'll secure Wilhelm and take him to Vienna. What about the operative?"

Gretchen's reply was measured. "Do not harm the operative. I need her to come in; there are other aspects of this mission I need her to handle. Get the location from Fritz and lock him up. Watch him and see if he has other moles in the castle. Send a team to the Hotel Bredleberg in Old Town. Use this number and I'll come out."

Rutger responded, "I'll have a team there in two hours."

Gretchen replied, "Make sure I know who you send."

Rutger was silent for a moment. "I will send Litz. I will call you back to confirm."

Gretchen disconnected the line. It was time to visit the boutique.

****

Gretchen took great care to pick out the most boring outfit she could find—a plain beige top with blue jeans and dock sneakers. She picked up a blue ball cap and made sure her hair would fit up under the top. A pair of brown sunglasses completed the ensemble making her the most unremarkable person in old town.

She sat at a table in Haus Schnitzel by the window and waited. The phone chirped. Rutger was on the line. "Litz will be coming alone. We have a safe house set up for you. Full communications package. Untraceable. We'll begin from there. I will always have two experienced operatives with you at the safe house. Very capable. Litz will be there in one half hour."

Gretchen responded, "Have you secured Fritz?"

Rutger chuckled. "Yes. It was quite entertaining."

Gretchen continued, "You'll need to find the location of Wilhelm and proceed there. I have not been able to locate the operative. I suspect they have been captured."

Rutger responded, "I'll take care of it now."

The line went dead.

Gretchen sipped on her espresso.

****

In precisely thirty minutes, a black Audi sedan pulled in front of the Hotel Bredleberg. Gretchen could see Litz sitting behind the wheel, unmoving. Gretchen surveyed the area from her window seat. There didn't appear to be anyone in the vicinity. Gretchen paid for her espresso and tipped the young man behind the counter a five Euro note. "Can I use your back door to leave?"

The teenager stuffed the note in his pocket and pointed his thumb over his shoulder.

Gretchen moved swiftly past the rest rooms and the kitchen and was out the back door in the alley behind the restaurant. She began to weave her way back to the front, where Litz was waiting in the sedan. She looked around before approaching the car. Litz was not in it.

Gretchen stopped; alarm bells sounded in her head. The hair on the back of her neck stood up. Something was wrong. She turned to retreat into the alley, but a tall sallow man blocked her way. There was a deadness in his eyes, despite his boyish facial features.

One handed, he lit an unfiltered cigarette and blew a plume of smoke into the air. "Do you know how long I've been looking for you? You're a very naughty girl. Naughty girls deserve to be punished." He drew an automatic pistol with a silencer from beneath his sky-blue windbreaker. "You play nice, I'll make this quick. If you don't play nice, well, just use your imagination." His smile was as lifeless as his eyes as he motioned with the gun.

Slowly, she began to walk toward him. As she drew closer, Litz came into view standing behind the assassin. Litz's gun was out and aimed. The trash dumpster was on the other side of the alley, she would have to time this perfectly. As she approached the dumpster, she dove and rolled into the corner. Bullets ricocheted off the dumpster and hit the wall by her head. The shooting stopped. Gretchen peeped above the dumpster in time to see Litz take the pistol from the dead fingers of the assassin. There was a growing pool of blood under the killer. Litz placed his pistol back into a holster under his sports coat. He stuffed the other pistol behind his back and dragged the man behind the waste container. He motioned for Gretchen to follow him. As she joined him, Litz asked, "Are you hit?"

She shook her head, willing herself to face forward and not look back at the growing pool of blood from the dead body in the alley. She looked up at Litz, his cropped blond hair framed a square jaw and ruggedly handsome face. "How did they find me?"

Litz kept his eyes moving. "Evidently there is a million-dollar bounty on your head. That amount of money encourages people to say anything to get a dollar. My guess is he bribed enough people to find you. The news only accounted for two people in your apartment when it was blown up. Neither of them was you. He's been looking for you ever since. We have a safe house set up for you in Salzburg. You will have secure phones and internet there. The apartment has a safe room. If they get past the guards, you will be safe there until the second team arrives."

Litz opened the back door to the sedan for Gretchen before easing in on the driver's side. "The windows are bullet proof. We have two teams escorting us." Litz opened the glove compartment and removed a small Walther pistol. "Can you shoot a gun?"

Gretchen replied, "Yes."

Litz handed her the Walther butt first. "It's loaded. Be careful not to shoot me in the back of the head."

Gretchen would have been insulted, but he had just saved her life. She dropped the magazine and examined the rounds. The thirty-eight caliber was loaded with hollow point bullets. She was armed and ready. She sat back in the seat and took a breath as the sedan eased away from the hotel. In the distance, she could hear police sirens getting louder. Someone had already found the body.

The house was in a well-tended section of town, a hedge hid the electric fence around the perimeter of the house. The gates remotely opened by a button on Litz's visor. As they proceeded into the drive, two black SUV's followed. Litz pulled into the garage. The door closed behind them. Litz looked back at her. "I need you to move to the driver's seat. I will go in and sweep the house. Stay in the car with the doors locked until I return."

Gretchen sat in the car every nerve tingling. The sun was beginning to set outside. The metal garage door popped suddenly from cooling and made her jump. Finally, Litz returned and motioned for her to enter the house. Inside, the house was clean and well decorated with silk flowers and tapestries covering hardwood floors. It was also very sterile, like a hotel room.

Rutger waited for her in the dining room at the table. He had papers spread out on the table with photos and emails. He looked up at Gretchen. "We have as much information as we're going to get. The Baron is holding Wilhelm in an abandoned warehouse in Innsbruck. There are about ten members of the Brotherhood holding the compound. The number doesn't seem very high, but these guys are handpicked as the worst of the worst. They're either ex-Russian military or former KGB. We can take them, but it won't be easy."

Gretchen looked at the pictures. "How did you get this so quickly?"

Rutger studied a picture of a couple handcuffed to

chairs in the middle of a warehouse. He looked up and replied, "One of Dr. Osterman's wonder drugs. It's like sodium pentothal on steroids. Fritz would have given us his bank account numbers if we had wanted them. We got access to his laptop and he had all this in his email. He's really a wanker when you get down to it. I don't believe we have much time before they move them. If we're going to rescue them, it had better be quick."

Gretchen looked over the pile of papers. "Do you have enough information and men to pull this off?"

Rutger nodded. "I've got twenty capable men. With the element of surprise, we can take them easily. Kill the power, some flash bangs, and take out every living thing except for the people being rescued."

Gretchen's eyes were steely. "Don't kill the Baron. We save him for the courts."

Rutger nodded. "No problem." He stood to leave. "Hans and Nabu will be here with you. If you have the slightest sign of trouble, get out."

Gretchen replied, "Rutger?"

He turned to face her. "Yes?"

Gretchen's face was sober. "Thank you."

He nodded and left. Rutger was not one for sentimental partings.

****

Rutger's team was assembled outside the warehouse. Rutger was positioned at a high point above the warehouse floor where he could see all angles. The lights would go out in two minutes. He would pull down night vision goggles five seconds before the ambush. He checked his watch: ninety seconds. Below, there was a commotion.

A burly Russian pulled a pistol and pointed at the

operative's head. Before anyone could react, the operative snapped the handcuffs behind her back and punched the burly man in the throat. Rutger's jaw dropped. The operative proceeded to pick up the burly man by his leg and slung him at the other members standing closest. He could see the Baron's double chin wobble as he screamed at the others to take the operative. The remaining five men in the room rushed at the girl. She vaulted into the air striking one of the men and landed for only a moment until she backflipped into the man behind her, crashing her feet into his chest. Rutger broke radio silence and ordered his men to kill the sentries outside, and hold cutting the power. The operative was back on her feet. She savagely struck the man to her right in the throat and sent a seamless spinning front kick into the temple of the man to her left. One lone member of the brotherhood stood between the operative and the door. She ran at him with full force diving at his throat with both hands. The pair landed on the floor with her hands still wrapped around his neck. She bashed his head into the floor repeatedly until he lay limp beneath her. It was over in less than a minute. She looked at the Baron for a moment as he cowered in the corner and turned and walked back to Wilhelm. What she did next surprised even Rutger. She sat on Wilhelm's lap in the chair and ran her tongue up the side of his face. It would have been seductive had he not just watched her kill eight men, who lay around her in a pile.

Rutger ordered his men to capture the Baron and hold him in one of the SUVs. Rutger eased down the stairs to where the couple sat in the middle of the room. The operative whirled around to face him. Her hair was wild, her eyes were blood red. It almost sounded as though she were hissing at him.

Rutger put his hands up. “We are friends of Gretchen. We were sent to rescue you.”

Wilhelm spoke to Gillian, “They are friendly; let them pass.”

Gillian stood but did not move away from Wilhelm. She hissed at Rutger. It made his skin crawl. Her glowing red eyes followed him as he walked past her to Wilhelm. Watching his every move like a wild animal. The cuffs holding Wilhelm’s wrists were standard handcuffs. Rutger removed them with a key from his belt. He watched Gillian as her eyes began to clear; within a minute they turned back to normal. She began to fall forward. Wilhelm rushed to catch her, easing her to the ground.

Rutger looked over Wilhelm’s shoulder and asked, “Is this normal for her?”

Wilhelm looked up at him. “Beats me, I’ve only known her for four days.”

****

Jeez sat in deep meditation. It felt good to control the human again. She could almost smell the blood as Gillian beat the thugs to death with her bare hands. Every strike brought her sensual pleasure.

Unexpectedly, she felt a tremor on Oronas as something broke through the dark matter shield surrounding the planet. Outraged at being disturbed, she broke from her meditation and uncoiled from the floor. She screamed in fury at the top her lungs in frustration.

****

Fredrick lay naked beside Luna. A tremor crossed the landscape, followed by an unnerving screech which resounded across the landscape, chilling him to his very core. Something had happened. Something big.

Chapter 10

Marty stood on an expansive plain. He surveyed the flat featureless grasslands in all directions. The air smelled sweet like honeysuckle. In the distance, he could make out an object on the horizon. He waded through the grass for an hour toward the outcropping in the distance. As he walked, he concentrated his thoughts on Jacob. *Son?*

Out of the ether, his son's response found him, *Dad?*

Marty stopped and responded, *Are you okay?*

A moment later Jacob replied, *I'm fine. I'm in a desert.*

Marty thought for a moment. They could easily be on opposite ends of this world. *Try to find a landmark. We'll triangulate from there.*

Jacob responded, faster this time, *Okay.*

Marty continued to walk to the object on the horizon. It was clearer now. It appeared to be vegetation, an oasis of sorts. The light never changed. His headache was a steady throb now, but he could visualize occasional color patterns he had never seen before. It was strange. He processed through the colors he knew; none of these colors seemed to be remotely similar to the red or violet spectrum. He considered the possibility that he was observing an unknown aspect of physics.

He could see the details of an oasis now. Short trees and broad green undergrowth stood out in stark contrast to the amber grasses of the plain. He could see movement in the trees. It was the first sign of life on this desolate landscape. At one hundred yards, the movement in the trees appeared to be primates. In the dim light they appeared red against the gray bark of the trees. The leaves did not appear to be any color he had ever seen before. As he drew nearer, the ape creatures did not appear to notice him or care. If they were like earth simians, they could probably tear him limb from limb. He had nowhere to escape to if they did. On Earth, he had a calming effect on animals. He hoped the same would apply here. At the edge of the tropical vegetation, he stopped to observe the apes. They stayed in one of the trees, bearing a brown ugly fruit, preening and grooming each other.

He watched as a blue sloth-like creature began to crawl up the tree. The apes began screaming and bouncing up and down at the blue sloth. The blue sloth continued its slow ascent into the tree. One of the apes broke a dead limb from the tree and swung with one arm toward the sloth, when it did not appear to have an effect, the ape jabbed the sloth, causing it to fall from the tree. Marty studied the sloth as it fell into oblivion beneath the tree. Marty looked at his feet. One foot beyond the foliage in front of him there was nothing. He was standing on the edge of a crater without a bottom. He stepped back in reaction. The apes took no notice of him and went back to their preening and napping. Other than the occasional grunt of the apes, there was no sound here, no bugs, no wind, no rustling. It was odd. Considering the flatness of the prairie, he expected there would be wind. The air was still.

He scrubbed along the surface of the grass around him until he finally found a stone the size of a large marble. He tossed the stone over the ledge and began to count. He listened for the stone to strike the bottom. At the count of five, he strained to hear the distant kerplunk as the stone struck the surface of water below. It had to be over three hundred feet. That would be a long trip to get water, and deadly if he were to fall.

Another blue sloth began to climb the tree beside the one the apes perched in. This tree looked very different. Its trunk was a beautiful iridescent aquamarine, the leaves were shiny and golden in the dim light, and the fruit was cherry red. The apes took little interest in the sloth as it climbed. It moved out on a limb traveling upside down under one of the branches until it reached a piece of delicious looking ruby red fruit. Slowly, it plucked the fruit from the tree and bit into the shiny skin. The juice dripped from the fruit as the sloth took a large bite. It chewed slowly and took another bite. The red apes stopped what they were doing to watch the sloth. As it chewed, it began to act strange. The sloth let go of the branch with one of its paws and now hung upside down from the branch with its rear paws, still clutching the ruby red fruit in one paw. Suddenly the sloth dropped the fruit from its paw and stopped chewing. The fruit fell far below, splashing into the water. Foam began to form around the sloth's mouth. Its eyes stopped blinking as it slipped from the branch into the pit below.

One of the red apes plucked a piece of the ugly brown fruit and began to eat. It finished the fruit and licked its fingers clean of the juice. The ape rolled onto its back on a large branch, covered its face with one hand, and took a nap. Marty made a mental note, brown ugly fruit good; beautiful red fruit bad. He took a sip from his canteen and bit off a small piece of camel jerky. This was going to be a long expedition, and he was not a gatherer. It didn't appear the apes would relinquish fruit without a fight. He decided he should move on. He scanned the landscape for another landmark. In the distance, he saw what appeared to be a pole. He would walk toward the landmark.

****

Jacob stood in a vast gray desert of dirt and stone. He scanned the horizon for a landmark or something which would indicate civilization. He could only find what appeared to be a faint trail in the dirt. He decided to follow it as far as he could. It was not hot here, but the landscape appeared uninhabitable. There were no signs of life, no bugs, spiders, or scorpions. Dust kicked up under his feet as he walked. He was careful to conserve his water, taking a sip of water to help ease his parched mouth. The trail was more pronounced now. It appeared someone or something used it. The surface looked like the moon, gray and devoid of life. The trail could have been left one hundred years ago for all he knew. In the distance, he could see something that could be a structure. For now, it was a distant marker against the landscape. As he moved closer, the structure became square, a small hut at best. Four dark walls stood out against the horizon. More importantly, a thin plume of smoke trailed up from the shack. It was sign of life, a sign of hope.

As he drew closer, he could see the walls were intricately stacked stones from the landscape around him. They rose only slightly over a man's head. There were no windows, only a doorway. Dirt filled the holes in the stone, providing it with the semblance of solidity. Smoke trailed from the structure as well as the smell of some type of food. Jacob's belly growled. His camel jerky and dates were long gone. An old man in tattered clothing appeared in the doorway, his eye sockets were black from burns. His voice crackled. "Who's there?"

Jacob was surprised he could understand the man, even though it was not a language he had ever heard. He replied, "I am Jacob, son of Martin. I am a stranger to this land. I mean you no harm."

The old man cackled. "Probably best for you that way, lad. I'm old and blind, but I'm not one to be messed with. I am Abrah, son of Aerat. I am called the Woodcarver. What do you bring to barter?"

The question made Jacob pause. "Barter? I supposed I have things that might interest you, I just don't know."

The old man nodded. "So you best come inside so we can trade." He turned and walked back into the hut. Jacob followed hesitantly but was amazed when he did. Inside, crudely constructed shelves of stone displayed intricate pieces of carved wood. Most were small enough to fit into the palm of Jacob's hand. The hut had no roof, so all were easily viewed. There were strange carvings of animals, a yak, an ape, and a panther. Others were perfectly formed eggs, jewels, and finally one resembled the Ark of the Covenant. He was surprised to see the Ark in the collection. Jacob tried to be polite, but his curiosity knew no boundaries. "How long did it take you to make these?"

The old man scratched the thin hairs on his chin for

a moment as if in thought before responding. "I would imagine it's been twenty seasons since they left me here to die. I started then. The Bots blinded me because I refused to stop carving. They killed my family and burned all my work, now all I have are the pieces you see before you. I was blinded and sent to wander the wasteland. They sent me here to die, but I fooled them." He cackled again, resulting in a rattling cough.

Jacob was quiet for a moment. "That's terrible, I'm sorry."

The old man replied, "Why are you sorry, you didn't do anything?"

Jacob responded, "No, but it's terrible for what they did to you. It's wrong."

The old man replied, "Yes, they wronged, but if I dwell on it, they still control me. I chose to move on. Then, they don't own my soul. If I dwell on what they did to me and my family, I give them the rest of me. My wife and kids did not die in vain. I live with their memory. But I was given a gift in exchange for what was taken from me. I was given a vision. A powerful dream that a boy would come to me one day, and this boy would change the world. All I had to do was carve one thing."

He walked over to the small carving of the Ark. He picked it up and extended it to Jacob. "Here, boy. The prophets gave me a dream of you. A sandy-haired boy, with gifts from the gods."

Jacob hesitated. How could a blind man know he had sandy hair? Hesitantly, he reached forward for the object. The old man clutched his hand with a strong leathery grasp. He placed the Ark in his hand and closed Jacob's fingers around it. He warned Jacob,

"You're going to dangerous places, boy. Keep your wits about you. Your journey takes you to the Dreaded Forest where the black witch waits. This is your key to her domain."

Jacob swallowed hard but didn't pull his hand back. The old man cackled again. "Let's get some stew in you boy. A little lizard mushroom soup should warm you up."

It didn't sound appealing, but then neither did starving to death. The old man pulled out carved stone bowls for the soup. The gray stew in the small caldron smelled like brussels sprouts and skunk. The old man took a sip of the broth. He smacked his lips in satisfaction. Jacob watched as the Woodcarver took a large gulp. Jacob took a timid sip of the stew. Strangely, it didn't taste as bad as it smelled; it tasted a lot like chicken. He learned to hold his breath as he ate. Before long the bowl was empty. Jacob felt better. The fire began to flicker so the old woodcarver picked up another brick and put it on the fire.

Jacob was curious, so he asked, "What are you burning?"

The Woodcarver poked at the fire. "Orn dung."

Jacob didn't press him for what an orn was or how he got its dung. He ate his soup and prayed that the old man had washed before he handled their food.

The small pot of soup diminished quickly with both eating. Jacob stopped eating and set the bowl down on a crudely constructed table of woven reeds where there were two small benches of stone. After a moment the old man asked him, "What is wrong, Jacob?"

Jacob replied, "I'm sorry. I have eaten your meal.

You could not have planned for two."

For the first time, the Woodcarver grinned. He had only a few teeth left presenting a gaping snaggletooth grin. "You are a special one, Jacob, son of Martin. No one could care less if I lived or died; you are worried that you have taken my food when you were starving."

Surprised, Jacob asked, "How did you know I was hungry?"

The old man sniffed the air. "I could hear your belly rumbling before you ever reached my hut. It is time for rest. You have a long journey ahead of you tomorrow. The monks wait for you."

Jacob replied, "Monks?"

The old man reached to a stone shelf, retrieved a mat, and threw it on the ground in a poof of dust. "Yes, monks. They bring me things and we barter for carvings. The monastery is one second from here."

Jacob was confused. "One second?"

The old man rolled the mat out. "Yes. We have first meal when we wake, second meal before we sleep. The time between first and second is the time it takes to get to the monks."

Jacob calculated it was a day's walk to the monastery.

The Woodcarver lay down and patted the mat beside him. "Sleep, boy."

Jacob lay on the mat beside the Woodcarver. He clutched the Ark in his hand. He was on edge until he heard the steady snoring of the old man beside him. He drifted off into a fitful sleep. He dreamed of snakes slithering into the hut and surrounding them. He lay paralyzed in fear, clamping his eyes shut as they crawled over his body to go after the old man. Chills ran down his spine as he heard the snakes repeatedly biting the old man. He heard the death rattle of the old man as the venom did its work on him. Jacob sat upright bathed in a cold sweat. The fire had died in the hut. He turned to the old man, who lay still beside him. He touched the Woodcarver's shoulder. It felt stiff. "Sir?"

He touched the old man again. The Woodcarver rolled over, his mouth agape. He was not breathing. Jacob recoiled instinctively. The old man had died while Jacob had slept. Jacob sat on the bench collecting himself, thinking about what the old man had said. He would use the trail to lead him to the monastery. Before he did, he would bury the old man. He moved outside and found a small depression in the rocky soil. He searched the hut for implements and found a metallic rod with a hoe-like implement on the end. It would do. He dug a space the old man would fit in, the stones and soil moved easily under the hoe. He searched through the hut and found tattered garments which would serve to cover the old man in the shallow grave. He found the old man's wood carving tools. The blades were razor sharp. Jacob unraveled the reed table and constructed a wooden cross; it was all he knew to do. It was time for the burial. He grabbed the old Woodcarver at his armpits. The body was cold and stiff, like a piece of wood. The body was lighter than Jacob had expected, but he still had to stop and rest as he dragged him through the loose soil. He made the final pull to the grave and eased him in. He covered the body with the garments and placed the woodcarvings around him. Jacob deliberated and changed the order of the carvings several times. He finally placed the carved wooden jewel on his chest, it just seemed right there. He pulled dirt over the old man. Jacob erected the makeshift cross at the old man's head and said a prayer over him. "Lord, thank you for my brief time with Abrah, son of Aerat. Please watch over him in Heaven. Amen."

He considered the old man probably wasn't religious, but it didn't matter. He gave him a proper burial, or as proper as he could. There was no shame in that; he did his best.

His belly grumbled. He had not eaten since he had gotten up. He would never make a day's walk like this. He searched the hut and found water, dried meat, and mushrooms. It looked like he would have another meal of skunk soup before resting. A small stash of grass, flint, and steel got the dung to catch on fire. It took an hour over the dung fire for the meat to be tender enough to eat. The old man must have cooked it all day to get it so soft, but then with no teeth, he probably had to.

The soup was tangier than he remembered from the night before. But it still satisfied his stomach. He watched as the fire died down and went over to the mat. He stared at the empty mat beside him for a while before rolling over and dozing to sleep. He dreamed he was sitting in the hut eating skunk stew. His mother and father were outside the hut calling for him. He yelled back, but they could not hear him. When he rose to find them, they had disappeared. As he went back into the hut, a flying craft flew overhead, its loud thrusters throbbed and pulsed as it landed. Robots marched off the craft and surrounded the hut. They began to move toward the hut and push the walls in toward him. As the walls began to fall toward him, he woke with a start.

He sat up on the mat and looked around; there were

no robots here. A sound caught his attention, a steady drip of water. In this arid place, it didn't seem possible. He rubbed the sleep from his eyes. Water was critical. He got up to investigate the source of the noise. He walked out the door to find the entire landscape enveloped in a dense fog. He followed the walls of the hut to the back where he found a stone gutter; the fog condensed on the stone and formed droplets which rolled into a small cistern the size of a gallon pail. Jacob ran back to the hut and gathered his canteen, filling it in the cistern. The water was clear; it tasted good to his dry lips. He refilled the canteen again and took a long drink.

He went back into the hut and gathered the remaining food and put it into his backpack. He placed the replica of the Ark in the side pocket. Last, he packed up the wood carving tools and placed them in the backpack. He might be able to use them for something. The trail outside the hut swirled in fog so thick he could only see ten feet ahead. He struck off without looking back. He walked until his feet were sore. He sat for a while on the dirt trail in the fog. It struck him there was no sun, no sunset, no sunrise. It was one constant day.

He reached out to his dad, *Dad?*

The thought came back to him, *Yes? Are you all right?*

Jacob responded, *I'm fine. I found a man. He gave me an Ark carved from wood. I am walking to where there are monks.*

His father's thoughts came to him. *He didn't hurt you, did he?*

Jacob responded, *No. He died from old age. I*

buried him.

There was a pause before Marty responded, *I'm sorry. I will find you as soon as I can.*

Jacob replied, *It's okay. Don't worry. I found water and food. I'm walking in the fog.*

He father responded, *Okay. Be careful.*

He thought, *I will. I love you, Dad.*

His father responded, *I love you too, son.*

Jacob rose and began walking again. The fog began to thin around him. Ahead, he could see a large structure rising out of the fog. Unlike the hut he had left, the walls rose to form a dome on top. The colors were not something he had ever seen before, but they were beautiful. Massive columns formed the structure on all four sides with an overhang which was ornately carved with vines and leaves. As the fog lifted, the structure glittered with condensate. Twelve men filed out of a massive doorway and formed a line along the front steps of the structure. The men wore hooded cloaks to hide their faces. The two men in the center spoke in unison, "Welcome, traveler. We are the twelve. Do you seek sanctuary?"

Jacob stopped. He thought through his response for a moment before responding, "I am Jacob, son of Martin. I was sent to you by Abrah, known as the Woodcarver."

The two men on each end asked in unison, "Do you hold the offering?"

Jacob pulled the replica of the Ark from his pocket and held it up for them to see. "He gave me this to bring to you."

One of the monks began to shake uncontrollably. The others broke rank to form a circle around the monk who had gone into a siezure. The monk was now convulsing. His hood fell back revealing lizard-like skin and reptilian eyes. The monks recoiled in horror. The lizard-like monk hissed at the other monks who ran from him, leaving the creature and Jacob alone.

The creature hissed at Jacob. "Give me the carving!"

Jacob placed the carving back in his pocket. "No!"

The creature moved toward him. Its voice rasped as it said, "Then I will take it from your dead body."

Without warning it dove at Jacob. Without thinking, Jacob waved his arm, casting the beast aside. It tumbled in the dirt away from him. From all fours, it launched into the air, springing toward Jacob. Jacob used his telekinetic power to propel the creature toward the solid wall of the building, the creature smashed into the wall with such force its head split open. It crumpled to the ground in a heap. A pool of black blood gathered around the body. Jacob looked at his hand. It trembled from the charge of adrenalin. He stared at the creature, and then at his hand in disbelief. He thought back to his time with the children in the Ark. He had done this several times when he played with the children. He had assumed this was merely a trick of the Ark and not anything to do with him. He faced the reality that he had many abilities.

The monks gathered around the lizard man. There was a murmur among them. Occasionally, they glanced at Jacob. The tallest monk turned to face Jacob. "You must be the chosen one. You have revealed a false prophet among us. We will follow you wherever you need us to follow, Jacob, son of Martin."

Jacob studied the men before responding. "Very

well, first things first, everyone drop your hoods."

The monks murmured to each other. The tall monk was the first to drop his hood. He was an average looking man, his father's age with an unremarkable face. He turned and looked at the other monks. "Do as he says."

Each monk dropped his hood. Each looked quite unremarkable, some had long faces, some had round faces, two had beards. No others had snake-like features. Jacob asked the tall monk, "Why do you hide your faces?"

The monk responded, "We keep our heads covered because we are not worthy of the ascension to the light in this physical form."

Jacob replied, "Well, it also keeps you from seeing your enemies when they are among you. No hoods."

The monks looked at each other. There was another quiet murmur among them. Jacob ignored it. "Do you guys have anything to eat besides skunk stew?"

The tall monk replied, "We do not know of skunk stew. Is it *good*?"

Jacob looked up in disgust. "No. No, it is not."

They all walked inside of the monastery and left the lizard man lying dead on the front doorstep.

****

In a chamber lit by unseen red light, the sorceress named Retch stared into a pool of black water. She watched as a blond-haired boy smashed her beloved Qua into the stone wall of the monastery. She felt the twinge of heat go up the back of her neck as anger filled her. For a millennium she had controlled the soft, useless monks with fear. None dared step outside the grounds of the monastery without facing the knowledge one of Retch's minions would rip them to shreds. Ever since the Day of Reckoning when the Dark Temple was finished and the demons were released in the Dreaded Forest, nothing had dared venture here without her permission. Jeez had given her complete autonomy in this realm. The appearance of this boy unnerved her. He was not like the others; he was not like anything she had ever seen.

She gazed into the black pool and watched the monks and the boy file into the monastery and the doors close behind them. She reached for the amulet centered over her heart. She lifted it where she could see her reflection in the black onyx. Her reflection dissolved as the amulet began to glow with purple light. She visualized the monastery and recited the travel incantation. The portal opened in front of her. She stepped into the swirling vortex of black energy. The swirling energy in the portal stung her skin like a swarm of angry bees on a summer day. She ignored the pain and moved forward. In an instant it was over. She stood outside of the monastery beside her beloved Qua. She had found Qua in the tunnels beneath the Dark Temple and raised it from a small, scared lizard. She had breathed human substance into its small, tiny body. It had grown from a small black reptile to an almost human-like form. She made it intelligent. She taught it to speak and walk like a human, and almost to feel like a human. It was the closest thing to a child she'd ever had. She stood beside its lifeless form and felt a cold, dark anger swell within her. She levitated Qua's body. A trail of blood dripped from Qua's skull where it had cracked open from the force of impact. This stranger would pay for this. She touched the amulet and passed the energy from the stone to heal Qua's broken head. Qua opened its eyes. He hissed and bit Retch on the arm. She took little notice of the wound. She spoke soothingly to her creation, "There, there, my sweet Qua. Mother's here. You must complete your assignment. Kill the boy. Bring his body to me and we will feast together on his bones."

Qua leapt up. He looked back and forth. There was a look of wildness in its eyes. One Retch had not seen since it was a fledgling. Part of her beloved Qua was back, but her creation had reverted to its wild roots. She looked at it for one last time and said, "Remember, stalk and kill the blond boy." She focused her attention on the amulet for the return to the Dark Temple. She could heal Qua with time, but there was none. She had to prepare for the stranger. The portal opened, and she stepped back into the swarm of bees.

****

In the distance, Marty could make out a distant object. He was drawn toward it. In the quiet of the grassland, he could hear something rustling behind him. He stopped and turned in time to see a red ape barreling up behind him. He held his ground. The simian was either going to kill him or sniff him. He hoped it was the latter. Marty lowered his head and was careful not to make eye contact. The last thing he wanted to do was provoke the beast. The ape stopped ten feet away from him. It held a brown fruit aloft for Marty to see. Marty raised his head enough to see the red ape and eased forward toward the beast carefully. He stretched his hand forward. The large primate dropped the fruit in his hand, turned, and left as quietly as he came. Marty stared at the fruit, and then at the tree where all the apes were observing him. He bit into the fruit. It was sweet, tangy, and salty all at the same time. He held it aloft so the apes could see him, and then returned it to his lips for another bite. The apes all hooted and called out to him. He breathed a sigh of relief. He turned and located the landmark on the horizon and began his long journey toward it.

He walked for what seemed like an eternity. The object now appeared to have the features of a person. Marty thought it odd anyone could stand still for so long, so he dismissed the possibility it was a person. At a close distance, he could clearly see the cloak-like hood. Marty slowed as he got closer. The cloaked figure waited for him. The face was hidden by a kabuki mask under the hood. The figure raised one arm and motioned him to follow, turned, and began to walk away. Marty followed at a distance.

Marty considered he should be scared senseless, but oddly he felt calm. He trailed the figure silently as they waded through the tall grass. He noticed they were walking toward a mound in the flat landscape and wondered if it was a dwelling of some sort. They began to descend into the mound, which quickly narrowed into a tunnel. The walls glowed in an eerie red glow. The cloaked figure stopped and turned toward Marty.

He said, "You must remain quiet until I tell you otherwise. If the sentries detect you, they will capture you. Follow me, and I will take you to Jacob."

Marty stood in shock. "How do you know my son's name?"

The cloaked figure placed a finger to his lips. "This is not the time for questions. You must do as you are told."

Marty was anxious, but he had little choice other than to follow quietly behind the figure. He navigated carefully through the tunnel which dropped at treacherous levels making it more difficult in the weird red light. They descended for an hour before a sound began to emanate through the tunnel.

Chink, chink, chink. The sounds of stone struck by metal, but the sound was not rhythmic enough for one person, it must be several people. As they drew closer, the sounds increased. A side tunnel appeared to their left; the cloaked figure slid into the side tunnel which was noticeably darker. Marty could barely discern the gravel path as they walked in near darkness. The chinking sounds grew fainter. As they approached the end of the tunnel, the sounds became strong once again. The cloaked figure moved forward. As they cleared the tunnel, Marty could see they were on a ledge high above a large cavern. In the cavern, hundreds of small figures toiled with pickaxes against the walls, extracting red glowing gems from the wall. Large robots scanned the crowd. One of the miners stopped and looked in Marty's direction. Marty ducked into the shadows out of sight. The robot extended a long metal rod toward the miner who had stopped digging. The crackle of an electric charge filled the room. The robot delivered a red bolt of lightning to the small figure. In the flare of light, Marty could see the miner was nothing more than a boy, almost the same age as Jacob. Marty stifled a gasp. The miners were all children.

He returned to the shadows and moved away from the sounds of the boy groaning and the constant chink of pickaxe on stone. They entered another chamber. Piles of jerky and pots of water lined the wall. The cloaked figure pointed to the dried meat. "Take as much as you think you can carry. It will have to last until you can find other food. Marty did as he was told; he grabbed handfuls of the dried meat and stuffed it in his backpack. He filled his canteen, drank deeply, and refilled again." The cloaked figure was on the move again. One hour later they could see the twilight of the plain ahead. The cloaked figure walked up the ramp which appeared to be designed for motorized vehicles. The cloaked figure led Marty away from the road and toward a dark stand of trees. The trunks were black in the dim light. They followed the tree line. The terrain dropped down in elevation, leading to a small ravine. A faint trail led into the black forest. The cloaked figure stopped.

He turned to Marty and said, "Wait here. Jacob will come to you in this spot. You will hear loud noises of large vehicles. Hide from them. When the time is right, follow the road near the mine."

Marty started to speak. As he opened his mouth, the figure disappeared. He was alone and puzzled.

****

In the center of the temple, Jacob sat on a circular bench which framed a firepit of glowing embers. In the center of the fire was a large metal pot which steamed with flower petals floating on the surface. The potpourri smelled better than the old woodcarver had provided. The monks sat around him. A tall monk asked, "Are you the child of the prophecy?"

Jacob deliberated for a moment. "I don't know. The old blind woodcarver seemed to think so. What I do know, is I came here with my father to stop an evil woman from hurting my mom. What I need is to find the snake woman."

There was a collective gasp from the monks. An older monk quieted his comrades and said, "You seek the high priestess of evil in this land. She holds dominion over everything you see. She is all powerful. None here dare challenge her."

Jacob looked the old monk in the eye. "I do, especially when she's messing with my mom."

The monk regarded him for a moment before responding, "There is a place of power two seconds from here. It is guarded by the black witch at the center of the Dreaded Forest. None dare enter. But you, Jacob, seem to have power beyond any I've ever seen. We will follow you there. We should leave after we've rested."

Jacob asked, "What do you call this place?"

The tall monk was quiet for a moment. "We do not generally speak of it, but it is known as the Temple of Darkness."

Jacob continued, "Will all of you be traveling?"

The tall monk replied, "Yes. But we must bury Brother Q before we leave. Even though he betrayed us, we owe him a proper burial. He lived here with us many seasons."

One of the monks walked up behind the tall monk and whispered in his ear. A look of concern crossed the tall monk's face. He announced loudly to the group, "It seems that Brother Q's body has disappeared."

This concerned Jacob. "Then I suggest we leave immediately."

The monks looked at each other and whispered. The tall monk asked Jacob, "But what of the food?"

Jacob looked the monk directly in the eye. "Then, I suggest we eat then leave."

The monk looked to his peers for consensus. One by one they nodded. He looked back at Jacob. "We agree."

The monks moved to the back of the monastery, where the large room divided into living quarters and a modest kitchen. Within the kitchen were various dishes on a large iron stove. The food smelled measurably better than the skunk stew the old man had provided. The pots had various vegetables, with gray meats. The monks provided stone bowls with small ladles. A large stone table was the center piece of the room. The table was set for twelve. Jacob sat in Brother Q's place. The tall monk introduced himself to Jacob, "I am Brother C. I am the elder of the monastery. Brother Q was the youngest convert of the Order. He was…a disappointment."

Jacob studied Brother C's face. He could see the emotions in the man's expressions—sad, but truthful. Jacob paused for a moment as he considered he could read the emotional state of the monk more so than he had ever been able to on Earth. He was a human lie detector. The thought surprised him. He focused back on his conversation with the monk. "Why do you use a letter instead of a name?"

Brother C replied, "When we were confirmed into the order, we abandoned our given names and were each known by only the first letter of our names. We left our family history behind in order to devote our lives to the Order."

Jacob considered this, and then asked, "Why was Brother Q a disappointment?"

Brother C thought for a moment. "We have few converts from the Nihilistic world outside. We believe there will be light again from the maker. Our people are caught in a world of deceit. We still believe we can help them see the truth. Brother Q came to us years ago as a boy; that thing was not Brother Q. It was impersonating Brother Q and only here to stop the prophecy."

Jacob considered this. "How many people know the prophecy?"

Brother C was silent for a moment before responding. "Fewer each day. The more people are possessed by the serqet and sentenced to the mines, the more the teachings of old slip away."

Jacob's stomach growled. "Can we continue this while we eat? We have much to consider, and little time to do so."

Brother C replied, "This is true. Let us eat."

One of the monks moved to the stove and carried a black pot of stew to the table. As was their custom, he ladled out a bowl to each monk starting with Brother C.

Brother C blessed the food. "He who provideth the food, so shall he bring the light and the redemption that comes with the light. Let us eat."

Each monk ate. The food smelled salty but tasted sweet and tart, much like sweet potatoes and rhubarb. It refreshed Jacob. When the first course was finished by each monk, a different monk rose and brought a second pot to the table. The second course tasted much like game meat. It was tangy but not unreasonably so, much like deer venison. Jacob began to feel sleepy. His ladle was almost to his mouth when he slumped over at the table. The monks rose silently and gathered the boy, carrying him to a cot. They laid him on the cot and bound him to it by wrapping a sheet around him. The monks sat on stools in a circle around him and watched

Jacob as he slept.

Jacob dreamed. He hung from a tree limb in a cocoon. The black trees of the forest surrounding him were engulfed with a low, dense fog from which the trees jutted straight up. He struggled against the cocoon binding him. The more he struggled against the binding the more the cocoon tightened around him. He stopped his struggling and turned his attention to a swirling mass of white mist which formed in front of him. The mist coalesced to the outline of a man, until the haze took a physical shape. The man formed from the mist cocked his head sideways as he observed Jacob squirming in front of him. His voice was gravelly, as if it were strained. “Hello, Jacob-san.”

Even upside down, Jacob was certain he did not recognize the man. He asked the old man, “Can you help me down?”

The old man’s expression did not change. “I can but I think it would be more useful if I taught you how to free yourself.”

Frustrated, Jacob replied, “I have tried. I can’t free myself.”

The old man replied calmly, “Perhaps you are trying too hard. The brute force of the body is no match for the power of the mind. Look within yourself, Jacob-san; what do you think would help you release yourself from your bonds?”

Jacob stopped struggling for a moment and thought about the binding around him. He thought about what it would take to free him completely, if he could melt the cocoon away from his body, he would be free. Even though he had not said a word, the old man responded to his thoughts. “Correct, Jacob-san. You can melt your bonds. Now, what would it take for you to do that?"

Jacob concentrated on the cocoon. He envisioned it burning away from his body without harming him. At the last moment when he released, he would swing his feet down and land as if it were a gymnastics landing. He focused his mental energy on the cocoon. He could smell the binding burning. The gossamer threads began to smolder and spark. At last, the cocoon burst into a million tiny explosions and released him, and he landed feet first on the fog-covered ground below him.

The old man bowed slightly to Jacob. "Very good, Jacob-san. You have learned to use your mind like a muscle in your body. You can move things and manipulate things with your mind. Those are the simple acts. It is time for you to wake now. The monks wait for you."

Without another word, the old man returned into the fog. Jacob called after him, "Wait!"

The old man stopped and poked his head from the mist. Jacob asked, "Who are you, how can I see you again?"

The old man replied, "I am Master Moto. I am a part of you, Jacob-san, I will always be here when you need me. Meditation is the easiest way to reach me. Now, go. Wake from your sleep and lead the monks to the Dreaded Forest."

Jacob awoke, his eyes wide. He tried to move but found he was bound tight against his cot. The monks had covered their faces with the hoods once again. Jacob looked at the closet monk and asked, "What is this?"

The voice of monk was not Brother C. "If you are the chosen one, then this binding should be no contest for you. If you are not the chosen one, then your fate has been sealed by the teachings. We must sacrifice you to the One."

Jacob stopped struggling against the binding. At first, there was nothing. He concentrated on the sheet holding him as he had the cocoon in his dream. He felt his body grow uncomfortably hot. He kept his eyes closed tightly. He heard a gasp from the monks around him. He opened his eyes in time to see the sheet disintegrate into a million tiny embers and fall to the floor. The monks backed away from him. He was free from the binding which lay in a smoking heap beneath the cot. He sat up and looked in the direction of the monk. "Is that proof enough?"

The monk lowered himself to his knees, angling his face to the ground. The other monks followed in succession.

Jacob swung his legs off the cot. He commanded, "Stand. Never bow to me again. When do we leave?"

The monk rose. He uncovered his face. It was the monk who had served the food. He replied, "I am Brother Z. We understand if you are upset but had to make certain. We will leave as soon as we have packed provisions for the trip. The journey through the Dreaded Forest will be long and dangerous. We have accepted our fate. Some of us will not return, but it is our destiny. We will follow you until the end. Until then, rest, Chosen One."

Jacob looked at Brother Z. "I understand. Call me Jacob, the Chosen One is a little over the top."

Brother Z replied, "As you wish, Cho…uh, Jacob."

The monks moved about with purpose. For several hours, they loaded a wagon with food, water, and blocks of dung for fire. Jacob watched with interest. He tugged at Brother Z's robe. "Brother Z, you said the trip was dangerous. Do you have weapons?"

Brother Z looked at him for a moment before responding. "Jacob, you are the only weapon we have."

Jacob blinked. It occurred to him for the first time that he was destined to be here. It was a sobering thought; he was a spirit warrior in a child's body. He stepped away from the monks and found a quiet corner. He sat and closed his eyes. He moved deep within his own mind not knowing what to expect. Before long, he found himself in a round chamber with many doors. With his telekinetic power he opened the first door with his thoughts. From the first door walked Master Moto. Moto's features were clearer; he was short for a man, only slightly taller than Jacob. His goatee was short and scrubby against his chin. His eyes reflected wisdom. He approached Jacob. "Hello, Jacob-san, are you ready for another lesson?"

Jacob replied, "We are preparing to leave, will it take long?"

Moto chuckled. "In this place, time is no longer an illusion. So let us begin with a very important lesson for you." He reached inside of his robe and extracted a blob of light. He released it into the air in front of him. It glowed with a powerful white light as it hovered. The amorphous blob floated and rolled as streaks of light escaped from it like pulses from a laser.

Jacob was fascinated by the blob. "What is it?"

Moto's face glowed from the light of the blob. "It is the Edajhia Root. It is the source from which all your powers manifest."

Jacob stared at it entranced by its light. "What does

it do?"

Moto replied serenely, "The Edajhia Root doesn't really *do* anything. It could be described as a toolbox of possibilities. Once you have learned to navigate within its realm, you will be free to travel to unexplored regions of your mind."

Jacob reached toward the glowing blob. Without looking at Moto, he asked, "Can I touch it?"

Moto replied, "Of course, it is as much a part of you as the blood in your veins and the bones in your hand."

It felt warm, soothing even. Jacob asked, "Can it be mastered?"

Moto considered the question for a moment before answering. "The Edajhia is a part of you, so what you are really asking is, can you master yourself. That is a question, and it is as old as mankind. My only answer can be, if you believe you can, then the answer is, yes."

Jacob allowed the Edajhia to swirl around his hand; it looked almost playful. Jacob replied to Moto, "I have done things that defy what I thought I knew. I believe, Moto."

Moto replied, "Then ask the Edajhia. What do you wish to know?"

Jacob relaxed his grip on the Edajhia. He thought about the trip ahead. It was a place the monks feared to travel to. He looked at the Edajhia and asked, "Can you show me how to summon a useful weapon against demons?"

Subtly the Edajhia changed colors to a blue hue. Jacob could sense the Edajhia begin to align thoughts in his mind. Jacob was frightened at first.

In a soothing voice, Moto said, "Relax Jacob-san.

Allow the Edajhia to take control, to show you new possibilities, it is what you asked for."

Jacob took a deep breath and let go. As he did, the chamber he was in seemed to melt away. He and Moto stood in a vast crystal room. The light from the Edajhia reflected from every surface making the chamber light up to an almost unbearable level. Jacob remained calm. The light grew greater and greater until the crystal room was filled with light. He could only see Moto and could not make out any features of the crystal room. Without warning the light collapsed into a tiny pinprick of light on his index finger. In a moment of clarity, Jacob knew the secret to fighting the creatures in the forest.

He looked at the speck of light on his finger, and then up at Moto. In the tiny glow from his finger was the concentrated reflections of the crystal room, Moto's features were hidden by the shadows. Jacob said, "I know what to do."

Moto placed a hand on his shoulder as he replied, "Then it is time to return."

Jacob took a deep breath and opened his eyes. The monks had all stopped and were staring at him. Jacob asked, "Is everything okay?"

Brother Z spoke. "Jacob, you glow as you meditate. We have never experienced that. It was…divine."

Jacob replied, "I was preparing for our journey. If we are going to fight the forces of evil, we need an arsenal. I was collecting our weapons."

Brother Z responded, "Indeed, Jacob." And carried the crate in his hands to the wagon.

****

Marty hunched in the ravine surveying the

landscape. On one side there was a serene plain of golden grass, on the other was a blackened forest laden with a dense fetid mist which clung to the ground. The faint throb of a large engine began to grow louder. The mysterious cloaked figure had warned him of others, but Marty wasn't sure what he should be looking for. The throb grew louder, so much so he could feel the vibration. Marty scanned in all directions trying to detect where the noise was coming from. He looked up at the tree line in time to see the front edge of a vast aerial craft flying over the forest. Marty dove into the fog. He crouched in the low-hanging mist. He rested on all fours poised to run if needed. The mist stank of sulfur and decay, and Marty struggled to breathe in the putrid fog. The air ship finally cleared the forest and was moving out of sight. Marty heard a growl behind him. He whirled to see multiple pairs of glaring red eyes observing him from the surrounding mist. He didn't wait. He vaulted from the forest and rolled onto the grassy prairie. Once he was out of the mist, he turned, prepared to fight whatever beast was in the woods, but nothing had followed him. He could feel the goosebumps on his arm and looked down to see his arm hairs standing on end. He backed away from the tree line and discovered the tingling energy he felt in the forest subsided. Curiously, he moved back toward the forest and watched as his arm hairs stood on end once again. As he backed away, he could feel the energy calm once again. He realized if Jacob was passing through this forest, he was in great danger. He reached out to his son telepathically. *Jacob?*

Jacob responded, *Yes, Dad?*

Marty thought, *The forest is very dangerous. You*

must find a way around it.

Jacob replied, *I know, Dad. But there is something I must do in the forest. I am prepared.*

Marty was more direct. *Son, there is something in the forest that will try to kill you. Find another way.*

Jacob responded, *I am ready. I have new powers. This is my destiny.*

Marty was desperate now. *Son, please don't do this.*

Jacob's thoughts were calm, almost serene. *Father, we knew this time would come. You must trust me. I am prepared, and this journey cannot be avoided. Trust me.*

Marty took a calming breath. *Okay, be ready for them.*

Jacob replied, *I am. Love you, Dad.*

With all his heart, Marty thought back, *I love you too.*

****

Jacob watched with keen fascination as the monks hitched a large beast resembling a buffalo to the wagon to pull it. They tethered the beast to the wagon while one monk stood in front of it with a handful of golden grass. The creature nibbled on the grass complacently, while the monks worked on the leather straps hitching it to the wagon.

Brother Z broke Jacob's reverie. "We're ready."

With no ceremony they started the long walk. The monks walked in pairs with Jacob in the middle with Brother Z.

As they walked, Brother Z began to explain the Order. "We have always been The Twelve. Twenty seasons ago, parents would bring their sons to the

Order. As monks of the Order passed on, we would send word to the city and parents would bring their sons to the monastery as candidates for the Order. Only one child could be chosen. When the child was chosen by the light crystal, he was given a robe and spent the rest of his days in the Order, praying and studying with the monks."

Jacob interrupted, "Light crystal?"

Brother Z explained, "The Order was founded based on a crystal which emanates light. When exposed to its light, others can see to the true nature of the person in the glow of the crystal."

Jacob murmured, "Interesting."

Brother Z continued, "Our order has practiced for centuries. But in the last twenty seasons, no one has come to join the Order; the people from the cities no longer come this way. We believe it is a sign. It was foretold there would be a Time of Chaos. It appears it is upon us."

Jacob asked, "What is the Time of Chaos?"

Brother Z explained, "The tumultuous end of an era. When the dusk that surrounds this planet dissolves. We have always known it is unnatural for this land to be in perpetual twilight. Demons rule this land. It was prophesized a child would come and usher in a period of reformation. We believe you are the one the prophecy foretold will end the twilight and move us into an epoch.

Jacob looked up at Brother Z. "Does that scare you?"

Brother Z said, "No. It scares me more thinking that everything will remain like this for eternity. There is no life here; there is no joy. The only people who experience joy here are the ones who carry the abomination known as the serqet. They celebrate carrying a demon seed within. Both men and women live to serve the Demon Jeez until their bellies are slit open like an animal to release the serqet."

Jacob frowned. "What is a serqet?"

Brother Z furrowed his brow. "Things not of this world. Jeez brought them here to find the red crystals under the sea so they can be harvested for her war machine. The serqets can sense the crystals. Children that are not suitable hosts are sent to the mines. Those are the same children who would have come here to be considered for the monastery. It is a travesty."

Jacob asked, "What are red crystals?"

Brother Z continued, "They are shaped like crystals, but hold mysterious power. Jeez's armies use the crystals to power the machines she has built for war. But we do not fight here. It is like she is preparing for something, but we do not know what."

Jacob stopped suddenly. The monks behind him almost piled up on one another. Brother Z looked at Jacob curiously. "What is it, Jacob?"

Jacob turned and looked up at Brother Z. "She is planning to invade Earth."

Brother Z looked confused. "What is Earth?"

Jacob replied, "That is the world I am from. She manipulates people on Earth. I think that's why she's interested in my family. We are sensitive to the power of the Ark."

Brother Z asked, "What is the Ark?"

Jacob continued, "There are people on Earth called Jews. They were instructed by God to create a box to hold His sacred laws."

Brother Z looked curious. "God?"

Jacob replied, "You would know him as the One."

Brother Z nodded in understanding while Jacob continued. "The Ark of the Covenant was so powerful only a chosen few could be in its presence. If you were not one of the selected few, the Ark would strike you dead. There was a man on our planet who found the Ark and tried to obtain ultimate power from it. My mother and father stopped him because he wanted to use the power to gain dominion over all living beings. My family is connected to the Ark, I'm not sure why, but we can communicate with Rachael, the entity is sovereign over the Ark's realm. She transported my father and me here to stop Jeez from hurting my mother. It sounds like we have the same purpose. Stop Jeez."

There was excitement in Brother Z's response. "Yes, Jacob, it is why you are the Chosen One!"

Jacob replied, "Perhaps."

The orn slowly paced the group through the grassland and into the twilight. Jacob walked, lost in thought. He toyed with the Edajhia in his mind, accessing more and more information, only occasionally looking up. He was surprised at the change in geography around him when the group stopped for the second meal. Jagged boulders randomly pierced the golden grass, creating a contrast in the landscape. The monks unhitched the orn to allow the beast to graze on the grass while the monks built a small fire to cook wassaw on. This was a stew made from fragrant green mushrooms that smelled like turmeric while it cooked. They pulled out flatbread to eat with the wassaw stew which tasted much like the shrak Jacob had eaten in

Amman. It was strange two completely alien cultures had such similar foods. The monks laid out mats of woven grass on the plain around the wagon near the fire and they slept.

Loathsome red eyes watched them from the grass as they slept, the creature waited with infinite patience to strike.

Chapter 11

Gillian awoke in a bed with soft linen sheets that smelled of lavender. The room was quiet, comfortable, and cool. She threw back the sheets and put her feet on the ground. Her head ached as if she were hung over. She sat for a moment on the side of the bed trying to remember how she got here; her attempt to recall the previous night's events was met with blackness. She eased off the bed and held on to the bedpost to steady herself before she walked to the bathroom. Her reflection in the mirror was clearly not her best moment. Hair matted to the side of her head in a clump, dark circles under her bloodshot eyes. Fresh clothes were folded on a chair next to the shower. They were her size and her colors, boring beige and drab olive. She stripped and dropped her clothes onto the floor in a heap. The steam from the shower peeled away some of the discord in her mind. She toweled off and dressed in the bathroom. As she flipped the light off, she noticed Gretchen sitting in an armchair, waiting with passive calm and staring out the window. Without turning in Gillian's direction, she asked, "What went wrong?"

Gillian replied calmly, "I don't know."

Gretchen turned and faced her. "Would you like for me to tell you?"

Gillian replied, "I'm sure you will, whether I want you to or not."

Gretchen ignored the jab. "You deviated from the directive. Why would you even consider allowing yourself to be captured?"

Gillian responded, "I don't remember anything after Milan."

Gretchen's eyebrow furrowed. "Do you remember our phone call?"

Gillian shook her head. "No. I've been having blackouts. Did we fail?"

Gretchen looked her in the eye. "No. Wilhelm is safe. And you are *disturbed*."

Gillian asked, "What do you mean?"

Without turning Gretchen explained, "You killed their entire team bare handed. It was perhaps the most frightening thing I've ever witnessed. Our team was poised, ready to intervene. Their video headsets captured the whole thing. It was like you were possessed."

Gillian's expression was passive. "Now what?"

Gretchen stood. "I don't know. I'm not sure what to do. And I will be honest. I am rarely in a position where I don't know what to do. I would send you home to your husband, but he's disappeared."

Gillian's mind was suddenly alert. Marty must have been able to travel to the other realm. She replied, "So I suppose my part of the mission is over."

Gretchen looked at her without expression. "Definitely. I can't risk another bloodbath like the last one. We captured the Baron as he was trying to flee. We've paid off the Russian mob, so they'll stop looking for you two. The only thing left is to make it to court and prove Wilhelm is the heir to the estate. My team will do that."

Gillian replied, “So let me go. I’ll blend into the shadows and disappear. No one will know where I am. Fair enough?”

Gretchen was quiet for a moment before replying, “Here’s what we are going to do. You will stay here for a couple of days until Wilhelm is validated in Vienna. When he is safely confirmed, you go wherever you want to go. Okay?”

Gillian considered the proposal. “Fair enough.” It would be a long two days.

Gretchen left the room. Gillian opened the window to feel the breeze of the alpine summer. She looked through the bars at the blue birds hunting bugs in the rose garden below. Nuthatches circled cherry trees in a mating dance. She listened as they chirped and twittered below. A voice broke her from her revery.

“Your work is not done.”

She whirled around to see a man in a black cloak behind her. She reacted, instinctively dropping into a defensive stance. He raised his hand toward her. “Stop. I am here to help you, nothing more.”

She stayed in her stance. “Who are you?”

The cloaked man replied, “It doesn’t matter who I am. What I need to tell you matters more than you can imagine. When you are released from this place, you will travel to Egypt. There you will begin your journey to recover three artifacts. Your first object will be within the statue of Ptah in Abu Simbel.”

Gillian’s eyes narrowed. “Who are you working for? Whose directive is this?”

The stranger replied, “I work for no one. I act in your best interest. I promise that who and what I am will be revealed someday, but not now, not here. Trust me."

Gillian opened her mouth to respond, but the figure de-materialized in front of her. She rushed to where the figure had stood. There was nothing. She looked for a projector. It had to be a trick. She found the surveillance camera watching her. She wondered if they could project from it. There was a small desk against the wall. She found a note pad and paper and scribbled a message on it. She held it up for the camera to see and walked back to sit by the window to wait.

****

Rolf's eyes narrowed as he watched the girl in the Rose room. Her actions became increasingly erratic by the minute. He eased forward in the chair and watched as she crouched in a defense posture, then she began talking to the wall. His hand hovered over a general alarm button. He scanned the room to verify she was alone. Finally, she scribbled a note and held it up in the direction of the camera. "Very Funny! Ha." She turned her back and sat down in the chair overlooking the rose garden. Rolf could understand why they had locked her up. She was a lunatic. The microphones in the room had been disabled by a higher-level security person. They had briefed him she may act peculiar, but he was not to act unless she tried to escape. This must have been what they were referring to. He eased back in his chair and waited to see what she would do next.

****

Gillian stared at her phone for the tenth time. No one called, no messages, nothing. It was her second day in the secure room of the castle. Her only visitors were the servants who brought her food with an armed guard as an escort. She resorted to doing sit-ups and push-ups in rotation for an hour until she collapsed from exhaustion. It was a good workout but only temporarily alleviated the boredom. On the second day, the lock clicked, and Gretchen walked in. There were no guards with her. Her face looked like a porcelain doll. Her tone was crisp as she spoke. "It's over. Wilhelm has been validated. The estate is secure, and the Baron is being counseled on his behaviors. You are released from the mission."

Gretchen handed Gillian a thick envelope. "There is enough cash to take you back to the US or wherever you need to go. We'll call if we need you."

Without so much as a goodbye, Gretchen turned to leave the room.

Gillian stopped her. "What about Wilhelm? Is he safe?"

Gretchen turned; her face was emotionless. "The staff security team is responsible for his safety now. They are highly trained. He will be fine."

Gillian asked, "Are you sure your staff in the castle can be trusted?"

Gretchen's eyes narrowed. "We have reconciled the inconsistencies with our staff. There should be no further trust issues with our team on site." Gretchen paused. "And I almost forgot, you may have your choice of cars from the garage. All of them are fueled and roadworthy."

Gillian replied, "Thanks." She followed Gretchen out of the room.

Rolf met her in the hallway as she walked out. He stood at attention when Gretchen walked past. He addressed Gillian, "Frau Wood, if you will follow me, I will take you to the garage."

Gillian followed the young man down the hall past the Ming vases which rested on Chippendale tables. The subtle blue of the Ming dynasty dragon contrasted against the rich walnut of the Chippendale. None of which Gillian cared about. All she could think of was the mysterious cloaked figure directing her to the Abu Simbel.

They walked down a ramp where the accessories became more austere. They passed through the door into the garage bay where a dozen cars were backed in diagonally ready to be driven out. Rolf continued to walk past car after car until he stopped at a deep burgundy British sports coupe. He opened the door for Gillian. She looked at the beige sedan next to it and asked, "I thought I could choose any vehicle. Wouldn't you be more comfortable if I were to drive that?" She gestured toward the sedan. "I don't seem to have a good track record with cars remaining intact."

Rolf's expression never changed. "I was instructed otherwise. I am to provide you with the coupe."

Gillian shrugged. "Suit yourself." She slid into the comfortable leather seats to find Wilhelm sitting in the passenger seat. Suddenly it became all too clear.

Wilhelm's eyes had a mischievous look as he asked, "Where are we off to?"

Gillian would not meet his gaze. She looked straight ahead over the hood. "We can't do this. I know some things happened between us, but I'm married, and I have a child."

Wilhelm replied, "I'm not trying to wreck your home life. I thought you could use some company. We'll take a quick trip to wherever and I'll be on my way."

Gillian pressed the start button. The engine rumbled to life. “No hanky-panky. Are we clear?”

Wilhelm looked out the passenger window so she couldn’t see his smile. “Crystal.”

Gillian eased the coupe out and proceeded toward the exit.

Chapter 12

Jacob drifted deep into meditation. As he felt his body lighten, he entered a state of tranquility. He visualized a room filled with soft cushions on polished purple wood floors. A brook flowed through the middle of the room tinkling into a small copper basin. The water was crystal clear. Master Moto entered the room with the Edajhia floating along behind him like a bizarre pet. Moto bowed to Jacob. “Jacob-san, the physical world attempts to intrude upon your transcendental world. Can you feel it?”

Jacob sat back in one of the cushions and envisioned the outside world. He saw the demon red eyes observing him from the grassland. The beast stalked him as prey. “I see the demon, Master Moto. What do you recommend I do?”

Moto replied, “You have the Edajhia at your disposal. It holds the answer to many questions. If I were you, I would ask the Edajhia.”

Jacob stretched out his hand. The Edajhia floated toward him and rested in his palm. In a moment, a fountain of all possibilities flowed before him. His perspective moved and changed moment to moment. Everything seemed so simple from the viewpoint of the Edajhia. He asked the question of the Edajhia, “*How do I drive away the demons*?” There were no words, only thoughts. The answer manifested all around him. In response to the thought, a perfectly formed ball of light, the size of a large marble, formed in his other hand. He lifted it to his lips and breathed life into the light ball to give it purpose, then he commanded, "*Chase the demon away*."

The small ball of light flew out of sight.

****

The monks surrounding Jacob in the grass woke with a start. Brother Z stared as Jacob began to levitate above the ground. Jacob opened his palm and a ball of light flew from his hand and into the grassland beyond the campsite. Brother Z watched in astonishment as the orb shot toward a dark figure hiding in the grass. The figure hissed at the light as it approached. Suddenly the orb began to touch the black figure in different places on its body. The black figure leaped and rolled, trying to escape the attack of the tiny spot of light. The orb was relentless, like an angry hornet it continued to sting the black figure as it rolled and hissed on the ground. Finally, the black figure hissed loudly and retreated as the light ball chased it through the tall grass. After a few minutes, the orb returned and entered Jacob's hand, sinking into his flesh.

Brother Z looked at Brother C and shrugged. They both returned to the grass mats and fell into a deep sleep.

****

Jacob floated above his body and watched the scene from above like a spectator in an arena as the orb stung the creature all over leaving small burns on the creature's skin. Giving up, the hell spawn fled on all fours like a dog. He summoned the orb back to him, closing the vision of the world outside. Safely back in his serene place, he watched the Edajhia glow and undulate before him. Jacob shifted his gaze to Moto. "I have an idea."

Moto looked intrigued. "And what would that be, Jacob-san?"

Jacob looked up as he replied thoughtfully, "I would like to share the Edajhia with my father."

Moto stared at him in disbelief. "You want to do what?"

Jacob replied with more conviction, "I am going to share the Edajhia with my father."

Moto raised one eyebrow. "I don't know if you can do that."

Jacob peered at Moto slyly. "I do. The Edajhia told me how."

Moto looked at the Edajhia and then at Jacob. "You are right about one thing: if it can be done, the Edajhia will know."

Jacob stretched out his hand for the Edajhia. The Edajhia nestled itself in his hand. Jacob stared into the Nexus and carefully worded the question in his mind. *How do I share Edajhia Root with my father, Martin Wood?* The answer formed all around him.

Your father must hold something of yours, and you must focus on that part of you. When you connect with yourself, you may invite him in. The Edajhia will create a twin for your father to have.

Jacob bowed his head. *Thank you, Edajhia.*

The Edajhia responded, *Most welcome, Jacob.*

Jacob exited the consciousness of the Edajhia. Moto asked, "And so, Jacob-san, is this possible?"

Jacob replied, "It is. I must reach out to my father."

Moto bowed. "You are very wise, Jacob-san. I

would offer one thought as you plan your next step. In this place, during these desperate times, ensure it is your father before you invite him into your mind."

Jacob realized the soundness of Moto's advice. "Yes. Thank you, Moto."

Jacob concentrated on his dad. *Father?*

It was a moment later when his father's voice replied, *Yes, son?*

Jacob asked, *Do you still have your backpack?*

Marty replied, *Of course*.

Jacob replied, *Can you tell me what's in it?*

There was a pause. *Camel jerky, water, a small bundle of rope, toothbrush, comb...*

Jacob interrupted with a thought, *Is that my comb?*

Marty responded, *Yes. You left it on the sink in Amman the last morning we were in the hotel.*

Jacob replied, *Is there anything on it?*

There was a pause before Marty responded, *There's some dandruff. You really need to start using a dandruff shampoo.*

Jacob would table the dandruff discussion for later. *Perfect. I have found a way to let you enter my mind. Put the dandruff in your hand and concentrate on it.*

A hesitant thought came back from Marty. *Okay. I have your dandruff and I'm looking at it. Really hard.*

Jacob visualized the tiny particles in his father's hand. He closed his mind to all else except to connect with the particles that had once been a part of him. Jacob felt a jolt. He felt his body shiver. When he came back to his sanctuary, Marty sat across from him, his eyes wide. "Hi, Dad."

Marty beamed. "Son? How did you do this?"

Jacob looked at him carefully. "Dad, this is going

to sound crazy, but humor me. When is the oil change due on the Massey Ferguson tractor?"

Marty stared at him, confused. "Son, we don't have a Massey Ferguson, we own a Ford. And we just changed it, or at least, I think we did."

Jacob stood and closed the distance between them. "I know. I just had to make sure it was you."

Marty looked around. "Where are we?"

Jacob gestured around with his hand. "Dad, you're in the mind of an eleven-year-old."

Marty gave him a sly grin. "Seems a lot more organized than I was led to believe."

Jacob arched an eyebrow, saying, "Stop it. I have something for you."

Marty asked, "And what would that be?"

Jacob stretched his hand and opened his palm wide. "This is called the Edajhia Root." The blob of light appeared in his hand.

Marty looked surprised. "What does it do?"

Jacob looked deep within the Nexus. "It's not what it can do, but more of what it shows you that you can do. It is a library of sorts. It knows about the latent things in you that are dormant. It is how I got you here."

Marty stared in awe. "Amazing."

Jacob focused on the light. He cupped both hands so the Edajhia rested comfortably between his palms. He focused on the light and made a simple command: *Share* and moved his palms apart. Now, there was a floating, glowing blob above each of his hands. Jacob handed the second Edajhia to Marty.

Marty held the floating shape gently above his hand as if it would break. "What do I do with it?"

Jacob looked at his dad. "Ask it how to do what you need to do."

Marty could not take his eyes off the Edajhia. "Do you mean like how to gain new powers?"

Jacob replied, "Exactly."

Marty murmured, "Amazing."

Jacob put his Edajhia away. "Dad, I have to send you back. I still have far to travel."

Marty looked at Jacob. "Son, I have one serious question."

Jacob replied, "What's that?"

Marty asked, "What do I do with this?"

Jacob laughed. "It doesn't matter, it's all in your mind. You could probably put it in your ear."

Marty looked around. "It seems so real." He looked back at Jacob. "But I get your point. See you soon, son. Love you."

Jacob hugged him. "Love you too, Dad."

Jacob released his father, and he was gone.

Moto stepped out of the shadows. "Well done, Jacob-san."

Jacob blinked and found himself back on the grassland. Strangely, the monks lay in a circle around him. All fast asleep. Jacob clapped his hands once. "Awake!"

The monks awoke simultaneously. They stared at one another, confused. They had moved while they slept. They rose from the grass looking around at each other.

Jacob looked at Brother Z. "Brother, could you organize a meal. We will need to begin again. We have many miles to travel."

Brother Z seemed to snap out of a daze. As he laid

a hand on each monk, they came to their senses. Two monks gathered the orn to hitch it to the wagon. One monk began to cover the fire pit with soil, while another prepared a meal of flat bread and cheese. They ate the bread and cheese, washing it down with water from leather bags. In a short while, the wagon was loaded and on its slow journey toward the Dreaded Forest.

****

Marty sat in deep meditation in the ravine outside the forest. He focused on the Edajhia and asked, *How do I protect myself from the demons of the forest?*

The Edajhia responded, *Creatures of darkness abhor the light. A shield of light protects you physically and psychically.*

Marty considered the answer. *Do you mean light will prevent the creatures from invading my mind?*

The Edajhia replied, *White light causes them great pain. The dark creatures do not push past pain. It is their weakness.*

Marty pressed on a little further. *Can they extinguish the light?*

The Edajhia replied patiently, *A point of light in the darkness chases away the dark. The same cannot be said for darkness. There is not a point of darkness capable of taking away the light.*

Marty asked, *How do I obtain a light shield?*

The Edajhia replied, *Imagine a bubble growing from your back and encapsulating you. You may make your bubble as large or as small as you like. And nothing can break through it, not another spirit, nor energy, nor matter. You must use your mind as a shield.*

Marty thought about this for a moment and

imagined a bubble growing from his back, surrounding him in a blue shield; nothing in his mind could penetrate the shield.

In the distance of the physical world, he could hear the hum of a transport approaching. It was time for him to practice his new skill. He imagined his shield growing from his back. It surrounded him as he walked straight into the forest. He noticed there was no foul odor as he entered the fog. All around him, red eyes appeared. He walked deeper into the forest until they surrounded him. One demon lunged, fangs bared, then another, each slammed into the wall of energy surrounding Marty. They backed away in fear and slunk back into the forest away from sight. One last demon stood on two legs and walked forward. Casually, it walked the perimeter of the force field staring at Marty with blood red slits for eyes.

It asked, "What are you?"

Marty stood his ground. "I am a mortal. What are you?"

The demon stopped walking so it could face with Marty. "I am Gar of the Serpent Clan. I feast on the souls of mortals. What is this magic that surrounds you, mortal?"

Marty ignored the question. "Are there other clans of your kind?"

Gar reached forward but would not touch the energy. "There are many clans of our kind. Some physical, some spiritual. It matters not, we all seek to feast on the souls of the living."

Marty considered his next question carefully. "And what of the demon called Jeez? Do you guard her?"

The demon spit on the energy field. It spattered and

sizzled like water in a hot frying pan. Gar replied, "Demons do not care about other demons. We only care about ourselves. Jeez feeds us with the souls of the dead. If she did not feed us, we would move on. And you, mortal, do you wish to feast on her bones?"

Marty answered civilly, "I wish harm to no one. But I will not allow another to harm the people in *my* clan."

Gar laughed. Or at least that's what Marty thought the dry hack which spat from Gar's mouth was. "Set her sights on one of yours, has she? Whoever it is will suffer unbelievably."

Marty controlled his anger. "Not if I have anything to do with it."

Gar's tongue tested the air around the shield. "Jeez will win. She always does."

Marty stared into the red slits. "And you, Gar, do you always win?"

Gar hissed loudly. Its body made a clattering sound from its scales opening and closing rapidly on its body.

Marty formed a ball of white energy in his hands. He stretched it until it was a long-pointed spear.

Gar leered at him. "Quite the dagger you have. How do you plan to use it and not pop your bubble?"

Marty did not reply. Instead, he focused a beam of light from his forehead which pierced through the bubble and through the chest of Gar, leaving a perfect circle burned through the creature's heart. It fell to the forest floor in a heap of seeping black ooze. Marty could hear the other demons in the forest hiss. Marty flicked the spear with his forefinger, and it disappeared. The ruse had been perfect. The demon had concentrated on the spear and not the real threat, which was Marty himself.

The throb of the ship had long since passed. Marty walked out of the forest leaving the corpse of the fallen demon behind. As he walked away, he could hear the other demons rending the flesh from Gar's fallen body as they feasted on him, followed by the crunching on his bones. Marty drew satisfaction from knowing there was one less demon on this world.

****

The slow caravan of monks reached the edge of the Dreaded Forest by the time they were ready for the second meal. The monks seemed relieved Jacob suggested they make camp and rest before entering the forest. Jacob looked at Brother Z. "No fire tonight. We leave the wagon here after we eat. I don't know if I will return with you to the monastery.

Brother Z replied, "What will you do, Jacob?"

Jacob replied, "I will meet my father on the other side of the forest."

Brother Z looked concerned. "How will we return through the grassland safely without you?"

Jacob was surprised by the question. "I'll let you know when I have figured it out."

The monks unloaded the grass mats, and the flatbread and cheese. This time they formed a circle around Jacob in the middle. While the meditation helped, Jacob needed sleep. For this period, he would have to do something different to keep the demons at bay. He walked the outer ring in the grass until the grass was beaten down in a circle. He placed his fingers into the soil at the starting point of the ring. As he concentrated on the soil, the ring began to vibrate. The monks exchanged concerned looks. Jacob pushed away the defensive energy from their fear as he concentrated on the ring in the soil. Within a minute the ring had begun to turn white. The monks watched. Some opened their mouths in amazement while others stared wide-eyed as the soil turned pure white. Jacob lifted his hand from the ring and touched it to his tongue. He could taste the strong alkali of the salt. It would have to do. On Earth, demons didn't like salt. He hoped it was true here. He settled on his grass mat and fell into a deep sleep.

In his dream, Moto appeared. He bowed deeply to Jacob. "Jacob-san, there is an important lesson for you tonight. It is the art of illusion."

Jacob sat on a wooden stump in a lush meadow. "Why, Master Moto?"

Moto's eyes glowed blue. "To defeat your enemy, you must first trick them with their own weakness before revealing your true strength."

Jacob looked into the deep blue of Moto's eyes. "Please explain, Master."

Moto replied, "I will show you instead." Moto reached into his robe and removed an orange striped kitten. The small creature purred as it saw Jacob. Small enough to fit into the palm of Moto's hand, it began to clean its face with its paw. Moto cupped the kitten with both hands and tossed it toward Jacob. In midair, the kitten transformed into a snarling tiger with bared fangs and huge claws. Startled, Jacob dove from the stump where the tiger landed and turned toward him, saliva dripped from its mouth as it snarled. Jacob picked himself off the ground as Moto snapped his fingers. The tiger disappeared. Jacob turned to face Master Moto, who had changed into an old man holding a cane.

Moto's eyes had changed, they now glowed with a brilliant white light. He motioned toward Jacob. "Come take me boy, if you can."

Jacob looked at him in shock. "I cannot strike you, Master."

Moto's eyes narrowed. "Then you will lose all you hold dear." Moto raised his cane, which transformed into a Samurai sword. Moto, himself, transformed into a young warrior. Moto lunged at Jacob with the sword. Jacob caught it neatly between his hands holding it there.

Jacob asked Moto, "So the lesson is to trick your opponent into a sense of false security before striking with a powerful weapon."

Moto returned to his normal form. The sword dissolved into glittering dust in Jacob's hands. "Indeed, Jacob-san. Your opponent must feel he has won before striking the first blow. It is only then that you can trick your opponent to underestimate you."

Jacob bowed respectfully to Moto. "Thank you, Master."

Moto bowed in return. "It is time to wake the others." Jacob awoke. He stretched and yawned, looking around. The monks stood within the salt circle in small clutches, whispering. Occasionally, one would make a furtive glance toward the grass plain and return to the group. Jacob stood and walked to Brother Z.

Brother Z bowed and said, "Good first to you, Jacob."

Jacob rubbed his eyes. "Good first to you, Brother Z. Is everything okay?"

Brother Z looked down. "There was an incident while we slept. The orn has died."

Jacob narrowed his eyes. “Died?”

Brother Z looked up. “Well, maybe *killed* is a better word.”

Jacob walked past Brother Z and looked at the orn lying in the grass. The flesh had been stripped away from the ribs. The beast had a large gaping hole in its side and its eyes were missing from the sockets. It was a horrible scene. Black, tarry-looking blobs surrounded the orn. Jacob inspected the salt line. Tar drops were evident at the salt line, but none passed into the area where they slept. Jacob realized the demons had visited them while they slept, but none was able to cross the salt line.

Jacob gathered the monks. “Monsters attacked while we slept but were not able to cross the salt. The salt will protect us. Gather as much as you can carry.”

Brother Z asked, “How will we move on without the orn pulling the wagon?”

Jacob thought for a moment before answering, “We gather what we need and carry it with us. Everyone must make a sling and store enough food and water to carry you for two meals. After we eat, we go into the forest.”

Silently a group of monks prepared a meal of dried fruit and flatbread, while the others took the tarp cover from the wagon and tore it into sections to make slings for food and water. Jacob could sense the unease in the group. He reached into his pocket and felt the carved edges of the Ark with his fingers. Somehow it reassured him.

****

Marty sat in a Lotus position meditating in the gulley of the grass plain. The floating orb of the Edajhia appeared before him. A calm filled him as he studied the amorphous glob of the Edajhia as it tumbled in front of him. He watched in fascination as the orb began to change. The amorphous blob began to stretch and thin in a string of pulsing light. It stretched until it was a thin vertical line. To his amazement, it opened. He was compelled to move into the opening. As he entered, it closed behind him. In this hidden realm was a soft, comfortable room. On the other side, there was a white barren plain, save two burgundy overstuffed chairs which faced each other. One chair was empty, the other occupied by the man in the black cloak. The man gestured toward the chair opposite him. He invited Marty, "Come and sit."

Warily, Marty studied the mysterious man. A Kabuki mask covered his face. Marty started to speak, but the man raised his hand and said, "I know you have many questions. I will answer what I can, but first you must know this…" The man dropped his hood and removed his mask. Marty was staring at an older version of himself. Marty's eyes grew large. The words tumbled out on top of each other. "You look, I mean you are, I mean, like, what the hell?"

The older version of Marty chuckled. "I am you. A much older version of you."

Marty looked at the older version of himself. "How is this possible, is this time travel?"

The older version of himself laughed. "No, physically, you can't travel in time. But what you can do is regress into past memories and manifest an image of yourself into a memory. This is the point in time you learn to do that. Because your memories are linked to the memories of others, they contain all the events that lead up to this moment in my life, your life, I can channel into those critical moments and act as a guide."

Marty asked, "So it was you who guided me across the plain and through the mine?"

The older Marty replied, "Yes. Given the critical nature of the events going forward, you could not waste time wandering around aimlessly trying to find your way. I am merely helping you be in the right place at the right time."

Marty thought for a second. "Can you tell me the future?"

The older Marty replied, "I can, but it could change your actions and cause you to do something which would change the future me. Even subtle changes could have far-reaching effects. For this reason alone, I will not."

It made sense. Marty asked, "What's next?"

The older Marty replied, "First and foremost, I need to teach you to cloak yourself. This will hide you from the transport ships moving the crystals out of the mine. Jacob will be traveling toward you in a short while. You will need to guide him through the tunnels beneath the forest. To do that, you will need to enter the forest without the demons seeing you. I will touch you on the forehead and you will understand how to do this."

Marty arched an eyebrow. "You can touch me?"

The older Marty replied, "Of course. None of this is in the physical world. I exist in the metaphysical world. My form is merely a projection to help you grasp the concept. I could appear as anything, but it would frighten you."

Marty considered this for a moment. "How do I

know you are not a demon trying to possess me?"

The older Marty replied, "Because no demon can cross the Edajhia's threshold. They would dissolve instantly."

Marty asked, "Why?"

The older Marty's eyes glowed blue. "Because this realm is made from God's first light. It is the oldest light, the purest. No creature of darkness could stand it here. It is what protected you from the demon in the forest."

Marty considered this for a moment and bowed his head forward toward his older self. The older Marty traced a small glowing circle on his forehead. Marty could feel a small shock followed by clarity of his inner self. The concept seemed so simple. He asked, "Can I do it now?"

The older Marty replied, "You *are* doing it now. You're invisible on the plain. Next, I need to show you how to project yourself. This will be more difficult." The older Marty placed his hands together, palms touching, fingers pointed toward Marty. The older Marty looked at Marty with his glowing blue eyes and said, "Do as I do." Marty mirrored his hands at his older self. The older Marty moved forward so the tips of their fingers touched. The older Marty said, "We will move our hands apart at the same time. You will feel some discomfort the first time you do this. In the future, there will be no pain." The older Marty began to move his hands apart. Marty did the same. As they did, Marty could see another version of his older self double as their hands moved apart. As he looked down, he could see a second set of hands from his own body. As their hands moved further apart, another version of himself appeared beside him. Now there were four of them standing in the space.

Marty stared wide-eyed at the new versions of him in the room. He asked the pair of older versions of him. "Am I crazy?"

The twins laughed in stereo. Only one answered, "Maybe. But until it's been diagnosed, you really ought to have some fun with it."

Marty felt a stabbing pain in his head, as if a knife had been driven between his eyes. His twin studied him intently. The second older twin responded, "Because you can now see through your clone's eyes, your mind is adjusting to this additional level of consciousness. It will pass. It's like the pain you felt when you first arrived on Oronas. The light here is different."

Within moments, the pain subsided. He could think clearly once again. His jaw dropped as he stared at his twin. His twin stared back mirroring his expression of wonder. The pair stared at each other for a moment. The newly created version of Marty asked, "So this means I can mirror my consciousness and project outside of my mind?"

Marty's older self responded, "Yes. But don't do that. Leave it to me. For now, you have much to do. As you arise from your meditation, remain invisible and go back into the forest to wait for Jacob. He is near."

Marty watched as one by one, versions of himself dissolved. He felt strange and wonderful at the same time. He opened his eyes to find he was still seated in the golden field, the only difference being, as he looked down, he could not see his body.

****

The monks shuffled in a single file behind Jacob

along the narrow path to the forest. The closer they came to the woodland, the narrower the trail became. At the first blackened stump, the trail had all but disappeared. Broken black tree trunks jutted up from the low hanging mist like jagged teeth in a rotting mouth. The path they followed had disappeared into a thick layer of green fog along the forest floor, leaving nothing to navigate other than the space between the trees. Jacob looked back at the monks to see them looking nervously from side to side. Jacob looked right to left, almost expecting an attack. But none came. It was eerily quiet in the forest. The mist had the foul odor of rotting flesh. The monks raised their hoods against the oppressive negative energy around them. In a short while, the black walls of the Temple of Darkness loomed before them in the gloom. A pair of red eyes appeared in front of them, and then a second set, and a third. Jacob stopped. He looked behind them. Red eyes glowed in the mist behind him. They were surrounded.

Jacob turned to Brother Z, who was close behind him. “Form a circle around me.”

Brother Z turned and spoke to the monk behind him. Quickly the men fanned out and surrounded Jacob in a tight circle.

Jacob removed his backpack. He reached inside and removed two jack-in-the-boxes. He wound the small toys by the handle. He picked up one in each hand and tossed one in the direction of the red eyes behind them, and the other toward the eyes in front of them. As the toys landed on the forest floor, the red eyes turned to the boxes as they played a bizarre tune from the mist. Jacob sang the words as the jack-in-the-boxes plunked their tune,

"All around the Mulberry Bush,
The monkey chased the weasel.
The monkey stopped to pull up his sock,
Pop! goes the weasel…"

Jacob whispered to the monks, "Duck and cover!"

The monks dropped to the ground and covered their heads. There were two successive thumps as each box flared out with brilliant white needles of light. The light ripped through the demons, rendering them into shreds. There were no red eyes left in the woods.

Jacob stood. "Let's go."

The monks looked at each other. Small bits of black tarry residue spotted their robes. They filed into a single line behind Jacob as he proceeded to maneuver toward the black structure. The smooth basalt walls towered from the forest floor in both directions with no apparent entrance.

Jacob pointed at the structure. "Fan out along the walls and find an opening or a doorway." The monks scattered in opposite directions. Jacob waited.

Shortly, Brother B sent word he had found something that could be a doorway. All the monks rushed toward him. As Jacob approached, Brother B proudly pointed to an opening next to a seam in the wall. "Here is an opening, Jacob." As he said it, he put his finger in the oddly shaped hole. A ball of red energy flung Brother B away from the wall. Only his feet were visible from the doorway as the mist swallowed him whole. The monks rushed and gathered around him. Brother B's feet smoked; his lips charred on his lifeless corpse.

Jacob knelt beside Brother B and closed his eyelids and rose; he returned to the opening. He reached into his pocket, removed the wooden replica of the Ark from the blind woodcarver, and compared it to the void. To his surprise, the opening was the shape of the Ark in his pocket. Carefully, he inserted the Ark into the slot and pressed.

A soft click released the door. It swung open to reveal a surprising interior of polished red floors, long rows of pews for seating, and a long aisle to the front. It looked like the interior of a church. Hidden lighting cast a soft amber glow up the walls, creating warm light throughout the sanctuary. At the front, a crone hovered over a book on a polished lectern of black wood. A red ape hunched at her feet like a gargoyle. It turned to look at them. Part of its face was missing, showing its jawbone and teeth. Its pelt had large holes showing the black putrid flesh beneath the fur. Its eyes had the milky look of death.

As they entered, the crone looked up, surprised. The red ape regarded them with glassy-eyed indifference. When she saw Jacob, she cackled in a dry, harsh laugh. “So this is your Chosen One as written in the prophecy? He looks like a child to me!”

Jacob ignored the jab. He continued to walk toward her. The crone closed the book and held it to her bosom. Halfway down the aisle, Jacob stopped. Something made him pause. He turned in time to see Brother Q, standing behind them at the entrance. His eyes glowed red, his head misshapen from the fatal blow at the monastery. He sprang at Brother R, landing on top of him. He drew back a razor-sharp talon to slash the monk. Jacob focused his energy on Brother Q. Brother Q hissed as he was struck with Jacob’s telekinetic force. He flew backward and tumbled out the door as if caught in a strong wind. Jacob concentrated on the door. It slammed shut with so much force it echoed through the room.

Brother Z helped up Brother R, who brushed himself off. Jacob looked up. Visible from the inside was a large stained-glass pentagram in the center of the roof gable. Where the roof should have been, a strange violet glow covered the roof of the building. From deep within him a voice began to chant, softly at first, and then began to grow until it resonated so powerfully he could think of nothing else: *Destroy the Portal, Destroy the Portal, Destroy the Portal...*

Jacob could see the stained-glass sparkle and glitter. He focused his energy on the pentagram. The glass sparked and shot hot coals toward them as if trying to resist Jacob's power. The crone watched in horror as the silent battle between Jacob and pentagram unfolded. Jacob focused with all his might; pure white light emanated from his forehead, centering on the pentagram. A crack appeared in the stained glass. Sparks erupted from the center of the pentagram; the glass cracked but held fast. Jacob dug deep. He reached out to the Edajhia to join him. He channeled all his energy on the broadening crack. In a single cataclysmic crash, the pentagram blew outward into unknown space.

Behind them, the witch screamed in terror. Jacob ignored the scream. He ignored everything except the portal. A bright light showed through the opening where the pentagram had been. The glowing roof above them evaporated. The amber light of the room flickered and winked off. Above them, gray clouds began to part; for the first time in ten thousand years, the sun's rays touched the surface of Oronas. The monks fell to their knees and chanted as Jacob looked up at the parting clouds to the opening and blue skies beyond.

****

Marty stood in the forest watching as six demons wandered about aimlessly around him. From his vantage point of invisibility, he could see them clearly. Black scaly skin, long serpent-like faces with piercing red eyes. If two demons encountered each other, they hissed angrily and move away from each other. He watched as all six stopped suddenly and stood still. Without warning, all six creatures vaulted forward and raced away deep into the forest. He stood alone in the foul-smelling woods. The forest was silent. There was no rustling or foraging by animals or the sound of birds. There was no wind, so the trees did not sway or move. It was unnatural.

Marty waited for a moment, then he heard two loud thumps like the sound of grenades in the distance. He waited. After what seemed like an eternity, a strange hum filled the forest. The resonance filled the air. The trees began to vibrate and fall away from him. The crashing moved closer, and trees fell away from the center of the forest in a broadening circle. Marty turned and ran out of the forest into the grassland and watched as the forest crumbled in front of him. As the sound of falling trees subsided, the ever-present cloud cover began to break apart. A round hole in the thick cover of clouds allowed sun to beam through the opening and touch the surface of the planet. Marty sensed Jacob had completed his mission. He watched in fascination as the mist dissolved from the forest floor. Light revealed the fallen timber and exposed a gray moss which covered the tree trunks. As the air cleared, Marty could see the black monolith looming in the distance. He wondered how Jacob would make it through the maze of fallen trees.

****

Jacob rested on a pew. His head swam, he felt nauseated from the strain. Brother Z gave him water and urged Jacob to drink as he patted his neck with a wet rag. Jacob recovered quickly. He focused on the door to the sanctuary. It snapped open to reveal Brother Q lay just outside the doorway trapped by a fallen tree. His body was crushed and pinned to the ground by the timber. Brother Q lashed out like a wild animal. Jacob frowned. "Zombies. I hate freaking zombies."

Brother Z asked, "What is a zombie?"

Jacob looked at Brother Q in disgust. "They are the walking dead. The witch must have reanimated him. You can't kill them because they're already dead. The only way to stop them is to take their heads off."

Brother Z replied, "Oh." Jacob realized Brother Z didn't understand.

Jacob stood and walked to the door where Brother Q lashed and hissed at him. He closed the door and walked back to the altar at the front of the temple. He weaved his way around the stage and saw a seam of light toward the floor. He reached down and felt a draft of air on his fingertips. It must be another doorway. The wall was smooth and solid. In the dim light, he could not see a catch or release. For the moment, they were stuck.

****

Marty waited patiently, watching for any sign of Jacob emerging from the forest. A grating sound caught his attention. A section of the grassland lowered, making a ramp into the ground just outside of the tree line. An old woman in black, her face weathered by the years, hobbled up the ramp followed by a rotting zombie ape. The ape followed the crone in its misshapen gait. Without thinking, Marty sprinted toward the opening. Slowly it began to close. Marty dove and rolled into the narrowing opening, landing on all fours on the smooth stone floor below. Soft amber light filled the corridor, which stretched out of sight. Marty followed the tunnel, stopping periodically to listen. The air was stale, but breathable. He walked for several minutes as the tunnel continued a steady, downward slope. He reached an intersection where a side tunnel connected to the main tunnel. He stared down the side tunnel and listened. It was as silent as a crypt. He concentrated on reconstituting his image. He watched as his hand reappeared, followed by the rest of his body. It was comforting seeing his body again. He reached into his backpack and tore a piece of paper from his last bit of camel jerky. He placed it at the opening and began walking down the side tunnel.

After a few minutes of walking, the tunnel began to level out and widen, flaring out in both directions. He could see a large opening ahead. He exited the tunnel into a chamber beyond any comparison. He tried to count the rows of giant aircraft but could not because of its expanse. Row after row of alien crafts followed precisely straight lines. He cautiously edged into the main aisle, wary of sentries. He looked to his left and spotted the robot standing at attention at the base of a large spacecraft. He jumped back instinctively, and then peeped like a child around the corner. The robot remained motionless. He eased out into the main aisle where he could get a better view of the chamber.

The alien craft were lined up out of sight in two directions as he stood at what was a giant intersection. He had stepped into a giant shaped tee. The aisle before him stretched on as did the aisles to his right and left. Rows of robots stood dormant beside each aircraft. There were no sentries or alarms evident. He was in a vast, silent chamber with an immense armada. Nothing seemed to notice or care he was there. It felt eerie to see such an enormous chamber of equipment standing idle.

Marty backed out of the chamber and went back to the tunnel. He found his scrap of paper and tucked it into his pocket. He turned right and followed the original tunnel onward. After a few minutes it began to slope upward. Marty walked until he reached a dead end. He walked back a few steps and looked around. He studied the wall on either side of the tunnel. After a minute he found a small depression. Cautiously, he put his finger in the impression and watched as a ramp silently lowered from the ceiling to reveal a room above. At the top of the ramp stood Jacob with a surprised look on his face. “Dad?”

Marty grinned. “Son!”

Jacob ran toward him and into his father’s arms. A group of faces peered down at them framed in the doorway above. Marty looked up, and then looked at Jacob. “Friends of yours?”

Jacob replied, “Kinda.”

One of the taller men in a long robe carefully came down the ramp. He spoke in a foreign tongue that sounded unlike anything Marty had ever heard. Marty looked at Jacob. “Do you understand him?”

Jacob replied, "Perfectly. You can probably reach out to the Edajhia to see if you can get a translator."

Marty grinned at his son. He was happy to see him. "So I guess there's an app for that."

Jacob chuckled. "I guess there is."

****

Fredrick sat up in the bed. Luna murmured sleepily beside him, "What's wrong?"

Fredrick looked down at her and asked, "Do you feel that?"

She rolled over and brushed blonde tendrils of hair from her eyes. "What is it?"

Fredrick's eyes were wide as he replied, "I feel a breeze." He rolled out of the bed and stood up, walking to the open window. He could not believe his eyes. In the distance the clouds were breaking up. Sunlight streamed through the clouds creating a line of golden crepuscular rays against the horizon, the image of which almost moved Fredrick to tears. People in the streets below them began to gather in small clumps staring and pointing. A hush fell on the busy street below. Luna joined Fredrick at the window. She slipped her hand into his. Softly, she asked, "What does it mean?"

Without looking at her, Fredrick replied, "It means everything is about to change. The Dark Lord is in danger."

Chapter 13

Retch limped across the uneven ground to Occul's Dingh. Her amulet had turned into wood as the stranger destroyed the dark energy generator. Her only thought was Master Jeez would protect her. She would seek sanctuary in the Dingh. Her reanimated red eck faithfully lumbered along behind her in its slow, awkward gait. She could see the floating tree above the entrance to the Dingh in the distance. At the base, its trunk was almost ten feet across. The limbs, long devoid of leaves and growth, were broken and jagged, as it floated weightlessly over stone stairs descending underground into the Dingh. She looked behind her. She could see the group far away. So long as she reached her Mistress first, she would be protected. She moved as fast as her bad leg would allow. The eck was close behind her. Ooze began to drip from the eck's open wounds. It was not used to so much activity.

Retch moved toward the black gaping entrance to the Dingh. She paid little attention to the enormous girth of the dead tree which floated over the entrance of the Dingh. The worn, roughhewn steps carved into the black basalt rock were underneath the giant tree trunk. The demons who guarded the tunnel were vaporous dark shadows and of no concern to her. They could do little more than scratch and screech. The human boy frightened her. The light that had emanated from him in the temple was first light, powerful light. She calmed as her feet touched the stone of the stair. She slowed her pace, not wanting to fall into the abyss beneath. The eck followed behind. Its vile smell wafted around her in the thick atmosphere of the stairway; she ignored the stench and kept moving.

The steps continued down until there was no light from above; instead, the walls of the cavern glowed red from the embedded crystals. She heard the screech of a demon close to her. She ignored it and kept moving. She called out to the demon, “Skinless bastard. Mind your own business. I come to speak with the master.”

The shadow landed on the stair in front of her. Its red eyes glowed angrily in the dim light. Retch never slowed as she walked through the demon without breaking pace. It screeched again and flew away. The stair was near the bottom. She could feel the chill of the master’s quarters. At the bottom was a single massive stone door. Rough hand-made carvings were chiseled into the door. Most resembled the seals of the goat’s head. Some she did not recognize. She waved her hand and the door lurched open. Bones littered the corridor to the main chamber. She shuffled through the tunnel, kicking a femur out of the way. Torches lined the walls, flickering in the sudden rush of air, making the bones dance in the torchlight.

The corridor opened into a large half-moon chamber. On the wall opposite the chamber, a large mass hidden by the shadows and just out of reach of the orange light of the torches scattered about. Retch moved to the center of the chamber and fell to her knees. “Oh Master, I come to you with news, the Dark Temple has fallen.”

The mass in the shadows began to unfurl. As it did, it took shape. A tall, beautiful woman approached Retch. Her hair, as black as her heart, cascaded over her nakedness. Her skin was flawless in the dim light. Her dark eyes sparkled with red lightning bolts. As she drew closer, Retch dropped her head. Jeez reached forward. Her soft fingers touched under Retch's chin. Her voice was not loud, but reverberated through the chamber. "Rise, my child."

Retch looked up into the pristine face of her Master. Her lips were full; her jaw was strong; her eyes piercing. Retch picked herself up from her knees and stood before Jeez.

Jeez took the back of her hand and ran it across Retch's cheek. She spoke in her full voice. "Retch, my child, you have served me faithfully for one thousand years. For that, I have given you many powers. But today you have failed me." Jeez's hand moved so swiftly Retch had no time to react as Jeez gripped her throat.

Retch felt her body lift from the ground. She gripped Jeez's wrist desperately as her feet flailed helplessly in the air. Jeez pulled her close as if Retch was a feather doll. She placed her flawless full lips against Retch's dry, cracked lips. Retch felt the power of blackness leave her. She twitched as the power drained from her until she hung like a rag in the wind. After what seemed like an eternity, Jeez released her hand and dropped her to the ground. Retch crumpled to the black sand at Jeez's feet. She watched with one good eye as Jeez leaned over and placed her lips against the putrid lips of the eck. She breathed new life into the eck. Her words stabbed Retch in the heart as she spoke softly to the eck. “Bring me Martin Wood.”

The eck’s eyes burned red in the dim light as it stood and walked out of the chamber. No longer did it walk with a misshapen gait. Jeez pushed Retch over with one foot; her words ran like ice through Retch’s veins. “Leave me, witch, and never return or I will boil you in oil for all eternity.”

With the little energy she had left, Retch pulled her body upright and staggered through the opening for the long trip back to the surface to die on the grassland. She mounted the first step. The shadow demon stood before her. Its red eyes glowed and a thin smile appeared on its pointed face, followed by a cold, harsh laugh. The demon disappeared. Retch felt it slice her cheek, followed by another small cut. She continued to climb. Each strike left a small cut, some on her exposed skin, some on her body beneath her black gown. She narrowed her eyes and forced herself not to cry out. A small cut above her good eye dripped blood. Her sight began to blur. She stopped for a moment to wipe the blood away, blinking until the stair was clear again. One step at a time, one small cut at a time, she moved forward. A long-dormant resilience surfaced within her. She wanted to live. She wanted to see the surface again. At last the glimmer of light appeared at the top of the stair. The demon grew bored of tormenting her as she rose toward the light of the surface, to a new world.

****

Marty and Jacob hurried side by side down the tunnel. Marty was happy. He had found Jacob. “Son, we still have to find Jeez and stop her.”

Jacob replied, “I know, Dad, but I don’t think it will be hard to find her.”

Marty asked, "Why do you think that?"

Jacob looked at his dad soberly. "Because we destroyed something of hers; she's going to get even."

Marty replied, "You have a point. We'll need a plan."

Jacob looked up at his dad. "Dad, you need to know one thing. The Edajhia is the first light. The demon cannot pursue you there. In your mind, you can escape to there. Does that make sense?"

Marty responded, "It does. I won't forget it."

They rushed past the tunnel which led to the squadrons of aircraft. Jacob asked, "Why are we rushing?"

Marty maintained his pace. "The old woman who came out of the tunnel when I entered. I suspect she might be headed to where we need to go. It's just a hunch."

Jacob replied, "That must have been the Black Witch. She ran when I destroyed the window."

They reached the end of the tunnel. Marty inspected the walls. He found the small depression and placed his thumb in it. The ramp lowered to the bright sunlight outdoors. Marty vaulted up the ramp. Jacob was close behind. The monks struggled to keep up. Marty looked in the distance. He could see the dot on the horizon. His hunches had proven well so far so he moved in the direction of the dot. For the first time since they had reunited with Marty, Brother Z spoke aloud to Jacob. "Jacob, where are we going?"

Jacob looked back. "To face Jeez."

Brother Z stopped in his tracks. "Jacob, we are not warriors. We are not prepared to fight demons and monsters."

Jacob looked Brother Z in the eye. "And yet, it is precisely what you've done. If you do not want to come, we understand. But I think your purpose is greater than being spoon fed your fate. You've been waiting for this moment your entire life. Now that it is happening, you're going to walk away from it. Does that make sense?"

Brother Z's jaw tightened. He replied, "Jacob, you are an old soul in a child's body. I will follow you." He looked back at the monks. "You must choose your path. No matter what you do, no ill will is wished upon you, my brothers."

Brothers C, M, and W stepped forward. "We will follow you."

Brother K stepped back. "Good travels, brothers. We will meet you back at the monastery." Several of the monks stepped back with Brother K.

The brothers embraced before parting ways. Brother K turned away from his brothers and walked toward the Dreaded Forest. He looked at his small band and said, "Brothers, it is time for us to return." He stared at the Dreaded Forest. The trees were no longer black and ominous. The fog had lifted. The air smelled clean and pure. Brother K marched forward into the fallen trees of the Dreaded Forest and an uncertain fate.

Marty set his sights on the smudge on the horizon hoping it would take them to the right place. He could hear the throb of the transport ships far behind them as they moved toward the mine. He stopped and pointed out the ship to Jacob saying, "They're mining some type of crystal out of the ground. Those ships are transferring it somewhere. Those ships might be our ride out of here."

Jacob studied the ship; it was large and clunky. They would need help piloting it. The monks stared at the ship in awe. As Marty moved across the plain, Jacob tugged the robe of Brother Z. "Come on."

The group could distinguish the dot was a floating tree with no visible trunk touching the ground. The gray trunk was weathered and cracked. Jagged limbs jutted out only a few feet from the trunk.

Marty watched as something moved away from the floating tree in the grass. It moved quickly as if trying to escape. He watched until it was out of sight. As they drew closer, a large black void began to take shape under the tree. Jacob was the first to spy the black witch emerge from the hole. Her face was covered with small cuts and dried blood. She struggled to make the final steps out of the hole. Brother Z stepped forward so that he was between the witch and Jacob. She stared at them; her face grimaced in pain. One hand reached forward. "Help…"

The witch fell forward onto the grass. Jacob pushed past Brother Z and ran to the old woman.

Marty called after him, "Son, don't! It's a trap." The witch lay on the ground. Her breathing was ragged. Her eyes closed.

Jacob looked at Marty. "No, Dad. Something's different." He reached into his backpack and pulled out a canteen of water.

Jacob gently lifted her from the ground. He touched the metal to her lips. He spoke softly to the witch. "Drink." He tilted the vessel to her lips being careful not to give her too much.

She swallowed and coughed. She opened her good eye and at him. A light breeze blew across the plain.

She was not dead.

She asked, "Why?"

The boy looked at her, confused. "Why, what? I don't understand."

She blinked to clear her mind. "Why do you not kill me?"

Jacob was confused. "Why would I want to? You have done nothing to me."

She took a breath. "You are the Chosen One. You are the destroyer of the Dark Temple. You are the only one my master fears. Why would you not destroy the agent of the Dark Lord?"

Jacob ignored the question. "Drink."

Retch drank. The clean water flowed. It was untainted, unlike so many things here. She stirred and looked at him steadily. "The Master seeks the one named Martin Wood. Are you him?"

The boy replied, "I am not. Why do you seek him, witch?"

She studied him. "I seek to live. I am no longer a witch. The master has taken those powers from me. I have nothing left but my will."

Jacob responded, "Then live."

Brother Z reached down with orn jerky and handed it to her. She chewed on the meat. She looked up at Jacob. "The Master seeks the one named Martin Wood. She has sent the eck for him. You should all be wary."

A man peered over the boy's shoulder. "And what does she intend to do with Martin Wood?"

Retch shook her head. "I do not know. Like all of us, she plans to use him and discard him. She will not rest until she has him."

****

Marty watched over Jacob's shoulder. He stepped back. Marty realized that his arrival was part of her plan. He tried to reason why she would influence him to come here, if he was the one who would unravel her source of control over this planet. It made no sense. There had to be something more. He stood behind the monks who gathered around Retch in curiosity. A sudden blinding pain in the back of Marty's head made everything go black.

Quietly the eck pulled Marty through the grass away from sight. The talisman fell from Marty's neck as the eck dragged him into a small hidden tunnel near the entrance to the Dingh. The eck pulled the grass away and pulled Marty inside and re-covered the tunnel entrance with grass. The eck began the long journey down the tube.

****

Jacob looked up from Retch for his dad. Brother Z stood over him. Jacob asked Brother Z, "Where's my dad?"

Brother Z looked behind him. Jacob gently lay Retch to the ground and stood. Marty was nowhere to be seen. He looked at Brother Z. "We need to find him." The monks fanned out looking for him. Marty had disappeared.

Before Brother Z could respond, Retch spoke, "You will not find him here. The eck has taken him below to see the Master. You will find him in the Dingh."

Jacob looked down at Retch. "Where is the Dingh?"

Retch closed her eye and lay back. Jacob asked again, forcefully, "Where is the Dingh?"

Retch opened her eye. She pointed to the blackness under the dead tree. “There. But you are not ready. The dead protect her.”

Jacob asked, “What dead?”

Retch took a deep breath and tried to sit up. Jacob reached over and grabbed her hand. It was thin and cold. He pulled her up. She paused for a moment from the exertion. “Like the eck, there are others. They guard her in the Dingh. You will need help rescuing Martin Wood.”

Jacob looked at her doubtfully. “How am I supposed to raise an army here?”

Retch squinted her eye at him. “The mines. The slaves there seek freedom more than anything. If you release them from the mines, they will follow you anywhere.”

Jacob asked, “Where do I find the mines?”

Retch pointed back in the direction that they had come from. “Go past the Dreaded Forest. The mines are beyond the forest.”

Jacob looked up at Brother Z. “I’m going. Watch her. I’ll be back as soon as I have people.”

Retch called after him. “Metal sentries watch the miners, beware of the red lightning bolts.”

Jacob nodded. He started off in the direction from which they had come. In the distance he could see the forest. He wished for a faster way to get there. He began to jog toward the forest. The years of working on the farm and sparring with his mother had hardened him. He was bigger and stronger than any of the boys in his class. It seemed like a million years ago since he was on the farm. He had reached the forest when he heard the throb of the transport ship overhead. He ducked into the fallen trees and waited. As the ship flew overhead, he waited until it passed, then he left the cover of the forest. He followed in the direction of the ship overhead and watched as it began its descent in the distance. He kept up the pace. He watched the ship set down beyond a small hill and lower a ramp. Automated buggies drove onto the ship one after another. He lay down in the grass and waited. After a short while, the ship was full. The ramp closed and the engines began to throb. The ship rose and flew back in the direction from which it came. It flew over him without slowing. He stood and jogged toward the mine.

At the entrance, there were no sentries or even signs of life. Jacob eased inside and moved deeper into the cool darkness of the cavernous opening. The tunnel was unlit, so he dug through his backpack until his hand felt the round cylinder of his flashlight. He turned it on in time to see a buggy moving in his direction with a load of glowing red crystals. He jumped to the side as it rolled past on its way to the loading area.

The tunnel descended sharply, winding its way downward. The passageway was quiet except for the steady drip of water. The rock surface beneath his feet was slick from the constant drip. After he had traversed down the winding tunnel several hundred feet, he detected the steady chink of metal on stone below him. A steady red glow ahead of him grew brighter as he moved forward. As he rounded a corner, he almost stepped into the open chamber, forcing him to step back by several paces to remain in the shadows. Before him, the enormous chamber was filled with small figures chipping away at the walls of the cavern. The cavity was the length of a football field. The walls were encrusted with red glowing gems. In the center of the room, a line of hopper buggies was staged at various levels of being filled. One of the miners stopped to wipe the perspiration from his brow. Jacob was shocked to see the miner was probably his age. A tall machine with track wheels and cylindrical arms quickly moved in the miner's direction. Without warning, the machine raised its arm and fired a bolt of red lightning at the boy, striking him in the back. The boy yelped, lifted the pickaxe, and began to chip at the wall.

Jacob watched as a creature emerged from a side tunnel in the chamber. It looked like a large white scorpion covered in red dust. As it came into the main chamber, it raised its pincers and emitted a high-pitched screech. The noise sent chills down Jacob's spine. Another robot moved toward the scorpion thing. It turned and moved back into the tunnel as the robot followed.

Jacob watched as the miners toiled without speaking. A girl with a dirt smudged face and blonde ponytail looked up at him silently. She made no attempt to say or do anything that would alert the robot sentry. She continued to chip at the wall in front of her, but there were noticeable glances of curiosity at him. He moved silently backward into the shadows to think about how to approach. In the dim light, he found a recess in the tunnel. It appeared to be an abandoned tunnel. It would be a perfect place to watch and plan. A loud buzzer sounded; all the miners laid down their pickaxes and moved into a single file. Each took a turn to move forward. Two robots emerged from a different tunnel in the chamber. One moved to one side of the cavern while the other proceeded to the opposite side.

They began to roll past the miners with a small hose. They stopped at each miner and shot a mouthful of green slime into the mouth of each of them. The children swallowed the mixture and stood in place. When the robot reached the end of the line, the buzzer sounded again, and the miners turned and picked up the pickaxes once again and began to chip at the wall. The robots disappeared back down the tunnel they exited.

Just as the children were beginning to start the work, the robot that followed the scorpion emerged from the tunnel. It stopped, and in a loud mechanical voice announced: "Team Lo, follow me. We have found another vein of crystals."

A group of the children stopped chipping at the walls and lined up behind the robot. It swiveled quietly on its base and moved back down the tunnel with a dozen miners following it. The other miners continued to chip away at the walls in silence. Jacob watched as the sentry robots began to move down the row of children, moving away from him. He watched and counted. There were four robots altogether, moving in parallel paths at the backs of the miners. With calibrated precision, they moved toward the end of the chamber, swiveled on their base, and moved back toward the center. All the miners remained within their sensors as they moved. Jacob considered his options on how to distract the robots.

He exchanged looks with the blonde girl. It was obvious he was out of the range of the robots scanning the area. Jacob continued to watch and count. The robots began their patrol about every three minutes, which would allow him enough time to pull off a daring plan. As the robots completed their patrol, he began to count again. A voice beside him startled him, making him jump. He whirled in the direction of the voice as a dark figure repeated, “Jacob?”

The voice sounded familiar; he strained to see a cloaked figure in a kabuki mask in the dim light. The cloaked man continued, “Jacob, you are the only one who can see or hear me. Your plan will work, but a word of warning: you must avoid the serqets.”

Jacob started to respond and thought better of it. Instead he whispered, “The what?”

The cloaked figure replied, “Serqets are the white scorpions you saw a short while ago. They are all linked telepathically, almost like a hive. If one sees you it will warn all the others. If you kill one, all will see you as a threat and attack. You have only a short while before the thing returns for more miners. You must move swiftly.”

Jacob started to ask about the robots, but the cloaked figure evaporated into a mist, like a ghost. He turned his attention back to the robots as they began their patrol cycle again. He waited until they were ten feet apart and he began to concentrate on creating an energy field between them. The robots tried to move forward to their set position before turning around and going back, but they couldn’t. The more they tried to move toward each other, the more the tracks driving them spun out in the gravel floor. The tracks on all four units began to spin in the loose stone. At the last moment Jacob released the energy and both pairs of robots vaulted toward each other in a synchronized collision course. Two pairs of robots collided with mechanical precision. Jacob focused his energy on the buggies beside them. He lifted one and flipped it over, causing it to rain down crystals on the first pair of robots, trapping them together under the open bin. He flipped the second buggy over the other pair of robots. He concentrated his power on the ones he had just bucketed. He turned the buggies over with the robots still in them. He moved to the second one and flipped it over. Now all four robots were on their sides in the buggies. Their tracks periodically spun in the air. Jacob cautiously moved forward. On the bottom of each robot, between the tracks, a large red switch was exposed. The robot's Achilles heel. He flipped the switch hoping it would work. Suddenly the robot stopped moving. Its systems went dead. He quickly proceeded to the other units. Within a minute he had disabled all four robots.

Some of the children dropped their pickaxes and stared while others held pickaxes in front of their bodies. The blonde girl walked up to Jacob. Jacob was intrigued. Her gaze was direct and unflinching. She asked, "Are you friend or foe?"

Several of the other children formed a small group behind her. They all held pickaxes. Jacob opened his hands to the girl. "I mean you no harm. I came here to free you."

The girl's expression never changed. "Why? Who are you? Why do you care?"

The question caught Jacob off-guard. "I am from another place. I came here with my father to stop the demon known as Jeez. My father was captured. I need help from you."

The girl replied, "So freedom with strings attached."

Jacob felt frustrated, but she had a point. "No, not

really. I can't force you to help me. I need your help in exchange for freeing you, but once you are free, I am not able to hold you against your will."

A distant whir of wheels sounded in the distance. The girl clicked her tongue and the other children immediately resumed their positions at the wall and began to pick at the stone wall. The girl picked up a spare pickaxe and handed it to Jacob. As she did, she said, "Act natural. The Bots are not very smart. They only look for odd behaviors."

Jacob glanced at the two robots face down in the carts. "What about them?"

She gave him a sly look. "You took out the first four. One more shouldn't be a problem."

Jacob picked up the pickaxe and began to chip at the wall. The robot rolled out of the side tunnel. A serqet was close behind it. It hissed in the direction of five miners. The robot rolled over and commanded the children in a tinny synthesized voice, "Follow me."

The children glanced at Jacob as they followed the robot, but none made a sound. When all five were gone from sight, the miners stopped again. A small group huddled around Jacob. The girl spoke, "We will consider following you out of here, on one condition."

Jacob asked, "What's that?"

Her face was expressionless as she replied, "You help us get our friends back."

****

Marty's head throbbed as he came to. He took a deep breath. The air around him was damp and smelled of spoiled meat. He coughed and sat up, looking around. The cavern was almost a perfect dome in the black rock. An amber glow lit the room with soft light.

The sand beneath him was coarse and black like volcanic beach sand on Earth. It was the chamber from his nightmare. From out of the shadows a woman's figure emerged. He focused on her face and was startled to see Gillian smile back at him. She said, "I've come for you, my love."

He stared at her for a moment before responding, "Gillian?"

She replied, "Yes, my love?" Her eyes flickered purple in the dim light. It was then Marty knew.

His voice was flat as he replied, "You can drop the act."

Gillian's expression was one of surprise. "What do you mean?"

Marty replied, "I know you're not Gillian."

The woman's face and hair changed as she walked toward him. "So you figured me out. I thought you might. You seem intelligent for a mortal, even though you came here to stop me in my own space. That wasn't very bright; it was brave, but poorly thought out."

Marty's eyes narrowed. "You didn't leave me with a lot of choice. Attacking my wife was a little uncalled for."

Jeez raised an eyebrow as she circled him. "Would you have come otherwise?"

Marty didn't move. "I suppose not. So now I'm here, now what? What do you hope to accomplish?"

Jeez stopped walking and plopped down in the sand in front of him. "The options are limitless, really. I could pleasure you for all eternity, or I could kill you and your child, or I could do nothing."

Marty stared into her red, glowing eyes. "I suspect you didn't go to all this effort to do nothing."

Jeez's laugh was deep and throaty. "What makes you think I put any effort at all into this? Besides, maybe you've got me all wrong. I'm a fun girl once you get to know me. I can party with the best of them. It's just that the people here are so unbelievably dull."

Marty's face was impassive. "So you brought me here to have a good time. Of all the humans on Earth, you picked me?"

Jeez shrugged. "There aren't many people on Earth with your ability. Even though you've convinced yourself you're not special, we both know you are. You *really* are. Let's just say, you're very well endowed, psychically."

Marty stared at her in disbelief. He wasn't sure what to think. *Was it possible she wanted him as a distraction?* He decided to pose a question. "So if I were to stay here and entertain you, would you release Gillian and allow Jacob to return to Earth unharmed?"

Jeez smile charmingly. "Of course. Why wouldn't I?"

A pain seared through Marty's head. His vision began to tunnel, and he fell backward into the sand unconscious.

****

There was no time for Jacob to deliberate. His father needed his help and the children around him needed his help. His concern for his father could not outweigh the immediate situation. He followed the girl into the tunnel after the miners. The tunnel descended sharply into the deep bowels of the mine. It glowed an eerie red from the crystals left in the walls. They were too small to be mined, but powerful enough to give off a red glow in the channel. They traveled down for what seemed like an eternity before they could hear the steady chink of pickaxes against stone ahead of them. The chamber ahead was twice the size of the one they had left. There were more miners here than at the one they had left. The five peered around the corner of the opening in time to see the serqet disappear into a jagged crack in the stone wall. The transferred miners were directed by a robot to work on a section deep into the chamber. The steady drip of water fell into the chamber, creating a growing pool of water on the floor. Most of the miners were standing in ankle-deep brackish water which dripped steadily from numerous cracks in the ceiling above.

Jacob whispered to the girl, “Where’s the water coming from?”

She looked back at him. “The ocean.”

It concerned Jacob they were thinning the walls holding back the water. Their best plan would be to get the others out of here quickly. Jacob surveyed the chamber. There were more robots here. It would be more difficult to repeat the ploy used to trick the other robots. Jacob felt a tap on the shoulder. He turned to see the other children had backed against him while they stared at an enormous spider peering at them from the other side of the shaft. The spider was as tall as his Tennessee coonhound with none of the same appeal. Jacob looked for a weapon of some kind. Instinctively, he prepared for the spider’s attack; instead, it raised its front leg and made a circle in the air as it motioned toward Jacob. He stared in disbelief. Was the creature trying to communicate or was it doing something else?

Again, the creature motioned, followed by a high-pitched voice, “Follow me, human.”

Jacob looked at the boy standing beside him. He trembled in fear at the sight of the giant arachnid. Jacob whispered to him, “Did you hear that?”

The boy didn’t respond. His eyes were fixed on the spider. The girl turned toward them. Her eyes grew large at the sight of the giant spider; she backed against the wall.

Again, Jacob heard the high-pitched voice. *Human, I mean you no harm. Follow me.*

Jacob whispered to the spider, “Are you talking to me?”

The spider motioned again. *Yes, human. There is no time, please come.*

Jacob walked toward the spider, as the creature turned and began to walk deeper into a narrow shaft. The girl caught Jacob’s sleeve. “Are you crazy? That thing will eat you.”

Jacob looked at her curiously. “If it wanted to eat us, it could have already done that. It asked me to follow it. I think it’s trying to help.”

She shook her head in disbelief. “This is nuts.”

Jacob shrugged his shoulders. “I don’t have a better plan. Maybe the spider can tell us how to defeat those robots.”

She gave him a dour look. “And maybe it has babies it needs to feed, and we’re the main course.”

Jacob ignored the comment and followed the spider as it moved down a side shaft in the tunnel. He expected to be alone and was surprised to find the others had chosen to follow him. He looked back to see their anxious faces behind him in the dim light. The spider found another side shaft and followed it deeper. The number of red crystals began to diminish. The light in the tunnel got dimmer. It was hard to make out the spider ahead of them. He felt his way along the tunnel as he turned a corner, and an amber glow appeared in the tunnel. It grew stronger as they proceeded. The air improved as they began to go up. Soon they were in a brightly lit chamber. Dried husks littered the floor. A small pile of brown fruit lay to the side of the chamber. The spider stopped in the center of the room. It motioned to the dried fruit. A strange tinny voice said, *Please, eat. I can gather more tomorrow*.

Jacob had to duck down under a rock ledge to pick up a piece of fruit. The spider said, *You must peel the husk.*

Jacob peeled back the brown husk and revealed the pink fruit within. He bit into the fruit inside, it was sweet like pineapple. He handed it to the girl. She watched Jacob for a moment before eating. She took a large bite and handed to the next boy in line. The spider lowered itself to the sand of the cavern so its body rested on its legs in the sand. It was the same pose Jacob had seen in dead spiders on Earth.

It spoke, *I am Mother Shadraq. Like you, I was drawn to this place by the underworld creature called Jeez. I wish to leave this place and return home to die with my kind.*

Jacob replied, "I am Jacob, how can I help?"

The blonde girl stared at Jacob. "That's great, Jacob, but who are you talking to?"

Jacob looked at her, puzzled. "Shadraq. She just told us that."

The girl stared at Jacob as if he had lost his mind.

Shadraq spoke again, *Jacob, the other humans cannot hear me. I communicate to you with my mind.*

Jacob suddenly realized Shadraq was a telepath. He looked at the girl. "The spider's name is Shadraq. She speaks telepathically. I can hear her in my head."

The girl raised an eyebrow saying, "My name is Ouna, and I think you're crazy."

Jacob tried to reason with her. "I may be crazy, but you're eating fruit that crazy led you to, versus the green goop in the mine."

Ouna replied, "Good point. Go on with your conversation with the spider. I'll eat my fruit over here."

Jacob cautioned her, "Don't eat too much."

Ouna snorted and wiped the juice from her mouth with the back of her hand and kept eating.

Jacob turned his attention back to Shadraq. *I'm sorry, as you were saying?*

Shadraq regarded him with ten sets of eyes. *I can help you defeat the robots and free the other humans if you will assist me in finding a ship to carry me home.*

Jacob replied, *My father has been captured by Jeez. I came here to get help to take back my father. We seek to leave this place as well. I believe my father found something in the Temple of Darkness, but we didn't have time to discuss what he found.*

Shadraq was silent for a moment. *I will help you free your father, Jacob. Jeez serves only her own dark soul. We will seek the ships when we have freed your father.*

Jacob placed his hand over his heart. *I am grateful.*

Shadraq stood and stretched her legs. *I have a sound that will disable the robots' communications system. When I make the noise, there is a disconnect switch on the base of the robot. You and your friends must run to the robots and disconnect them. Can you do this?*

Jacob replied, *I know where the switch is.*

Ouna spoke, interrupting his train of thought with Shadraq. “So do you have a plan?”

Jacob turned to her. “Shadraq will make a sound that will disrupt the robots. We will need to go to each one and turn the switch off. Can you help me?”

Her eyes were steady as she looked at him. “We’ll all help.”

Strengthened by the fruit, they began the trek back to the mine shaft.

****

Marty opened his eyes to the blinding white light of the Edajhia. He stood alone in pure light. Two human shapes began to walk toward him and take form. Barb and Bess stood before him. The three hugged. As they broke their embrace, Bess smacked him not so gently on the side of his head.

Marty winced. “Oww. What was that for?”

Barb placed a hand on Bess’s arm. “Honey, you know better than to make a deal with the devil. No matter how good it sounds.”

Marty looked a little surprised. “So you heard that?”

Bess looked at him dourly. “Of course, we heard it, Martin. You can’t deal with this demon. She’ll keep her promise in a way you didn’t count on. Don’t you remember your Mark Twain?”

Marty replied, “But my whole reason for coming here was to stop her.”

Barb responded, “This is true, my dear, but taking the first deal is not the answer. She’s a trickster. It’s why she was sentenced here. When she tempted Eve, God banished her to this world. She has lived here plotting her return for millennia. Earth is the crown jewel. She wants it, and like every thief, she plots how she will steal it."

Marty looked frustrated. "So what am I supposed to do? She's killing Gillian. I can't let her do that."

Bess replied, "This is true, but giving her your soul in trade is an equally bad idea. You must consider your powers. Jeez is strong, but you have untapped powers she would use to make herself even more powerful. She cannot have you. Besides, why are you giving up without a fight? I didn't raise you to be like that, boy!"

Marty replied, "Point taken. So how do I fight her on her own turf?"

Barb flashed her gentile southern smile. "Fight back, not too hard, but keep her at a distance. I see help coming your way. Just hold out as long as you can, and we will help you as much as we can. Don't quit fighting."

Marty opened his arms and they embraced. "I love you guys. I'll fight with every fiber of my being."

He closed his eyes. When he opened them Jeez was an inch from his face, staring into his eyes. He pushed her back, throwing her off balance. "Back off, crazy woman."

Jeez hissed at him and circled around. It was going to be a long, hard fight.

Chapter 14

The elderly Arab squinted at the car that rolled into the pump followed by a cloud of dust. It was not the condition or even the type of car causing him to stare; it was a gut feeling that the people in this car were not typical tourists. The woman got out of the driver's seat and walked to the gas cap. She opened the hatch and walked to the pump. The old man picked up speed and raised his hand and shouted, "Wait!"

The woman looked up. He waved his hand. She stood calmly beside the car waiting for him. In Arabic she replied, "Yes?"

The old man panted as he stopped at the car. She waited patiently for him to speak. She looked like an American. Her accent was Iraqi. His breath slowed a bit so he could talk. "I must operate the pump. It is the law."

She stepped aside for him. "High test, please."

He nodded. "Certainly, miss."

She looked past him at the aged adobe building and asked, "Do you take American dollars?"

He nodded. "We take any currency. So long as it is not counterfeit."

The woman's gaze was steady as she replied, "My money is good. Do you have bottled water?"

The old man nodded. "It is not refrigerated, but we keep it underground, so it is cool."

The woman replied, “That’s fine. How much is the petrol?”

He looked at her. “Only one dollar per liter.”

She shook her head. “Is this robbery? I’ll give you one dollar for four liters.”

He shook his head. “My children will starve. I must have at least three dollars for four liters.”

The woman scowled. “Two dollars for four liters or I’ll have you take it out and I’ll leave.” It was a hollow threat and they both knew it. Meanwhile the gauge was approaching eighty liters.

The old man shook his head. “Three dollars for five liters and I’ll throw in two bottles of water.”

The woman narrowed her eyes at him. “Filtered?”

He smiled. “Of course. By the finest reverse osmosis system in the country.”

The woman raised an eyebrow. “We’ll see about that.”

The old man pulled out a rag and wiped his hands. He held his palm open to the woman. She handed him a fifty-dollar bill. “Keep the change for your starving children.”

The old man bowed to her. “May Allah bestow one thousand blessings on you and your friend. One moment and I will return with water.” He hobbled back to the adobe. In the back he opened a hatch door and pulled up a rope with a box of water bottles. The bottles felt cool to the touch from storage underground. He hurried back to the woman, who stood leaning against the car. She stood away from the car and dusted her backside off. He handed her the bottles of water. She asked, “How far to Abu Simbel?”

He replied, “Not far, maybe an hour from here. It is

at the dam. You'll have to drive around the lake to get to the entrance. So you come to Egypt to see Rameses?"

She gave him a sly smile. "More so to see Ptah."

A chill went up his spine. Ptah was one of the gods of the underworld. He backed away from the woman. "Have a good day."

He turned away and didn't look back. Nothing good came from saying the names of the gods of the underworld. He heard the car door slam behind him, and the engine roared to life. The cloud of dust from the car caught him before he could make it back to the adobe, making him cough.

****

Wilhelm watched Gillian as she climbed back into the driver's seat. "How far to location?"

Gillian looked forward as she cranked the car. "Not far." She handed Wilhelm a bottle of water. "We should be there in an hour."

The coupe eased down the highway and fell in behind a cattle truck. Wilhelm wrinkled his nose at the smell of cow manure. He asked Gillian, "This car will do at least two hundred miles per hour, do you think you could work around the truck?"

She gave him a sideways grin and looked ahead. They glided around the cattle truck with no issues. For days they had avoided the subject of why they were going to Egypt. Principally, Wilhelm was glad to be free of the castle, but his curiosity was becoming unbearable. The landscape outside began to change. Clumps of green palm trees could be seen in the distance at they neared the Aswan dam. He asked, "Why are we coming here?"

Gillian glanced at him, and then back at the road. "It's going to sound crazy."

Wryly, Wilhelm replied, "Try me."

Gillian sighed. "I had a vision I needed to come here to retrieve something from Abu Simbel. I don't know what it is, or why we need it."

Wilhelm furrowed his brow a bit. "So how are we supposed to know what to look for?"

Gillian shrugged her shoulders. "I can't tell you how. From experience, I can tell you it will be clear to us at some point."

Wilhelm pressed, "Is it big or small?"

Gillian replied, "I don't know."

Wilhelm replied, "You're right, it does sound a little crazy."

Gillian rolled her head toward him. "I told you it would. We'll figure it out when we get there."

A billboard in English and Arabic along the road advertised the museum at Abu Simbel. Gillian commented, "It looks like it's about fifty kilometers. We should be there in about thirty minutes. You had better drink up. It will be a hot afternoon."

Wilhelm glanced at his phone. "Holy crap, it's one hundred and five out there!"

Gillian replied, "Yes, but it's a dry heat."

Wilhelm responded drolly, "So it's like an oven?"

Gillian glanced at him. "Yes, but it's only set to warm."

Wilhelm shook his head as they traveled in silence to the parking area for the museum.

Gillian pulled into a parking space close to the entrance. Both she and Wilhelm stretched as they stood beside the car. He looked at Gillian. "Dry heat, huh?"

They laughed and headed toward the entrance. Two armed guards languished on a bench at the entrance. Neither gave them a second glance as they walked by. A young Egyptian woman stood close to the entrance. As they walked up, she asked in English, “Would you like a personal guide today?”

Gillian shook her head. “I believe we can find our way.”

Wilhelm flashed a toothy grin. “How much?”

Gillian stopped and glared at Wilhelm.

The girl replied, “Only twenty US dollars.”

Wilhelm fished out two twenties. “Here, we should get an extra special tour with this.”

The girl’s smile was stunning. “Most certainly, sir!”

Gillian shook her head and continued toward the entrance.

Wilhelm asked the girl, “Where do you recommend we start?”

The girl responded, “At this time of day, the large temple. There are very few people there now. It will be a good time to see the monuments without the crowds.”

They passed through the entrance before Gillian finally stopped and looked at the girl. “Is there a statue of Ptah?”

The girl’s expression changed for a moment. “Yes, ma’am. He is in the sanctuary.”

Gillian’s gaze made both Wilhelm and the girl pause. “Take us there first.”

The girl dropped her head. “Yes, ma’am.”

Gillian walked on. The girl looked at Wilhelm. “I am sorry to have angered your wife.”

Wilhelm arched an eyebrow. “She is not my wife.

We are friends. What is your name?"

The girl looked up. "I am Jhazelle. I am from Edfu, north of Aswan. I am here to earn money for Cairo University."

Wilhelm looked into her incredible emerald green eyes. "Why do you want to go to Cairo University?"

She looked straight ahead. "My father is a fisherman. No one from my family has ever gone to a higher university. I would be the first."

Wilhelm replied, "I'm sorry. I didn't mean to offend you."

She looked up. "I am not offended. I will work hard. I will make my family proud. I will be the first to graduate from the School of Law."

Wilhelm changed the subject. "You seemed a bit upset when we asked about Ptah. Why?"

Her expression was serious as she looked at him. "Ptah is the god of the underworld. He is the creator, but he is also the destroyer. We respect him, but we fear him."

Wilhelm looked at her, really looked at her. She held her head high, giving a full view of her oval face, which was deeply serious and hauntingly beautiful. She wore no makeup but didn't need it. Her lips were full and dark, her olive complexion was flawless, even in the strong light. Her most striking feature was her eyes, which were deep and green in stark contrast to most of the dark-eyed Egyptian women. He asked her, "Why are you hustling tourists when you could be modeling?"

Her expression never changed. "Isn't that kind of shallow?"

Wilhelm felt the sting of the comment. "You're right. I'm sorry. It's just that you're really beautiful."

Jhazelle shrugged. "It's hard to think that way when you grow up on a fishing boat hauling in nets by hand and shoveling fish into bins. It's difficult to see yourself as a beautiful woman when you're ankle deep in fish guts."

Wilhelm replied, "I see your point."

Jhazelle pointed to Gillian, who was far ahead of them. "And what of your friend?"

Wilhelm shook his head. "Her husband is away on business. I asked to ride along. Partly because I like her, partly because I didn't want to stay home."

Jhazelle asked, "Is it bad where you live?"

Wilhelm replied, "The worst. It's all business. People wait on you hand and foot. It's so boring it makes you want to scream."

Jhazelle stared at him with her large green eyes. "You have servants?"

Wilhelm nodded. "Yes, but it's not as good as you think it is. The best time I ever had was at sea with my friend, Chris. Chris and I sailed around the world. I wish I were at sea with him now."

Jhazelle replied, "I understand. Even though the work was hard, the open water has a rhythm that creeps into your soul."

Wilhelm nodded. "Indeed. So let's catch up to my friend before she tries to release my soul."

Jhazelle laughed. Even her laugh was pretty. Gillian was at the steps of the main temple waiting. Her face was emotionless.

As they approached the steps Gillian asked, "Where is the sanctuary where Ptah sits?"

Jhazelle walked past Gillian. "Follow me."

Inside the temple, the air was moderately cooler.

Jhazelle guided them to the back of the great hall and turned down a smaller corridor. She gestured to the room around them with a sweep of her hand and began her rehearsed dialog. "The original structure was relocated here in nineteen sixty-eight by Polish archeologist…"

Gillian interrupted her. "This isn't the original structure?"

Jhazelle responded, "No, ma'am. The original structure is below the water line on the lake before the Aswan dam was constructed. The site was taken apart piece by piece and reconstructed here. All the pieces are original.

Gillian's eyes burned into Jhazelle. "We'll see."

Jhazelle continued walking toward the small sanctuary. "The four divine ones: Ra-Horakhty, Ramses, Amun-Ra, and Ptah are side by side. Ramses was deified here with the other gods."

As they entered the sanctuary Gillian stopped. She stared at the statue of Ptah covered in the shadows. She was almost breathless as she asked, "Do you see it?"

Wilhelm and Jhazelle stared at her for a moment. Wilhelm asked, "See what?"

Gillian's eyes were glued to the statue of Ptah. "The heart. The heart of Ptah."

Jhazelle's eyes grew wide as Gillian pushed past the rope keeping tourists away from the statue and walked up to the seated Ptah. Jhazelle backed against the wall of the sanctuary, fearful she would be seen with the brazen American woman approaching Ptah's statue.

Jhazelle stammered, "Ma'am, that area is forbidden. We cannot go there. Ma'am?"

****

Gillian paid no attention to Jhazelle. Her eyes fixed on the red pulse beating inside the breast of Ptah. She could see it as clearly as the scepter he held to his chest. Gillian was drawn to the red glow. She reached through the stone into the chest of the statue and gripped the red glow. She could feel the tightening around her hand. Her hand had passed easily through the stone only to feel it solidifying around her fingers. A black mass began to rise from the statue. The glowing red eyes glared at her. It drifted toward her, gripping her around the neck. She felt her throat beginning to close. She could feel someone behind her tugging at her waist, trying to pull her back. She ignored everything except for the red glow her fingers had grasped within Ptah's chest. She slammed her other hand against the statue. The grip on her neck grew tighter. The black mass began to take shape. An angry face formed in front of hers, its red eyes burning into her. She would not release the heart. With all her might she wrenched her hand free of the chest. A blast of sandstone showered her with debris. The black mass disappeared, and she fell backward. As she landed on the floor, she heard a "Humph!" She had landed on top of Wilhelm.

Gillian sat up and shook her head free of the sand and rocks. She stood and grasped Wilhelm by the hand and hoisted him up. Jhazelle stared at them with a horrified look. Gillian turned to look at the statue of Ptah. There was now a black crater where her hand had been. In her hand was a flat half disk of gold encrusted with rubies. She shoved the disk into her pocket. She looked at Wilhelm. "Let's go."

Jhazelle stared at them. Wilhelm stopped for a

moment and shoved a wad of cash in her limp hand. “Good luck with the college thing.”

She stared at the cash for a moment and shoved it into the folds of her *sebleh.* She ran behind them, as they cleared the entrance into the bright sunshine, Jhazelle ran in the opposite direction. Once outside there were no guards to be seen. Gillian stopped running. She turned to Wilhelm. “How do I look?” Without a word, he reached out and brushed sand from her shoulders and hair.

He stopped for a moment and stared at her. His voice had a different tone than Gillian had heard from him before. “The experience we shared is possibly the scariest moment I’ve ever had in my life. I watched your hand disappear into solid rock. This black shadow rose from the statue and grabbed you by the neck. After you fell on me and I saw your face, it was different. Your eyes were glowing violet. You and I have been through some weird stuff together, but it felt different—*you* felt different. For the first time since we met, I was afraid of you. I know it sounds weird.”

Gillian looked into Wilhelm’s eyes as she spoke. “I would love to tell you everything is fine and it will all work out in the end, but I can’t. As strange as it is for you, it is ten times as weird for me. I don’t know if I’m sane anymore or if this is some bizarre construct in my mind. When I walked into the temple, I was being guided by a figure that may or may not exist in the real world. When I looked at the statue, I didn’t see a stone figure carved three thousand years ago, I saw the beating heart of an entity. I wish I could say I understand any of this, but I don’t. All I can tell you is my husband risked his life to travel to another world to fight a demon for me. I can't even comprehend what would drive anyone to do that other than unfathomable love. I know we have some chemistry, but the reality is the man I love is millions of miles away from here facing an unbelievable evil because he doesn't want to see me suffer. Has anyone ever done that for you?"

Wilhelm stared at her in stunned silence before responding, "I couldn't even get my dad to listen to me for five minutes, much less throw himself into the abyss for me. So no. No one has ever even considered doing that for me."

Gillian placed a gentle hand on his face. "Me neither. So you and I have to consider this is bigger than the both of us combined, and we need to put our passions aside for something that may be greater than everything we think we know about the universe."

Wilhelm took a deep breath. "I have never even considered myself worthy of something like this. What do we do now?"

The sound of whistles blared in the distance. Gillian smoothed her hair back. "Right now, I think we need to fire up the ride and blow this joint."

Gillian pressed the fob and the engine growled to life as the pair ran toward it. Two uniformed guards ran toward them blowing whistles and yelling in Arabic. Gillian slid into the driver's seat and jammed the car in gear. Wilhelm barely closed the door before the tires were spinning the coupe in a circle, leaving the two Egyptian guards waving at a cloud of dust in their wake. Gillian sped toward the highway passing a slow farm truck and barely making it back into the lane before a car of tourists met them head on. Wilhelm placed his hand on Gillian's arm. "Slow down, there's no one after us."

Gillian kept her eyes focused on the road ahead. "For now. But they'll come, they always do."

A voice from behind them spoke, "I can take you to a place where you will be safe."

Startled, Wilhelm whirled his head. Jhazelle sat in the small storage compartment behind the seat. She grinned at him and said, "Hello, again."

Gillian never turned. "Where?"

Jhazelle replied, "My parent's home in Edfu."

Gillian's tone was flat as she asked, "What makes you think they won't turn us in for a reward?"

Jhazelle replied, "They won't, they trust the government less than they do Americans."

Gillian snorted. "I guess some things are universal. Death, taxes, and nobody believes their government. So where are we going to in Edfu?"

Jhazelle pointed ahead. "Go two kilometers and turn left on Trader's road."

The road turned quickly from a paved road to a limestone road to a goat path. Gillian slowed the car to keep it from bottoming out in the ruts in the road. Wilhelm looked back at Jhazelle. "Why, exactly, did we go this way?"

She looked straight ahead as she replied, "It is shorter, and none of the ENPs use this road."

Wilhelm asked, "ENP?"

She looked at him for a moment before concentrating back on the road. "Egyptian National Police."

Jhazelle tapped Gillian on the shoulder and pointed ahead. "Bear right at the fork."

Gillian squinted into the blistering sun and could

barely see a faint trail to the right ahead. She slowed just in time to ease through a deep rut in the road. The car shuddered but kept moving. She made a mental note: the next time she decided to go on a tour of Egypt, she would bring a jeep. After a few minutes they could see the highway ahead. Jhazelle placed her hand on Gillian's shoulder. "Slow down and wait here." Gillian slowed the coupe to a stop. They watched the highway for a moment. In a short while, two dark blue Egyptian police cruisers screamed by on the highway, the light bars flashed but no sirens. Gillian turned toward Jhazelle. "How did you know?"

She shrugged. "The closest station for support to the park is Aswan. This would be the direction they would travel. We took a short cut and beat them here. We should be fine from here. We will need to change cars, though. This one will easily be recognized."

Gillian looked at Wilhelm and they both grinned. It was Gillian who spoke. "Just like old times." She asked Jhazelle, "Is it safe now?"

Jhazelle nodded and pointed straight ahead toward the highway. "We will need to go south first and go to the first turn around."

Gillian eased the car forward. The trip was uneventful to Edfu. As they motored into the edge of the city, Jhazelle pointed to a side street. "Go there."

Gillian slowed and eased behind a horse-drawn carriage. Jhazelle pointed to a building with a dirty white awning. "There is an alley beside that building. Go into the alley."

As Gillian eased into the alley, she wondered if they would be able to open the doors because it was so narrow. Gillian focused ahead but asked, "Are you sure about this?"

Jhazelle replied tersely, "Yes. There will be a courtyard ahead." Jhazelle pointed at the opening. "Pull in there."

As Gillian turned the coupe through the narrow limestone gates, she was surprised at the opening within. It was half the size of a football field, with junk cars piled on three sides. Some were in various states of disassembly.

Jhazelle said, "Go to the end and stop."

Gillian eased through the junk yard and stopped. A young man walked out. His clothes were covered in grease and grime. He wiped his hands with a rag that didn't appear to have any surface left to remove the grime. A scar ran across his chin. His dark eyes were forbidding. He began to walk around the car.

Jhazelle nudged Wilhelm. "Let me out."

Wilhelm didn't move. "What makes you think I want to get out?"

Jhazelle poked him harder. "It's my cousin Rhys. He's harmless, now let me out."

Wilhelm opened the door and stepped out keeping the car door between himself and Rhys.

When the man saw Jhazelle, he opened his arms for a hug. He was missing his front two teeth. He called out, "Jhazelle! What brings you here?"

Jhazelle ran to Rhys and hugged him. "Nothing. Just wanted to see you."

His toothless grin never faded. "Liar."

She poked him. "Where is Uncle?"

He thumbed toward the open bay in the wall. "Working. As usual."

Rhys's focus returned to the coupe. He looked at

Wilhelm. "What kind of car is this?"

Wilhelm blinked. Gillian stood from the car. In Arabic she replied, "It's an English car."

Rhys continued to inspect the car. "Did you drive it all the way here from England?"

Gillian laughed. "I guess it looks that way. But no, we drove here from Germany."

Rhys nodded.

Jhazelle returned from the building. A portly older man with graying temples walked behind her. He whistled when she showed him the car. His voice was deep. "Very nice. I have only seen these in pictures."

Jhazelle asked him, "Do you have anything we can trade for it?"

A look of concern crossed his face. "No, little Jha-Jha. I have nothing that would equal such a fine car, and if I did, I could not afford to buy parts for it."

Jhazelle took the man's hands in hers. "Uncle Baram, do you have a car we can borrow then."

He smiled at Jhazelle. "I do, but it won't be fancy like this one."

Jhazelle replied, "Anything will be fine."

Baram chuckled. "Perhaps for you, but I don't know about your friend."

Gillian replied, "We would be very grateful for anything you could help us with. My friend here would be pleased to pay you for accommodating us."

Baram looked at Wilhelm and back at Gillian. "He doesn't understand a word of this, does he?"

Gillian shook her head. "No. He doesn't."

Baram scratched his chin. "A beautiful thing is never perfect."

Gillian asked, "Pardon me?"

Baram replied, "A car this unique will not go unnoticed. I'll hide it for you. We can trade back when you are ready."

Jhazelle hugged her uncle. "Thank you, Uncle!"

The older man nodded. "Rhys, go get the VW."

Silently, the young man disappeared into the debris field of cars only to return in moments with a nineteen sixty-seven beige VW Beetle. Paint was missing from numerous places making it look like a Dalmatian, but there was no rust evident. Gillian and Wilhelm threw duffels into the trunk and climbed in. Wilhelm climbed into the back and looked around the backseat, and Jhazelle sat in the front for easier navigation. Wilhelm shrieked. Jhazelle looked back in time to see a small black scorpion walking toward him. She reached back and deftly caught it by the tail and flung it out of the window. Wilhelm's eyes were wide. Jhazelle looked at him with serious, beautiful eyes and said, "You are fine, sit back." Wilhelm's eyes were still wide. He looked around the backseat to see if there were other scorpions but found none.

Gillian eased the Beetle into reverse and backed out of the junkyard. Jhazelle waved good-bye to her uncle and Rhys as they left. They maneuvered through the open-air market of Edfu and toward the river. With no windows in the Beetle and no air conditioning, Wilhelm nodded off to sleep in the heat of the afternoon sun, as the Beetle jostled along the dusty streets of Edfu. Jhazelle pointed to the street where she lived with her father. As they eased down the narrow street of brightly colored mudbrick homes, Gillian asked, "How do you get all the way to the temple every day? It seems pretty far to go without a car."

Jhazelle nodded. “I catch a ride on the vegetable truck going to Sudan and hop off to make the walk to the temple. The farmers are nice to me, my father provides them with fish for their families. It is a good arrangement for all.”

Gillian replied, “Are you ever afraid?”

Jhazelle looked at her curiously. “Why? They are all cousins, we played soccer together as kids. Why would I be afraid of my family?”

Gillian apologized. “I’m sorry. I didn’t realize they were family.”

Jhazelle pointed to a red and white mud dome house. “Stop there.” Gillian pulled into the driveway and killed the engine, which backfired in protest. Wilhelm sat up with a start, looking around him. Gillian looked back. “Relax, it was just the car.”

He blinked at her and rubbed his face, trying to wake up. Jhazelle got out of the car and motioned to them. “Come inside where it is cool.”

The door was unlocked as she walked in, removing her shoes. The inside of the home was a contrast to the outside. The dome made it look small, but once inside, the rooms were spacious and comfortable. The large living room was lined with comfortable sofas and plants. The floors were inlaid tile with mosaic geometric patterns. Gillian looked around and said, “You have a beautiful home.”

Jhazelle gave her a polite smile. “Thank you. Father will be home soon. I will tell him you are tourists and have paid extra to see a real Egyptian home. He will not be happy if he thinks you are being sought by the police.”

Wilhelm plopped on a sofa. “I can see how that

could be a problem."

Gillian looked around. "I need to use the washroom, if I may."

Jhazelle motioned for Gillian to follow. She opened the door to the narrow washroom. Inside the squat toilet was clean. Jhazelle looked at her curiously. "Have you ever used one of our toilets?"

Gillian nodded. "I have. Thanks."

Gillian closed the door. She sat in the floor and assumed the Lotus position. She reached out to Marty in her meditation. A fog was between them she could not penetrate. She concentrated harder. From out of the mist she was met with glowing red eyes. A hiss made her shudder. The voice from the mist chilled her. *He is mine. I will send your beloved back to you in pieces.*

Gillian swallowed hard but stood her ground. She pushed past the fear and made a clear resounding thought, *I will save you, my love, no matter what.*

Gillian retreated away from the fog, resolved to finish what she had started. She opened her eyes to see the black cloaked figure sitting across from her.

Even though he sat directly across from her, she could not see his face. His voice was strangely familiar. "You will see him again. He is alive."

She couldn't hide her look of surprise. *How could anyone know?* "I'm not sure how you keep popping in my life. And I certainly don't know how you can know what I'm thinking. You're freaking me out."

The black cloaked man replied, "I realize you have no reason to trust me. So I will not waste your time asking you for trust. I can say you are in this place for a reason. What you need from this home is a plank of acacia wood. You will take this wood to Jaffa. There you will find the catacombs. The Heart of Ptah should be placed on the back of the acacia board. It will act as a compass to the next key. The girl will help you find the Poseidon Stone."

Gillian reached forward in time to grasp thin air, and the figure disappeared. The voice from the cloaked man lingered in the air around her. "You must hurry. They are coming for you…"

A light knock on the door sounded. Gillian's voice was distant as she answered, "Yes?"

Wilhelm replied, "Whenever you're through in there, I need to visit the latrine. Please. They only have one toilet in the house."

Gillian stood and flushed. As she opened the door Wilhelm stood looking at her curiously. "Who were you talking to?"

Without expression she said, "The voices in my head. Don't be so judgy."

He put up his hands defensively. "I'm not judging, I'm just asking."

She walked past him and said, "Don't ask. The answer would scare you more."

Gillian entered the living room as the front door opened. A wizened, middle-aged man walked through the door. As their eyes met, he placed his hand on the knife in his belt. Jhazelle rushed into the room and put herself between the man and Gillian. "Father, it's okay. They are with me. They are tourists, they paid extra to see a real Egyptian home."

The man's eyes narrowed. His gaze never left Gillian as he asked, "How much extra?"

Jhazelle placed a soothing hand on his arm. "Two hundred, American."

He looked in her direction. “To see a poor fisherman’s house? Do you expect me to believe that?”

She kissed him on the cheek. “Yes, Father.”

He took his hand from the knife. “Do they expect you to feed them as well?” He looked at Gillian. “We are not a hotel. I’m not sure what my daughter has told you.”

Gillian smiled charmingly. “We don’t expect a thing. I am a journalist; my story is about the middle-class Egypt of today. I wanted to break the typical mold of how the media has painted about Middle Eastern life. So much is written about the violence here, I wanted to show a more normal life. Jhazelle was kind enough to provide us with her plans for the future to attend college and perhaps work in the legal world.”

The man snorted. “Yes, I suppose I can’t expect her to take over my fishing business. Even though it puts a roof over her head and food in her belly.”

Jhazelle scowled. “I’m not saying being a fisherman is not good enough for me, I think I can be more.”

The man opened his arms to his daughter. “I know. I’m sorry. I didn’t mean for it to come out like that. It makes me afraid for you to go off to Cairo by yourself. You are my life.”

Jhazelle went to him. “I know, Father, we will work it out.”

He looked at Jhazelle. “So what did you promise them for two hundred dollars? And are you sure they can afford it? The old car in the driveway looks like something your uncle would try to sell.”

Jhazelle replied, “Oh, just stories about our life here, how you fish for income, this and that.”

He gave her a dubious look. “Really? I am a fisherman, not a fool.”

Jhazelle looked surprised. “I don’t understand.”

He placed a hand on her cheek. “My darling daughter, I traded that heap to your uncle ten years ago for a new motor for the Isis. The only way your uncle would let you take a car is you had to trade him something for it. This woman you’re with is not a journalist. She looks like she is ex-military. So let’s start again. What is going on here?”

Wilhelm walked through the door. The man looked at him. His hand did not go for the knife. Gillian replied before Jhazelle could speak, “You’re right. We are not journalists. I can’t really explain everything, because I don’t really understand it myself. Let’s sit.” She motioned toward the sofas.

The man placed his hand over his heart. “I am Solah.”

Gillian responded in kind. “I’m Gillian.” She pointed to Wilhelm. “He is Wilhelm.”

Gillian opened her hands to him. “My husband is a farmer from America. He and I traveled here many years ago. He has disappeared, and I am trying to find him.”

Jhazelle returned with coffee. Gillian continued. “I cannot explain how, but I am led to clues. Jhazelle witnessed me finding something.”

The old man raised an eyebrow. “You travel with a man who is not your husband? What is this clue you have found that would influence my daughter to bring you to my home?”

Gillian thought for a moment. She had to give Solah some credible evidence or he would not believe them again. She took a deep breath and pulled the Heart of Ptah from her pocket. Solah gasped. He looked at his daughter. "What have you done? The woman has stolen an ancient treasure, and you have brought her to our home?"

Jhazelle lowered her eyes. "I'm sorry. I did not think. I was drawn to the piece. I cannot explain it."

Her response struck Gillian. The man in the black cloak had said the girl would lead them to the next piece. She realized the connection. "Jhazelle."

Jhazelle looked up. Gillian handed the piece to her. "Take this."

Both Solah and Jhazelle looked surprised. Jhazelle's hand trembled as she reached for the piece. As it touched her hand, it began to pulse. It suddenly all made sense to Gillian. Jhazelle was part of the puzzle. She asked, "Do you have a piece of acacia wood here?"

Solah could not take his eyes off the relic pulsing in Jhazelle's hand. Distantly he responded, "What?"

Gillian pressed. "A board or a plank made of acacia wood."

Jhazelle stood transfixed on the object pulsing in her hand.

Solah tore his eyes from the pulsing Heart of Ptah. "We have a family blessing. It has been here as long as I can remember. I don't know what type of wood it is on."

Gillian replied, "Show me."

He nodded; his eyes were fixed on the pulsing object as he rose from the sofa. Gillian watched him as he struggled with pulling away from the Heart of Ptah. He walked to the kitchen and pointed at a hand painted square plank of wood hanging from a leather strap from the wall. On the face it read in Arabic:

Bless This House

Bless this house and everyone who lives within. This house will be safe and sound against all storms. Misfortune shall not enter here. May laughter and joy echo throughout every room and love and peace dwell here forever and ever.

Gillian stared at the blessing for a moment. "Could you take it down?"

Solah furrowed his brow. "Why?"

Gillian studied the blessing. "I'm just curious."

Solah reached up and removed the blessing and handed it to her. She turned it over. On the back was an embedded gold Eye of Horus. Solah gasped. He looked at Gillian. "I inherited this home from my parents. It has always been there. I have never seen the back of it. I didn't know what was on it."

She studied it for a moment. "Let's take it back to the other room."

Gillian carried the blessing back to the living room where Jhazelle stood fixated on the pulsing relic. As Gillian entered the room, the Heart of Ptah began to move in Jhazelle's hands toward Gillian as she carried the house blessing toward Jhazelle. When they were within one foot of each other, the Heart of Ptah flew out of Jhazelle's hands and landed on the Eye of Horus. There was a stunned silence in the room as everyone stared at the two relics. The Heart of Ptah began to glow at one tip and pointed to the north.

Gillian set the wood and relic down on a wooden coffee table in the center of the room. She began to turn the wood on the table only to have the Heart of Ptah continue to adjust to the north. A quiet filled the room no one was willing to break. It was Jhazelle who broke the silence. “What does it mean?”

Gillian replied, “I believe it’s a compass to something.”

Solah looked at Gillian. “Are you a Sufi?”

Gillian blinked. “A what?”

Solah repeated the question. “A Sufi, an ancient mystic.”

Gillian shook her head. “I’m a housewife trying to find her husband.”

Solah looked at her. His gaze was direct. “It doesn’t matter what you think you are, the universe knows you, even if you don’t know yourself. You are being called. And for that matter, so is my daughter. I cannot stop that. I can only hope Allah loves us enough to bring her back to me.”

Jhazelle broke her gaze on the relic. She moved toward her father and wrapped her arms around him. “We will never be apart. So long as there is breath in my body, I will always be your loving daughter.”

Wilhelm watched the two. Deep within him there was a twinge, a subconscious pang of loss. One he would never have. Both his parents were gone. The only person he felt close to was Adalyn, Captain Chris’s mother. It was debatable if he would ever see her again. He took a deep breath and decided he needed something more in his life. For right now, he would need to survive. He spoke out, “So what are the next steps?”

Gillian looked at him. “We follow the compass to Jaffa. It is leading there.”

Solah looked at the group. “If you are going to Israel, you will not make it in that piece of crap my brother gave you. You will need a better vehicle."

Jhazelle looked at her father strangely. "And where do you plan to get another vehicle?"

Solah smiled for the first time since they had met. "This old fisherman may still have a few tricks up his sleeve."

Jhazelle raised an eyebrow as Solah said, "Follow me."

Solah led the three of them to the back of the home, and they filed out the back door. Jhazelle's eyes narrowed as she caught her first glimpse of a crudely constructed pole shed with tarps on all four sides. She looked at her father and said, "This is new." Solah's grin broadened as he pulled back the tarp on one side, revealing a beige Cherokee beneath.

Jhazelle eyed her father. "And when were you going to tell me about this?"

He grinned. "When you said you were planning to leave for college. You could not simply walk to Cairo."

****

Officer Zaher stood at attention at Captain Nimr's desk. Nimr looked over the photographs of the ruined statue from Abu Simbel as he eased back in his chair and looked up at the junior officer. "So what exactly happened?"

Beads of perspiration dotted Zaher's forehead as he replied, "Two Anglo tourists entered the park. They went to the great temple. We believe a local girl from Edfu led them to the temple. There was a loud bang from the temple and the Anglos fled from the park in a sports car."

Nimr looked at the officer. "And what became of our intrepid pair?"

Zaher shuffled his feet nervously. “It is unclear, sir.”

Nimr’s eyes narrowed menacingly. “Then return to me when it *is* clear, Officer Zaher.”

Zaher saluted. “Yes, sir!”

Nimr picked up the close-up photo of the gaping hole in Ptah’s chest. He studied the geometry and edges. The edges looked like there had been force applied from the inside out. More importantly, it appeared there was a cavity where the hole had been placed. *How was this possible?* It was conceivable someone could have drilled a hole and used a tool to pull the section away, but there was no record of anything being concealed in the statue. The original x-rays from the relocation project had carefully surveyed the statues to determine the best way to move them without damaging them. Nothing had shown up. He picked up a half-smoked cigar from the ashtray and lit it. He blew smoke rings at the ceiling and thought about what should be done next. If someone had found an artifact, it was probably already on the black market on a sell list somewhere. Finding black market artifacts was like finding a needle in a haystack. There seemed to be something about this case that didn’t feel right. His gut told him there was something more to this. He picked up the phone and dialed his friend Jhahar at UNESCO.

The phone rang several times before the gravelly voice of Jhahar sounded on the other end. “Hello?”

Nimr replied, “Old friend, it is Nimr.”

Jhahar rumbled back, “Old friend? I would debate that. No cigars, no imported scotch. What kind of a friend does that?”

Nimr snorted. "I owe you a trip. And I'll bring some good scotch from the UK the next time I'm in Cairo. But for right now, we have a bit of an issue at the temple in Abu Simbel."

Jhahar's tone changed. "What is wrong?"

Nimr stayed on topic. "One of the statues was desecrated. I'm trying to see if you have any of the images from the original project. I need some detailed images of the statue of Ptah in the small temple."

Jhahar replied, "Yes, yes, I have them here. What are you looking for?"

Nimr continued, "The people made a fist size hole in Ptah's chest. Is it possible something was hidden in the statue?"

Nimr could hear papers shuffling. Jhahar was quiet for a moment. "No. There's no indication of that. I worked there for a year before they reassigned me to supervise the relocation of Ramesses. I can't remember any antiquities left in the temple. Everything was looted years ago. Why would you think they found something?"

Nimr responded carefully, "The hole was not drilled. It appears it was forced from the inside out."

Jhahar replied, "That's impossible."

Nimr flicked an ash into the tray. "I know. That's why I'm calling you. I can't trust anyone else with this kind of case. You and I have seen a lot of strange things over the years, but this is the strangest. I'm not sure what to look for."

Jhahar replied, "There was an old tale about how the Gods created a heart for Ptah and it was the key to something greater than the underworld. There was very little detail about it, and nothing was mentioned about what it meant. I'm not sure if it helps."

Nimr replied, "It's more than I started with. Thanks. I owe you some good British scotch."

Jhahar laughed. "Don't wait too long. I don't have too much longer before I'll be visiting the Pharaohs in person."

Nimr snorted. "You'll probably outlive us all, you old goat."

Jhahar replied, "I'll wait around long enough for you to bring me some decent scotch."

Nimr hung up and sat back in his chair. The heart of Ptah. Maybe it wasn't an old wives' tale.

****

Back in the spacious living room Gillian, Wilhelm, and Jhazelle sat in the comfortable overstuffed furniture talking about leaving the next day. Gillian watched as Jhazelle shifted uncomfortably in her seat. She asked the young woman, "What's wrong?" Jhazelle looked at her with troubled eyes. "I want to touch it. I feel like I must touch it." Gillian removed the Heart from her pocket and handed it to Jhazelle. Gillian could almost swear she saw a ripple of power go across Jhazelle's hand. Jhazelle's eyes glazed over for a moment as she began to chant in an ancient language. Wilhelm stared at her from the other side of the room. Without warning, a flash emitted from the Heart with a wave of energy as it passed across the room, rattling shelves and glassware. Then all was quiet. Gillian took the Heart of Ptah from Jhazelle's hand and eased it into her pocket. Jhazelle sat on the sofa staring into space. Gillian asked, "Are you okay?"

Jhazelle blinked and looked up at Gillian. "I think so. I feel strange. I'm not sure what happened."

Her father rushed into the room. He looked from one to another. "What happened?"

Wilhelm shrugged.

Gillian placed her hand on Jhazelle's shoulder. "I've been there. You've been chosen by a greater power. It will take some time to adjust. Did you have any visions?"

Jhazelle blinked and tried to focus on Gillian. Mists swirled past Gillian and began to coalesce next to her. Jhazelle watched as the mist formed into a shape and then a figure. Her mother stood beside Gillian. Jhazelle gasped.

Gillian asked, "Are you all right?"

Tears formed in Jhazelle's eyes. "Mother?"

The form stretched out her arms toward Jhazelle lovingly. Jhazelle reached for her mother's hand to find frigidly cold air where her mother's touch would have been warm and welcome. She drew back her hand. Her mother's lips moved, but no words came out. She could read her mother's lips. *I love you. We will guide you.*

Jhazelle responded, "I don't understand. Have I gone mad?"

Her mother's voice sounded in her head. *No, my love. You can see what others cannot. Hear what others cannot. Understand what others cannot. For the first time in your life, you are aware.*

Gillian asked Jhazelle, "Are you sure you're all right?"

Jhazelle looked at Gillian. "I can see my mother standing beside you. She passed away when I was six. I don't know if I am crazy." Tears streamed down Jhazelle's cheek.

Gillian replied, "You're not mad. You are gifted."

Jhazelle focused back on her mother, who began to fade in the light. "Mother, what am I supposed to do?"

Her mother replied, *Follow the heart. It leads to the eternal one.* Before she could respond, her mother faded from sight.

Jhazelle stood. She looked Gillian in the eye. "I need to be alone."

She ran to her bedroom and shut the door barely in time before she sobbed out loud.

****

Solah looked at Wilhelm. His eyes narrowed. He touched the hilt of his knife. Wilhelm stood and walked to the other side of the room. Gillian turned her attention to Solah. "Jhazelle is gifted. Now she is aware, there will be an adjustment for her."

There was anger in Solah's eyes. "What have you done to my daughter?"

Gillian met his gaze steadily. "*We* have done nothing. Jhazelle has always had the gift, she just didn't know it. Now she does. Whatever powers are at play here choose to manifest when the time is right. This is her time."

Solah glared at her. "She was not ready."

Gillian didn't back away from him. "No one ever is. And yet we still meet the challenges life throws at us. Being alive is facing the challenge of the moment, and not backing away. When you back away in fear, you die a little bit on the inside."

Solah stomped away to the kitchen, muttering to himself. Gillian walked to Jhazelle's room and tapped lightly on the door. "Can I come in?"

A soft reply from the other side answered. "Yes."

Gillian eased the door open and walked in and

closed it behind her. Jhazelle sat in a chair by the window. Mascara runs left long streaks down her face. She was even beautiful when she cried. Gillian asked softly, "Are you okay?"

Jhazelle looked up. Her eyes begged for an explanation; her lips remained silent.

Gillian sat on the end of the bed. "I have been where you are now. In the beginning, I struggled emotionally with my new abilities. What helped me the most was accepting I had changed and I could not go back. I've thought back on that day many times. What I have come to realize, is before I understood my powers, I lived in the dark. When you can see the world in a different light, it forces you to accept your new reality. Denial will make you crazy. Most people go an entire lifetime choosing to deny who they really are, and they live miserably because of it. Or you can accept how wonderfully unique you really are. It's a choice you have to make."

Jhazelle's eyes shifted from Gillian to something behind her. She stood. Gillian whirled around to see a large black shadow figure looming behind her. She turned and backed toward Jhazelle to protect her. Jhazelle placed her hand on Gillian's shoulder and moved her aside. With her other hand she turned her palm up. A small white flame erupted in her hand. The flame grew to the size of a small melon. Jhazelle drew back and threw the white flame at the shadow figure, which immediately engulfed the shadow being. The shadow figure was consumed in a million tiny balls of fire before it disappeared.

Gillian looked at her. "That was impressive."

Jhazelle looked at her empty hand, and then at

Gillian. "It appears I have been given more than I originally thought."

Gillian nodded. "It doesn't surprise me. Once you open the door, there are many rooms to be explored. Keep looking."

Jhazelle squared her shoulders and held her head high. "I'm ready now. I know what I need to do."

Gillian put her arm on the girl's shoulder. "Welcome to the nexus."

****

Captain Nimr admired himself as he straightened his hat in the mirror. Egyptian National Police was lucky to have him. As he walked past his secretary, he didn't even look at her as he said, "I'll be out the rest of the afternoon."

His secretary, Palma, looked up from her paperwork and asked, "Where shall I say you've gone, sir?"

As he reached the door, he replied, "Edfu."

Chapter 15

Fredrick gazed in fascination as the riot unfolded on the street below. Lightning crisscrossed across the sky as Oronians ran and screamed as though the planet were coming to an end. Perhaps for them, it was. It was the first weather event Fredrick had seen since being on the planet. Luna's hands caressed his back from behind. He looked back. "I guess this is the first weather they've ever seen."

Luna replied, "It's the first I've seen since I've been here, and that's been a very long time. What do you think it means?"

Fredrick thought for a moment. "It means the balance of power is shifting for some reason. Jeez is distracted by something."

Luna stood beside Fredrick and watched the carnage below. Centurions tried to control people; a troop of Centurions formed an arc around the crowd as a tall dark-headed Oronian tried to break through the police line. A Centurion fired a bolt of energy, killing the man. People screamed and trampled each other as they scrambled to escape. Luna stared at the melee below. Without looking up she asked, "What should we do?"

Fredrick looked at her. "I say we take advantage of the situation and get out of here."

Luna nibbled on his shoulder playfully and said, "I

thought you might say that. I have a plan."

Fredrick urged her on. "And what might that be?"

Luna stepped back into the room. Fredrick turned and leaned on the windowsill. "There is a tunnel that leads out of the city underneath the altar. If we can make it to the Temple in one piece, we can follow the tunnel to the edge of the city and into the wastelands. From there it's a short journey to where they keep the transport units."

Fredrick looked at her curiously. "How do you know all this?"

Luna looked down. "I was a traveler. My sensors picked up an anomaly that turned out to be this world. Before I could react, gravity from this planet pulled me into the atmosphere and I crash-landed. I was promised that if I assisted them they would allow me to leave. I helped them design the first transport unit, then I was injected with a monster as a reward. The robots took my design and mass-produced a fleet of warships. I can only imagine what she is planning."

Fredrick nodded. "I'm beginning to see the plan now. Jeez plans to invade something. The question is what? How will we get one of the units? I'm sure they're guarded."

Luna laughed bitterly. "Why? No one knows about them except for the robots and me. I'm certainly not a threat to her here. But I do know how to fly them."

Fredrick thought for a moment. "If we can get to Earth, I have doctors there who can remove these wretched things from us."

Luna nodded. "Gather as much food paste as you can. It will have to last us as we cross the wasteland."

Fredrick fashioned a backpack from a tunic. He

tied a knot in the bottom and tied the arms together, so it would hang across his shoulder. They filled it with tubes of food paste from the apartment. They eased down the stairs and out of the back side into the alley behind the street. Luna guided him through the back alleys until they reached the Temple of Ascension. They slipped into the temple and crept to the altar stair. Tucked beneath the stair, behind a purple velvet curtain, was a hidden doorway. She opened the door and stepped in. The smell of rotting flesh almost made them sick. Fredrick covered his mouth. Decaying bodies lay scattered about in the dim light. Luna hurried to the back of the chamber where she touched the wall. A pocket door slid open silently, and they passed through it, closing it behind them. The tunnel was wide enough to drive a car through, but the ceiling was low. The walls were covered in black growth and dripping with an unknown fluid that didn't look like water. Glowing red crystals gave them just enough light to see ahead. Uneven cobblestones made walking difficult. Luna finally spoke. "I think this is part of the original Oronian architecture. It is far older than anything above."

Fredrick squinted in the dim light. "How do you know all this?"

Luna replied, "Like you, all I've thought about since I got here was escaping this place. I would go out exploring when everyone else slept. I found this tunnel but could not follow it all the way."

Fredrick stared at the bones along the wall. "Is there anything down here we should be aware of?"

Luna replied, "I don't know."

Fredrick's senses were on high alert. They moved

deeper into the tunnel; a sound ahead made them stop. The low growl grew louder as two red eyes appeared in the dim light. The creature made its way forward. Fredrick looked around quickly for a weapon. A triangular-shaped piece of cobblestone was at his feet. He inched down and picked it up. The beast moved into the light. It had an odd assortment of features. It had a long, muscular jaw with short, pointed ears. Its short, muscular legs were striped like a tiger, while the brown fur covering its body was matted and knotted.

Luna moved behind Fredrick. The beast charged forward with no hesitation. It jumped at Fredrick's belly. Fredrick turned as the beast neared and struck down hard with the stone, striking it in the shoulder. It yelped and landed hard on the cobblestones. He turned to face the beast. It shook its head and turned on him again. It lunged, striking Fredrick in the chest, knocking him to the ground. Fredrick instinctively grabbed the doglike creature with both hands at the throat. Its muscular neck was unyielding to his grip. He could not choke it. It snapped at his face. Saliva dripped from its mouth onto Fredrick's face. Fredrick could smell the rotting flesh from its breath. He looked up in time to see Luna raise a large stone above them. She crashed the stone in the center of the dog's back. It yelped and rolled off Fredrick, snapping at them from the floor. Its back broken, it could not stand. Instead, it pulled itself forward with its front paws, snapping at Fredrick's feet. Luna raised the rock once more and threw it with all her strength at the creature's head. A sickening thud was followed by silence. Luna helped Fredrick to his feet. He brushed himself off and looked down at the dead animal lying at their feet. "I see why they don't guard this place."

They moved forward. Large black spiders skittered along the walls as they passed. Occasionally one would drop from the ceiling and run to the wall. A mile from the temple, the tunnel split. Down one side it was completely dark. The other showed a light faintly in the distance. They moved in the direction of the light. Small luminescent creatures that moved and pulsed began to appear on the wall. As Fredrick and Luna moved forward, the tiny creatures' mass grew thicker. Then they reached a place where the small worms had occluded the tunnel in a solid writhing web of worms. The walls beside them were covered in the writhing worms, and the pulsating glowing wall of small creatures blocked the front.

Fredrick looked at Luna. "Now what? Do we go back or keep moving forward?"

Luna looked at the worms, and then at Fredrick. "If we go back, the other tunnel was completely black. There's no telling what's in there. Maybe we can break through this?"

Fredrick looked around and found a large stone. He flicked off a small worm from the rock. A burning sensation on his finger was almost immediate, and a blister appeared where he had touched it. He showed the blister to Luna. "It appears our luminescent friends here are not limited to glowing." He spat on the blister, washing some of the irritant away. He hefted the rock and threw it forward. It crashed through the writhing wall, revealing the other side of the tunnel. They worked together to gather and throw stones until a large opening was cleared. Occasionally, worm secretion dripped in the opening. Fredrick looked at Luna. "We run through at the count of three. One, two, *three*. He held her hand as they vaulted through. Luna cried out as several drops of secretion landed on her neck. She reached for the spot when Fredrick grabbed her wrist. “Wait!”

She looked up at him. “But it burns.”

Fredrick spat on her wound and wiped it with the sleeve of his tunic. “If you touch it with your hands, you will spread it. Any other places?”

She shook her head.

They moved away from the worms quickly. A light ahead of them grew brighter. As they drew closer, they could make out the rocky landscape at the mouth of the tunnel. The storm had passed. They shielded their eyes against the bright sunlight on the wasteland. A faint trail appeared in the barren landscape. Luna pointed. “This is the way to the temple.”

They trudged in single file through the wasteland until the city was out of sight. Heat shimmered off the rocks as the sun grew stronger and temperatures rose. Ahead, Fredrick spotted a shack. If there was water, they could refill the water sacks. Luna stopped behind him. He turned to her. “Are you all right?”

She concentrated on the wasteland. Without looking at him she said, “There’s something out there tracking us. I can see it move every now and then.”

Fredrick’s eyes narrowed. “Something we should be concerned about?”

She began walking toward him a little faster. “I think it might be.”

****

He bore the countenance of a madman. He pulled his long unkempt hair back and tied it tightly with a leather cord, never taking his eyes off his quarry. His skin was pale, making him blend in with the desert stone around him. He removed a honed German jungle warfare knife from a worn scabbard. He looked down and spoke to his empty belly. "Gonna get us some sweet ripper meat. Yes, yes, we are. Sweet, sweet meat."

His prey was almost invisible against the landscape. It moved on six legs, its skin reflected the landscape, making it almost invisible in the bright sunlight. When it turned its head, he could see rows of razor-sharp teeth lining powerful jaws. The creature was a small throwback to the dinosaurs that once dominated the planet. Its long front claws did the killing while the back four legs propelled it forward at remarkable speed. This was the first time he had seen one above ground. The creature was either brave or hungry, but he didn't care. It was young and tender, unlike the older, larger rippers. His mouth watered at the thought of it.

The ripper stalked two humans on the path. The crazy man stalked the ripper. The creatures had amazing eyesight but were practically deaf. Being stupid like sheep made them easy to strike. Rippers were vicious, making them unlikely prey. The ripper and the crazy man watched the couple from the city as they made their way to the old woodcarver's shack. He had not seen the old man for several days now. He watched as the couple drew nearer to the shack. The ripper crept closer to them.

The woman spotted the ripper and screamed. The man pushed her forward to the shack and they ran as the ripper closed in. They were slow, while the ripper moved quickly across the landscape. It was time to strike. While the ripper was focused on the humans, he would strike it from behind. Nimbly, he vaulted from the rock he hid behind and sprinted after the ripper. The humans slammed the door shut to the shack while the ripper tore at the door with its claws. It shredded the wooden door into toothpick size shreds as it shrieked in an eerie high-pitched screech. The crazy man closed the gap and leapt high into the air and landed on the back of the ripper, sinking his knife between its shoulders and leaving it there. The creature screamed in a high pitch and rolled to the side, trying to throw the man off. The man wrapped his legs around the ripper's belly, and he grabbed the creature's lower jaw, pulling it back. With its head back, the ripper could not reach him with its front claws. He held the beast until it quit struggling. The man's naked belly dripped with the black blood of the monster in his death grip. The iridescent skin turned green as the ripper died in his hands. Its eyes glazed over as its body convulsed in death throws. The man unwrapped himself from the creature and stood. He removed the long knife from its back and grabbed the front of its snout while slitting the throat.

He rolled the creature over and made a slit along the torso and began to dress the creature, removing its entrails. As he made the first cut, the door eased open and the man inside the shack peeked out. After a moment the man swung the door wide and exclaimed, "Viktor?"

He stopped butchering the ripper and looked up. "My meat, it's my meat, sweet, sweet ripper meat."

Fredrick eyed him before replying, "Well played. Are there any other men left?"

Viktor continued to eviscerate the ripper. "No. Only me. Which means all sweet, young ripper meat is mine, all mine."

Fredrick nodded. "Indeed."

The woman peeped from behind the Duke. "You know this man?"

Fredrick replied, "He was one of my original team. I assumed all had been lost. We recruited him from the German Fourth Platoon."

Viktor cut a large hunk of white meat from the ripper and offered it up to Fredrick, "Sweet, sweet meat. Have some."

Fredrick smiled. "Would you mind if we cooked it first?"

Viktor pulled the meat back and stuffed it into his mouth, and replied, sputtering meat as he spoke, "Suit yourself."

Viktor stopped his butchering and looked up at Fredrick and Luna. His eyes narrowed as he focused on their bellies. "You've got those devil bugs inside you, don't you? Devil bugs…" His sentence drifted off as he stuffed another piece of meat into his engorged mouth. He chewed and swallowed before saying, "That's how this beastie found you. They can smell the devil bugs two kilometers away. They love eating devil bugs as much as eating humans. You're like a prize."

Fredrick responded, "I would certainly like to be removed from the prize list."

Viktor looked up. "Are you sure about that?"

Fredrick arched his eyebrow. "Yes. Most certainly."

Without warning, Viktor jammed the knife into Fredrik's belly. Fredrick's eyes grew wide. The pain was sudden and sharp. He felt the serqet shudder within him from what appeared to be a mortal blow. Viktor let go of the knife. It stood out of Fredrick's belly as the blood dripped. Fredrick stared at the wound, and then at Viktor. "Now what? Am I supposed to walk around with the knife sticking out of my belly from now on?"

Viktor stuffed another piece of meat into his mouth. "No. Now we build a fire and seal you up."

The raw pain of the cut wormed its way past Fredrick's resolve. He sat back on a small stone bench against the wall of the shack. He tore a strip from his tunic to pack a dressing around the knife.

Viktor looked at Fredrick's belly. "I need my knife back. I'll build a fire so I can seal the wound."

Fredrick raised an eyebrow. "Am I supposed to leave this creature in me?"

Viktor wandered around the shack and picked up orn dung for a fire. "Up to you. I can cut it out, or you can leave it in."

Luna stared at the two in disbelief. She didn't understand the dialog between them. She asked Fredrick in Oronian, "What did he say?"

Fredrick looked at her and took a deep breath trying to swallow back the pain. "He said I could leave the serqet in me or he could cut it out. He doesn't care. Right now, he just wants his knife back."

Luna blinked. "Are you serious?"

Fredrick nodded. "Quite."

Luna placed a hand on his shoulder. "When we get to the ships, there are medical robots. They can surgically remove these things. He will most certainly not be taking care of mine today."

Fredrick agreed, "A wise choice on your part.

Believe me."

Viktor removed a piece of flint and steel from his BDU's. In a short while he had a fire in the hearth of the shack. He walked over to Fredrick and without a word, snatched the knife from his belly. Fredrick pulled the makeshift tunic bandage over the wound and held pressure. Viktor held the blade over the fire. The blade smoked as the blood burned free.

Fredrick looked at Viktor. "Now what?"

Viktor moved toward Fredrick with the smoking blade. Without a word he pulled the tunic up and seared the open wound, closing it. Fredrick fainted and collapsed backward on the bench. Viktor walked back over to the ripper and began to carve meat again. He put a piece in his mouth. "Hmm. It does taste better cooked."

Luna sat beside Fredrick on the stone bench. She inspected the wound where the knife had been. It was a raw burn, but now sealed and not bleeding. She watched Viktor was he stripped back a section of skin from the ripper and piled the meat he had been cutting into the skin. Fredrick's eyes fluttered open. For the first time in ten years, there were no voices in his head. With Luna's help, he rose to his feet.

"Viktor, we have a plan to leave this place. Do you want to come?"

Viktor looked up with a mouth full of meat. "Where would we go? There's no place like home. There's no home in this place. Where would we go?"

Fredrick replied, "To Earth. Where we came from."

Viktor shook his head as he continued to carve meat from the ripper. "No place for home, no home for place. Where to go, where to go…"

Fredrick responded, "Come along Viktor. We will find your home."

Viktor continued to carve at the ripper. "Sweet meat. Such sweet meat. I shall take some meat as we find our home, our sweet, sweet home." He looked at Luna. "We must kill the Devil bug in her, or others will follow. Devil bugs are like candy to them. Sweet, sweet, candy bugs."

He started toward Luna with the knife. Fredrick stopped him. "It is only a short way to the ships. The creatures can follow us there, but they are battle ships. We can defend ourselves there."

Viktor stroked his long straggly beard with greasy hands. "Guns. It will be nice to have guns again. I ran out of ammo long ago. Lost my guns, long ago. Nice to have guns again. Let's go find our new guns." He wrapped up his pile of meat in the ripper skin and tied it closed with a leather strap. Fredrick and Luna began the long trek forward. Viktor disappeared into the rocks behind them. Occasionally, Fredrick would hear him move, but they could not see him as he followed. The old Fredrick would have cared less as to the fate of Viktor. Now he felt responsible for the man's madness. Alone, on a foreign planet, surviving off the land for a decade, it was no wonder he was a lunatic.

The skies turned to amber hues as the sun moved toward the horizon. Ahead, Fredrick could make out the shape of a building. They could take shelter in it and begin once more in the morning. As they approached, a solitary figure stood outside of what appeared to be a monastery. When the man looked up and saw the pair, he ran inside the building and shut the door. The wasteland blended into grassland around them. Fredrick could hear something behind them in the rocks. He assumed it was Viktor. They kept moving toward the monastery. Fredrick turned once again to see if Viktor was behind them. In the distance he could see a large ripper coming out from behind a rock. The ripper stared at Fredrick for a second, and then began to run at full speed. Fredrick pushed Luna forward. "Run!"

They neared the door. The ripper was gaining ground quickly. As they reached the door, there was no catch to open it. They beat on the door and screamed for the caretaker to let them in. This ripper was twice the size of the last one. Fredrick looked around for something to defend themselves. He could hear the ripper snorting as it ran. Its skin shimmered in the setting sun. It would have been beautiful had it not been so terrifying. He moved Luna away from the door to the wall. He waited until the beast was in the air before he pushed Luna away. The ripper smashed into the wall where, curiously enough, there appeared to be a previous bloodstain. The ripper struck the wall with such force its black blood spattered the stone wall, covering the previous stain. As the beast lay, stunned for the moment, its nose bled. Viktor erupted from the grass plain and leapt up, landing squarely on the ripper's back. He jammed the knife deep in the creature's back above its front legs. Its eyes opened and it twisted, trying to reach Viktor. Viktor rolled free of the beast, agilely landing on his feet in a crouched position. The ripper attempted to stand but staggered and fell over. Its eyes clouded and it shuddered one more time and lay still. Viktor eased up to the beast cautiously and yanked his knife from its back. Black blood dripped from the blade as he held it ready.

Confident the ripper was dead, Viktor began to butcher the monster at the opening of the building. Black blood streamed across the washed stone porch, filling cracks and seeping toward the door. Viktor was oblivious to the carnage as he sang to himself, “Got me sweet meat twice in one day, twice in one day, twice one day…” He continued with humming the macabre tune as he eviscerated the ripper.

Fredrick held Luna to him as she wept at the madness of it all. He looked across her shoulder, and in the distance a group of robed men walked toward them across the grass plain. Their robes were like the man who fled inside the building and had yet to open the door.

Viktor stopped butchering the ripper for a moment to look up at Fredrick and Luna. He held out a piece of freshly cut meat. “Want some?”

Fredrick shook his head. “No. Thank you.”

Viktor looked at Fredrick with what seemed like a moment of sanity. In perfect Oronian, he replied, “You know they’ll keep following us until the devil bug inside of her is dead.”

Luna stopped crying and her eyes grew large. “You are not stabbing me in the belly to kill this thing. I will find another way to remove it!”

Viktor shrugged. “Suit yourself. I may not be there to save you the next time. It’s a bad way to die.” He went back to butchering the ripper while humming his little tune quietly.

Fredrick spoke to Viktor and Luna quietly. “We have people approaching from the rear.”

Viktor never looked up as he shoved another piece

of meat in his mouth. With a full mouth he said, "Monks. Harmless, useless lot. Can't fight, can't run. No good for nothing. Might let us sleep inside when it gets dark. Should keep the rippers at bay."

Luna's jaw clinched. "Fine! Kill it! But understand this, if you kill me, you kill your chances of getting off this God-forsaken rock."

Viktor looked up. "Time to build another fire."

When the robed monks were within clear sight of the ripper lying on the doorstep of the monastery and the carnage surrounding the group, they stopped. They gathered in a huddle. Occasionally one would peep toward Fredrick and Luna and go back into the group. Fredrick watched them patiently. Viktor had abandoned dressing the ripper and wandered off in search of fuel to make a fire. He returned a short while later with a tightly bound bundle of straw grass which looked remarkably like a log. The monks continued to huddle and look over at them furtively. Fredrick looked at Viktor. "Keep working on the fire. I'll open a discussion with our friends over there." Pointing at the monks.

Using the thinning flint rod from the jungle knife hilt, Viktor showered the dried straw with sparks, leading to a small flame almost immediately. He urged the gentle flicker of flame with a gentle breath, coaxing it to grow. By gradually feeding it straw and blowing, he soon had a cozy fire in which he began to heat his blade.

Luna called after Fredrick, "Oh, Fredrick, dear! Please hurry along, I have no desire to do this alone."

Fredrick looked back and nodded. One of the monks looked up at the sound of Luna calling out and saw Fredrick moving toward them. He poked his head back into the huddle and spoke loudly enough even Fredrick could hear his high-pitched voice. "One of the strangers approaches!"

A monk stepped out of the huddle and faced Fredrick. "I am Brother K of the Monastery of the Enlightened. We are peaceful and mean you no harm."

Fredrick was amused. "As are we. I am Fredrick. My woman and I are traveling. We seek shelter in your monastery for the night. We bring the gift of food for you and your brothers." He gestured toward the ripper.

Brother K cleared his throat. "I see. And it is a magnificent offering. A little frightening perhaps, but quite splendid indeed."

Viktor looked up from the fire. The knife smoldered in his hand. In German, he said, "You give away sweet meat, Fredrick. Not good. Not good at all."

In German Fredrick replied, "Not the time, Viktor. We must negotiate with what we have."

Viktor grumbled under his breath as he stood and walked toward Luna with the smoldering knife.

Luna called out to Fredrick, "Fredrick, dear, I need you. Sooner rather than later!"

Fredrick turned his attention back to Brother K and smiled like a used car salesman. "Brother K, as you can see, we have a bit of a situation here that must be dealt with. Would you be so kind as to excuse me for one moment while I attend to the procedure at hand?"

Brother K's eyebrows arched up as Viktor walked toward the woman with a smoking knife. "Most assuredly, kind traveler. By all means, do whatever it is you need to do there."

Fredrick turned and jogged back to Luna's side.

Viktor's knife was still smoldering. Fredrick held up his hand and stopped Viktor. "Please, dear Viktor, give us a moment here."

Viktor looked disgusted at having to wait. "Need to get meat before useless monks."

Fredrick looked at Luna reassuringly. "Why don't we raise your tunic so he doesn't have to go through your clothing as it did with me, my dear. Close your eyes and it will be over in a quick second." The serqet squirmed in her belly sensing something was not right.

Luna looked peeved. "Don't patronize me, Fredrick, I'll lift my tunic. You hold my hand."

"Of course, dear."

She closed her eyes and raised her tunic revealing her naked belly underneath. The monks gasped. Viktor studied the position of the serqet and jabbed the knife in the center of the mass above her navel. The smell of burning flesh and Luna's scream filled the air. The serqet stopped moving. Two monks fainted and collapsed to the ground. Fredrick tore another section from the bottom of his tunic and dressed the wound as Viktor removed the blade. Beads of perspiration dotted Luna's forehead. Her voice was shaky as she asked, "Is it done?"

Fredrick used his sleeve to blot the perspiration from her brow. "You're all finished."

She opened her eyes. There was an aspect about her Fredrick had not seen before. Her eyes had changed to an azure blue. They almost glowed. A faint smile traced her lips as she said, "The voices have stopped."

Fredrick kissed her gently on the forehead. "It's wonderful, isn't it?"

She closed her eyes. "It's lovely. I have control of

my mind again."

Fredrick pulled her tunic to cover her again. Viktor went back to carving meat, giving the monks a sullen look as they passed him. Brother K approached and said, "Fredrick, we would be pleased to offer you shelter and a place to rest." He looked up. "We have noticed the skies are turning dark. We are concerned it is an omen of evil portent. Please follow us inside." He stepped over the pool of thickening black blood at the door and pressed a small depression in the stone wall. The door opened silently. He motioned for Fredrick and Luna to follow him. He made a fleeting glance back at Viktor. "Do you think your friend will need help with preparing the animal?"

Fredrick shook his head. "I believe he is happy. We'll let him work on it until he's satisfied with the task at hand."

Brother K nodded. "There is wisdom in that. So where are you traveling to?"

Fredrick replied carefully. "There is a complex near here. We are inspecting it."

Brother K replied, "We just came from the Temple of Darkness with two other travelers like yourself."

The statement tweaked Fredrick's interest. "Really. Can you tell me more of these travelers?"

Brother K continued, "They were strangers to this planet. A boy and his father. They sought to battle the demon Jeez."

Fredrick urged Brother K, "Please continue."

Brother K looked thoughtful. "It seems Jeez is attacking the boy's mother in a place called Earth. His name was Jacob. His father was Marty."

Fredrick's eyes narrowed. "Did they say how they

traveled here? Were there others like them?"

Brother K shook his head. "I don't believe so. They landed in different places, but somehow found each other. The boy has many powers. More than I have ever seen. He rivals the most powerful sorceress from the Dark Temple."

"Thank you, Brother K." Fredrick began to think back to the time he had arrived. Was it possible Martin Wood had survived the night he had been transported through the wormhole to Oronas? Could the child of a gifted parent be gifted at birth? Could it be Martin Wood was here on Oronas? What would it mean if they were to meet? Luna moaned and stumbled beside him. Her color did not look good. He smoothed her hair. Blood dripped from her tunic to the floor. Viktor must have nicked a blood vessel when he killed the serqet. She needed surgery, soon.

He looked at Brother K. "The woman needs medical help."

Brother K nodded as he looked at the growing pool of blood under Luna. "We might be able to help. We are not warriors, but we are healers. I will make the preparations."

Within moments an unknown monk arrived. He led Fredrick and Luna to a room deeper in the monastery. It appeared to be a primitive surgical unit. A monk entered the room and approached them. "I am Brother O, the healer. May I see the wound?"

Luna raised her tunic for the monk to inspect the wound. He prodded it with a gentle finger making Luna flinch. He looked up. "You are bleeding inside. We will need to repair the blood vessel."

Fredrick looked at him, his eyes were hard. "Can

you do that?"

Brother O replied solemnly, "Yes. We are far from the medical units in the city. We have learned to treat such things. We will provide you with some tea which will help relieve the pain. We should be able to do this quickly."

Brother O left. Fredrick looked at Luna. "Do you want to chance it?"

Luna looked at him. Her hand stretched out and caressed his cheek. "I don't think we have a choice. I feel weaker by the moment. I don't think I'll make it to the ship in time."

Fredrick kissed her on the lips. "Then I'll be here with you."

Luna smiled.

Brother O returned with a steaming cup of liquid in a brown bowl. "You must drink this."

Luna leaned forward and winced. She sipped the liquid and made a face. Fredrick asked, "Does it taste bad?"

She looked at him and replied, "Imagine burnt hair soup with a side of poop. It would taste better than this."

Fredrick made a face. "I'll pass."

Brother O urged her. "You must drink it all. It will help you."

Luna took a deep breath and began to sip it methodically. She finished the bowl and said, "That's weird."

Fredrick asked, "What?"

"After the first sip it wasn't all bad. It tasted like mint at the last."

Brother O gently patted her arm. "Good. You

should be feeling better shortly."

Luna's eyes glazed over. She laughed deliriously and poked her finger in Fredrick's mouth playfully. "How's my finger taste, sweetie?"

Fredrick pulled his head back. "Like finger."

She laughed even louder. "Finger food!"

Fredrick raised an eyebrow. "I think she might be ready."

Brother O nodded in agreement. "I believe you are right. We can begin."

Another monk moved a small table with surgical instruments on it over to them. Brother O rinsed his hands in green liquid. "This will prevent infection in the wound."

With a fine bladed knife, he opened the scar from Viktor's blade. Inside, blood ebbed from a vein across the head of the serqet. With a small loop of thread, Brother O closed the open vein. He then placed a small amount of green paste to the area. The blood stopped flowing. With careful precision, he closed up the small section with thread, applying more green paste. Luna chattered and made animal sounds the entire time but did not move. Brother O placed a small plaster of blue material over the incision site.

He looked at Fredrick. "She should be fine. The creature inside of her is dead, but it should be removed, it will lead to tumors."

Fredrick patted his belly. "That was the plan. How long before she can travel?"

Brother O replied, "It will be a while before the Gowha tea wears off."

Fredrick looked around. "I will sleep beside her. Can we move a cot in here?"

Brother O motioned to one of the other monks. “Bring us a bed in here.”

The monk disappeared.

****

Jacob followed Mother Shadraq down the narrow mine shafts until they arrived back at the first chamber. The group moved quietly to the side shaft the serqet and robot had led the children down. The shaft was wider and higher. The ground was smooth, indicating it had been in use much longer. It was easy for the group to walk side by side. Shadraq stopped without warning. Jacob asked, “What’s wrong?”

The response was in his head, *There is water ahead.”*

Considering the dampness around them, Jacob asked, *Why is that a problem?*”

Shadraq insisted, *Lots of water.*

Jacob considered this. *What do we need to do?*

Shadraq responded, *Carry me. The water burns my legs.*

Jacob turned to Ouna. “We need to carry Shadraq.”

She looked at him as if he had lost his mind. “You want us to do what?”

Jacob pressed, “She said there’s a lot of water ahead. The water burns her legs, she needs for us to carry her.”

Ouna rebutted, “Or easier for her to eat us.”

Shadraq turned and let out a low screech. Jacob could hear the message, *My kind does not eat other living beings. The children are in danger. We must hurry.*

Jacob looked at Ouna. Before he could speak, she said, “I know, she promised not to eat us.”

Jacob glared. "Yes. But more important, your friends are in danger. Are we going to argue or are we going? We don't have time to debate."

Ouna's eyes flashed with anger, but she didn't argue. "Fine! You get the front near the mouth. One funny move and we leave you with her."

Jacob turned away. "Whatever."

He got down on all fours in front of Shadraq. She placed her legs on his shoulders. He could smell her, she smelled sweet like peaches. The other children got on either side, linked arms under her, and raised up. She was lighter than they expected. The makeshift litter carried the enormous spider down the tunnel. Jacob felt the splash of water beneath his feet. By the time they had gone one hundred yards, the water was ankle deep.

The group could see the opening into the large chamber ahead. Shadraq said, *Jacob, there is a ledge ahead, you can put me there.*

Ahead on the right there was a large outcropping of shoulder-high rock. He led the litter team to the ledge. Shadraq stepped onto the ledge. She said, *We must work quickly. They have thinned the walls too much. The ocean will flood the chamber soon. All will die.*

Jacob replied, "How do we proceed?"

Shadraq's eyes glowed in the dark corner. *I will emit a sound. You must reach under the robot and disable the switch. There are ten robots altogether. I can make the sound for one minute of time.*

Jacob surveyed the chamber. Ouna crouched beside him. "So what's the plan, smart guy?"

Jacob looked over the chamber. "Shadraq says the chamber will flood soon. Too much rock has been removed. She will make a sound to disrupt the robots.

We will have a short while to disable them. I will run to the farthest one since I know where the switch is. If you can start moving the others out, I'll work my way out making sure each robot is disabled."

Ouna replied, "That's pretty good." She pulled the rest of the group together. Jacob held his fingers in two L's. Quietly he showed the group where the button should be. "You must turn it a half turn. It will be stiff. If it doesn't turn in one direction go the other way." Ten pairs of eyes regarded him anxiously. He tried to reassure them. "Look. I did four by myself. All you must do is one. This is for your friends; you can do this."

He put his hand in the center. They stared at him. Ouna was the first to place her hand on his, slowly each followed suit. They were united. Jacob looked at Shadraq. "We're ready."

The group lined up in two rows. The sound Shadraq emitted was a high-pitched hawk's screech that sent a chill up Jacob's spine. He was stunned for a moment, and then he began to slosh through the calf-deep water. The frigid water numbed his legs. They would have to go underwater to disable the robots. This might be problematic. He made it to the end of the row and faced the robot farthest away from the exit. It stood frozen, every light blinking erratically. He braced himself as he ducked his head in the ice-cold water. The unit had tracks like a bulldozer. He reached between the tracks and fumbled with the switch until it turned.

As he arose, there was pandemonium in the room. Half of the miners, who were supposed to turn off robots, were running with their friends toward the tunnel exit. Only half of the robots were turned off. He started to work his way back toward the tunnel. He secured three more. He looked to his right. Ouna was doing the same. They reached the robot closest to the exit when an eerie quiet filled the room.

The circuit lights cleared on the robot as it assessed its quota of children was gone. It immediately zeroed in on Ouna. Jacob could see red bolts of electricity on its exterior electrodes charging as it prepared to shock Ouna. Jacob dove under the robot and jammed his hand on the switch. It seemed frozen in place for a moment. He struggled against it. He could see the electrodes getting brighter. He made one final twist and the switch turned, shutting the robot down. He rose from the water. Ouna stood before him. Her eyes were different, almost tearful. "You saved me. Maybe I was wrong about you."

He grinned. "Maybe you weren't, but that's neither here nor there. For right now we've got to go." They waded out of the chamber only to stop in their tracks. A large serqet clung to the ceiling and snapped its claws menacingly. Its abdomen quivered. Ouna never took her eyes off the monster. "Now what, smart guy?"

Jacob's eyes were fixed on the serqet. "I'm thinking."

The water rose around them. Ouna moved slightly away from Jacob. The serqet matched her move. "You need to think faster."

"I need you to trust me."

Ouna glared over at him. "You're starting to use up all your good boy credits, buddy."

Jacob focused on the serqet. "It seems to be following you as you move. It can't reach you from the ceiling if you duck down. Which means it will have to drop on you in the water. I can catch it and fling it when it does."

Ouna backed a little farther away from Jacob. The serqet followed her move. Her eyes were locked on it as she replied, "Have you ever seen the pincers on this thing work? I saw one take a boy's arm off once. It was gruesome. If you miss, this thing will take my head off. That's a lot of trust."

Jacob replied, "I can do this."

The serqet edged closer. She turned and looked at Jacob. "You had better not miss."

Ouna splashed as she ran straight toward the serqet. With only inches to spare she dove into the water. The serqet dropped from the ceiling. Jacob waved his hand and directed the creature toward the wall with as much force as he could muster. The serqet landed on the wall with all six feet and skittered behind him. Now he was the prey. He sloshed through the water toward the opening to the tunnel. The serqet was gaining ground fast across the open ceiling. He could hear Shadraq in his mind. *Hurry, Jacob, the devil bug approaches.*

His head pounded with adrenaline as he responded, "I'm working on it!"

He could feel the serqet snipping at his neck. As it followed him into the tunnel, Ouna stood there with a pickaxe. Before the serqet could turn, she hit square in the middle of its face. It fell from the ceiling and into the rising water. Blue blood clouded the water.

Jacob looked at Ouna. "Are we even now?"

She smirked. "Not quite, smart guy. You still owe me for being human bait."

He looked around. "Where are the others?"

Ouna jabbed her finger at the tunnel. "Probably on

the surface, kissing the ground."

Jacob's face was solemn. "How will we get Shadraq to the surface?"

She shrugged. "Maybe you and I can carry her."

Shadraq's voice entered his mind, *I'm sorry Jacob, but you are wet. That will not work.*

Jacob looked around. In the distance, he could see two objects. They might do. "I'll be right back." He ran ahead to where two metal rods were stuck in the ground above the water line. He wasn't sure what they had been used for in the past, but he knew what he would do with them. With some effort, he pulled them from the ground and ran back. The water continued to rise.

He held the rods up toward Ouna. "Put one on each shoulder."

With no time to lose, she shouldered a rod on each side.

He placed one on each of his shoulders. "Okay, Shadraq, hop on." Carefully the spider lay on the makeshift litter. She curled her legs to stay on while they moved up the tunnel. Shadraq was much heavier between the two of them and soon his shoulders began to ache. He called to Ouna, "You okay back there?"

She answered, "Considering I've got the biggest bug butt imaginable in my face, sure."

The water began to get shallower; it was only ankle deep now. A sound behind them made a low roar. He shouted back to Ouna, "Run!" The fissure had opened, and the water was rushing in behind them. As soon as his feet hit dry land he shouted, "Stop!"

He went down on his knees in the gravel and yelled at Shadraq, "Run!"

She skittered across his back and traveled quickly

up the tunnel out of sight. Jacob looked behind him, and Ouna was already moving past him. She grabbed him under the arm and pulled him up. They dashed ahead of the rushing water. The sound grew louder behind them. They were headed up the last incline to the surface. He could see the light ahead. The roar of the water stripping loose rock from the tunnel wall was almost deafening behind them. Jacob's breath came in jagged gasps. Ouna for all her toughness was beginning to fall behind. He grabbed her arm and pulled her forward. Within feet of the entrance the water caught them. With his hand still on her arm they were vaulted into the air by a plume of water. A group of children watched as Jacob and Ouna flew ten feet into the air propelled by the jet of water. They slammed into the grass below and rolled followed by the hammer of water. The pressure below pulled the water back into the hole and it ebbed at the entrance like the tide. Jacob coughed and sputtered. Ouna lay beside him. She wasn't breathing. Jacob turned her on her side and slapped her on the back. Water ran from her mouth onto the wet grass around them. He rolled her onto her back and raised her chin and breathed into her mouth. On his second breath she coughed and sat up. She blinked at him for a moment, and then slapped him. "You call that a plan?"

He grinned. "Yep."

She spit into the grass beside her.

The group gathered around them. Jacob looked through the crowd. "Where's Shadraq?"

The children looked at each other. Finally, one boy asked, "Who?"

Jacob reached out with his mind, *Shadraq?*

Her tinny voice came back to him, *I am safe,*

Jacob. But I am injured. Can you come back to the mine? Bring the children.

Jacob looked around. Everyone stared at him.

Ouna sat beside Jacob in the wet grass. She wiped the water from her face and stared at him. It was the first time he had seen her at a loss for words. Finally, she reacted. Tears formed in her eyes. She sniffed and wiped her eyes. "You saved my life. I was dead."

Jacob shrugged. "I guess so. I wasn't going to let you die."

With tears in her eyes, she asked, "Why? Why would you save me?"

He struggled for the right words. "Lots of reasons. We worked together, I respect you, and I…like you."

She stared at him for a moment in disbelief. "Why would you like me?"

"I don't know. I just do."

The right side of her lips rose into a half a smile. It was the kind of smile people make when they don't normally smile. "You like me?"

Jacob furrowed his eyebrows. "Yeah. Don't make a big deal out of it, okay?"

She hugged him. Jacob hugged her back. They held each other for a while. The other children watched them. Some looked on curiously. Ouna didn't seem to want to let go. Finally, he whispered, "I think it's time to go."

She let go reluctantly. "Where?"

"We need to go back into the mine."

Ouna drew back. "Why?"

"Shadraq needs us." He could see her eyes narrow. He could tell she was thinking it through. "Shadraq did help us escape. We owe it to her."

She looked at the others. “We need to go back in to gather supplies for the journey. Follow us.”

It was odd to Jacob there was no dissent in the group. A few nodded, but most just looked at them. Jacob whispered into her ear. “No one is arguing with you. Is that normal?”

She moved toward the entrance of the mine. “They’ve been programmed to follow orders, there is no freedom of thought here. I’m not like them. My mother was an engineer who worked on robots. She died because of an illness. I was sent to the mines because there was no other place for me. I’m not emotional like the people in the city.”

Jacob rubbed his chin where she had slapped him. “That remains to be seen.”

She gave him a sideways look. “So where are we going, smart guy?”

Jacob directed a thought at Shadraq. *Shadraq, where are you?*

Follow the main entrance to the first side tunnel. It is small. You will need to walk single file. It will open into a large chamber. I will be there.

Jacob stepped up to lead. The water had washed away a layer of rock exposing thousands of crystals. The tunnel glowed in red light. He walked until he noticed a side tunnel he had not noticed on his previous trips through. Shadraq spoke to him, *This is the tunnel you need to follow.* She seemed to know where he was.

It became very narrow as they walked. In places the group would turn sideways to navigate down the narrow shaft. The ceiling was lower, so the group walked stooped over. Finally, the tunnel opened into an enormous cavern. Jacob could make out a lump against the wall. He sensed it was Shadraq, but she looked different in the dim light. As he drew closer, he could see her injuries. She had not escaped the water entirely as it ravaged the tunnel. Large holes on her torso bubbled with fluids. She was dying. Jacob ran to her. He placed a hand on her head. *Shadraq, is there anything we can do?*

Ten eyes regarded him. She could not show emotion, but he could feel her pain. Tears filled his eyes. She spoke but her voice seemed very distant in his mind. *I do not have much time. I came here because my planet was dying. I had to find a place for my race. I have failed them. I am the last of my kind. When we spawn, we are food for our children. I have no children here. Can you partake of me?*

Jacob was reviled, he responded carefully, *You want us to eat you?*

I know it is not a custom of yours, but I would be honored to feed you as my own. It is the only time we partake of another in our lives. She bristled the hairs on her torso. *Pluck a single hair and swallow it. It will nourish you and give you strength to fight the Black Guard.*

Jacob asked, *Who are the Black Guard?*

They are the thirteen warriors that protect the Dingh. Their souls are black, like hers. You must hurry. I am in front of the door to the ancient armory. Jeez does not know this exists. Take a piece from my torso. Have the others do the same. Open the wall behind me. The weapons can kill the Black Guard.

Jacob plucked a hair from her torso and placed it in his mouth. As it dissolved in his mouth, it was bitter but then turned sweet. He felt strength enter his body.

Shadraq spoke again, *At death, I give all my energy to my children so they will have my strength and that of our ancestors. Have the others eat as well; it will harden them for the battle.*

Jacob looked at Ouna. “Pluck a hair from her torso and eat it.”

She raised an eyebrow. “Do what?”

He plucked another hair and handed it to her. “Eat it.”

She took the coarse hair from him and eyed it dubiously. Hesitantly she placed it in her mouth. She made a grimace, and then he saw a look of calm replace the grimace. She motioned to the others. She plucked hairs and gave them to the others. There was a palpable electricity in the room. Some ate more. Some began to smile at the gained strength.

Shadraq spoke, *You are the closest beings I will ever have as children. Remember me.* And she was silent. Her body sagged into the floor. The hairs on her back began to curl. Jacob spoke out loud so all could hear, “Stop eating. Mother has passed.”

He kneeled beside her and said a short prayer for Mother. As he rose, the others stared at him. It was Ouna who asked, “What did you do?”

“I prayed for her.”

“What is praying?”

“Well, you talk to God and ask him things.”

“Who is God?”

He paused for a moment. It was not a question he was prepared for. “My people believe in a supreme being. We call him God.”

She looked at him curiously. “Do you mean like a giant?”

He thought about the question for a moment. "In our belief, God is not a physical being, he is spiritual."

"What is spiritual?"

"You know, it's your soul."

"What is a soul?"

He sighed. "We might need to continue this later. We need to bury Mother."

She raised an eyebrow. "Okay. But she's just a big bug."

Jacob scowled. "No, she wasn't. She was the most amazing creature I've ever met. And a part of her is in you now. Think about how great you feel. She gave a part of herself to help you feel that way. She considered us as her children. For her, it was a great honor."

Ouna shrugged. "Big bug."

Jacob took a deep breath and held his temper in check and pointed. "That's a good spot over there. Dig a hole and place her in it."

Ouna went to the others. Using their hands in the loose sand, they dug a hole large enough to hold Mother and moved her in. After she was covered and Jacob said another silent prayer over her, he turned his attention to the wall where she had been. He looked at Ouna. "There are weapons behind this wall. We need to break it down."

She looked at him drolly. "We're miners. It's what we do."

Ouna looked around. "We don't have any tools."

Jacob inspected the wall. "We won't need them." With one foot he kicked a small crack in the wall. His foot went through what appeared to be solid rock. He pulled his foot free. "Help me." He grabbed a section and pulled. A large section came out easily. The rest of the children joined in, pulling sections away and throwing them into the chamber. Soon a large arsenal of weapons glittered in the dim light. Swords, knives, shields, and bows. All the edges glinted in the dim light. Jacob picked up a sword that resembled a Roman broad sword. It felt light in his hand. "Everyone, grab a weapon."

****

Marty hung in shackles in the center of the Dingh. The metal dug into the flesh of his wrists and ankles. The blood dripped into red spots beneath him. The pain of hanging spread eagle did not compare to the claw marks and cuts covering his body. Jeez had tortured him steadily since he had been dragged down the tunnel by the eck. She had tortured his body, but his mind was protected by the Edajhia. He opened one eye. The other swelled shut by her fist as he had tried to grin at her. "Didn't hurt." He said this one time too many. She circled him now. With one eye, he could see her squint as she studied him. Finally, she stopped pacing. She stood where he could see her. Her question was simple. "Why?"

He blinked. His vision blurred and then refocused. "Why, what?"

Her eyes narrowed. "Why do you resist so? I can give you anything. Am I not attractive to you? I could make you a king." She stepped close to him. She touched the open wounds on his chest. Her touch was like multiple needles on an open wound. "I can make all of this go away. All you have to do is say, 'yes'."

He swallowed the best he could. His throat burned from the screaming. "T-the price is t-too high."

She glared into his good eye. "What price? What

are you paying for this? Nothing! I ask you to be my companion eternal. To join me as the ruler of all the known universes. And your pathetic excuse is a family? Let me explain something to you. In the end, they will all die anyway. And you? Your soul will be mine to torture for as long as I want it to be mine. I can keep you alive for another thousand years, torturing you like this every day. So your family will die anyway, you are tortured for all eternity because of some ethical nonsense?" She looked up and spoke to some unseen entity. "You said humans contained the seeds of the universe in their souls. So far all I've found is ignorance and stupidity. Worse yet, stupid stubbornness. They'll never get it!"

She returned her attention to Marty. "Suit yourself. I don't sleep or eat. I will do this twenty-four hours a day for the rest of eternity. You will hold up for a while, but eventually you'll fall. They always do. And when you do, I'll have both you and your beloved family."

He squinted to keep her in focus. "If I am so useless, why are you going to this trouble?"

Jeez looked thoughtful. "Very good question. I don't really care about you at all. I will admit I was a bit curious at first. But that waned after a while. What I'm really interested in is something you are connected to. Something I want. Something that will change everything."

"And what is that?"

"What? And ruin the surprise? Don't worry. You'll know soon enough."

She gripped his cheeks with her hand and kissed him fully on the lips. Her long serpent tongue slid into his mouth and down his throat, almost gagging him before she pulled it back out. She broke the kiss and walked away laughing.

Marty wanted to vomit, but there was nothing left to throw up. Instead he broke into a cold sweat. With sudden fascination he watched a cloaked figure step out of the shadows and follow Jeez.

She stopped at a floating black orb. She gazed into the black orb and watched children walking in the sunshine outside the mine. Weapons glinted in the sunlight. She made a face of disgust. The cloaked figure peered over her shoulder. Jeez sensed the presence and growled, whirling round. She squinted into the dim light, turning her head back and forth to see. She looked right at the cloaked figure without seeing anything. The man in the cloak never moved, he was invisible to everyone except Marty. The mysterious figure watched the scene in the orb. Young Jacob began to rally the children, he began to speak. Jeez focused on the boy. The cloaked figure reached out and stroked her hair. She hissed and whirled around. Thrashing at the air with her long taloned fingers. Her talons passed through the cloaked figure. The enigmatic man watched as his arm turned to dust as her claw raked through him. In the instant her hand was free of him, his arm had re-formed as though nothing had happened. She whirled back to focus on the black orb, but it was too late. She had missed the critical information the boy had given the other children. She watched as the children nodded. The entire group rose in unison and began to follow the blond child. They were moving toward the Dingh.

Jeez spit into the floor. The sputum sizzled and boiled on the surface of the black sand. She muttered out loud to no one in particular, "This is really beginning to annoy."

In a loud voice she commanded, "Black Guard, rise!"

The Dingh began to rumble. In a ring around the room, one after another, coffin doors opened from beneath the sandy floor. A ring of thirteen coffins opened. The commander of the Guard was the first to rise. His black skin was like leather, his eyes glowed red in the dim light. His voice croaked like an old bullfrog as he asked, "What are your orders, master?"

Marty blinked. Her face was emotionless as she said, "Defend the Dingh."

The other guardians rose from their shallow graves. They formed a ring around the Dingh. Silently they stood, swords pointed out, waiting for any and all attackers.

Chapter 16

A crowd gathered around Jacob in the open field. His voice was strong, his message direct. "Today, you are free. Free to fight for the freedom of another. More importantly, you fight for the freedom of your world. Jeez has held this planet in a dark cloud for over a thousand years. Isn't it time for her rule to end? Isn't it time to stand together and show her you will not stand for her tyranny? You are the first. You are the only ones able to do this. My father and I came here with nothing more than our belief we could stop her. We still believe, and we entrust that with you. You were once the oppressed, now you are mighty. Only those who are mighty can fight for freedom! You have won your freedom from the machine, now it is time for you to win freedom for Oronas! It is time for you to take back your planet!"

For the first time in a thousand years, a rally cry rose from the grassland. No one had stood in opposition since the Dark Temple had been built. For the first time, the people believed in something worth fighting for. For the first time, they were united against a common cause.

The sound of the mining transport sounded overhead. The children looked on it without fear. Ouna looked at Jacob. "I believe our ride has arrived."

Jacob looked at the unit as it landed. "How are we

going to take control?"

Ouna replied, "It's easy. They're self-guided. There is no one at the controls. The unit is designed to wait until the buggies are offloaded and full ones are loaded in place. Since nothing is going to come out of the mine, I can hack the controls and fly it manually."

Jacob stared at her in disbelief. "How could you possibly know that?"

She shrugged. "Mom was an engineer; I spent my entire childhood watching and copying her as she worked on hardware and sub-systems. Most of the programming is on a common platform. None of it is encrypted. No one here has a reason to steal one. I'm pretty sure I can take it off autopilot and fly it manually."

He grinned at her. "You're pretty amazing."

She shrugged. "It's a system. I can't move things with my mind or speak to creatures telepathically. I am a little intimidated by you."

Jacob looked a little taken back. "Why? I'm just a farm boy from the deep South. Plain and simple."

She started moving toward the transport. The unit had already off-loaded the buggies for the mine and sat idling. Huge engines throbbed as the group walked onto the back of the transport. Ouna moved forward to the cockpit. Inside, several indicator lights blinked and cycled. Nothing was labeled. She scratched her chin. "This might be a bit more of a trick than I first thought."

She studied the panel for a minute and mumbled to herself. "Engine thrusters over here, nav system over here," she looked up, "door controls here…"

She yelled back into the cargo hold. "Everyone,

stand clear of the door and hold onto something. It might get bumpy."

Jacob looked around the cabin. "There are no seats for the flight crew."

She never looked up. "There is no flight crew. Now be quiet while I think."

He stepped back and was silent. She punched a few buttons and the door closed. She pushed a few more buttons and the doors opened. She closed the doors again. She pressed another button and the engines revved up, but the rig didn't rise. Instead it shot dirt out from under. Ouna grinned sheepishly. "Sorry. Those were the landing thrusters."

She pressed the next button, and the unit began to rise. The sudden lift almost threw them off their feet. Jacob looked a little alarmed. "Are you sure you can fly this thing?"

"Relax. I used to fly the simulators. I'm just a bit rusty. Working in a mine will do that to you." The rig smoothed out and began to ease forward. They floated along the grassland. From this altitude they could see a dot in the distance where the Dingh was. They eased toward it at a slow pace. Jacob looked out the side window and could see the Dark Temple from his vantage point. He considered they would be fighting for their lives shortly. He tried to chase the thought from his mind.

****

Luna had slept for hours. It was daylight again. Fredrick looked at Brother O. "We need to move to the temple. There are machines located there that can help us with removing the creatures."

Brother O nodded. "Very well. I will guide you

there. We will use a cart for the lady."

Within an hour, the orn-drawn cart was loaded with food, water, and extra medical supplies. Luna was loaded onto the back and laid in a bed of straw and a hand-woven mat. They began the trek toward the Dark Temple. Luna's temperature had gone down. Brother O pointed to the place where they had stopped with Jacob. "We camped here the first trip. Do you wish to stop?" Fredrick looked ahead. "We keep moving. We can be there by dark."

The slow orn kept moving. Viktor would periodically appear, chewing on something. Fredrick asked him, "Viktor, what are you eating?"

Viktor shook his head. "Don't ask. Things we shouldn't eat but must, but must…"

Fredrick shrugged and kept moving at pace with the orn. At twilight, they reached the edge of the Dreaded Forest. Brother O stopped. He looked at Fredrick. "The forest has monsters. I will go no farther. Follow the path. When you arrive at the Dark Temple, turn the orn around and it will follow the trail back to the monastery."

Fredrick replied, "Thank you for your hospitality, Brother."

Brother O bowed. "It was my pleasure." He turned and started on his long trek back to the monastery. Fredrick led the orn into the forest. The trail was too narrow for the cart. He veered off the trail and tried to keep track of where it was in the waning light. He looked for Viktor, who was nowhere to be found. The cart jarred and Luna moaned from the back. Fredrick was forced to make a decision; it was too dark to move forward without a torch and there was nothing with which to make a torch. The orn mooed loudly. They had been traveling all day with few breaks. The beast was probably hungry and tired. A low, dense fog now covered the forest floor. There was no chance to see the trail. They were stuck. From the darkness a voice made him pause. “Fredrick.”

Fredrick whirled around. It was not Viktor’s voice, but it seemed familiar for some reason. As he turned to face the front of the wagon, a cloaked figure stood before him. The cloaked man repeated, “Fredrick.”

Fredrick squinted in the darkness. “Are you one of the monks?”

“No, Fredrick. I am someone from your past here to help you.”

Fredrick’s stomach knotted in fear, but he acted confident. “What makes you think I need help?”

The cloaked man replied calmly, “Because you’re lost. You know that. We need to turn the wagon around and move you back to the grassland for the night. It is too dangerous to be here. There are creatures that patrol this forest. Terrible creatures.”

Fredrick’s reply was laced with bravado. “What makes you think I am afraid of this place?”

The cloaked man held up one hand. A globe of white light lit the area around them. Red eyes glowed back at them. “Don’t let your ego put the ones you love in harm’s way. We both know what that will lead to.”

Fredrick wanted to come back with a snide remark, but the eyes scanning them made him think otherwise. “What do I need to do?”

The man in the cloak said, “Follow the light in my hand.”

As the man in the cloak began to move forward, he

guided them in a gentle arc until they were back on the trail. Fredrick couldn't understand how the man seemed to know where to go, but he didn't argue. He followed behind until they reached the vast grass plain. The cloaked man said, "You will need to go some distance from the forest. The creatures will not stray very far from the cover of the woods."

Fredrick asked, "Who are you, stranger?"

The cloaked man replied, "You wouldn't believe me if I told you."

Before Fredrick could respond, he disappeared. Fredrick could still hear the sounds from the forest behind him. The low growls and hissing noises made him cringe. He wished he had not walked into the forest at all.

When the forest was behind them, he stopped the wagon and unhitched the orn to graze in the grass. Luna sat up for the first time since they had started to travel. She yawned and said, "I'm hungry. Do we have anything to eat?"

He opened the sack in the back of the wagon. He sorted through a selection of dried fruits and jerky. He poured water into pottery cups. They drank and ate quietly in the darkness of the prairie. He lay back on the wagon with her. She nestled against him and they stared at the sky. For the first time since either of them had been on the planet, they could see the stars above. Both stared in silent wonder. The constellations looked different from here, but many of the stars he knew were there. The thought made him pause. Was Oronas in their solar system? How would it be possible for it to be there all this time and no one had detected it? And yet, he could see the Big Dipper over him. Luna snuggled closer to him. Soon they both slept under the starry sky.

Dawn cast an orange glow over the horizon. A breeze made the grass ripple in the wind. There was a crispness in the air Fredrick had not noticed before. Luna shivered in the cool morning air. He covered her with a blanket left by the monks. As he climbed off the wagon, a pair of worn jungle boots protruded from underneath the wagon. Viktor was sound asleep. Fredrick kicked his boot. “Do you want food?”

Viktor sat up and hit his head on the underside of the wagon. “Ow! Sheisse!”

Fredrick repeated his question, “Do you want anything to eat?”

Viktor crawled out from under the wagon. “Yes.”

Fredrick rationed out fruit, jerky, and water for each of them. He carried a bowl over to the orn and poured water for it to drink. It slopped the water and drank the bowl dry. The creature allowed Fredrick to lead it back to the cart to be hitched up once again. It was an incredibly docile creature. They began the slow journey back to the forest. The night creatures were all gone, but the dense black forest was no less foreboding. The fog thinned to the point where Fredrick could make out the trail. Even so, the wagon would occasionally swipe a branch, making Luna dodge the black limbs. They had only traveled a short while when the Dark Temple came into view. The smooth black obsidian walls appeared seamless as they rose to the sky. They followed the wall until a downed tree blocked the path. A creature pinned beneath the tree hissed and lunged at them. It lashed out with such ferocity Fredrick wondered if it was worth challenging. It was Luna who pointed to the seam in the wall. “That’s the door.”

Fredrick looked at Viktor. "This seems to be your area of expertise. What do you think we should do to get past this beastie?"

Without uttering a word, Viktor disappeared into the surrounding forest. Luna looked at Fredrick. "Now what?"

"Let's give him a moment, shall we?"

A moment later Viktor returned from the forest with a crooked black limb the size of a baseball bat. He walked up to the creature which lashed out and hissed furiously. Keeping himself out of range of the talons, he raised the club and smashed downward into the creature's head. There was a sickening thud and the hissing stopped. He raised the club and struck it twice more. A thick pool of green ooze glistened on the stone steps beneath the creature's flattened skull. Viktor threw the club aside. "That's how we get past the thing."

Fredrick helped Luna off the wagon and onto the ground. She struggled for a moment but smiled reassuringly to Fredrick. He walked to the seam and looked around for a way to open the door. A small carved piece of wood was protruding from an indentation in the wall. Fredrick removed the carving. His blood ran cold. The carving was a replica of the Ark. Without reacting to it, he said, "This must be a key." He replaced the carving in the slot and pushed it in. He could feel the catch give and the door cracked open. He pushed on the solid obsidian wall, which floated effortlessly inward. Viktor and Fredrick worked to unload the wagon and turn it back. In no time, they had moved the supplies into the Temple and turned the wagon in the direction of the monastery. Fredrick slapped the orn on the rump and watched as it moved slowly out of sight.

Inside, Luna led them to the front of the sanctuary. Past the altar, she studied the wall for a moment before depressing the indentation in the wall. With a quiet click, the door opened. They followed the smooth stone walls of the tunnel, stopping occasionally so Luna could rest against the wall. Fredrick asked, "How much farther?"

She replied wearily, "Not far."

She found the side tunnel and led them down the short ramp to the hangar. As Fredrick came into full view of the hangar, he let out a low whistle. "That's a big fleet."

Luna moved toward the closest ship. "She intends to conquer your Earth. It's all she thinks about."

Fredrick frowned. "Why?"

Luna shook her head. "That is a question for her. I don't know what the obsession is."

A single robot stood at the head of the flagship. With some effort, Luna got down on all fours and reached under the tracks and turned something underneath. She rose and pushed a button on its back. The panel dropped to reveal the circuitry inside. Viktor walked toward the rear of the ship. Luna called after him, "Viktor don't touch anything until I say it's okay. Do you hear me?"

Viktor grunted and sniffed the underbelly of the craft. This ship was longer than the others. It was easily the length of a soccer field and forty feet high.

Luna continued to work inside the panel, turning knobs and flipping switches. After a few moments she said to the others, "When I turn this thing back on, I need you both to remain silent while I give it voice commands."

On all fours she twisted the power control. The robot lit up like a Vegas light show. Luna spoke in her native tongue, Elterian. Fredrick had never heard her use the language before.

"*Oot frak nom deis fro nom Rose.*"

The robot responded, "*Nom Rose, oot frak.*"

Luna rose. She commanded the robot, "*Nok fremen dos nona explack dow.*"

She looked at Fredrick. "I'm done. We can board the ship now."

Fredrick asked, "What did you say?"

She closed the panel. "I reset the previous commands and set the control word to Rose. Which is something you could use if you needed to take over the ship. I disabled the security protocols on the Flag ship. No one can command the ship except for us."

Fredrick raised an eyebrow. "I don't mean to be insulting, but it seemed relatively simple."

There was a gleam in her eye as she replied, "Like every programmer, I wrote code as a back door. It's normally much more difficult. The robot protocol is linked to the flag ship."

He chuckled. "Smart girl."

She spoke in Oronian, "Lower the personnel hatch."

With a hiss, the bottom section of the ship tilted down into a ramp.

Luna motioned Fredrick to follow her. She moved to the forward section of the ship where the command center was. She began to power up the main consoles. There were no seats on the command deck, save one.

The captain's seat. Luna keyed in a seven-digit cipher on the console in foreign characters. A mechanized voice sounded throughout the flight deck, "Systems are at thirty percent, what are your orders, captain?"

Luna responded, "Bring systems to one hundred percent. Notify me in the infirmary when complete."

The ship responded, "Yes, captain."

She pushed herself up from the command seat and exited the bridge. "Let's get these things out of us."

As they walked down the corridor to the infirmary, lights continued to come on ahead of them. As they moved farther down the passageway, the lights behind them would shut off. Luna turned the handle on the infirmary door and opened it. Two bipedal robots approached them, identical except for color. The gray robot asked, "What is the nature of your problem?"

Luna responded, "This is Commander Luna Luxan. My logistics captain has a foreign body embedded in his torso. The object must be removed."

The white robot moved a gurney over to Fredrick. "Lay back, please."

Fredrick looked at Luna. "Why am I going first?"

She raised an eyebrow. "Do you know how to command the robots?"

He lay back on the gurney. "I see your point."

The white robot slit his tunic from the bottom to the top. With machine like efficiency, it scanned his torso with an x-ray matrixing system. Fredrick watched the screen as it mapped the image of the serqet inside him. The robot said nothing. It clamped a mask over his face and within seconds Fredrick began to see the light tunnel until there was nothing but blackness. It seemed like a moment later he was waking up. Luna was by his side. She patted the back of his hand. "It went very well. We only had to remove half your stomach and thirty percent of your intestines."

Fredrick's eyes grew large. "You did what?"

She laughed. "I'm joking. They removed the serqet with no complications."

He looked down and could barely see the incision mark. "That's impressive."

"I'm next. While I'm out, you can ask for food and drink and they will bring it to you." He eased off the gurney and to the floor. His belly was sore as he slid off the gurney, but he could walk without assistance. He rubbed his eyes and yawned. "How long was I out?"

Luna looked at a digital readout above his head. "In your time, I would estimate ten hours."

"So now that we know how to do it, I guess you'll be next?"

Her face was tight. "I guess so. I've given them a command to let you know when it's over. You don't have to watch."

Fredrick sensed she wanted him there. He reached over and kissed her on the lips. "I'll be here with you the whole time. I wouldn't leave you here by yourself for all the gold on Earth."

She touched his cheek gently with her hand. "You're sweet. A bit thick, perhaps, but sweet."

He laughed. "Let's get this moving. We need to launch as soon as possible."

She hopped onto the gurney. "Robot, advanced surgical protocol. Remove foreign obstruction in the anterior torso."

The robot responded, "Executing advanced surgical protocol. All clear."

****

Ouna set the mining transport down with expert precision. Jacob stared in awe as she deftly maneuvered the controls to set the ship down within twenty yards of the Dingh. He opened the hatch for her and asked, “How did you learn to fly one of these?”

She shrugged. “When my mom was the chief engineer on the larger ships. I grew up in a lab around these things. The controls are pretty easy once you understand the principle.”

“It’s a pity they don’t have spacecraft here.”

She blinked. “Well, they do. Lots of them. They’re in a hangar not far from here.”

Jacob’s eyes grew wide. “You mean like a spaceship we could fly away in?”

She nodded. “Is there any other kind?”

Jacob’s mind raced. “How do you navigate them?”

She thought for a second. “I think they have navigational programs. Mom worked on one of the nav systems for a while. She made it very simple, because they were intended to be flown by robots. Why? What are you thinking?”

Jacob looked her in the eye. “I’m thinking once we get Dad out of the Dingh, we try to find a way to plot a course for Earth. We could take everyone.”

He could see her eyes light up. “So we could leave here and go to another place?”

He nodded. “Yes. All of you.”

She hugged him again. It didn’t feel awkward this time. He hugged her back. In the open bay the other children just stared. After a moment a tall red-haired boy in the back shouted, “Enough already! Are we going to do this or not?”

Jacob and Ouna parted reluctantly. Jacob replied, "Let's go kick some demon butt!"

A cheer went up. Ouna lowered the bay door and the children flooded down the ramp and into the shadow of destiny.

****

Jeez brooded on her obsidian throne. The Black Guard stood with swords drawn, ready for anything that entered the Dingh. The eck fed Marty and gave him water. Surprisingly, he felt better. Some of his strength returned. He closed his eyes and meditated, blocking the pain and fear of the Dingh. The light of the Edajhia appeared before him. He entered the light and passed through the portal. Barb waited for him inside the portal. She sat in her favorite rocker with her Bible in hand. She reached out and patted the arm of a comfortable old tweed couch beside her. "Come here, honey."

Obediently, Marty sat next to her. She leaned forward and placed her hand on his. It was warm and tingly. Her eyes sparkled and shimmered as if energized with electricity. Her smile was comforting in such a dire situation. "Sweetie, from the time you were a little boy, I knew you would be a good and decent man. And you are everything I ever dreamed you would be. You are as dependable as a Swiss watch. And that is our problem."

Marty recoiled at the statement. "You're saying it's a *bad* thing that I'm dependable?"

She patted his arm reassuringly. "No, honey. It's not bad. It's predictable, and Jeez is using your predictability against you."

Marty was confused. "What do you mean?"

She carefully closed the Bible and set it beside her where there should have been an end table, but wasn't. The Bible sat in mid-air. "What I mean is, she attacked your wife, because there is a part of Gillian that is useful to her. Jeez is using Gillian's warrior instincts to carry out something she needs on Earth. You and Gillian are pawns in a much larger campaign."

Marty probed, "Are you saying she's manipulating us?"

"Yes, dear. She needs Gillian to recover a lost relic. Without giving it a second thought, you sacrificed yourself to come here to save her. Your selfless act is driving Gillian to reconcile her internal struggle. But *you* need to understand that Jeez is using you both."

"So what is this relic? What is she supposed to find?"

"It is not for me to say what the object is, all I can say is, it is vastly important to both sides. That is why it is so carefully hidden."

"So I've been duped because I'm a stand-up guy. Is there any way to get out of this mess?"

"Of course, dear. Hold your hand out."

Marty did as he was told. An orb of light appeared in Barb's hand. She gently placed it in Marty's palm and folded his fingers around it. She instructed him, "Blow into the orb."

Marty blew into his hand and to his surprise the orb began to grow larger. It grew until it was as tall as him. The orb began to take shape. The shape formed and refined until it was a replica of himself. He was staring at his twin. He moved his hand in an arc and the twin matched his move. It was as if he were staring into a mirror.

He walked around the figure and studied every detail. It was his exact double including cuts, bruises, and abrasions. He looked at Barb excitedly. "This is amazing!"

She chuckled. "I couldn't show you this before, because Jeez was eavesdropping. She's too distracted now. You can channel into anyone's past memory and make this doppelganger appear in any form you like, even the memories others tell you about."

"I don't understand. How does that help?"

"You can influence the right outcome. You can guide others to safety or where they need to go."

"You mean like time travel?"

"Sort of. While you can't physically go back in time, the echoes of the past are always resonating in the present. Let me give you an example. How did you find your way through the mines?"

Marty considered the question for a moment. "I saw a cloaked figure. He guided me through the tunnels." His voice trailed off at the end as he realized what she was saying. "You mean I guided myself?"

She replied, "Smart boy."

"So the cloaked figure I saw behind Jeez was really, *me*?"

Barb patted his cheek. "You're catching on fast."

Marty thought for a moment. "So logically, it means my future self was able to project an image behind Jeez. Which means I survive this somehow."

Barb stood and kissed him on the forehead. "I think that is enough for today's lesson. Now get back out there and play this game for real. No contest has ever been won sitting on the sidelines trying to survive, waiting for victory to come to you. So I need you to get up off your duff and get back into the game and show her what you've got."

Marty took the chiding in stride. "Got it, coach."

****

Brother Z sat over Retch. Her breathing was shallow, her color ashen. He watched the mining ship come toward them. He shielded her face with his robe to protect her from the turbulence of the thrusters as it landed. As the gate lowered, a large group of children flooded down the ramp. He watched in amazement as they formed a circle around him. In their small hands were weapons of every type. Some carried swords. Others carried bows. Some of the larger children had wooden-handled maces. The weapons glinted in the sunlight. The last person from the ship was Jacob. Brother Z breathed a sigh of relief. As Jacob approached Brother Z and Retch, the circle of children opened for him. Jacob looked at Retch and said, "She looks worse."

Brother Z nodded. "She's gradually gotten weaker. Age and stress have caught up with her."

Ouna stepped forward. "We have a medical kit on the ship. I'll get it."

Retch forced one eye open and in a faint voice, she said, "Let me die. It is my time. I have waited for you to return. She will summon the Black Guard." She took a breath and swallowed. "Your weapons can harm them, but the only way to stop them is with fire through the heart. Use your bows…" Her eye rolled back, showing only white. Her frail body went limp. A silence fell over the group. Jacob took her hand and said a silent prayer over her.

Brother Z stood. "Jacob, why do you care for this

witch? A short while ago she would have killed you if she could have."

Jacob looked up. "True. But that was then; this is now. In her final moments, she tried to help us. Anyone who has a change of heart should be forgiven. We should respect that. We need to bury her." He motioned to three of the larger boys to come forward. "Go get shovels. We must dig a hole."

The three boys ran back to the ship to retrieve shovels. In a short while there was a hole large enough to fit Retch. Gently, they lowered her into the ground and covered her face with her shawl. They shoveled dirt back into the hole. After a brief prayer, Jacob gathered the others around. "This is a dark place. I will lead us down with a white light. As we enter the Dingh, there will be soldiers waiting for us. Use your swords to defend until we can use fire to kill them."

He looked at two girls holding the bows. "Have you ever shot a bow before?" The dark headed girl shook her head. He reached for the bow. "Here, I'll show you." Jacob began using a skill Marty had taught him at an early age. He picked up the bow and aimed for the tree floating over the opening to the Dingh. His arrow centered the trunk. The children looked at each other, and a murmur rose up from the group. Two other children came forward with bows. Jacob looked at Ouna. "We need to set up some targets for the archers. What do you suggest?"

She considered the question for a moment and replied, "I say we keep it simple. We dig up some dirt into a pile and aim for that."

Jacob looked at the group. "Okay, guys, we need to start with making some piles of dirt. Who can help?"

The four boys who dug the grave stepped forward. The tallest one said, “We’ve got it. Where at?” Jacob pointed away from the group and the ship. “Over there.”

He turned back to Ouna. “We’ll need a battle plan. And some practice with the swords. This will be dangerous.”

Brother Z watched the group pull together under Jacob’s leadership. It was amazing to him the children could launch an attack on the Dingh without adults telling them how to do it. He sat quietly contemplating how he and the monks had hidden away in the monastery for years waiting for someone to come to them. Perhaps it was their faith, or perhaps it was their fear. It was time for his order to do something to help. “Jacob.”

Jacob looked up from their battle plan sketched in the dirt. “Yes?”

“It is time for me to return. I see now our order must go to the city and try to help people. It is a time of great unrest. We will travel there and try to do what we can.”

Jacob rose and hugged Brother Z. The action surprised him. No one had given him a hug since he was child. Jacob looked up. “Thank you for everything. You made all this possible.”

Brother Z was surprised. “I did?”

Jacob responded. “Of course. You fed me and guided me to the places I needed to go. You’ve been a great help.”

Brother Z hugged Jacob back. “Thank you, Jacob, for everything. You will always be the Chosen One. You have done more than you know. For that, we will always be grateful."

"Safe journey, Brother Z."

"Safe journey, Jacob."

Brother Z gathered up his remaining food and water and walked across the grassland to return to a different Oronas. A neglected world in need of direction. A direction he and his brothers could provide.

As he departed, he could hear the excited buzz as the children planned. He said a silent prayer for them. It was the first prayer he had uttered in years. He assured himself a higher power was listening to him. He resolved to himself the prayer would be answered. It was part of his new beginning.

Chapter 17

The president was greeted by Rex Logan, head of the National Security Council, as he approached the Oval Office. "Mr. President, we need you in the situation room."

President Franklin Lee Pierce sized up Rex with a calm gaze and replied, "Who made the coffee, Rex?"

Rex smiled. "It's French roast, sir. Just the way you like it."

The president knew from the response he would be spending most of his day in the situation room. There would be no house bill reviews today. The President's valet, Hans, trailed behind them on the way to the West Wing. Hans never left the president's side. Rex tried not to dwell on the six-foot-five behemoth following them. It was just part of who President Pierce was. Before he was president, everyone knew him as Uncle Frank. Everyone in power knew who he was and respected him. It was only after a landslide victory in the election that the rest of the American public knew him. Oddly, the press left him alone. He was the first widowed president ever elected. He was also the first who had no previous history in politics and the first who neither the House nor Senate challenged. He was an enigmatic character everyone seemed to embrace. Uncle Frank made it clear he would be president, not because he wanted to, but because the country needed him. It was like George Washington had been resurrected.

As they entered the Situation Room, everyone stood. The room went silent as the president settled into his chair at the head of the table. "All right, why am I here?"

General John Blackstone, head of the Joint Chiefs of Staff, replied, "Mr. President, at Oh-Three-Thirty-Three EST, the Black Spider reconnaissance satellite positioned over the Indian Ocean observed a planetary body of unknown origin in a mirror orbit to Earth."

The president lit his ever-present cigar and took a puff. "You're telling me a planet popped up out of nowhere?"

General Blackstone replied, "That is correct, sir. We immediately took control of SETI at Hat Creek, California, and blacked out all press. We have been monitoring the radio signals from the space and found there is considerable RF traffic coming from the planetary body."

The president blew a smoke ring at the ceiling and stared at the ceiling while deep in thought. "General, we've been staring at the skies for as long as mankind has been around. How do you think we missed something like that?"

"That's a great question, Mr. President. One we don't have an answer to yet."

The president scanned the room. They were all ranking military personnel or NSA directors. He focused back on General Blackstone. "Jack, it seems we have a healthy representation of armed forces here, but I don't see one single scientist. I want to see a fifty percent ratio of security professionals to scientists in this room. I need you to reach out to the best astronomers and physicists in our network. Invite them here. If we have spotted this planet, then it won't be long until our friends to the east will as well. What we don't want to happen is for one of our allies to report this to the public before we do. The people have a right to know. Work with the Press Secretary on how to word the press release this so it doesn't cause a panic. Now, how about some images of this new world?"

General Blackstone projected his screen so everyone could see. He began to circle areas of the image for emphasis. "As you can see here, it appears to have cloud cover in areas, meaning there is the presence of water in the atmosphere. We do not have detailed images to see if there are signs of organized life forms, but we are receiving radio signals. We haven't been able to translate those yet, but there is a clear modulation to the signals that are representative of intelligence."

There were circles and arrows and boxes all over the image. The president stopped him. "Jack, erase all of that crap. Let's look at this world for just a second. This is the first time we've seen a new planet in our solar system in ninety years. Let's just take it in for a moment, then you can get back to your tactical analysis, okay?"

General Blackstone replied humbly, "Yes, Mr. President." All the markings went away leaving an unobstructed view of the new planet.

After a moment of silence, Mark Russo, the Director of the NSA, spoke up. "Mr. President, since it was one of our satellites that observed the new planet, we can claim first knowledge and name the discovery."

The President thought for a moment. "Well, Mark, if there is intelligent life there, they might already have a name. When we meet them, we will ask. How about that?"

Russo nodded. "Yes, Mr. President."

"Jack, you might want to consider getting ahead of the press on why our fourteen-billion-dollar Black Spider, charged with keeping an eye on the enemy, was looking off into space."

General Blackstone cleared his throat. "Uh, yes, Mr. President."

Blackstone motioned to one of his aides. There was a hushed intense conversation after which the aide left the room.

The president studied the planet, taking in the swirls and colors of the low-resolution image. "Jack, how long before we can get the Goliath telescope in range, or even Hubble? Anything is better than this."

General Blackstone sat back. "Yes, sir. The Black Spider was designed to focus on Earth-bound images. The refractor quality was not intended for deep space. We're working with NASA to turn all guns on this new planet. For now, we have named it Planet X until we have a definitive name. Our initial thoughts were if Planet X has developed stealth technology, or if this is not a planet at all but a large ship, then we are at a disadvantage."

The president puffed again. "True, but if you had a tactical advantage that significant, why would you turn it off? Unless someone on the inside of their system is a saboteur. That would indicate unrest. If there were hostile intentions on the part of the population, we could leverage that to our advantage. At this point, it's all speculation. Let's refine what we know. I will be back in two hours. I want a full briefing on staffing strategies of how we will gather more information. That is all."

The president stood. As he left the Situation Room, he whispered to Hans, "I need to make a call in private. Let's head to the booth." The booth had been installed in recent years as a secured room incapable of intrusion by listening devices. After the White House systems were hacked by a group of cyber terrorists, a stand-alone system had been developed that was impenetrable by outsiders. It was a small, austere room with a single desk and thick, soundproof walls. A gunshot could not be heard from the outside when sealed. The president stepped into the room while Hans waited outside.

He keyed in the number near Geneva. It rang twice before a gravelly male voice answered, "Bonjour?"

"Hello Jacques, it's Frank."

"Hello Frank, or should I say Mr. President?"

"Very funny. I suppose you heard about what we found?"

"You mean the planet no one seems to know anything about? Yes. We got wind of it from a Russian deep space telescope studying the sun. They were making adjustments, and it came into view. They were all quite surprised."

"As were we. Have you noticed any anomalies at CERN?"

"Interesting you should ask. We had special plates made to capture collisions with Bailor—Ortez particles. We were going to use them in the collider and noticed they were ruined."

"Are those the dark energy particles? How were

the plates ruined?"

"Yes, the hypothesis is BO particles are trace energy signatures made by decaying dark energy. The best description we can come up with is anti-photons. They are extremely hard to detect, because while we have models that can predict the wave patterns of photons, it appears that the BO particles travel in a double helix pattern, which we're not able to calculate. We normally run the collider to generate the proper field to capture the images of the BO particles, however, this plate had never been used in the collider and it was riddled with the BO particle collisions. Some were so dense they could almost be seen with the naked eye. We are quite confused. It's as if a dark energy explosion happened somewhere close by."

"That is interesting. Is there any way to assess trajectory?"

"As it stands now, no. Why do you ask?"

"Just a hunch. I find it interesting that you have an anomaly showing evidence of a large release of dark energy and now can suddenly see this new planet."

"Humm. If I were to read between the lines, I would say you have an interesting hypothesis, Frank. So you think this planet was under the cover of dark matter and something caused the dark matter to catastrophically fail?"

"Something along those lines. It should give you a puzzle to work on for the next few days, yes?"

"Indeed. I'll call you when I have some thoughts."

"Au revoir, Jacques."

"Au revoir, Frank."

The line went dead. Frank sat for a moment pondering. He relit his cigar and blew a smoke ring.

Instantly the ventilation system sucked it out and there was no trace of the smoke. Frank blew another smoke ring at the ceiling and watched it quickly dissipate. He smiled with satisfaction at the thought.

He pulled the door open and moved toward the Oval Office with Hans close behind. Behind the Resolute desk, he picked up the handset and called the Deputy Director of the CIA. The phone rang only once before a female voice answered, "Yes, Mr. President."

"Hi, Shelia. Can you swing by sometime today? We need to talk about our small operation in the Middle East."

"Certainly, sir. I have some interesting footage that might be good for you to see. I had planned to put it in the report."

"Bring what you have. The report can wait."

"Yes, sir."

"Meet me in the Oval Office at eleven."

"Very good, sir."

He dropped the phone in the cradle. He streamed the image from the Situation Room to his computer. It was a beige-looking planet and rather unappealing at first glance. He sat back and studied it in detail. A small black speck on the planet's surface was almost undetectable. It caught his attention. Of all the possibilities the new world had to offer, the one black spot made him pause. It was a melanoma on the skin of that world. He wondered if it would spread its cancer to Earth. He reached into the bottom drawer of the Resolute desk and pulled out a bottle of twenty-five-year-old Macallan single malt scotch and poured a single shot into a cut crystal glass set on the desk for that purpose. He sipped the scotch and looked at the black dot on the screen. His finger tapped the glass as he thought.

Hans spoke for the first time this morning. "Frank, it's time."

"Thank you, Hans."

He tossed down the scotch and stood. He was curious to see what Blackstone had put together. He hoped it was something better than he had seen earlier.

****

Gillian noticed the drone for the first time as they stopped to refuel the Cherokee. It seemed to be too high tech for the Egyptian police, but out of character for Gretchen. It hovered at a discreet distance but maintained line of sight. She got back in the Cherokee and waited. Wilhelm wandered out with a sugared-down frozen blue drink of some kind while Jhazelle sipped from a bottle of water. She handed a spare to Gillian. In the seat between Gillian and Wilhelm rested the Heart of Ptah on the acacia wood. It continued to point north. Jhazelle looked at the road sign and said, "We're about one hundred miles from Tel Aviv. Jaffa was annexed by the Israelis. If we stay along the coast, we will miss the West Bank and there will be fewer check points."

Gillian replied, "I like that idea." She kept her eye on the drone in the rearview mirror.

Wilhelm noticed her watching the mirror. "Relax, we'll be out of Egypt in no time. The Egyptian police will have no jurisdiction in Israel."

Heat shimmered off the road as they moved across the Sinai. She kept her eye on the mirror. "I'm not so worried about the Egyptians as I am wondering who is controlling the drone that has been following us for the last five miles."

Wilhelm jerked his head around. "Drone? What drone?"

Gillian's voice was calm. "About one hundred yards behind us on the passenger side. It was originally much higher. It went down in altitude when we stopped. It looks like a military grade, long-range observation drone. We'll have a better idea when we reach the border."

Wilhelm strained his neck to catch a glimpse of the drone. Gillian continued to glance in the rearview mirror. As if it were appearing from the ether, a black Saab turbo emerged from the shimmering heat of the scorching Egyptian highway with blue and red lights flashing. Gillian knew there was no way they would outrun the Egyptian police car in the Cherokee. Wilhelm's eyes widened at the sight of the police cruiser bearing down on them. "Are they after us?"

Gillian replied calmly, "Do you see anyone else out here they might be after?"

Wilhelm stared at her wide-eyed. "What are we going to do?"

Gillian patted him on the knee. "When he pulls up behind us, we'll pull over. Then we'll talk."

"But what if…"

Gillian cut him off. "Wilhelm, you control one of the most powerful economic syndicates in the world. I'm sure we can figure something out."

Jhazelle watched the scene unfold from the back seat. The banter confused her, the influx of things pursuing them frightened her. She wondered silently why she had ever involved herself with these people. She looked behind her. The dark form of the driver of the Saab was clearly visible. The car was barreling up on them. She felt like she was going to vomit. She sat back in the seat and looked forward, stemming the tide of panic rising in her throat. When she looked in front of them, she could not contain the scream. Two black SUV's were on a collision course with them. She felt the jerk as Gillian slammed on the brakes in the Cherokee, throwing her forward in the jeep. As she vaulted forward everything around her melted into slow motion. Her head went between the bucket seats and wedged between Gillian and Wilhelm. Gillian's arms were locked on the steering wheel. She watched as Gillian's hair fell forward and covered her face. Wilhelm grabbed the Heart of Ptah before it fell into the floorboard. Both SUV's moved around them on either side, missing them by inches. Jhazelle stared in horror as they shot past. The smell of burnt rubber as the tires screeched on the road filled the cab of the Cherokee causing both her and Wilhelm to cough violently. Only Gillian turned in her seat to watch the scene unfold behind them. Jhazelle heard the wrenching jolt of metal behind her. She pried herself from between the seats. Gillian unbuckled her seatbelt and shouted, "Stay here."

Gillian exited the vehicle, careful to keep herself behind the Cherokee for cover. Skid marks on the pavement were evidence one of the SUV's had swerved the rear end of the vehicle into the Saab. The driver of the Saab wasn't moving. Two men from the other SUV aided the driver of the crashed SUV from the vehicle. The driver of the wrecked SUV wobbled a bit as they guided him to the other vehicle, but there was no blood evident. The police officer behind the wheel of the Saab had not fared so well. Gillian could see the blood streaming from his ears as his forehead rested against the steering wheel. A cloud of steam flowed from the front end of the Saab. One of the men from the SUV started walking toward the Cherokee. He raised his hands in the air and held out a cell phone toward Gillian. She stood still as the man approached.

He called out, “We mean you no harm. I have a call for you.”

Gillian replied, “Stop there. Set the phone on the ground and back away with your hands in the air.”

The man stopped. He carefully laid the phone on the ground and backed away. Gillian cautiously stepped away from the cover of the Cherokee and eased toward the phone, never taking her eyes off the man. She picked up the phone and said, “This is Gillian.”

Gretchen’s voice was on the other end. “The men are with the Mossad. Go with them. Tell them where you need to go. They will take you there.” The line went dead.

Gillian walked back to the Cherokee. “Come on, we’re switching vehicles. Grab your gear.”

****

The roar in his ears competed with a pounding headache and all but overpowered any chance of concentrating on the situation. With superhuman effort, Captain Nimr focused on what the emergency services technician yelled at him. It was like the man was yelling at a jet engine. “Don’t move!”

Nimr took a deep breath and looked around. The twisted metal of his Saab turbo wrapped around him was contrasted by the chimney of steam coming from under the hood. The smell of burning wires and hydrocarbons riveted his attention back to reality. He watched as the rescue workers argued over how to crank the giant cutting tool intended to free him from the wreckage. He assessed his options: Wait on a contrary extraction tool, or free himself and jump from the vehicle which was about to explode. The latter of the two options seemed logical. He released the seatbelt and pulled himself upright. The smell was getting stronger. Two technicians yanked desperately at the pull cord trying to get the cutter running. Nimr maneuvered himself away from the steering wheel toward the passenger side and struggled to climb under the collapsed passenger dash and crawl out the opposite window. He finally worked himself free, fighting back the intense pain in his right leg. It was probably broken. None of that would matter if he was trapped in a blazing inferno. He gritted his teeth and pulled himself through the shattered passenger window. The technicians, still focused on the cutting tool, yelled at each other, trying to get the contrary cutter started. Nimr yelled out, “Hey! Come over here and help me!”

Startled by his shouting, the larger man holding the tool dropped it and it landed on his partner’s foot. His partner screamed in agony. Nimr shook his head in disdain. The technician ran to the passenger side and helped him crawl free of the car. As he fell toward the technician, the man caught him under the arm, sending a shock wave of intense pain through his body, almost making him vomit. He wondered how many ribs were broken as he kept moving. A loud whistle from under the hood grew louder. The technician’s partner cursed as he limped behind them. As the trio moved behind the ambulance for shelter, the explosion from under the hood of the Saab rocked the ambulance and melted the paint on the exposed side to the blast. Nimr collapsed to the ground. The two technicians began to argue on the best course of treatment. After listening to them for a minute, he placed two fingers in his mouth and whistled. The men stopped arguing and stared at him. Nimr looked at the man who had pulled him from the wreckage and said, “Just put me in the truck and take me to the hospital.”

Two fire engines arrived and began to fight the inferno of the burning car. Nimr watched from the back window of the ambulance as the fire fighters hosed his car. He had loved his car. It irked him it was a total loss. What irked him more was he was about to close in on the kafirs when the black SUV ran into him. He would find them if it was the last thing he ever did.

****

Shelia Collins waited on the Victorian sofa made of walnut and beige satin outside the Oval Office. The turn of events in the Middle East was dramatic and mysterious. The president entered the Oval Office with Hans close behind. She stood as he entered. The president motioned her into his office. “So, Shelia, what do you have for me?”

She handed him an “Eyes Only” file sealed with red tape. “Well, Mr. President, we had an unexpected turn of events. As you’ll see in the file, Gillian Wood and two companions, Wilhelm Lindenspear and an unidentified Egyptian female, were traveling along El Arish Rafah Road as an Egyptian National Police vehicle was in pursuit. It appears that two unmarked black SUV’s turned onto the highway from a secondary road and moved in a collision course toward the two vehicles. The two SUV’s maneuvered around Wood’s vehicle, and SUV One swerved the rear quarter panel into the front end of the ENP vehicle."

The President scratched under his chin and commented absently, "Fascinating." He stepped over to the Resolute desk and removed a bottle of scotch from the bottom drawer. He held the bottle up. "Would you care for a taste, my dear? It's a safe zone here."

Shelia remembered the rumors of the president drinking scotch. He only offered a drink to those he trusted. She replied, "That would be lovely, sir."

Without looking up he asked, "Ice?"

"Neat is fine, sir."

She walked over to his desk and sat in the chair across from him. The president sat back and took a modest sip. He looked up at the ceiling for a moment, as if in thought before returning his gaze to Shelia. "So it appears that someone is working to protect Ms. Wood. Without committing, who would you think that someone would be?"

Shelia took a sip of an exquisite scotch. "Sir, I have been able to isolate all assets we have in that area. All our CIA and deep cover operatives are accounted for. The assets were not ours. Data from our signal sweepers correlates to an increase in traffic from Israel to their agencies. The vehicles in question are standard issue Mossad transport. If I were betting, my money would be on Tel Aviv ordering the intervention. Why, is the bigger question. We simply don't have enough depth within that organization."

The president took another small sip. "It's interesting that Wood is traveling with Wilhelm Lindenspear. He was just reinstated to his father's estate by the German court system. As I remember, his father, the Duke, had deep ties to Israel for many years. I can't imagine that his organization would have left that relationship idle after the Duke's disappearance ten years ago. The important thing now is to keep tabs on where they're going. Our concern is not who rescued them, but more, where are they headed next. Mossad agents are quite crafty. Watch them carefully. They will pull a shell game to misdirect us. As a side note, how is the driver of the ENP vehicle?"

"Rescue workers extracted him from the wreckage before it blew up. He is being transported to Cairo for treatment."

The president nodded. "And what type of vehicle was the officer driving?"

Shelia's eyebrow furrowed for a moment while she tried to remember. "A Saab turbo as I recall."

The president inspected his cigar. "That is not a standard issue ENP vehicle, which means the person pursuing them was a ranking commander. To take someone out of the office to chase our friends means he's fixated on them. He will not stop until he has some closure. It is their way. You will need to keep an eye on him."

Shelia tried to contain her surprise. This was the first president she had ever dealt with who knew her business as well as she did. "Yes, sir. We'll assign a watch detail."

"Very good, Shelia. Keep me updated as you have new developments."

"Yes, sir." She started to leave but stopped. "Sir, if I may take the liberty?"

The president raised an eyebrow. "Of course."

"Sir, I've known many presidents over the last

twenty years. I have never met anyone, president or director, who has your insight. How do you do it, sir?"

The president responded, "I'll tell you someday, Shelia. But today is not that day. Go dig up what you can."

"Yes, sir."

The president returned his gaze to the file she left for him. She left the scotch glass on the table beside the door to the Oval Office. She couldn't help thinking he was truly one of the most interesting men she had ever met.

****

The driver of the black SUV used an access card to enter a parking deck of a luxury apartment building in the Dokki district off Damascus Street. They grabbed their bags as three of the agents in the team walked to a parked SUV, leaving behind one tall, muscular agent. The agent guided them down the hall to the spacious apartment. He addressed the group. "My name is Benjamin. My instructions were to intervene and protect you. I will not interfere with your primary mission, but respectfully, I must guide you through the territories."

Gillian scrutinized his face to look for signs of stress. "So you're assigned to help us?"

Benjamin replied, "Yes."

Gillian replied bluntly, "We're not really sure what we're going to find, but it might be an artifact that is historical and significant. Is that a problem for you?"

Benjamin's expression never changed. "Everything in this region is historic at some level. My purpose is to support you, so long as you are not here to deliberately injure our people."

Gillian looked at him evenly. "We don't want to hurt anyone. That is not our purpose."

Benjamin replied, "Then there should be no problem. We will rest here overnight and leave by boat in the morning. We have a fishing trawler that will take us to Tel Aviv."

Gillian asked, "Can we dock at Jaffa?"

Benjamin furrowed his brow. "Of course. There is little there. It is a fishing village."

Gillian replied, "That's where we need to start."

"Very well. Jaffa it is."

Jhazelle tugged at Gillian's T-shirt. "Can we speak?"

Gillian looked around and moved to one of the four large bedrooms. Jhazelle looked down as she spoke. Her voice almost cracked as she said, "I-I'm afraid. I don't know what I've gotten myself into, but I'm in way over my head."

Gillian rested her hand on Jhazelle's forearm. "It's okay to be afraid. I've been doing things like this since I was sixteen. I don't know any other way of life. But it doesn't mean that I can't respect you just because you're afraid. We'll look out for you. Together we can be very strong. I saw something in your home that makes me believe you were destined to be a part of this. Let's work together to help you find that strength. Okay?"

Jhazelle nodded. She looked up and her eyes welled with tears. "Would you stay with me in my room tonight?"

Gillian touched her hair. "Of course. But if this is going to be a slumber party, we probably need some supplies."

Jhazelle cocked one eyebrow. “Slumber party?”

Gillian’s grin grew larger. “In America, when teenage girls get together for a sleep over, it’s called a slumber party. Girl talk, fashion trends, boys…”

“Oh. I’ve never had a slumber party with friends.”

“Neither have I. It’ll be a first for both of us. Unfortunately, all I’m good at is guns, choke holds, and explosives.”

For the first time, Jhazelle smiled. “Me too!”

Gillian laughed. “Should be quite the party. I’ll get the wine.”

Without a word, Gillian walked through the living room to the kitchen. She stopped at the stove and opened a pot slowly bubbling with a spicy aroma. She replaced the lid and systematically opened each purple wooden cabinet until she landed on one with several bottles of wine. She grabbed a bottle and two drinking glasses from the cabinet next to it. Benjamin looked up from a copy of The Times of Israel and eyed her from across the living room. “Is there anything you need?”

Gillian opened the drawer beneath the wine cabinet and dug through kitchen implements to retrieve a corkscrew. “Nope. I’ve got everything I need right here.” She held up the wine bottle and glasses. “Jhazelle and I are bunking together tonight. We’ll see you guys in the morning.”

She started to walk back to the room and stopped. “What’s on the stove?”

Benjamin resumed reading the Times and replied from behind the paper, “Lamb stew. It’s my mother’s recipe. I hope you like it.”

Gillian looked at the label on the bottle of wine. “After a bottle of this Basque, I could probably eat an old army boot and think it was good."

Wilhelm watched the scene silently from his chair. His heart sank at hearing the girls would be spending the night tucked away in their room. It surprised him to realize he might have feelings for one or both of them. His crush on Gillian had not waned since Italy. He tried to deny his feelings, telling himself she was attractive, and he was just following his instincts. But now, he was forced to face his feelings he was developing for Jhazelle. He turned back to his phone and flipped through internet sites on sailing ships to distract him. Bored, he looked at Benjamin, who was still buried in the newspaper. "Benjamin, are there any night clubs around here?"

Benjamin lowered the paper and looked at him. "There are a few. But I suggest that we get some sleep tonight. We don't know what we will encounter tomorrow on the way to Jaffa."

Wilhelm sighed. "All right. Do I get my own room, or do I have to bunk with you?"

Benjamin raised an eyebrow. "You have your own room." He pointed to the room closest to the balcony. "You even have you own private balcony if you would like to sit outside."

Wilhelm pushed himself out of the lounger. "I'm good."

****

At six a.m. Benjamin rapped on the door. Gillian pushed through the lingering effects of two bottles of the Basque wine and lamb stew from the night before. She sat up and poked Jhazelle in the back. "Come on, kid. We've got a boat to catch."

Jhazelle snorted and rolled over in the bed. Gillian

walked to the bathroom and climbed in the shower, washing away the cobwebs. As she stood under the hot water, she heard rustling in the bathroom. She pulled back the curtain to find Jhazelle's head poised over the toilet. The girl retched a second time and flushed but not before the smell made its way to Gillian. Suddenly, the water in the shower turned scalding. Gillian yelped and pushed the lever down, turning the water off. Jhazelle rinsed her face in the sink and looked over at Gillian soaking in the shower. "Sorry."

Gillian toweled off and asked, "Are you going to be okay?"

Jhazelle rinsed and spit. "Yeah. I'm the daughter of a fisherman. I've felt worse. I'll be fine once we're on the water. It's calming to me to be on the water. I was born there."

Gillian replied, "Say what?"

"My mother sailed out with my father the day I was born. My father delivered me in the back of the fishing boat. He said I was the greatest catch he ever had."

Gillian laughed. "Well let's see what we can catch today in Jaffa. Maybe we'll be as lucky." Gillian stepped out of the shower and Jhazelle disrobed and climbed in. Gillian asked, "Do you want me to flush one good time?"

Jhazelle poked her head from behind the shower curtain. "You had better not."

Gillian finished dressing in the bedroom. Benjamin waited for them in the spacious living room on an overstuffed couch. A large urn of coffee sat beside the tray of falafel and goat cheese on a wood inlaid coffee table in the middle of the room. Wilhelm watched as

Gillian spread some cheese on a crusty falafel and bit into a satisfying crunch. She poured coffee as Jhazelle walked out of the bedroom drying her hair. He almost gasped as the light streamed through the balcony windows making Jhazelle's hair glitter in the morning sun. Everyone in the room stopped to stare at her for a moment. She frowned and asked, "What?"

Wilhelm chimed in from an armchair across from Benjamin, "You're glowing, darling. Literally."

Jhazelle made a "Humph" sound and moved to the coffee table where she poured a cup of coffee and drank it black.

Benjamin glanced at his watch. "We need to leave in three minutes. The morning rush will jam up traffic."

Gillian shoved the falafel in her mouth and carried the cup of coffee to the bedroom. She retrieved her backpack. Jhazelle followed and stuffed clothing into her bag. The girls emerged from their room, ready to go. The trip to the docks only took a few minutes in the early morning traffic. Benjamin parked at a private pier and opened the rear door to the SUV where everyone grabbed their bags.

The black boat was tied off at the pier. The name was painted in Arabic on the aft of the boat. A large crow squawked noisily at them as they walked up. Jhazelle stopped dead in her tracks. Gillian turned back and asked, "What is it?"

Jhazelle stared at the letters on the thirty-foot sailboat. "The name of the boat is the Black Jinn."

Gillian shrugged. "You mean like the drink?"

Jhazelle looked her in the eye. "No. It is the English equivalent of 'demon'."

Gillian's eyes turned hard. "It's just a boat. I live

with a demon inside of me every day. Let's go so we can stop this thing."

Jhazelle looked Gillian in the eye. "It's a bad omen."

"And we'll make it through. Trust me. Let's get going."

Jhazelle moved forward, never taking her eyes off the ship's moniker. The captain was a large, jovial man in a Chicago Cubs ball cap. "Come along, girls. I'm your captain. My name is Izzy. There's nothing haunted about my boat. The name keeps the river pirates away."

The first mate, Jumah, was casting off lines for them to make ready. He almost lost his balance as he stared at the girls walking up the rickety gangplank to board the ship.

Jhazelle whispered to Gillian, "Why does that man stare at us?"

Gillian whispered back, "He's a sailor, honey. I suspect if we were forty years older with a peg leg shared between us, he would still stare."

Jhazelle giggled. "Probably more so."

Gillian called out to the captain, "Captain Izzy, where do we put our bags?"

He pointed at the door leading into the cabin. "There's a storage closet in the cabin, toss them in there." He turned and yelled at Jumah, "Get those lines cast off so we can make way, Jumah!"

The thin young man scampered around the dock like a rabbit. He jumped back and forth, throwing off the remainder of lines before hopping back onto the boat. Jhazelle watched him thinking about how much energy he had.

Benjamin pulled Izzy to the side. Gillian watched a

brief, tense discussion between the two just out of earshot. She tried to read Izzy's lips but it was impossible because of his angle. She moved into the cabin and stowed her bag in the small, cramped closet, then moved to the tiny galley where a pot of strong Turkish coffee was on the small stove. She poured a cup and sat on a sturdy wooden bench at the table. She sipped the coffee and considered what to tell the captain. Jhazelle sat beside her on the bench. She placed a cup of coffee in front of her.

Gillian asked, "How are you feeling?"

Jhazelle gave her a weak grin. "Better. I probably should not have cracked that second bottle of wine. I'm not much of a drinker, but it was so *good.*"

Gillian bumped her with her shoulder. "It was, wasn't it?"

Quietly they sipped their coffees.

Wilhelm poked his head in the galley. "So this is where you got off to. Did you save any coffee for me?"

Jhazelle looked up. "No."

He grinned. "That's cold." He grabbed a tin cup and poured some. He looked around for creamer and sugar. Finding none, he shrugged his shoulders and sipped the dark, rich blend. He made a low whistle. "Wow. I don't guess I should plan to sleep for the next couple of days. So what's the plan?"

Gillian looked up. "We go to Jaffa and follow our compass."

His brow furrowed slightly. "That's it? That's your plan?"

She replied, "I know it doesn't sound very precise, but it will work out. You'll see."

"Uh, okay. What if doesn't?"

Her face lacked expression as she replied, "You fly back to Austria and call it a day."

He sipped his coffee again and made a face. "How do you drink this stuff?"

Gillian replied, "It's an acquired taste."

He pushed his cup toward her. "No kidding."

They felt a gentle lurch as the ship moved away from the dock. Wilhelm chatted with the girls about Tel Aviv night life and the incredible beach parties on the Metzitzim Beach. Jhazelle peeped out the windows as Wilhelm droned on about The Havana Club. Calm seas ushered a smooth launch as they headed north. Jhazelle yawned and looked at Gillian. "If you don't mind, I'm going to take a nap."

Gillian nodded, while Wilhelm took little notice. Jhazelle walked to the forward section with hammocks. She slid into the bottom hammock and fell asleep almost immediately; the sounds of the ocean lapping against the hull were balanced against the steady hum of the big diesel engine. She dreamed of the Heart of Ptah spinning in the air in front of her like a top. The half-moon shape spun faster and faster until it formed a perfect circle. As it floated, the Heart modulated and morphed until it appeared as a sphere, half blood red, half aquamarine. She watched in fascination as a thin vertical line of pure light began to form in the center, growing brighter and brighter until the intensity of the light almost blinded her. Fixated on phantasmagoria, she was startled by warm hands caressing her shoulders. She tore her eyes away from the event to find her mother behind her. Her touch was comforting. Her mother moved her hand to her cheek. She leaned forward and whispered into her ear, "Only the worthy can see Poseidon's Stone."

Jhazelle looked into her mother's eyes. She was young and beautiful, like Jhazelle. Her features were translucent as if she were made of glass. "What do you mean, mother?"

Her mother traced her finger under Jhazelle's chin, like she had done when Jhazelle was a child. "Not all of those you travel with are worthy. Not all that seem unworthy are so."

"What does that mean?"

Her mother moved her finger to cover Jhazelle's lips. "You will understand when the time is right. For now, awake and be ready. Mother Earth will test you. Trust your heart. It will always lead you to the truth."

She awoke with a jolt as the hammock swung and struck the wall in the small quarters. She heard shouting from the deck above. The boat groaned as if under some tremendous strain. Jhazelle struggled to push her legs free from the hammock as she reached out to wood frame for steadiness. She reached out again to pull herself free from the hammock. Her hand caught something warm and strong. She looked up to see Wilhelm standing before her. The happy go lucky charming playboy was gone. His eyes were like steel. "We've run into some sort of squall. We need to move to the deck above."

As they moved through the galley, Wilhelm held her hand to steady her while he kept the other hand on anything that would keep them upright. Pots clamored to the floor in the galley as the ship lurched again. Gillian appeared before them with life vests. Jhazelle looked at Gillian's cargo shorts. The Heart of Ptah glowed through the fabric, making an eerie image on her leg. Gillian spoke above the groaning of the ship, "Izzy said we might have to abandon the ship. They're preparing lifeboats."

Jhazelle asked, "What is wrong?"

Gillian helped her with her life vest. "It appears to be some type of large whirlpool the ship is trying to stay out of. It's all Izzy can do to keep it away. If the engine fails, we're goners."

The timbers of the ship groaned again. Gillian looked at them and said, "Let's move above before we get caught down here."

They moved up the stairs to the deck above into a pelting rain just in time to hear a large timber crack. The back of the boat shuddered under the stress. Izzy worked frantically at the wheel to turn the ship as the diesel engine below roared. Izzy gave the throttle one more kick to break free. The back of the ship began to sag. One of the main timbers of the hull had broken. Water was coming in as they limped free of the vortex. Jumah struggled with Benjamin to get the rubber dinghy in the water. A final backfire signaled the end of the engine below deck. Izzy jumped from the wheel and shouted to Jumah, "Let them get the dinghy in the water, come help me fix the leak!"

Jumah handed the second rope to Benjamin and scooted below deck with the captain. Wilhelm ran to Benjamin's side and took the second rope from him. Together they lowered the dinghy. Benjamin looked at Wilhelm and said, "Get the girls, I'll get the dinghy started."

With that, he jumped over the edge into the water below. Wilhelm waved to Gillian and Jhazelle to come over. They heard the engine start on the dinghy.

Benjamin moved away from the ship and throttled the engine up. Wilhelm stared in disbelief. “Where’s he going?”

Gillian scowled. “On his way to Hell if I have anything to do with it. Let’s get this other boat in the water.”

They unhitched the second dinghy from the deck and quickly moved it over the edge of the boat. Gillian looked at Wilhelm. “On three, we lower together.” They lowered the ropes in tandem. As the dinghy lowered, the Black Jinn began to list to the other side. This made it difficult to position the dinghy for a safe exit. A scream from below deck did not bode well for Izzy and Jumah. Jhazelle looked back and forth between the dinghy and the cabin, appearing uncertain on what to do. Gillian made it clear. “We can’t help them now. Get to the dinghy.” Wilhelm climbed down the rope ladder and held it steady for Jhazelle. Gillian followed. Once on board the dinghy, Wilhelm began to pull the rope on the outboard engine. It sputtered but did not crank. The ship began to roll beside them. Gillian grabbed an oar and pushed them away. Jhazelle followed suit with the other oar. Wilhelm primed the engine one more time and began to pull the cord. On the fifth try, the engine coughed to life. It smoked terribly but continued to run. Slowly, they began to move away from the ailing ship just in time to see the stern sink below the waterline followed by the bow slowly submerging.

Jhazelle whispered, “Only the worthy can find Poseidon’s Stone.”

Gillian stared at her. “What?”

Jhazelle looked up at her. Her eyes were distant. “I

had a dream. My mother told me only the worthy could find Poseidon's Stone."

Gillian's eyes narrowed. "Then that is what we are supposed to find in Jaffa."

Jhazelle's eyes grew wide from panic. "How can you know that? It was just a dream."

Gillian consoled her, "I know someone who is led by dreams. I've learned to trust those dreams. I can't understand it; I just know we must follow the guideposts."

Wilhelm brought them back to reality. "Where should we head?"

Gillian pulled out her phone and looked at the compass. She pointed east. "Go back to shore. We don't have enough gas to get to Jaffa. I hope we have enough to get back to the coast."

Wilhelm kicked a can at his feet. "The spare can is half full. That should get us close enough."

The engine sputtered along. An hour later they could see the shoreline in front of them. The engine coughed its last drop of fuel and went silent. Without a word, Gillian grabbed an oar and began to paddle. Wilhelm grabbed the other oar and followed suit. Slowly, the shore took shape. The beach was deserted save a few men fishing from the surf. Between strokes Wilhelm asked, "Where do you think we are?"

Gillian looked in both directions. "We must be close to Gaza. There doesn't seem to be very much here."

Wilhelm scanned the shoreline as he rowed. "How do you know we're not in Gaza?"

Gillian gave him a sideways glance. "If it were Gaza, you would know it."

They kept paddling. Gillian kept her eyes fixed on the shore looking for Israeli military. Fishermen stopped and stared at them as they rowed in on the waves. When they were close to shore, Gillian hopped in the surf and began to pull the dinghy forward. On the beach, they walked away from the dinghy toward the beach access. The sun was high in the sky and the beach hot as they slogged through the orange sand to the road. Jhazelle looked at Gillian, and then at Wilhelm. "Now, what?"

Gillian looked in both directions. "First we get a car, then we get food." The tired and hungry trio walked for a mile before reaching the outskirts of the village of Zikim. An old man slept in his cab in front of the small restaurant with an Israeli Defense Forces armored carrier parked in front. Gillian nudged the old man through the open window. He snorted and sat up. He squinted up at Gillian. "Yes?"

"Can you drive us to Ashkelon?"

The old man rubbed his nose. "It depends."

Wilhelm handed him two hundred dollars. The old man took the cash and counted it. "Welcome, friends. It would be my pleasure to drive you to Ashkelon." He cranked the engine on the old Volvo. Wilhelm and Jhazelle hopped into the back seat and Gillian slid in beside the old man. She looked at him saying, "We're trying to avoid any confrontation with the IDF."

The old man turned the car around in the street and said, "As are most of us."

As they rode, Gillian looked straight ahead. "Is there a place where we can get food and water?"

"We'll go by Cali's. You can eat without people asking many questions. Where did you come from?"

Gillian looked forward. “Our boat sank at sea. We escaped on a raft and came to shore. We were headed to Jaffa.”

“That’s too far north for me. But we can find you a car in Ashkelon.”

The barren landscape along the desert road to Ashkelon provided little to look at save scattered rocks and orange sand. They passed less than ten cars on the way to Ashkelon. The Cali Restaurant was on the outskirts of Ashkelon and thrived in the local economy. As the old man dropped them off, he parted by saying, “Ask for Hiram. He can arrange to take you to Jaffa. Shalom.”

Inside, the restaurant was cool compared to the desert sun. Patrons chatted and paid little attention as the odd trio entered. There were only a few patrons in Cali’s who looked up as they seated themselves at the counter. A young, dark-haired server eyed Jhazelle suspiciously. She asked, “What do you need?”

Gillian responded, “Food and a driver. We were told to ask for Hiram.”

The young woman’s face softened. “The kebabs are good. Our mint tea is delicious.”

Gillian smiled disarmingly. “Then, kebabs and mint team it is. And Hiram?”

She wiped the counter in front of Gillian. “I’ll send him out.”

She poured all three of them mint tea. Though hot, it was amazingly refreshing.

Gillian swung around and stood to meet a portly older man with a fraying black and white yamaka. “Are you Hiram?”

“I might be. Who are you?”

"My name is Gillian. This is Wilhelm and Jhazelle. Our boat sank off the coast. We're trying to find a driver to Jaffa."

"That's a very long journey."

Wilhelm stuffed four hundred dollars in Gillian's waiting hand. She handed the bills to Hiram, who made no pretense of counting them in front of her. Finally, he looked up at Gillian. "I'll have the car out front in fifteen minutes."

When she returned to the counter, her food was waiting. There was no conversation as they ate the lamb kebabs and humus. As he scraped the last morsel from the plate, Wilhelm stood and motioned to the darkly tanned woman behind the counter. She stared at the three clean plates on the counter. She looked at Wilhelm. "Either the food was very good, or you were very hungry."

He replied. "Both."

Hiram waited out front in an old beige Mercedes with the engine running. Gillian climbed in the front. Hiram cocked his round head in her direction. "Where to?"

Gillian looked straight ahead. "Take us to the old port in Jaffa."

"We should be there in an hour." He put the car in gear and hit the gas, throwing Wilhelm and Jhazelle backward in the back seat. Jhazelle's hand landed on Wilhelm's belly. She was surprised at how tight it was. He had the belly of a fisherman, not a playboy. She pulled her hand back and said, "I'm sorry."

Wilhelm grinned. "I'm not."

Jhazelle giggled.

Gillian ignored the two. The Heart of Ptah was

getting warmer in her pocket. The ride along Highway Four was remarkably different than the road from Zikim. The barren desert evaporated and made way for palm trees and lush undergrowth. It was like a different world here. Gillian's eyes remained alert for being followed. As far as Benjamin knew, they had died on the boat along with Izzy and Jumah. She was curious about what Benjamin would report back to Gretchen. If Wilhelm were thought dead a second time, it would prove to be a greater problem for Gretchen. For the moment, it wasn't her problem. They would find a phone in Jaffa and report in. But not before they found whatever it was they were supposed to find. Jhazelle giggled again from the back seat. As they entered the outskirts of Tel Aviv, Gillian glanced in the side mirror again. She caught a sudden movement from behind. She lowered the vanity mirror on the driver's side and watched as a large Israeli Army jeep came up behind them. "Hiram, we have some company coming up fast."

Hiram looked in the mirror. "So I see. Let's add some excitement to their day." He eased over in front of an old man in a produce truck. The timing was perfect. Hiram jammed on the brakes, causing the old man to swerve in front of the Army Humvee. The Humvee swerved to the left to avoid the produce truck. Hiram jerked the wheel to a hard right and down the off ramp out of the line of sight from the Humvee. At the bottom of the ramp he swung into traffic, then maneuvered into a residential neighborhood. He drove until he could cross back under the interstate from behind where they had exited. The Humvee was hopelessly trapped on the interstate with dozens of cars honking for them to move on.

Gillian was impressed. “That was quite a tactic.”

Hiram grinned. “Nothing an old cabbie can’t handle.”

Gillian met him with a sly grin. “Not bad, cabbie, not bad.”

“I’ll get us there through some of the old neighborhoods. It will take a few minutes longer, but not too much.”

The Heart of Ptah was getting more uncomfortable in Gillian’s pocket. She looked at Hiram. “Could we stop somewhere? I need to use the restroom.”

Hiram chuckled. “A little too much excitement for you, huh? No problem. There’s a park a few blocks ahead. We can stop there unnoticed.”

Hiram eased in between two large delivery trucks in the parking area. Gillian hopped out of the car. “Jhazelle, do you need to go?”

Jhazelle looked away from Wilhelm for a moment. “No, not really.”

Gillian narrowed her eyes. “Are you sure?”

Jhazelle got the message. “Uh, sure, now that you mention it.”

Wilhelm looked at Gillian. “What about me?”

“You should be fine.”

Wilhelm sat back in the seat with a glum look on his face.

Gillian grabbed Jhazelle under the arm and pulled her along toward the restrooms. She burst through the door, startling two teenage girls preening in the mirror. Jhazelle was startled when she pushed her into a stall with her and locked the door. Gillian dropped her pants revealing a red mark on her leg. She looked at Jhazelle. “Can you touch it?”

The two Israeli girls fell silent at the mirror.

Jhazelle reached over and touched the Heart. "It feels normal to me."

There was a snicker from one of the teenagers.

Gillian replied, "Well, you can have it then. I can't stand it anymore."

The other teenager tittered.

Gillian sighed. "Let me deal with those two twits." Gillian concentrated on the overhead fan in the room. She diverted the energy to the water faucet beside one of the Israeli girls. The spigot came on abruptly, splashing her. She jumped. There was a low dialog between the girls and Gillian heard them leave the restroom. She returned her attention to Jhazelle. "This thing is burning me every time I get near it. I need you to carry it."

Jhazelle shrugged. "Okay."

Gillian sighed. "You'll need to get it out of my pocket."

"Oh. Can we open the door now that those girls are gone?"

Gillian undid the latch and peered out. The water was still pouring from the spigot. Jhazelle exited the stall and waited for Gillian to follow. Gillian removed her shorts, careful not to touch the Heart. She held the pocket toward Jhazelle, who fished it out with great care. She stuck it in the front pocket of her jeans. "Are we good now?"

Gillian got a funny look on her face. "Yes, except for one thing…" She turned and lunged back into the stall, throwing up in the toilet. She spat and wiped the sweat from her face. She knew the feeling. It was the same feeling she had when she was first pregnant with

Jacob. Morning sickness. This was going to be a problem.

Jhazelle looked at her, her eyes were large. "Are you okay?"

Gillian replied, "I'll be fine. Must have been the kebabs."

On the way back to the car, Gillian stopped at a vending machine. She leaned against the machine for a moment staring at the symbols in Hebrew before asking, "Jhazelle, can you help me get a bottle of water?" Jhazelle dug in her handbag and pulled out a credit card. She swiped it and pulled a bottle of water from the machine, handing it to Gillian. Silently, Gillian cracked open the top and drank nearly all the contents of the bottle. "Thank you."

At the car, she motioned to Wilhelm to open the window. A rush of cold air washed over her from inside the car. It felt wonderful against the hot breeze across the parking lot. "We're going to let Jhazelle sit in the front with Hiram and I'll sit with you in the back."

Wilhelm opened the door and slid over so she could sit beside him. Jhazelle looked a little confused but moved to the front of the vehicle beside Hiram. Gillian sat and rolled the window up. Hiram called from the front, "Where to?"

Gillian looked at Jhazelle and said, "Show him the way, Jhazelle."

Jhazelle stared at her, puzzled for a moment before her look of confusion turned to understanding. Gillian guessed she had connected to the lifeforce in the Heart. She watched her for a moment as she began to guide Hiram through the complex of back streets toward old Jaffa. She turned to Wilhelm. "What happened in

Milan?"

He met her gaze directly. "That night in the hotel, it was like you were someone different. You awoke from a nightmare. When I went over to check on you, you got really…physical."

"Just how physical?"

"Let's just say that I've never experienced that kind of intensity from a woman in my life. And I've had my fair share of experiences. This was different, though. It's almost as if you were someone else. I can't really describe it in a way that makes any sense."

Gillian was quiet for a moment. "I think I'm pregnant."

Wilhelm's eyes grew wide and his mouth dropped.

Tears formed in her eyes. "My husband is risking his life on a foreign world to save me, and I'm carrying another man's child."

Wilhelm placed a hand on her arm. "It wasn't your fault. If you weren't in your right mind…"

Gillian jerked away from him and looked out of the window. A mixture of anger and shame filled her. Her mind raced. *What had she done? What would Marty say? What would Jacob think?*

Wilhelm moved away, giving her some space. He stared straight ahead. The weight of her statement settled on him. Gillian was pregnant with his child. In all his years, he had never had children. The thought drilled through his cavalier armor; he was going to be a father.

Gillian composed herself and turned back to him. "I'm sorry I reacted. This is not your fault. I'll deal with it. You don't need to worry about this."

Wilhelm turned toward her. His countenance was

different, and his eyes bore a seriousness she had not seen before. "I've been a ne'er do well all my life. Everyone has bailed me out of one fiasco after another. Adalyn, Chris's mom, was the first person to show me what a true parent's love is supposed to be. I was in her home in Kingston; they lived in a suburban home. Her neighbor's son, whom she had cared for as a baby, was grown and a drug addict. One evening I was sitting in the kitchen with Chris and Adalyn and the young man burst into the kitchen through the back door with a butcher knife to rob them. I started to stand, and Chris placed his hand on my shoulder. I watched as Adalyn picked up an iron skillet, knocked the knife out of his hand, and proceeded to backhand him with the same skillet on the side of his head. She picked him up by his shirt and sat him in a chair. When he came to, she made him apologize, and then fed him some pea soup. When he finished, she sent him home to tell his mother what he had done. When I was a drug addict, no one made me address my addiction. She showed me what it was like to be accountable while still showing him she loved him. Up to this point, I've never made a decision that was anything other than self-serving. I think the time has come. Please let me help you with this."

Gillian was silent for a moment. She was unprepared for Wilhelm's response. Carefully, she replied, "I want my husband back. I want all of him. I would appreciate you helping him to see that this was not a casual affair."

Wilhelm nodded. "I will do everything in my power."

The cab lurched suddenly as Hiram jerked it back into the lane. He was busy eavesdropping on Gillian and Wilhelm. Jhazelle reached over and pinched his ear, twisting it. "You need to pay attention to me. I'm giving the directions here."

Hiram swallowed hard. "Yes, miss."

She pointed ahead to a single turret piercing the sky. "Go to that tower."

"You mean to St. Peter's Church?"

"I don't know what it is, just go there."

He pulled the Mercedes into a parking lot and stopped. "This is as far as I can go with the car. You'll have to walk from here." He pointed to a stone path that wove through a lush green lawn.

Wilhelm pulled out several one hundred-dollar bills. "Do you take American money?"

Hiram licked his lips. "Certainly."

Wilhelm shoved five hundred in the man's hand. "Is that enough to keep quiet on where you dropped us?"

"Well, my mother needs surgery. We might have some unexpected expenses." Wilhelm handed him another five hundred. "Will this cover your pain and suffering?"

Hiram grinned, showing large yellow teeth. "This will certainly help mother rest comfortably."

Wilhelm's voice was flat as he replied, "Best wishes to your mother."

Hiram counted the one hundred-dollar bills and answered distantly, "Many thanks."

The three stood on the walk as the Mercedes accelerated out of the parking lot.

Wilhelm looked at Gillian. "How long do you think we have before he rats us out to the authorities?"

Gillian glanced at her watch. "We've probably got

a half-hour head start. Which isn't much, considering we don't have an exit strategy. Let's concentrate on finding the artifact, whatever it is."

Jhazelle looked at the tower. "It's somewhere over there, but it's underground."

Gillian finished off her water and tossed the bottle into a waste container. She started following the path to St. Peters. As they approached the modern white edifice, she looked for something less modern. They began to circle the complex. As they followed the cobblestone stair to the street below, she pointed to two stone arches leading under the church. "I think that's our best bet. What about you, Jhazelle?"

She looked absent. "Yes. The feeling is stronger there."

Inside the arch, the air was cool and damp compared to the heat of the late day sun outside. Jhazelle stopped at a rough-hewn cyprus door with a chain looped through two large iron eyebolts terminating in a rusted lock. "We need to go in here."

Gillian pulled out a small lock pick kit from her cargo shorts. Because the lock was so rusted, she struggled with the tumblers for a moment before she heard the satisfying *click* of the lock opening. She pulled the door open to cobwebs and utter darkness. From another pocket she removed a small, powerful flashlight. She motioned the others into the chamber. The tunnel was filled with pipes, and conduits stretched for thirty feet ahead before turning a corner. She pulled the door closed behind them. The trio walked carefully in the single beam of the flashlight amongst the littered remains of debris on the tunnel floor. Broken cobblestones, pipes, and trash created a treacherous path ahead. They eased down the narrow tunnel to the turn where it seemed to widen slightly without the debris field at their feet. After several minutes of walking, Jhazelle said, "Stop!"

Gillian looked back. "What is it?"

"There's another opening here."

Both Wilhelm and Gillian scanned what appeared to be a solid wall. Gillian scanned the wall with a flashlight. "I don't see it. Are you sure?"

Jhazelle nodded. "I can't explain it, but I can see it. There was an opening here once. It's been stoned up. This is where we need to go."

Gillian sized up the wall. "Where is the center of the opening?"

Jhazelle pointed. "It is here."

Gillian gingerly kicked the wall. Her foot went through a thin facade. They could hear water running on the other side. She pulled her foot free. She looked at Wilhelm. "Help me push these rocks in." Between the two of them they cleared the opening in a few minutes to reveal an aqueduct on the other side.

Gillian stepped across the threshold onto a small ledge. She held out her hand to guide Wilhelm and Jhazelle. As the three settled on the ledge that traveled along the aqueduct, Gillian moved the flashlight around them for a moment to evaluate their surroundings. As she moved the light beyond Jhazelle, a thick, coiled yellow viper was less than five feet from her feet. Without thinking, Gillian drew a throwing knife from a hidden pocket in her cargo shorts. In one fluid motion the blade flew with deadly accuracy behind the head of the viper, sticking upright in its body. Jhazelle shrieked. The tunnel reverberating along the closed channel. The snake's body spasmed, almost falling off the ledge. Gillian worked her way past Wilhelm and Jhazelle and retrieved the razor-edged black throwing knife from the body of the snake. She bent over and rinsed the blood off in the water of the aqueduct before returning it to her hidden pocket. She moved the light around the aqueduct to look for other creatures lurking in the dark before saying, "Keep your eyes open. It appears that there are other crispy critters down here. Jhazelle, lead the way."

Jhazelle's eyes grew wide in the dim light. "What?"

Gillian leveled her gaze on the girl. "You are better connected to this place than we are. Lead the way."

Jhazelle blinked. Her hand trembled as she took the flashlight from Gillian and worked her way past Wilhelm, grazing his hard belly with her nails. She could see the goosebumps rise on his arm. She began to move down the ridge carefully. She moved steadily, holding the flashlight down so all three could see their footing. The Heart began to vibrate lightly. As she moved forward, it became almost violent in its movement. The farther she moved, the more it subsided. She stopped abruptly, making Wilhelm bump into her. She looked back at Wilhelm and Gillian. "I think we need to go back."

Wilhelm arched an eyebrow. "Why?"

"We've gone too far."

"How do you know?"

She narrowed her eyes. "I just know. Now, go back."

She handed the flashlight across to Gillian, careful not to touch Wilhelm. She looked at Gillian. "I'll tell you when to stop."

They began to backtrack toward the opening. Jhazelle could feel the Heart begin to lurch in her pocket again. "Stop."

She reached into her pocket and pulled out the stone, which pulsated red. As she stretched her hand out over the water, the stone began to move more violently, almost tugging itself free from Jhazelle's grip. As she pulled it back to her, it calmed. "We need to cross over here."

Wilhelm looked at her. Even in the dim light she could see his eyes were wide. "What about snakes?"

Jhazelle looked back at Gillian. "Watch me when I go in the water."

Gillian nodded. Jhazelle hopped into the water without knowing how deep it would be. She was able to touch bottom easily and spring back up. She reached the other side easily and followed the ridge. There was a cavity in the wall at her feet. She turned to Gillian and held up one hand. "Throw me the light."

Gillian made a deft underhand toss and the light landed squarely in Jhazelle's hand. The stone was moving wildly in her pocket. She took a deep breath and went under water. The cavity was a narrow tunnel, just large enough for her kick her way through. After a few kicks, she emerged in a large stonework chamber. Even without the flashlight she would have been able to see the glowing aquamarine half-moon piece embedded in the wall at the end of the chamber. She swam back through the tunnel. As she popped up, Gillian and Wilhelm were sitting on the ledge with their feet dangling in the water.

She called out excitedly, "I found something!"

Gillian slid into the water and Wilhelm followed. In a moment they were beside her. Gillian pushed her hair out of her eyes and said, “Lead the way.” Jhazelle took a deep breath and swam through the tunnel again. This time as she exited, she held the light so the others could see. Triumphantly, she pointed. “See?”

Gillian squinted her eyes in the dark. “Not really.”

Wilhelm’s eyes were wide. “Oh, wow.”

Gillian turned to him. “You can see it?”

Wilhelm nodded. “Goodness, yes. It’s amazing.”

Gillian looked at the two of them. “Work together to see if we can obtain the piece. I’ll hold the flashlight.”

They swam to the back of the chamber. As they drew closer, roughly hewn stone stairs were under them. The three approached the relic cautiously. Jhazelle reached out and tried to touch it. Her hand was repulsed by an invisible force. She tried again. This time her hand was thrown back more forcefully. Jhazelle looked at Gillian. “You try.”

Gillian reached forward with no better result. She looked at Wilhelm. “Your turn.”

Wilhelm stared at the aquamarine half-moon imbedded in the marble face. He reached forward. He winced as his hand was drawn to the relic with so much force it slapped as it landed on the disk. He wondered if it had broken his bones. There was an audible *crack.* He stared at the aquamarine, which was glued to his hand as he drew it away. The chamber swirled around him with sparks of light. A low rumble began to resonate through the chamber like an earthquake. Bits of debris fell from the walls and ceiling. Wilhelm opened his hand to reveal the smooth aquamarine disk with a gold

Trident in the center. A confusing cacophony of voices ripped through his mind. One voice became clear. *Kneel to the power of Poseidon.* Wilhelm dropped to one knee holding the disk forward to no-one. The girls stared at each other.

Gillian looked at him curiously. "What are you doing?"

"I don't know. The voice inside my head told me to kneel."

Gillian placed her hand on Jhazelle's shoulder. "He has been chosen."

Jhazelle looked from Gillian to Wilhelm. "Chosen for what?"

Gillian's eyes narrowed. "To wield the power of the object."

A sound behind them made Gillian pause. She grabbed the flashlight from Jhazelle and pointed to the back of the chamber. Multiple black objects were coming their way. She recognized the Uzi barrel on the object to the front. "Wilhelm, we need to leave this place. What do we do?"

Wilhelm blinked. He reached out with his hand and touched the wall beside them. The shockwave passed through the chamber like an explosion. The men coming behind them screamed as the concussion hit them with unparalleled force. The wall under Wilhelm's hand collapsed into rubble allowing light to stream in from the bright sunlight outside. The bright light cast shadows across the men floating face down in the water.

Jhazelle stared at Wilhelm wide-eyed. "How did you do that?"

Wilhelm shook his head. "I wish I knew. Let's get

out of here."

They exited on a hillside facing the ocean. A group of tourists stared at them as they filed through the opening half the size of a door. Gillian waved at a group of tourists that were clearly American. "Hey guys! That was an amazing part of the grotto tour. It has a pretty darn dramatic finish. You really should inquire at the front office."

A rotund man in a red Hawaiian shirt, black socks, and white leather athletic shoes nodded. "Uh, yes, ma'am. We'll be sure to do that." His wife and children peeped out from behind him like chicks under a mother hen.

Gillian led Wilhelm and Jhazelle down the path away from the opening and into the narrow cobblestone streets of Jaffa. They stopped at a small coffee shop along the portside and gathered around a small worn table aged with stains. The shop owner brought them Turkish coffee and falafel balls, then hurried away from the table to help the next customer.

Wilhelm stared at his hands, as if he were seeing them for the first time. He looked up at Gillian. "What has happened to me."

She placed one hand on Wilhelm's hand and the other on Jhazelle's. "You have awakened something deep within you. You have had a glimpse of what you are truly capable of, now it is time for us to finish what we set out to do."

Jhazelle stared at Gillian, her eyes were wide. "What is that?"

Gillian shared her motherly side she reserved for Jacob when she reassured him everything would be okay. "We go to where the disk leads us. And we wait for whatever happens next."

Wilhelm looked at Gillian. The concern in his eyes was unmistakable. "What do you mean?"

Gillian's voice was solemn as she replied, "We are being led by a power beyond our understanding. Everything we are doing at this moment has a purpose, we just don't have the perspective to see it. What we do now is trust an unseen force and let it guide us where we need to go. Because we are being shown the way, we will also know when we've reached our destination."

Jhazelle's deep green eyes widened. "How will we know?"

Gillian squeezed her hand reassuringly. "We'll know. We always do."

Chapter 18

Jeez perched upon an obsidian throne like a gargoyle and glared at Marty from across the Dingh. Torturing him was not nearly as rewarding as she thought it would be. He continued to defy her worst attempts to break him. It was unlike anything she had ever experienced from a mortal. She hurt him and healed him so she could hurt him again. And yet, he refused to break. More frustrating still, he seemed capable of shielding her from his mind. Humans were so easy to manipulate. No human had ever been able to block her. She suspected Rachael had given him some divine trick to keep him sane, but whatever discipline he was using, it had none of her resonance. It was a puzzle, and puzzles annoyed her. She considered killing him, but a thought nagged her he was more valuable alive than dead.

The Black Guard stood stoically waiting to defend their keep. Their hearts were black with hate. Their swords yearned for the taste of blood. But they stood like memorial statues in a cemetery. She weaved in and out of the Black Guard as she worked her way around the Dingh. She wondered if she should try to seduce Marty again, but decided after all the torture it would be as wasteful as her last attempt. She had turned his skin inside out, and then returned it to normal. She knew the pain had to be excruciating and yet, he stared at her, his eyes never wavered. He never looked away.

He watched her now. Calmly. Silently. Her frustration with him was behind her now. She was annoyed at herself for not breaking him and bored with the whole charade. She sensed the boy was mounting a rescue. Her guards would deal with him and whatever rabble he had managed to pull together. She would fight them off and make them die painfully. The screams of children were always satisfying. The messages that Mine Number Four had been destroyed had reached her. It was of little consequence. She had mined enough red crystals to fight ten thousand wars. If she needed more, she knew how to get to them. She didn't care if it took the remaining population of Oronas to do it. None of it mattered anyway. Once she launched the fleet, she would leave this place behind.

****

Jacob conducted drills throughout the day and into the night. The miners fenced, shot arrows, rolled, and tumbled until they were weary. They learned quickly and were the most serious group of people he had ever met. He guessed being a prisoner in a mine for any amount of time hardened you. He stopped them from training when the sky was black, and the stars shone brightly. Traces of the dark matter shield around the planet floated by and blocked out the stars. It was eerie for Jacob to look up into fathomless black. It was more eerie for the others because none of them had ever seen the night sky.

Jacob led them back into the mining ship to sleep. Tomorrow they would attack. The ship had been made for humans at some point. They found unspoiled metal containers of food chips and water.

As the door closed on the ship, Jacob addressed the group, "For your whole life you have lived as prisoners on your own world. You've done nothing wrong. And now you have a chance to be free. What we're going to do is dangerous. No one knows what is in the Dingh. The only thing I know is that we are the only things standing between my father and certain death. I will get him out of there or die trying! When we win, when we leave, you are welcome to come to Earth. It's a good place where people don't try to hurt you all the time. Get some sleep, and we fight in the morning."

One hundred pairs of eyes stared back at him. None knew what to say. No one had ever given them a notion of freedom. A dark-haired girl with torn, dirty clothes rose from the crowd and eased her way up to him through the others. All eyes were upon her. "Jacob, what is this place like?"

He looked at the group thoughtfully. "There are trees and birds and lakes to swim in. We grow food, we celebrate good times, and we're sad during bad times."

The dark-haired girl shook her head. "I don't know what any of those things are."

Jacob paused for a moment. He began to understand when his dad tried to explain to him about Aunt Barbara and the farm and all the things he had done there as a boy. He had never understood why his dad had been frustrated when Jacob couldn't relate to any of those things. Now he understood. He took the dark-haired girl's hands. They were rough from using a pickaxe. He gently kissed the top of her hand. She blinked at him. Ouna raised an eyebrow at him. He released her hands. "Was that gentle and nice?"

The dark-haired girl nodded silently. Jacob said,

"Earth is a thousand times gentler than that."

The dark-haired girl worked her lips into an awkward smile. It was the first time she had ever smiled. "Oh." She returned to a small clutch of girls who gathered around her. They chattered quietly among themselves. Occasionally, one would look away from the group toward Jacob, and then turn back to the group.

Jacob looked back at Ouna. Quietly he asked, "Did that help or hurt our cause?"

She whispered back, "We'll know in the morning. If half of them are gone, we'll know. We've been surviving for so long from one minute to the next, what you said doesn't even make sense to them. We were all with our parents to a certain age but were removed when we didn't pass the emotional exam."

Jacob raised an eyebrow. "What's an emotional exam?"

"An interviewer asks a bunch of questions and if you don't react to enough of them, you're sent to the mines."

Jacob's look of revile was obvious to Ouna. "That's barbaric."

"It is, but none of us knew that until we failed. Evidently, the parasites they call the serqet feed off dopamine. The faster you get excited, the faster they grow."

Jacob shook his head in disbelief. "Let's get some sleep. We'll see what we have in the morning."

Jacob went to the cockpit of the ship. He sat upright and concentrated on his father. Within seconds, his dad greeted him.

"Hello, son."

"Dad, I'm coming to get you. I've got help."

"I know, son. So does she. She is waiting for you with the Black Guard. There are several of them. I can only see the ones in front of me, but there are more. They are the undead."

"Retch said we can kill them with fire through the heart."

"There is a secret tunnel the eck dragged me through. Split your group into two. Half come straight ahead through the main opening; the other half comes down the tunnel. Son, Jeez lives for torturing the living. Are you ready for that?"

"I can't leave you here. We know of a way to leave the planet. I've promised them they can come with us."

"If we live, I would welcome them. Son, I was wrong to come here."

"No, Dad. We did this for Mom. You did the right thing."

"When you arrive, I will fight with you. Don't hold anything back."

"I won't."

****

The early dawn light streamed through the cockpit windows waking Jacob and Ouna. Jacob opened the hatch to the cargo area and looked over his army of little people. He was encouraged when he saw no one had fled during the night. They exited the transport unit to find purple hues and crimson streaks washed the break of day. Jacob gathered the people around him. "We have two ways to enter the Dingh. One is a secret tunnel; the other is the spiral staircase." He pointed to the boys who had dug the grave for Retch. "Can you make it through the tunnels?"

The tallest boy nodded. "What do we do when we get there?"

Jacob asked, "What is your name?"

"Ook, sir."

"Ook, follow the tunnel to the end. It will lead to the Dingh. Wait until you hear us attack and come in from behind. My dad will be in the center of the room. We need you to free him, while we attack from the front. We will go down the main stair. Archers, wrap your arrow tips in straw. Torchbearers will light the arrows. Archers, aim for the Black Guard's chest." He pointed to the center of his chest. He pointed to the swordsmen. "When you attack, fight in pairs. It will be harder for them to fight two. Stay far enough away that the archers can get a clear shot. Do you understand?"

The young men with swords nodded solemnly. The dark-haired girl looked at Jacob. "Tell us about Earth again, Jacob."

Jacob looked at one hundred pairs of expectant eyes. He took a deep breath and relaxed. "There are insects that have colorful wings. We call them butterflies. We have places people our age go to called school. They teach us things. Best of all, we have people who love each other. We take care of others because we love them. I don't think there is anything better than that."

The dark-haired girl looked at him. "What is love?"

Jacob thought for a moment. He looked to his right, and then to his left. Ouna stood behind several others. He moved toward her. She stared at him with wide eyes. He took her hand and led her back to the center. "This is love."

He kissed Ouna on the lips. It was awkward and ill

planned, but it was a kiss. She pushed away and looked at him for a moment. “That’s not love, this is…”

She wrapped her arms around his neck and kissed him back. It wasn’t nearly as awkward the second time. He rather enjoyed it. It wasn’t bad for an eleven-year-old. But then, he was almost twelve and on a foreign planet. It counted.

The two broke their embrace. The dark-haired girl stared at them; her eyes were wide. She ran back to her friends and they discussed in frantic chatter. The dark-haired girl turned and yelled, “Let’s go get some love!”

The crowd broke up into groups.

Ook led a small band around the grassland to find the entrance to the secret tunnel. With spades they spread out and poked at the ground around the Dingh entrance. Within minutes, one of the miners found an amulet lying on the ground next to a hollow spot. “I found something!” He held up the talisman for Jacob to see. Jacob took it from his hand. “This was the last thing that was given to my father on Earth.” He slipped it over his neck. Jacob looked at Ook. “Make the hole bigger.”

Soon, the team had cleared the entrance and opened the tunnel. Ook waited for Jacob to enter the spiral stair before entering, and he led them into the eerie red glow of the tunnel. It reminded Ook of the mineshafts. It smelled of rot and decay. The five boys eased down the tunnel. They moved carefully along the gravel floor until daylight was completely gone and the only light was red crystals embedded in the walls. There was the faint light of an opening ahead…the Dingh. As the light grew larger and brighter, something blocked the view. The smell of the eck reached them before the shuffling sound. Even in the dim light, Ook could see the dull glowing red eyes of the eck. It shuffled toward him without breaking stride. He readied the shovel for the eck. A voice within him steadied him. *You are strong. You are fearless. You are the legacy of Shadraq.* The voice forced back the rising bile of fear. He visualized striking the eck. Suddenly the eck sprung at him with both arms extended. His timing would need to be perfect. It was as if time slowed. The eck was hurtling toward him. The voice in his mind said, *Wait for it...* The eck moved with incredible speed for one so dead. The shovel was poised, waiting for the perfect moment.

The eck was almost in front of him when Shadraq's voice sounded in his mind, *Now!* With deliberate force he shoved the spade into the eck's neck, severing the head from the shoulders. The body propelled forward as Ook sidestepped the rotting corpse. The head tumbled and rolled along the floor of the tunnel. The eyes and tongue still moved while the body lay motionless in the dirt. Ook stood over the head staring at the bizarre thing gnashing its teeth. He raised the spade and smashed downward. He smashed downward twice more. When he raised the shovel there was nothing left but a pulverized mess. He motioned for the others to follow. He moved down the tunnel and waited just outside of the Dingh for Jacob to arrive. The Black Guard stood poised and ready. Inside his head, the voice of Shadraq chanted, *You are strong. You are fearless. You are the legacy of Shadraq.*

****

Jacob's legion followed him in pairs down the stair into the dark. There was a chill in the air as they descended worn stone steps. A mist formed in the air around them. The mist sized them up with seething hatred. The demon tried an old trick to stop them. It materialized on the stair before Jacob as a small boy in ragged clothes. "Can you help me, master? I am lost."

Jacob eyed the boy. He sensed what it was. He stopped. And looked back. The second demon had landed behind them. Its black wings and red eyes moved toward the miners in the back. Jacob recognized the trap. "Yes, young one, I can help you."

The little boy in the ragged clothes reached toward him. "Thank you, master."

Jacob closed his eyes and took a deep breath. The Edajhia appeared before him. He reached out and touched the light. Before he could ask the question, the answer appeared to him. *They hate their own reflection. It reminds them of who they are.* Jacob considered his options. He could not simply conjure up a mirror, but the chamber was damp. He could collect the water. He concentrated on the water in the air and began to swirl in front of the lost boy. Soon, a shimmering film of water formed before him. He could see his reflection so he deduced the lost boy could see his own reflection. The demon spit into the water's reflection, hissing irritatedly at Jacob. Jacob motioned for a torch Ouna carried. He held it before him and concentrated on the light it made. He turned the glowing torch into a brilliant white light. He continued to concentrate on it until a bolt of light shot from the torch and through the heart of the lost boy. The demon howled in pain and disappeared. He turned to face the black mass behind them. It loomed over the dark-haired girl. He concentrated on the torch and fired a bolt toward the demon, striking it between the eyes. It howled and disappeared. The dark-haired girl's eyes grew wide. She shrieked and ran back up the stairs and out of the Dingh. Her friends followed her.

A boy with curly red hair behind Ouna stood frozen in fear. Ouna touched his arm. "It's going to be okay."

Before the boy could rebuke her, he heard a voice in his mind, *You are strong. You are fearless. You are the legacy of Shadraq.* He blinked.

Jacob watched as each of the miners changed. He wondered what was happening. He heard Shadraq in his mind, *Jacob I am with you. You fight to save your father, just as you fought to save me. I will help you fight the demons. We are as one.* Without a word he moved down the stair.

The black sand at the bottom of the stair was littered with white bones. Skulls, femurs, and ribs were scattered in disarray along the fifty feet to the chamber door into the Dingh. He turned to the group. "The Black Guard waits for us. Aim for the heart. Strike for the sword hand. We are strong. We are fearless. We are the legacy of Shadraq."

Jacob pushed on black stone doors that didn't budge. He motioned to the boys with pickaxes. "Take them down."

Four strong boys took aim on striking the hinges. In pairs, on opposite sides, they chipped away at the black rock. The double doors to the Dingh began to crack. The top hinge broke free. They struck at the bottom hinge. It broke free. The boys shouldered the door and it fell in with a crash, creating a cloud of dust in the Dingh. The Black Guard stood, swords in hand.

They were giants compared to the children. The red-headed boy behind Ouna screamed a war cry that even startled Jeez on the other side of the room. He vaulted forward ducking and weaving around the Black Guard. The Guard stood without moving. Jacob wasted no time in assembling the archers. The first arrow flew toward the Guard directly in front of them. It bounced off its chest harmlessly. A low, deep rumble rolled out of the giant's broken lips. It laughed at them. It raised its sword and slashed downward, barely missing one of the strong boys. The boy struck back with his pickaxe. It bounced harmlessly off the arm of the giant. The giant swung back, knocking the strong boy off his feet and into the range of the next giant. He rolled quickly into the circle. Without waiting, he struck the giant from behind. A large gash appeared. The creature roared in anger but would not turn from facing front. He yelled at Jacob, "Their backs are weaker!"

He struck again. Once more the creature roared.

Marty opened his eyes. He was facing the entrance to the Dingh and witnessed an army of children coming to rescue him. Jeez slithered past him to attack the boy in the middle. Marty collected his light and fired a bolt at Jeez, striking her in the back, which sizzled and burned her. She turned to hiss at him. For the first time he could see her real face. The face she had hidden from him. Her eyes were black which framed the hole where her nose once was. Her gray skin was covered in scales. Her mouth was wide and full of jagged, broken teeth. Marty wasted no time in sending another light bolt at her. She moved quickly so it missed her, but it struck the Black Guard behind her. The light seared a hole through the giant, making it go to one knee.

She hissed again but turned back to the advancing army of children. She was unprepared for their ferocity. Nimbly, they dodged and scrambled past the Black Guard and began to pounce on her. She would sling off two only to have three more leap on her. Jacob landed on her back and with Ouna beside him, struck with swords, cutting into her flesh. Marty could hear them chanting, "We are strong, we are fearless, we are the legacy of Shadraq!"

Frustrated and angry, she howled. She flung Jacob from her back. Jeez's nails had grown into daggers. She raised her hand, prepared to strike Jacob on the ground. She paused as she looked at Jacob. She recognized the strong white aura around him. It was the same light as the aura of Gabriel the Archangel. Ouna struck her hand and Marty fired another light ball at her head, breaking her from her reverie. The compounded effect of the sword on Jeez's hand and the light ball striking her head made her scream. Her hand bled and her head smoldered from the blistering pulse from Marty's light bolt. She shuddered and turned to glare at Marty one final time as she peeled the other children off her like fleas. She retreated toward the back of the Dingh. Three of the Black guard lay face down in the dirt, with pools of black blood beneath them. Children lay dead at their feet. From behind, Marty felt small hands around his shackles. He looked down to find children with pickaxes at his feet. The tallest boy looked at Marty and said, "I am Ook, we are here to free you, Jacob's father."

****

On the opposite side of the sun, Rachael froze the realm. Nothing moved within it.

She looked deep into Digger's eyes and said, "I must leave for some time. I will return."

Frozen in position, Digger could not move his body, he could only move his eyes and speak. He asked, "What?"

"The planets are aligning. I am being called."

"What does that mean?

"Every five thousand years, Earth and Oronas align at the Realms. The Chambers where the Ark and Jeez's Sarcophagus are aligned physically. It is a time when she and I can travel freely. And we are drawn to do so."

"How long does it last?"

"In your world, only a fraction of a second. In our world, it will seem like an eternity."

"But you will come back. Right?"

Rachael placed a gentle hand on his cheek. Her lips were full and rich as she kissed him on the lips. A slight charge passed between them. "Yes, my love. I will return to you and the children."

****

With pickaxes and sheer will, the strong boys broke the links to Marty's shackles. The last hold on his hand broke free and Marty fell to the ground. He rested on all fours in the sandy floor. He focused his energy on the Black Guard. The miners continued to fight until there was only one of the Black Guard left standing. The children struck at its legs from behind until it toppled like a tree to the black sand below. It lay face down in the floor of the Dingh. It continued to lash out with its sword at anything it could reach. The red-headed boy leaped onto its back and stood with his sword poised over its heart. His blade was white-hot, heated by the flame of a torch in the Dingh. He plunged the blade into the back of the giant and through its black heart. The white-hot metal found its mark and the last of the Black Guard fell still. The putrid smell of burned decaying flesh filled the Dingh. The cry went up in unison: "We are strong. We are fearless. We are the legacy of Shadraq!"

Marty sat back in the sand staring across at Jeez who coiled against the wall of the Dingh. Her eyes were uncharacteristically white and not focused on the destruction around her. She seemed detached from the surrounding chaos. Jeez's wounds dripped black blood that mingled with the remains of the Black Guard and slain children. Marty knew better than to think she was defeated. But she seemed subdued. He looked at the strong boys and said, "Help me to my feet."

Jacob ran to his father. He hugged him around the neck and cried over his numerous wounds. When he could finally speak, he said, "Dad, you're naked."

Marty gave him a lopsided grin. "I don't need you to tell me that. Where did you find all these kids?"

Jacob straightened up. His head held high. "Dad, this is the Legion of Shadraq."

"Okay. I am forever in your debt. Now let's get out of here. Something is wrong." Weakened from hanging, he could barely walk. With the support of the children, he moved toward the opening. The Dingh began to rumble. At the top of the dome, a violet light began to swirl above them.

Marty urged the miners to move. "Come on, guys; let's move out of here, fast!"

The children ran from the chamber. As Marty reached the door to the chamber, a beam of purple light appeared in the center of the Dingh. The beam crackled with energy, dissolving anything under it. Bodies instantly vaporized in the shaft of light. Jeez moved toward the beam. Marty didn't know what to expect, he only knew they needed to escape.

As Jeez entered the beam, she dissolved into a million red particles of light.

Marty urged Jacob, "Let's go, son."

****

Earthquakes rumbled on both Earth and Oronas. A beam of pure energy passed through the sun connecting Oronas to Earth. Solar flares erupted from the sun in all directions.

Rachael bathed in the sustained plasma oceans on the sun. She looked down through the pool of light and into dark fusion of the Sun's core. A pair of red eyes peered back at her from the black depths of the Sun's core. The voice resonated from behind the red eyes. "Hello, sister. I'm coming for you."

Rachael floated above her in a pocket of solar wind. "I know. I will be waiting for you."

****

The miners helped Marty to the surface as the Dingh shook violently, causing the walls to crumble around them in a cloud of dust and debris. They exited the Dingh just before the stairs collapsed into the black hole below. Marty rested in the bright sun, relieved to have escaped the Dingh. He was moved to tears to be free and with Jacob. Jacob placed a gentle hand on his shoulder. "Just a little farther, Dad, we have food and water in the transport ship."

Marty squinted in the light, seeing the transport ahead. "You secured a transport ship? How long was I down there?"

Jacob shrugged. “I don’t know. A few days I think.”

Marty wiped the tears from his eyes and marveled at it all.

The group stopped dead in their tracks. A large iridescent monster stalked back and forth at the tail of the closed transport unit. It stopped occasionally to sniff the transport unit. The strong boy stepped forward. “Don’t worry, sir. We’ll take care of it.”

Marty placed his hand on the boy’s shoulder. “Let’s not attack it just yet. Let me have a go at him.”

The strong boy’s eyes narrowed. “No offense, sir, but you’re in no condition to fight a ripper.”

Marty smiled weakly. “Not all solutions require violence. Come with me, Jacob.”

With Jacob’s help, Marty made his way over to the ripper. It paced back and forth, its fangs bared, dripping longs strings of saliva. Marty and Jacob could feel the low growl. As Marty and Jacob drew near, the beast stopped pacing and turned to face them. Its lips quivered into a snarl. It lowered itself down, preparing to pounce on the pair. Marty stopped and raised his hand toward the ripper. He thought of the ripper as a cub, with its mother. He pictured the mother cleaning the small, vulnerable creature. The ripper’s snarl relaxed, and the growling stopped. It stood still and waited for Marty to approach. Jacob looked back to see the others staring in fascination. Marty moved closer. As he neared the ripper, it lowered itself flat on its belly and looked up at him. Marty reached down and ran his hand along the beast’s back as if he were petting a tame animal. The creature’s body rippled in response to the stroking. To the group’s astonishment, it rolled over on its back and allowed Marty to stroke its belly. Marty spoke to the animal as if it were a pet. “There’s a good boy. Let’s run along now. We don’t want the children to get the wrong idea about you.”

The ripper rolled back onto its legs and rose. It nudged Marty’s hand to pet him again which made Marty smile. A long snake-like tongue slipped from its mouth and touched Marty’s bare leg. Its large reptilian mouth grinned at him before it backed away and disappeared in the tall grass. Marty looked at Jacob. “I think we’ve taken care of that problem; now, how do you open the door on this thing?”

Jacob motioned to the others to come on. Ouna arrived first and out of breath from running. As her breathing calmed, she said, “That was amazing! How did you do that? Rippers kill everything they meet.”

Marty shrugged. “I don’t really know. What I do know is it’s best to meet others on their own terms. It opens them up to being reasonable about things.”

Ouna slapped the tailgate release with her hand and lowered the ramp of the ship. The dark-haired girl stood with her friends. Her head was lowered. “I’m sorry. I was afraid. I ran away.”

Jacob placed his hand on her shoulder. “It’s okay. We all get scared sometime.”

As the others passed them on the ramp, none of them looked at the dark-haired girl or her friends.

Jacob scrounged through some of the lockers on the ship and found a worn jumpsuit for Marty. It smelled musty, but it fit. The red-headed boy brought him water and another boy brought him brown food pellets as he sat back in one of the few crew seats in the back.

In the cockpit, Ouna and Jacob stood in the pilot and co-pilot positions and prepared for takeoff. Ouna raised the ramp. She fired the thrusters and the ship shuddered as it lifted off. Marty lay back in the seat and closed his eyes. Over the roar and vibration of the engines, he drifted to sleep. He dreamed of being in the Dingh; the eck paced back and forth. He stood in the center of the Dingh. The Black Guard surrounded him. Their leather-like faces and red eyes glared at him angrily. Jeez stood from her obsidian throne. Her body, morphed into a snake, slithered toward him. The right side of her face was supple and full, the left bore dark scales, a thin reptilian mouth with a yellow slit of an eye. When she reached him, her long taloned fingers pierced his abdomen. She tore up through his chest, grabbed his still beating heart, pulled it out, and showed it to him. Her voice hissed as she said, "Your soul will always be mine. You will never be safe from me."

Marty watched the blood drip from his beating heart in her grasp. His voice boomed as he spoke, "You will never possess me. You didn't break me. You have no power over me, demon. I own my soul. Be gone!" A beam of powerful light exploded from his forehead.

She screeched loudly. Her hand and his heart turned to dust. He directed the beam at her face. The screeching stopped and her body coiled and writhed without a head in the sand below him. He directed the beam at the Black Guard behind her which turned to dust. The eck continued to pace in front of him. He focused the beam on the eck. "That means you too."

The eck turned to dust and blew away in a hidden wind. Marty opened his eyes. He was surrounded by children. They stared at him intently. It was as though they had never seen anyone like him before. He reached forward. “Help me up.” Several of the children eagerly grabbed his arm and pulled him upright. He rose painfully and moved toward the cockpit. Ouna deftly maneuvered the controls while Jacob stood by her side. Marty greeted them, “Hey, guys.”

Jacob looked back at his father. “Are you okay?”

“I’m okay. I need to know something. Have these children been drugged?”

Ouna replied without turning. “Not exactly. If you mean that they act differently than other children you’ve seen, it’s for a reason. When they are sent to the mines, the robots wiped away their memories of the past so they would not know to run away. When they entered the mines, they were programmed to believe they have always been there.”

Marty replied, “That makes sense. But what about you?”

Ouna glanced back at him and grinned. “The unit they used didn’t work on my brain because I’m alien to this world.”

Marty scratched his chin. “Interesting. Anything else we should know about you?”

“No. Not really. Other than that, I’m a pretty normal kid.”

Marty chuckled. “That’s an arguable point.”

Ouna pointed ahead. “We’re here.” She depressed a button on the upper console, which activated an enormous ramp in the side of a hill. The grassland lowered into a gaping hole, large enough for the ship to pass through. As she eased into the opening, lights began to illuminate ahead of them, revealing a large underground tunnel. She eased the ship forward until they reached a fleet of ships stored in the hangar. She set the transport unit down carefully on the concrete deck and powered down the engines. A figure darted between ships on the deck in front of them. Marty narrowed his eyes. "Jacob, we need a small team with us. Make sure they're armed."

"Sure, Dad." He moved past Marty into the back.

Marty looked at Ouna. "You're very talented at flying this rig. What about one of those things?" He pointed to the lead ship.

Ouna looked back at him. "The controls are very similar. The only difference is the thrusters to break free of the planet's gravity are different. We'll have to make sure everyone is strapped in."

"Hang tight until we come back for you. You're the only one who can fly that thing. We need you to be safe."

Ouna pouted. "But I want to go with Jacob."

Marty lowered his voice. "We need you to get us out of here. Stay on the ship."

"Humph!" She turned away from him.

Marty moved to the rear. Jacob was huddled with a small group of boys. "Okay, Dad. We're ready."

Marty would have felt odd taking children with him to secure the area, had it not been for him witnessing how hard they fought in the Dingh. He was confident in them. These kids were not children.

The tailgate of the ship opened long enough for them to hop off. It then closed back. Swords drawn, the group eased through the hangar quietly. It was Jacob who noticed one of the ships was lit up. A wild-eyed man ran past them toward the lighted ship. Marty and the team eased toward the ship cautiously. A ramp was lowered, and at the top of the ramp, just inside the ship, a man blocked out the light to the interior. A familiar voice spoke, "Hello, Mr. Wood."

Marty looked up and squinted against the glare of the ship. The man took a step down so Marty could see him better. His eyes widened. "Duke Lindenspear?"

The man replied, "It's just Fredrick, now. I thought you were dead."

Marty replied cautiously, "Same here. We have someone who can fly the ship. Are you trying to leave?"

Fredrick eyed him coolly. "As do I. And yes, we plan to leave this place as soon as possible."

Marty's mind raced. *What if the Duke tried to kill him again? What if he was in league with Jeez? Should he risk it or just take another ship?*

As if he were reading his mind, Fredrick said, "Mr. Wood, I have been trapped in this hell for the last ten years and all I have dreamt of is leaving this place. I would not think of leaving you stranded here if you wish to leave. My time here has been life altering, to say the least. I realize that my actions on Earth were foolish. That demon made me believe something about myself that simply wasn't true. She betrayed me and left me to a horrible fate. You have my word that I will not harm you, if you wish to travel with me."

Marty's eyes narrowed. Fredrick could sense his conflict. "Your men have weapons. If I let you board, is that enough of a show of good faith?"

Marty considered the offer. A lone figure silently eased up behind Marty's group. A woman walked up behind Fredrick. A voice behind Marty exclaimed, "Mom?"

The woman behind Fredrick replied, "Ouna?"

The woman pushed past Fredrick and came down the ramp. Ouna pushed past the boys and ran to her mother. They locked in an embrace. Luna's tears fell onto Ouna's hair as she kissed her on the head. Ouna sobbed and pulled her mother tightly, causing her to groan. Ouna pushed back briefly. "Are you all right?"

She cradled her daughter's face in her hands. "I'm okay, just sore."

Ouna wiped the tears from her eyes, leaving streaks in the dirt on her face. "Mom, they told me you were dead."

Luna replied, "That's what they told me about you. I gave up after that."

Marty interrupted. "Guys, this is great, it really is, but I don't know how much time we have before Jeez returns. Fredrick, we have a few passengers we need to include. Do you mind if we get loaded and get out of here?"

Fredrick looked at the boys with Marty. "Still trying to rescue the downtrodden, I see. Very well. Let's get your men on the ship and leave this place."

Jacob piped up, "I'll go get the others."

Fredrick raised an eyebrow. "Others?"

Marty nodded. "Just a few. I'll explain on the way."

Fredrick and Viktor stared as one after another children filed on board. He looked at Marty and asked, "How many did you say?"

"A little under one hundred."

"How long have you been here?"

"A few days. They're adopted, Fredrick."

"Uh-huh."

The last one on the ship was the little red-haired boy, who reported, "All accounted for, sir."

Marty smiled at the boy. "Very good. What's your name?"

"Arn, sir."

"Good job, Arn."

The boy grinned shyly and followed the others. The hatch raised silently and secured into position. A voice sounded overhead. "Everyone, strap in. We're headed for Earth."

****

Rachael stood safely back in the realm with Digger at her side holding her hand. He raised her hand and kissed it gently as he asked, "So what's next?"

Rachael stared into nothingness as she replied cryptically, "From the darkness a shadow comes."

A word about the author…

As a career professional spanning the disciplines of corporate security, safety, and environmental management, Darren has spent 30 years in technical fields. Born and raised in North Carolina, he has experienced a diverse background of supervisor, police officer, husband, and father. As an international traveler and marathon runner, he has experienced physical and mental challenges. His lifetime experiences have seasoned his view of the world and provide a unique blend of cultural perspective with a thirst for understanding the human condition.

Thank you for purchasing
this publication of The Wild Rose Press, Inc.

For questions or more information
contact us at
info@thewildrosepress.com.

The Wild Rose Press, Inc.
www.thewildrosepress.com

www.ingramcontent.com/pod-product-compliance
Lightning Source LLC
LaVergne TN
LVHW020525100826
845148LV00010B/1347

* 9 7 8 1 5 0 9 2 3 4 3 9 4 *